Ceae

D0286247

Outside the Limelight

Ballet Theatre Chronicles, Book 2

Terez Mertes Rose

Copyright © 2016 by Terez Mertes Rose
www.terezrose.com

All rights reserved. No part of this publication can be reproduced or transmitted
in any form or by any means, electronic or mechanical, without permission in
writing from the author and publisher, except when permitted by law.

Outside the Limelight is a work of fiction. The West Coast Ballet Theatre is a
fictional dance company, a composite based on information culled from five major
U.S. dance companies. All events, schedules, individuals, organizations and
incidents are either products of the author's imagination or have been fictionalized.
Any resemblance to actual San Francisco events or persons is coincidental.

Published in the United States
Classical Girl Press - www.theclassicalgirl.com
Cover design by James T. Egan, BookFly Design, LLC
Formatting by Polgarus Studio

ISBN 978-0-9860934-3-2
ISBN (ebook) 978-0-9860934-2-5

For my wounded warrior sister, Maureen, with all my love

This is part of what a family is about, not just love. It's knowing that your family will be there watching out for you. Nothing else will give you that. Not money. Not fame. Not work.

— Mitch Albom

Family love is messy, clinging, and of an annoying and repetitive pattern, like bad wallpaper.

— P.J. O'Rourke

Prologue

Dena - Spring 2006

When Anders Gunst, artistic director of the West Coast Ballet Theatre, told nineteen-year-old Dena Lindgren he was promoting her to soloist, all she could think was that she'd misheard him. They were standing backstage, post-performance, at San Francisco's California Civic Theater. Partial lighting streamed from the overhead fixtures, casting the furthest wings in shadows. The stagehands, immersed in their nightly cleanup routine, swept the floor, inspected cables and called out to one another across the empty stage. Anders always spoke softly, and right then, it was hard to hear over their voices.

"I'm sorry," she stammered, clutching and unclutching the towel she'd used to mop up her sweat from *Arpeggio,* the ballet she'd just finished. "I misunderstood what you said. Because you're promoting my sister. Not me. Right?" She felt foolish even suggesting otherwise, like the newbie first-year corps dancer she was. At five-foot-two, she was a petite dancer, and right then she felt her smallness. Anders himself, while not particularly tall, was dressed tonight in a sleek charcoal Italian suit and tie that enhanced his refined looks and made him seem all the more intimidating, even as he smiled at her.

"No." He shook his head. "It's you I'm promoting to soloist."

She began to shiver in her costume, a pale, glittery, silken tunic that clung damply to her skin. "That's not possible. There's just that one position open."

"Yes." Anders didn't seem bothered by her aggrieved tone or the way everything about her had scrunched up in resistance.

"But... but," she sputtered. "That wasn't the *plan.*"

He chuckled. "I think, as the artistic director, I have a fairly good sense of what the plan should be."

And still she stared at him, incredulous, unable to process it.

While he continued speaking, a part of her mind detached and hastily scrolled over the past two hours, this performance of *Arpeggio*, the unexpected triumph of it in the aftermath of the terrible news she and her older sister Rebecca had just received. Their parents were divorcing; their father already had plans to remarry. Dena hadn't seen it coming, and this destruction of their family of four had devastated her. Rebecca, dancing *Arpeggio* too, had taken Dena by the shoulders in the dressing room, given her a shake, told her fiercely to take that pain and pour it into the performance. This crucial performance in which they both had soloist roles, even though they were both only corps dancers. The big, huge, this-could-be-career-changing opportunity for the two of them that they simply had to excel at.

They'd excelled, both of them. And now, by all rights, the career change belonged to Rebecca, three years Dena's senior, in age and company status. The promotion was to be hers. Everyone in the company knew it.

"Anders," she said, more vehement now. "What about my sister?"

Anders gave her a thoughtful nod. "Rebecca is a very strong dancer, graced with extraordinary beauty. You lack your sister's looks—most of the girls do—but it's that very omission that makes you a more interesting dancer to watch. You can embody a number of different moods and personas, all so decisive and convincing. You have a talent that draws eyes to you. Rebecca fits seamlessly into any ensemble she's placed in. She blends in. You stand out. I see that now. To keep you in the corps would only hinder what's flowing from you so naturally. Soloist rank is where I want you."

He glanced over to the front of the backstage area where Ben Marlborough, ballet master and assistant to the artistic director, was gesturing to his wristwatch. Anders looked at his own watch. "I'm expected over at L'Orange in ten minutes," he told Dena. "I'll leave you to your cleanup. Congratulations, again."

The implications began to sink in. "Wait! How... how can I possibly tell her?"

A touch of impatience crossed Anders' face. "Rebecca and I understand each other. I'll have a word with her."

He didn't wait for her reply, but instead strode away to where Ben stood waiting by the door with the green glowing "exit" sign above. The two of them disappeared from sight.

She remained there, rooted to the spot, still trying to process it all.

"Excuse me, miss," one of the stagehands called out, gesturing to the mop he was pushing along.

"Oh. Sorry." She stepped out of his way and watched him mop. She studied the backstage area in a daze, as if seeing it for the first time, the sets and backdrops all pulled up, making the space cavernous, so different from the enclosed space they performed on. All mystery had been wiped clear of the space, all illusion and artifice dispersed and packed away for the night.

Deep within her, a bud of euphoria hovered, hesitant to unfurl, like a bud in late winter that appears during a warm spell. Everyone knows early warm spells don't last, and that the bud is screwed if it starts to unfurl.

Don't think about it. Not yet.

As if on autopilot, she made her way off the stage, down the hallway, the stairs, through another, more narrow hallway with its scuffed linoleum floors and pale green walls, to the corps dancers' dressing room she shared with her sister and six other females. An overcrowded place, inconveniently located, because the soloists and principals got the more premium ones, three to a room instead of eight.

There, at the doorway, she stopped. Rebecca sat, finishing up her makeup removal. She was beautiful, strikingly so. She didn't even need makeup to accentuate her deep-set brown eyes, expressive brows, sculpted cheekbones. She spied Dena's reflection in the mirror and smiled. "Hey, why the down face?" she asked. "Are you thinking of Dad's terrible news still?"

The divorce. She'd nearly forgotten. What had held her in such a dark, powerful grip earlier in the evening now just seemed like an average piece of bad news that wafted in and out of a person's life.

"No," Dena said. "I mean, yes. I mean, I just feel all muddled inside right now. And exhausted."

Rebecca's eyes went soft with sympathy. "You gave your all in that performance. I could tell. But you did it—you channeled that pain into your dance, and you were incredible. The way the crowd roared when you took that curtain call? Omigod, Dena. It gave me chills. I'm so proud of you. You may still be low on the totem pole in the corps, but your job security with this company is *sealed.*"

Dena looked at Rebecca's beautiful, untroubled face and began to cry.

"Oh, look at you!" Rebecca rose and swept Dena into a hug. "You're all full of emotion still." She stepped back, but kept her hands on Dena's shoulders, eyes fixed on her face. "I'd say let's go out together and have a celebratory glass of wine and dinner out, but the truth is, I've got plans."

She leaned in, eyes bright with excitement. "Anders said he wanted to share a word with me. He invited me to join him at L'Orange for a drink. I think this might be it, Deen. The news."

"Oh, Becca," Dena said, and began to cry harder.

"Aww, Deen," Rebecca said, and gave her one last hug. A quick one. One that said her mind was already on the meet-up at L'Orange, on the news she'd be receiving.

Stop the damned tears, Dena told herself fiercely. But what do you say to your happy, excited, older sister who, Dena knew, was off to hear not the news she was expecting but something quite different?

"Becca," she tried. "It might be for another reason he wants to talk to you."

Rebecca smiled at her. "Trust me. I think I know Anders a little better than you. Mark my word. What he tells me tonight is going to change everything."

"You're right," Dena said softly. "I'm just not sure either of us are ready."

"Well, I, for one, am." Rebecca deposited the last of her supplies in her theater trunk and closed it. She gathered up her dance bag and beamed at Dena. "Don't worry. It won't change a thing between the two of us. I mean, we won't share the same dressing room anymore. But we're family. Even after Dad's shitty news and the way he just utterly ruined Mom's life. But you and I, we'll always be sisters."

Rebecca took one last, critical glance at herself in the mirror. "Okay, I'm off. G'night, sis."

"Good night."

Dena sank to her own seat. In the mirror's brightly illuminated reflection, she studied her tear-streaked, makeup-smudged face. The younger, lesser Lindgren sister. The same color eyes and hair as Rebecca, but the resemblance stopped there. Dena's features were bland, neutral. What made her stand out, in the family and onstage, was her fierce spirit, which shone out through her eyes. Eyes that displayed fire and stubbornness and yearning and aching.

Right then, especially the aching.

The other corps dancers were preparing to leave the dressing room as well. Pam, one of the older ones, cast Dena a sympathetic glance. "This is the cycle of things," she said. "Good dancers get promoted and move up and out. Be glad for your sister."

A pang shot through Dena. "It's more complicated than that," she told Pam.

"Well," Pam said in a less friendly voice, "you'll get over it."

The three of them left. Dena heard them murmuring to each other as they walked down the hall.

"What a little princess," she heard one of them, a dancer named Charlotte, say. "She's not even glad for her sister. Wants the limelight all to herself."

They were Rebecca's friends, not hers, all of them seasoned dancers. Dena was only in their dressing room because Rebecca had requested it. As a result, she'd never made close friends with the corps dancers her own age. Right then, it made her feel so alone.

When the news got out, these dancers would hate her for usurping her sister's promotion. The promotion that half of the corps de ballet females were secretly wishing would land on their own laps.

Socially, she was screwed. Guaranteed to be friendless.

She commenced her makeup removal in a teary silence. Once her face was clean, she unpinned her bun and brushed out her long, shiny brown hair, her best feature. The halls were quiet now, most of the dancers having left the theater already.

"Dena? You still around?" she heard a female voice call out from the hallway.

"In here," she called back.

Lana, one of the soloists and a fellow dancer in *Arpeggio*, poked her head into the room. "Hey," she said. "I heard Charlotte and Pam mentioning you as they passed my dressing room a few minutes back. It sounded like you were upset about something."

Dena drew a steadying breath, rose and faced Lana, who was taller than she. Pretty much all the dancers were.

"It's true! You've been crying." Lana's hazel eyes, big and round like a child's, were wide with concern.

Lana had been a new hire the previous fall, and was probably the only other dancer in the company who could appreciate both the thrill and the burden of a surprise promotion. A former soloist from Kansas City, she'd been anticipating a position in the corps, but Anders had taken one look at her dancing and decided nope, soloist all the way. Even though Lana was kind and friendly to all, her assimilation into the company had been anything but easy.

"What's going on?" Lana asked.

"Anders spoke to me backstage after the performance," Dena said. The heaviness released its grip on her insides. She could feel the corners of her mouth twitch into an almost smile.

"...And?" Lana breathed.

The almost-smile grew bigger. To watch Lana's expression change from concern to anticipation to barely suppressed excitement made that little bud of euphoria inside Dena explode into bloom.

"He promoted me to soloist."

"Oh my *God!*" Lana screamed, and grabbed at Dena. They stood there, hugging, laughing, crying, rocking back and forth, both babbling "oh my *God*" and "I know, right?"

She'd been right. Lana was the one person who'd get it, who could share all this with her.

One person, in the end, was all you needed.

Spring 2010

Chapter 1 – Dena

It all starts and ends with the artistic director. Casting in ballets. Daily rehearsal schedules. Careers. One word from him, an index finger raised, a frown creasing his brow, could change everything. Case in point: Anders' murmured words to Dena backstage, four years earlier. The nods of approval since then, a *good job* and *I think I'd like to see you rehearsing Nikiya this season*, all catapulting her career forward, ever forward. It was intoxicating beyond measure.

Today had brought Dena further attention, although maybe not the good kind. He'd called a rehearsal for her alone, onstage, while he, Ben, and the technical director stood in the tenth row of the darkened 2000-seat theater and watched.

"Take it again, please," Anders called out.

From the upstage left corner she began the same eight-count passage from the ballet *Spirit Hour*, elegant, classical fodder with a sweeping Tchaikovsky accompaniment, in which she shared the female lead for the six-night run. Performances had commenced and it worried her, this impromptu rehearsal. It could only mean she was doing something wrong, which she was desperate to undo, if only she could figure out what it was Anders had found fault with.

Anders didn't seem to know either. He had her run the passage again: a series of quick chaîné turns interspersed with double piqués and a slower, more graceful one with her back leg high in attitude, culminating under the downstage lights with a sustained piqué arabesque. Again. Again. Finally he held up one finger. She paused, hands on knees, panting, as the three men talked among themselves in low tones. They did not consult her.

"The angle of her head?" she heard Ben murmur.

"It could be the way the light's falling on her right there," the technical director said.

Anders shook his head. "I don't know. I think it's something else." The three men vacated the auditorium and trooped up the steps to join her on the stage. "Dena," Anders commanded. "One more time, please."

She repeated the passage, distilling her attention to a tiny pinpoint of concentration, those eight counts, getting it right. She felt Anders watching her closely, almost stealthily, and she prayed it didn't show, the off balance feeling that soon began rising in her.

Here, then, was the disquieting element in her otherwise perfect life: a disturbing sensation that hovered over her of late, a nameless, fuzzy disequilibrium. It had been going on for months now, maybe a year. She was only twenty-three, too young for such health problems. She'd been worried enough to visit a doctor, who'd been less concerned about her dizziness-but-not and more so about hearing loss on her left side. He'd referred her to an ENT specialist, who in turn had ordered an MRI. The procedure had taken place four weeks ago. No call back. No news meant good news, she decided, admittedly an ostrich-with-its-head-in-the-sand attitude, but a workable one. The most effective solution to her problem was simply to try harder. Work harder. Not ever give in to fuzziness, fatigue or pain. That was how you became a principal in the company, the goal to which she devoted all waking hours. Lana, her roommate of three years, had just gotten engaged, calling it a dream come true. Not for Dena, that. She'd excelled as a soloist for four years now. She'd just made *Dance Magazine's* annual "25 to Watch" list. Her own dream come true—a promotion to principal—just might happen too.

The three men conversed a minute longer before Anders looked at his watch. "Thank you, Dena," he called out, and began to walk away with the technical director, leaving her alone on the stage with Ben.

She wasn't sure what he'd seen, what had been wrong that he now found acceptable. Only a tossed out "good work there" over his shoulder just before he disappeared from view comforted her. That, and the fact that this was her last rehearsal for the day. It gave her time to slip back to the apartment and nap before the night's performance.

Rest and dance. Nothing else mattered.

When she returned to the theater two and a half hours later, Lana and Sylvie were already in the dressing room the three of them shared, applying their makeup. Lana was recounting a story to Sylvie, a new soloist this season, a petite, russet-haired Canadian. Lana paused to greet Dena. "You're late," she said, balancing a false eyelash strip on her fingertip. "And you look like you need a nap."

"Ironically, I had one, back at the apartment." Dena slung her overloaded dance bag down on the couch. "It didn't help."

"Oh, don't worry. You'll be less foggy within the hour and perform all the better for having rested." Lana beamed at her.

"You're right." Dena offered her a bright smile in return. It was easy to hide her health worries from Lana these days because Lana lived in a bubble of happiness, ever since getting engaged. It was all rainbows and sunshine, Gil did this and Gil said that. Dena, relationship-less since her love affair with Nicholas, a fellow soloist, three years earlier, didn't know how to relate to Lana's besotted couple's bliss. It was starting to hurt their own closeness.

She rearranged the night's costume on the rack behind her and sat down to apply her makeup. Lana had returned to telling Sylvie her story, related, no surprise, to wedding preparation. But Sylvie, unlike Dena, relished every last detail.

Apparently, Lana had found The Dress. She and her old housemate Alice, a former company dancer and administrator, had gone to a boutique shop where Alice had bought her own wedding dress three years earlier. The Dress had been the first one Alice had pulled from the rack, and had proved perfect in every way. Upon hearing this, Sylvie gave a little coo of pleasure.

"Ooh, more details, please. You took a picture, right? I can't wait to see whether—" She paused when she saw someone hovering at the door. "Oh. Hello, Rebecca." Her voice grew cool. "Looking for Dena again?"

Dena turned to see her sister, standing at their doorway, arms folded. Rebecca didn't look happy. A preemptive wave of fatigue washed over Dena.

"Yes, I am," Rebecca said. "Did you tell her I'd stopped by and was wanting to speak with her?"

Sylvie's chin lifted a notch. "No, I'm sorry. She came in just a few minutes ago. I didn't get the chance."

Sylvie and Rebecca did not get along well. New-hire soloists rarely made friends with the old-timer corps dancers, and this was no exception.

"A minute of your time, please?" Rebecca asked Dena.

"Sure. Here I am," Dena mumbled.

Rebecca's gaze swept over Lana and Sylvie before returning to Dena. "In privacy, maybe? The hallway?"

"All right."

She could feel Sylvie's disapproval as she rose and followed Rebecca. "Don't let her push you around," Sylvie said to Dena in a low voice. "She's just a corps dancer."

But Sylvie didn't have an older sister. She didn't understand the unspoken rules that superseded company etiquette.

Rebecca was waiting for her in the hallway, an impatient look on her face. She was already in costume and makeup, hair pinned and sprayed into submission. She looked beautiful, as she always did. They said corps dancers aged faster, but Rebecca only became more lovely as the years passed. Not exhausted in the least, no physical sign of stress or wear.

Behind her stood Pam, Rebecca's best friend and housemate. Pam, unlike Rebecca, looked worn, her thinness more haggard than pretty. But she'd been in the corps for over ten years, after all.

Dena gestured to Pam with her chin. "What's she there for?"

"Backup support."

Pam spoke up. "Rebecca's here to confirm she's taking the car on Sunday afternoon and night, and I'm her witness that she's left you several phone messages. I heard her call you."

The car: their father's gift to his daughters after he'd remarried three and a half years ago, a gesture that had endeared him to Dena, but had only made Rebecca more wary and cynical toward him. Which hadn't stopped Rebecca from enjoying the car.

"I didn't notice any new messages," Dena said, which was only a half-lie. She hadn't bothered to check for them. Resting had been a much bigger priority.

It annoyed her, the private look of mirth Rebecca and Pam exchanged. "Well," Rebecca said, "if you look, I'm sure you'll see and hear all four of them. Boyd and I have Sunday night out-of-town plans. A nice hotel. The car is a must."

Another wave of fatigue, laced with that semi-dizzy feeling, overcame her. "Fine. Fine," she said, leaning against the wall. She let her eyes flicker shut. "Just take it. Whatever."

"Sounds like you've got things covered," she heard Pam tell Rebecca. "I'm out of here."

"Thanks," Rebecca said, and Dena steeled herself for more demands from her sister.

None came. When she opened her eyes, Rebecca was studying her suspiciously. "What's wrong with you?" she demanded.

This woke Dena from her torpor. "Nothing's wrong. What are you talking about?"

Rebecca sized her up. "Something in you seems… off. It has, lately."

How was it that sisters could notice something even your best friends couldn't? For an instant, she found herself melting back into the girl she'd once been, the one whose big sister could protect her, make things better, chase away the demons. She could tell Rebecca about her symptoms right now, unburden the worry.

But who was she kidding? They'd been kids back then. That particular closeness had ended years ago, never to return. Now, it seemed, only the car kept them connected and engaged.

Dena drew herself taller. "Nothing's off. I'm tired, that's all. I've been working hard."

Rebecca studied her for a moment longer and shrugged. "Oh, well. Get more rest."

"I plan to try."

"And I'll pick up the car Sunday afternoon."

"Fine."

Rebecca turned to leave but then paused. "Why the rehearsal with Anders this afternoon?"

"I'm not sure. He just wanted to watch me run through one of my solo passages a few times."

"Well, whatever it was, I'm sure you'll do a stellar job tonight. Like you always manage to do."

It sounded like a double-edged compliment. Rebecca was good at those.

"Um, thanks," she told Rebecca. "Merde, tonight."

"Thanks. Merde to you, too."

Dancers wished each other "merde" before a performance instead of "good luck" or "break a leg" for reasons of theater superstition. All in an attempt for good luck onstage. Tonight, however, the wish didn't help.

She tripped, over her own foot, during the simplest of steps. Despite her windmilling arms, she lost balance and crashed down to the marley floor. The bright lights from the side booms seemed to redirect their aim to focus on her and her blunder. Over the orchestra's swell of music she could hear gasps of dismay, both from the audience and the dancers backstage who'd been watching. She popped right back up, but there it was, this ugly blight on the night's performance.

The set of graceful waltz turns that followed helped her regain her composure. "Shit, are you all right?" Nicholas, partnering her that night, murmured into her ear a moment later as he prepped her for a grand jeté lift.

"Yes," she murmured back just before he launched her overhead, carrying her a half-dozen steps before setting her down, downstage right. She kept her smile fixed and bright. Stumbling happened; gaffes happened, an unfortunate facet of live performing. The worst thing she could do right then was wallow in it, allow it to taint the rest of her performance. She ratcheted up the wattage of her smile, the quality of her ensuing petit allegro work, until the corps dancers returned and she and Nicholas exited stage right. There, in the cool dimness of the wings, she avoided eye contact with the dancers hovering behind her. She didn't want anyone's concern or pity. She just wanted to get back out there, dance for all she was worth. She accepted a bottle of water from the backstage assistant and took a sip with shaky hands. Afterward she tested her ankle and knee joints gingerly. No stabs of agonizing pain, so nothing sprained or torn.

Nicholas glanced over at her for the third time. "I'm fine," she growled. "Stop doing that."

"Sorry," he said in a hurt voice. "I care."

He did; in that respect, she'd been lucky. Although he'd been the one to end their love affair three years earlier, he'd been careful since then not to let her get hurt, physically or emotionally. He was still her favorite partner for a reason.

"Thank you." She reached over and gave his hand a squeeze.

Back onstage they went, the bright stage lights recommencing their assault. She danced better now, affecting a relaxed, blissed-out expression, even as her muscles ached with the strain of so much effort to appear effortless. The stumble, she told herself, had been a one-time fluke. Nothing to do with her health issues at all. The mantra served her well, through the ballet's second and third movements, through her increasing fatigue.

No problems at all.

Until one happened again.

She was running upstage, a flurry of little steps, in preparation for a partnered passage from the diagonal. There, rounding the corner, she felt herself slip, like a little kid in stocking feet taking a turn into the kitchen too fast.

This time Nicholas, right by her side, caught her before she could fall. A gasp rose from the wings, from the nearby dancers watching. "Jesus, she almost fell again!" she heard one of them exclaim.

Commanding herself to ignore them, she and Nicholas shot

downstage on the diagonal. Her adrenaline had kicked in from the near fall, giving her razor-sharp precision now. There were no further stumbles. Through the final minutes, she pulled energy and focus from some previously unknown source and made herself excel, because that's what you do when you're performing, no matter how ghastly the performance had been up to then. And this had been one for the books.

Backstage, after curtain calls, she assured everyone around her that she was fine, just tired, and pushed her way through the milling dancers, frantic to get to her dressing room before Rebecca could confront her. There, in the safety of the room, empty of Lana and Sylvie, she studied her made-up face in the mirror, its painted prettiness, and burst into tears.

Something was indeed wrong with her. She could no longer afford to pretend otherwise.

Five minutes later, Anders knocked at her dressing room door, as she'd suspected he would. She swallowed her trepidation and invited him in. Lana, who'd come in to check on her and help shoo away a concerned Rebecca, slipped right back out. In this enclosed space, it was impossible to hide anything from Anders. He had this way about him, of studying a dancer with his alert grey eyes, wordlessly retrieving data he needed to know, as if he could log into their bodies without the dancer having any say in the matter. In truth, she'd never lost her intimidation of him. He was not a chummy, gregarious artistic director. He was, simply put, God.

He greeted her, asked if anything had been physically compromised by her fall, and when she responded no, he told her to stand.

"Look straight at me," he said in that commanding way of his. He had the voice of a radio broadcaster: low, clear, and improbably sexy.

Even though he was a native Danish speaker, his English was accentless. He began to walk around her. She turned her head to follow his next words, and he told her, no, look straight ahead. He started speaking more softly, telling her to tendu her right foot to the side, raise it six inches and hold. Lower. Repeat on the left. His voice grew softer, more difficult to hear, and she started to tremble, in fear, in that nameless fatigue.

He came back around to face her. "You're tired," he said.

"Yes," she admitted.

"We have you onstage for how many more performances of this program?"

"I'm off tomorrow night. The Sunday matinee I'm on. And Tuesday I finish up."

He nodded. "Sit," he said, and she sank gratefully into the battered couch behind them.

He joined her. "How long has this been going on?"

"I'm not sure. I've just felt more tired than usual this season. And then comes this light-headed feeling, and... I don't know how to explain it. This blocked feeling behind my ear. But that would affect sound, not this dizzy sense. I went to a specialist, and he ran tests. I guess nothing conclusive came from them. His office never called me back."

"I don't want you taxing yourself tomorrow. Class is fine, but no rehearsals. Instead, go home and rest."

"I will."

"And I'm pulling you from the cast list for the Sunday matinee."

"Anders, please! Tomorrow's rest is what I need. On Sunday, I'll be fine."

He shook his head. "Monday I want you to call that doctor's office, find out how soon they can get you in again. Tell them it's an emergency. Mention you never heard back from them."

"It's nothing. I'm sure."

"It's not nothing, Dena. There's something serious going on. I can see in the way you turn your head. Your hearing is compromised."

She'd been found out.

"I was thinking it could be some kind of inner ear infection," she confessed. "The hearing… you're right. It's muffled on the left." She wanted to cry. "I didn't think it could show."

He looked solemn. "I'm a fairly good judge of what's going on with my dancers." He rose. "So. Sit the Sunday performance out. Talk to that specialist again. We'll consider Tuesday night's performance once you report back to me."

"All right."

She wanted to fight back, but one did not fight with Anders Gunst. It was her job, as one of his fifty-five dancers, to heed and follow his direction.

Anything. Anything, just to keep dancing.

Chapter 2 – Rebecca

The first thing Rebecca did when she and her boyfriend Boyd checked into their Sonoma Valley hotel on Sunday late afternoon, after she'd oohed and aahed over the luxury touches and Victorian-style decor in their room, was fill the bathtub with steaming, sudsy water. Sinking into it, she winced at the heat, but a few moments later got her reward, a blissful lavender-scented release, an unclenching of all the muscles that had congregated around the hurt places. And there were plenty: her hip joints, the left ankle, her right knee's medial collateral ligament, the groin injury from last year, the aching quads and calves from the day's performance, the throbbing toes with their blisters beneath calluses, two small but vicious corns, an ingrown toenail. All of these pains now easing up, melting away.

The human body holds 600 muscles, 206 bones and 900 ligaments.

That meant 1706 opportunities to get hurt.

Boyd brought her a glass of wine, perched himself on the marble counter, and together they continued their analysis of the day's earlier performance. Orchestral tempi had been on the too-quick side, they both agreed. In spite of that, Katrina and Javier, senior principals and the lead couple in *Raymonda* Act III, had given an exceptional performance. In *Logic of Life*, the corps dancer next to Boyd had overstepped his cued spot for the ensemble work and their fingers kept touching when their arms were extended à la seconde. Most noteworthy had been Laurel's performance as Dena's understudy in *Spirit Hour*.

There'd been last-minute rehearsals on both Saturday afternoon and Sunday morning to help ease Laurel, a second-year corps dancer, into the role, but she'd been a nervous performer. She'd taken everything conservatively, double pirouettes instead of triples, slowing down the chaîné series, the tension apparent in her rigid upper body port de bras. The overhead grand jeté lifts had seemed sluggish. Rebecca could tell Nicholas had struggled to get Laurel high in the air the way he managed so effortlessly with Dena, who knew how and where to help.

Rebecca rotated her ankles back and forth in the sweet-smelling, sudsy water and took a sip of her wine. "She did great under the circumstances but she never really warmed to the role, did she? The aura of a soloist, and all."

"What would you have expected, instant familiarity?" Boyd said. "It takes a while for a corps dancer to translate into soloist material."

"It only took Dena the one performance."

She'd been nineteen, a new corps member subbing for an injured principal, and it had been like watching a different dancer step into her sister's skin—a bolder, more decisive one, charming and utterly fearless, her technique flawless, her lyricism heart-rending. Rebecca, watching from backstage, had wept. The audience had gone wild. Even Anders had looked stunned.

Boyd snorted. "Princess Dena finally takes a stumble. About time."

The wine glass paused midway to Rebecca's mouth as she stared at Boyd. "Excuse me, we're talking about my little sister here. She could have gotten seriously hurt. Do you think I enjoyed watching her trip and fall?"

Boyd laughed. "I don't know. Did you?"

"No!"

He shrugged, unconcerned, and reached over to pour more wine into his glass.

Berating him was pointless. To Boyd and her other friends, Dena was an enemy, one of The Privileged, recipient of Anders' attention, career potential without limits. For Rebecca, it was more complicated. She'd tried, really tried to stay allied with Dena following that promotion four years earlier, swallowing her own bitter disappointment at being passed over. For a while it had worked, particularly as their parents' divorce had just occurred, a pain the two sisters could share, understand. The ensuing season had proven more trying, however, as Anders dropped any focus he'd had on Rebecca and redirected it onto his new soloist and his principals. For the two years prior, she'd been on his radar, and then, not.

Poof. Gone, like that.

The downgrade in Rebecca's status had not gone unnoticed by the other company members. Pam, a corps dancer two years her senior, pulled her aside after rehearsal one day and, over coffees, told her how she understood, how there was a group of them who'd so struggled with the pain of being overlooked that they'd created a club: the Disaffected Ballet Dancers' Club, the DBDs for short. Theirs was a clandestine operation, never letting any negativity show around Anders or the other dancers. They would welcome Rebecca with open arms, Pam told her.

Rebecca was appreciative but initially resistant. "No," she wanted to tell the members, who, one by one, let Rebecca know who they were. "I'm still very much promotable. Anders and I have a connection, a strong one. He's just distracted right now." But she couldn't bear the thought that it might produce more pity, more "oh, honey, I've been there too. No dancer wants to believe it ends here, in the corps." She shared with no one her feelings of infatuation over Anders, this sweet, unbearable fire in her soul. It would have destroyed her to be told that he had that effect on all the girls, and that those feelings, too, would pass. She needed to believe that what had transpired between the two of them had been special, unique.

She finally accepted the DBDs' invitation for a night out and discovered they weren't a sulky, resentful bunch in the least. They were lively and had opinions and talked about current events, international goings-on, college classes, books they'd read and enjoyed. And through them, Boyd came into her life. Or, better put, into her bed, because she'd known him and danced with him for several years. He was passionate, principled, easy on the eye, and when he made the moves on Rebecca, there was a sense of "oh, well, why not?" Five years spent pining for one's boss was, in truth, rather pathetic.

They'd been a couple for nine months now. In many ways, this was as close to happy, a contented kind of happiness, not the fiery kind, as she'd been in a long time. It made her feel less alone in the world.

Boyd's cell phone chimed out and he left the bathroom to answer it. "Hey, Pammy, we're in Sonoma," she heard him say. "We're living the genteel life for the night. ...Yeah, we did hightail it out of there, didn't we? So, what's up, what should we have waited for? ... You sly little bitch, you didn't! Why didn't you tell me earlier? Oh, man, I wish I could have been there."

Rebecca rose, dripping, from the tub, wrapped herself in a towel and hurried out of the bathroom.

Boyd turned her way. "Pam's got a contract with Oregon for next season. As a soloist. She just now told Anders."

Words eluded her. She could only gape at Boyd.

"I know," he said, grinning at her.

"What... what...?" she began, but Boyd shooed her away.

"Later. Let me finish here."

She left him to retrieve her wine and get dressed. When she returned, he was sitting on the bed, studying the phone in his hand.

"Wow," he said. "So she did it."

"I'm in shock. She has another year on her contract, like us."

He nodded, his expression grim. "Well, I guess Oregon's shown interest in her for a while now, but she was hesitating. Too long, actually. Two years ago, she might have been considered for future principal material. Now her age is an issue. So, anyway, she told Gunst about the offer and apparently he was cool as you please and told her that she should go for it, because he didn't see himself using her all that much next season. Said she was starting to look shopworn."

"God. Ouch."

"Seriously." Boyd shook his head. "I'm glad she did it. She's been really unhappy."

She'd assumed Pam was fine, that she'd found the same acceptable level of happiness Rebecca had. This news presented itself like a tremor, an ominous warning of things about to irrevocably change.

Boyd poured them more wine and they stepped out onto their balcony to take in the view, acres of rolling vineyards and just beyond them, hills that morphed into the bluish haze of the Sonoma Mountains. The sun cast its last golden ray before sinking below the mountains. Boyd was silent until the sun had faded from view.

"I wasn't going to tell you about this yet, but Pam's news sort of calls for it. Tulsa and I are talking." He turned toward Rebecca. "For a soloist position, but after two years, maybe principal. Principal! Pay is lousy, and it's only a thirty-two-week contract. But hey, time to stop and smell the roses. And things are so much cheaper out there, so that'll be okay."

Encouraged by her stunned silence, he continued. "It's too late to do anything for next season and besides, like you said, we both have one more year on our contracts. But they want me to come out for a few days and take some classes with the company. More as a confirmation than an audition, that's what my friend Bruce there told me. They really liked my audition tape." He held up a hand as if to stop her from commenting.

"There's more. They told me to bring out a partner, that they'd consider two of us."

Oklahoma? *Oklahoma?*

He studied her. "You don't look excited by the thought."

"It's a lot of news to process."

He seemed bothered by her lack of enthusiasm. "I assumed you wanted to get the hell out of the corps."

"Well, yes. But I spent the first thirteen years of my life in the Midwest. The weather's horrible. I don't want to go back. I love California."

"I love California too. But I hate Gunst. I have to get away." Boyd plowed his hands through his thick gold hair. "He's sucking my artistic soul dry. He's not using me to the limits of my capabilities and we both know it. If I stay here, my dance career will end with a whimper. And I don't intend to let that happen."

She shivered, whether from chill or from unease, she didn't know. Because the truth was, even if Anders wasn't noticing her anymore, she wasn't sure she could ever leave his company. She'd sooner quit the business entirely, the thought of which produced an even greater frisson of unease.

Boyd noticed her shivering. "Let's go back inside."

"Let's. And can we maybe talk about something else?"

"Fine. I just wanted to plant the idea in your head."

"Okay. Idea planted."

"Good."

An accident on the Golden Gate Bridge and subsequent traffic backup had them arriving back in San Francisco late on Monday, which meant Rebecca missed her college biology class. It left her time, at least, to hunt down her teacher in his office to beg his forgiveness. He'd warned her, just two weeks previous, about her shoddy attendance. Mondays ordinarily weren't the challenge; the company never performed on Monday nights. Her degree program, offered by a private university, was geared toward performing arts adults, designed to fit their schedules and interests. Several of the dancers were enrolled. Most classes met on Sunday and Monday nights in eight-week sessions. However, she needed fifteen hours of general coursework, which was cheaper to obtain through public colleges. Thus the biology class, which was partially convenient, meeting on Monday afternoons. The other half, though, the Wednesday class, was harder to make. Missing today was simply a case of bad luck.

She dropped off Boyd and made her way to the college campus. Once there, she parked and walked, her footsteps heavy and reluctant. She was a foreigner here in this world, an imposter. In her teens, at the professional children's school she'd attended, she'd scoffed at academics, convinced they would never again play a part in her life.

Silly clueless girl.

Her biology teacher, Misha Lavigne, was a puzzling entity, a science type, possibly her age, possibly a few years older. He was good-looking in an unconventional, Johnny Depp sort of way, with disheveled, glossy black hair long enough to have to tuck behind his ears. His brown eyes seemed to have a permanent startled look, as if someone had stepped into the room and surprised him while he'd been engrossed in his molecular specimens beneath the microscope. The first time she stayed after class to talk to him about her schedule constraints, she'd called him Mr. Lavigne and he'd grimaced.

"You can call me by my first name."

"Sorry. Misha, then," she said, and he nodded. She smiled. "Ballet dancers like that name."

"Because of the dance guy. Baryshnikov."

"You know who I'm talking about!" she exclaimed in delight.

"Yes. I know who Mikhail Baryshnikov is. I even know who George Balanchine was. Despite how it might look, I don't live under a rock."

"Oh. Sure. Sorry."

He smiled; it made him look younger, more like a friend than her teacher.

Today, however, he was not smiling, nor did he look like a friend. He was in his office, a tiny room crowded with books and stacks of papers. He looked up and saw her hesitating by the door. His jaw tightened but he continued the task he'd been focused on, leafing through a stack of turned-in assignments. She continued to stand there nervously.

"Why weren't you in class today?" he finally said.

"I was out of town and traffic back into the city was a nightmare. Backups everywhere. I'm sorry."

"Why weren't you in class last Wednesday?"

"They called a last-minute rehearsal. They know I've requested that time slot off, but I'm one of fifteen dancers in the ballet and the scheduling couldn't be avoided."

He lifted his gaze. "Do you know that, as things stand now, you're close to failing?"

How had it gotten that bad? A knot of sick anxiety formed in her gut.

"Sit down." He gestured to a nearby chair.

Once she was seated, he swiveled around to face her. "Why are you doing this?" he asked.

"Doing what?"

29

"Going to school."

"Well, to earn my degree."

"Fine. Admirable. But if you're not going to take it seriously, give college classes your all, why bother, when you've got a full working schedule already? If you're 'too busy' to come to class, over and over, what's the point?"

She decided to attack with candor. "Do you know how long a ballet dancer's career is?"

"I know it's short. Maybe till you're thirty-five or something?"

She shook her head. "Most of us are eighteen when we join the company, usually as apprentices. By age thirty, that would make twelve years. If you've made it to soloist or principal, you could go comfortably till thirty-five, and even beyond. But if you stay in the corps, it wears the body down much faster. I don't know any corps dancer who's made it past twelve years and is still going strong. Around ten years, you're pondering retirement, what comes next."

"How long have you been there?"

Eight years. Nine if you counted her year as an apprentice.

That was getting close to ten.

Reality rose up and hit her in the face. Why had she never looked at it quite that way before? She had less time than she'd thought.

To her dismay, her reply seized up in her throat.

Misha noticed. "I'm sorry. That wasn't fair of me to ask. It's just that… well, I get kids in my classes who just don't care. And sometimes I need to pound it into them, the importance of education, of working toward a college degree, and how every class should matter, whether or not you're a 'science' person. I just want my students to try. To make a genuine effort to learn, to profit from the opportunity."

He gave a self-conscious shrug. "Listen to me, rambling on."

"No, I understand. I appreciate your honesty. And I'll do my best."

"Good to hear. So. Show up. Catch up on your back work. I'll give you a week and if it's not in, well, you'll get the grade you deserve, and I'll have no sympathy."

"I'll have it in."

With the more awkward business taken care of, the strained air between them cleared. Misha relaxed into his chair, commenting how, back in college, he'd had a girlfriend who was into the performing arts. He'd taken her to see a touring company's production of *Swan Lake*.

"Watching that stuff is amazing," he said. "The way the female dancers skim across the stage in those pink satin shoes. They look so delicate and quiet."

Rebecca thought of the stiff, dangerously slick, peach-colored torpedoes she had to break in before ever wearing them, hammering the new pointe shoe against a concrete wall to soften the box, slashing the shank with an X-Acto knife, ripping the satin off the toes, darning the tips to provide some traction, inwardly wincing when the still-rigid sides pressed against her bunions every time she went en pointe. Hardly delicate.

But that was ballet for you. All about the image.

"So," Misha said, and now he looked a little flustered, tucking his hair more neatly behind his ears as if to spruce up his appearance. "How does one go about attending the ballet here in San Francisco?"

She smiled. "One gets a pair of comp tickets left at the will-call window at the California Civic Theater."

"Oh, I'm not begging for a freebie." He waved his hands.

"It's absolutely no big deal. I get comps all the time."

"Serious?"

"Yes. Just say the word. We finish a program on Tuesday, but we'll be back onstage a week from Friday."

"Well. Maybe a weekend night would be a very cool thing to do."

"A week from Saturday, two tickets?"

"Sure. If you can make it happen."

"Consider it done."

He hesitated. "This isn't tickets in exchange for a good grade here. I don't work like that. You still have to fully participate, Rebecca."

"Of course."

"And study for the final in four weeks—it's worth thirty percent of your grade."

"Our season ends in three weeks. I'll be in good shape for the final."

"Good. Because it's important. No excuses, no absences. And I'm no pushover."

"I believe you."

After the meeting, Rebecca drove to Dena's apartment to drop off the car. Dena and Lana's apartment came with a parking space, one more staggering bit of good fortune bestowed upon her little sister. Dena was home, acting cagey, broody.

"I won't be in company class tomorrow," she told Rebecca. "I have a doctor's appointment."

"See? Something's up with you—did I call it or not?" Rebecca didn't know whether to feel triumphant or worried. "I told you something looked off."

"Nothing's wrong with me. I'm only doing this so Anders will let me dance tomorrow night." A fierce, decisive look had come over her face, the kind she used to wear so much when they were kids. Dena had been so stubborn, so strong-willed and single-minded that it seemed she could make something happen by sheer force of will.

"This is the specialist you saw, who never got back to you with results?"

"Yes," Dena admitted.

"How'd you get an appointment back in so fast?"

"Anders told me how to phrase it when I called them. And I mentioned who he was, so I guess that was worth a lot. That's the only reason."

The worried feeling lingered. Anders had clout, but not that much. "Do you want me to go with you to the appointment? For support?"

Dena frowned at her. "No. I told you. Nothing's wrong with me."

Why had she been thinking Dena might relax her guard? Rebecca sighed. "Okay. Whatever. I'm tired, I'm going home. I guess I'll see you at the studios some time tomorrow afternoon."

"I'll be there," Dena said in a steely tone. "You can count on it."

Chapter 3 – Dena

Even dragging her feet for her ten o'clock doctor's appointment, Dena managed to arrive early. She checked in with the receptionist, who responded to Dena's name by straightening in her chair and beaming at her. "Oh, *you're* Dena Lindgren," she said. "Of course! Hello, Dena. The doctor will be with you shortly!"

The receptionist hadn't been so friendly the first time. Probably she'd caught on that Dena was a soloist with the WCBT. People tended to treat her differently once they knew that.

She took a seat and looked around. The room's beige, blocky furnishings were made blander by the fluorescent overhead lighting. A sickly potted ficus sagged in a windowless corner. Even though there were a half-dozen people waiting, stillness hung over the room.

She hated medical clinics and doctors' offices. She hated feeling unhealthy.

Her cell phone had chirped while she'd been speaking with the receptionist and now she saw that she'd missed a call from her mother. She drew a fortifying breath and listened to the voice message she'd left.

"Dena, this is my third call to you, what on earth is going on? Rebecca's worried as well. You tripped and fell during a performance, you're seeing a specialist and you couldn't let me know? Dena, a mother gets worried. Call me, as soon as your appointment's over."

It was a command, not a request. That was Isabelle Lindgren for you.

At least she could look at her relationship with her mother and the pain of those early years more objectively now. She better understood, as an adult, the sacrifices her mother had made to move them out to San Francisco, set up a second household so that the fourteen-year-old Rebecca wouldn't have to live alone while attending the WCBT's ballet school. Had they stayed put in the suburban outskirts of Chicago through those years, it would have consigned the girls to regional instruction and dance opportunities. But what eleven-year-old harbored such farsighted vision? Instead, when Rebecca had been accepted on scholarship into the school, prompting Isabelle's decision, Dena had begged to be allowed to stay behind with their father. An absurd idea, as he traveled over fifty percent of the time for business. With a West Coast base, he might see his family just as much, he'd promised Dena, but that hadn't been the case. Sometimes it was weeks between visits, periods of agony for Dena, missing the Chicago area and her friends, listening to her mother criticize her sloppiness, her moodiness, while in the same breath praising Rebecca and her potential.

While Rebecca attended the ballet school, Dena took ballet classes at a local studio, and regularly tried out for one of the few privileged positions at the WCBT ballet school. She was rejected, not once but twice, told she didn't match the body profile they were seeking. Lovely extensions and beautiful feet, true. Peerless flexibility. But she was short and lacked Rebecca's spectacular good looks, her long-limbed lines, their way of saying she was chubby. Finally she was accepted, as a paying student for the spring term, but Isabelle was dismissive, even cruel in her rejection of the invitation.

"If they don't think you're good enough for a scholarship, good enough for them to invest in you, what makes you think they'd ever consider you for their company?" she said to Dena. "Money. Right now they want you for your money. We're not biting. But we'll let you do their summer intensive."

Four weeks when she wanted year-long, life-long? She hated her mother for that; she screamed and ranted for hours upon hearing Isabelle's final dictate. Her thirteen-year-old self was sure her mother had acted out of malice, because she only wanted Rebecca to succeed, and didn't care what happened to Dena. Rebecca, kinder about it, tried placating her, but gave up a few hours later. Isabelle only rolled her eyes and turned her attention back to Rebecca.

Her father finally saw how it was. On his next visit to San Francisco, Dena overheard her parents talking. "Jesus Christ, Isabelle," her father was saying, "it's Rebecca this and Rebecca that. You've got two daughters, you know."

Isabelle's murmured reply was too low to reach Dena's straining ears.

"Then give her to me for two weeks," Conrad said. "Right when school ends, before that damned summer intensive starts up for her. I'll cut out travel those weeks.... No, not both girls. You want to run Becca's life, I won't stand in your way. This is about Dena. ...Well, send Becca out to your sister for a week if you're so burnt out. You chose this for yourself. You took the girls from Chicago."

She'd forever adore her father for his support, and he'd been true to his word. She flew back to Chicago for two weeks and while he still had to work every day, farming her out to aunts and cousins daily, he was there every evening, every morning, booming out his greeting to her. And lo and behold, puberty hit, seemingly overnight, and brought with it astonishing changes. Not increased curves, but length to her limbs, a melting away of body fat, revealing cheekbones, a slim torso and delicate shoulders.

She returned to San Francisco looking like a ballet dancer. Rebecca and Isabelle stared, gape-mouthed at the change. Two months later, at the end of the summer intensive, Dena was offered a place in the ballet school. On scholarship.

And here she was, almost a decade later, living the life of her dreams. Except that her dreams had never included debilitating disequilibrium and an emergency doctor's visit.

"Dena Lindgren?" a nurse sang out, startling her from her reverie. The nurse stood at the doorway, folder in her hand, smiling brightly at her. Dena rose, smiled back at the nurse and followed her into the back area. "So, you're a ballerina, are you?" the nurse asked as she took and registered Dena's weight, temperature, blood pressure. "That's something else!" She didn't wait for Dena's response, but simply continued on talking, a nervous flow of chatter, about exercise, the importance of living healthy, the value of family support. It grew exhausting to listen to. She wanted to tell the nurse there was nothing to be nervous about. Dena wasn't a star, she was merely a hardworking professional dancer. The woman was making her, in turn, feel nervous.

The nurse led her to the examining room and told her the doctor would be with her shortly. Dena settled into a chair with a magazine; they always told you "shortly" and it never was. Particularly since they'd squeezed her in today, between other appointments. But to her surprise, less than a minute later, the doctor knocked at the door and entered the room. He greeted her in a cheery, relaxed fashion, dispelling her unease that something was amiss. Tucked under his arm was Dena's file. He took a seat in his chair and after a brief, chatty exchange, apologized for the delay in getting back to her regarding the MRI results.

"Our mistake entirely. Your file got placed in the wrong pile." He looked grim as he spoke; someone had clearly been chewed out over the error. "I'm very sorry about that."

"No problem. I'm here now," she said cheerfully. "Thanks for getting me in right away. That means I'll be able to perform tonight."

Instead of a reply, he pulled the MRI image results from the file and tacked two of them up against the viewing panel.

"All right. Here's what we have—"he began, but when Dena leaned in, the magazine she'd placed on her lap slid to the floor. "Whoops, I'll get that for you," he said, and bent to retrieve it.

Dena hardly noticed. Her eyes were already locked on the first MRI image, trying to make sense of it. A pale, bumpy mass against a grey surface. It could have been a map, a close-up of dividing cells, a work of modern art. Impossible to interpret, except for one thing: a chunk of the pale mass stood alone, apart from the other tentacling mass. Like a little peanut-sized island.

The second image was easier to decipher. It was a view from the back of her head. Brain mass, grey. Background, black. And close to where the brain met bone, the same little nugget, showing up as white.

It was a tumor. She had a brain tumor. The room swayed.

"Here you go," the doctor said, handing the magazine back to her.

The swaying stopped. Now the doctor would tell her no, that wasn't a brain tumor, it was simply a growth of muscle or fiber or brain stuff, or whatever. She didn't know her brain anatomy; why the hell should she?

"Now." He tapped the pen against the peanut-sized island. "Let's talk about this."

"Yes. Let's."

"What you have here is an acoustic neuroma. A vestibular schwannoma."

Relief made her light-headed. "Oh, that's all. God. I thought it was a brain tumor."

He offered her a sympathetic smile. "Well... It is."

Through the roaring numbness settling over her, a few of his words stuck. A tumor, benign, slow-growing; she'd probably had it for years, a decade even. Pressing into the brain stem between the seventh and eighth cranial nerves. The latter, the vestibulocochlear nerve, a word he wrote out for her, underlining it twice, had to do with balance and hearing. The nerves were being squashed, thus the imbalance, the hearing loss. If left untreated, the symptoms would only get worse and might even become life-threatening. He'd give her names of specialists. Neurotologists, they were called—another word he wrote down and underlined—and they would discuss treatment options with her.

"What kind of treatments?" she managed, her words barely beyond a whisper. The magazine slid off her lap again, but this time neither of them bothered to pick it up from the floor.

"Radiation is a possibility, but given the tumor's size and placement, they'll most likely recommend a craniotomy to remove it."

The news rattled around in a mind that had gone blank.

She had a brain tumor. They wanted to operate on her brain.

He continued speaking in a brisk tone and a sense of exquisite regret came over her, that she'd turned down Rebecca's offer to accompany her. The doctor was handing her slips of paper with names, information on acoustic neuromas, saying that he understood that this was all a lot to take in, to call if she had further questions on what came next. Because something would have to give here. A tumor was crushing her brain stem. It would have to go.

He left, and she rose, collecting her things in a numb state, barely registering the white hallway, the cheery framed prints that now seemed ugly, foreboding. She passed the first nurse, the nervous chatterer, only now understanding that the nurse had been nervous for *her* sake. The receptionist, too, had risen and now stood in the hall, watching her anxiously. They hadn't recognized her today because she was a talented dancer. Instead it was because they'd known she had a brain tumor, and was about to find out.

She took an unsteady step and promptly bumped into the wall. Both women reached out their hands as if to steady her. Inside, she bristled. Outside, she righted herself and tried to laugh it off, a sound that came out more like a bleat. "Clumsy me," she said.

"Are you okay?" the nurse asked. "Do you need to call someone for a ride?"

"Oh, no, I'm fine. Thank you, though."

The receptionist had remained silent, her eyes brimming with pity, which bothered Dena worse than bumping into the wall. The nurse had opened the door leading to the reception area, and Dena offered her a bright smile.

"Thanks! Have a nice day," she told the nurse.

"I sure will. And you, too."

Right.

"I will," she lied as she stepped into a waiting room now full of people. Sensing everyone was watching her now, she sailed through the area, head high, holding that bright smile, just like when you fall onstage and have to get up and keep dancing. Competent and unconcerned until your final exit.

Outside, the morning traffic on nearby 19th Avenue sent a low hum through the air as she navigated the clinic parking lot. Once inside her car, she sat there, unseeing, without turning on the ignition. The news felt like too much to process alone. What she wanted more than anything right then was her father by her side, strong arm slung over her shoulders, telling her everything would be all right, that surely it had all been a mix-up, and it was the next patient who had the brain tumor, not Dena, and how about he go in there and double check things for her?

Anders was expecting her call. So was her mother, but right then those calls seemed like too much. So she did the next best thing to conjuring up her father physically; she called him.

She'd thought she'd be able to say it and remain strong, but the moment she heard her father's voice, his cheerful, assured, "Hi, this is Conrad," the tears began. "Oh, Daddy," she sobbed, like she was nine and not twenty-three. But he kept talking and she realized it was a recording, his voice mail, telling the caller to leave a message.

"Dad," she squeaked out after the beep sounded. "Please call me. Something's up."

Chapter 4 – Rebecca

La Bayadère was the company's next featured full-length ballet, and final show of the season. Rehearsals were in full swing, concurrent with the final performances for the current program. The corps rehearsal for the Kingdom of the Shades scene had stopped while April, the ballet master in charge, helped the audio-visual technician set up a video player and monitor. They were in the largest rehearsal studio, the one whose parameters mimicked the stage. Rebecca and Pam had left the twenty-two other dancers and wandered over to the bank of east-facing windows, issuing in morning sunlight, that looked out onto the city street below.

She'd been wrestling with low feelings all morning long, trying to pretend like it was just any other day, any rehearsal, but what had seemed so mundane the previous week was now tinged with bittersweet. Pam was leaving the company. She and Rebecca would not attend rehearsals together beyond this season. For eight years they'd rehearsed and performed and laughed and wept together, lived in the same house for the past few years even, as close as sisters. Which, given her contentious relationship with her own sister, wasn't saying enough.

"I can't believe you're leaving all of this behind," she said to Pam, gesturing to the other twenty-two dancers.

"Yeah. No more corps de ballet. Finally." Pam grinned.

"You'll miss us."

Pam pondered this and her expression grew sad. "You're right. Of course I will. You're my friends. But I've had enough of being overlooked. It's my turn to claim center stage while the corps hovers behind me."

"I'm jealous," Rebecca said, and Pam gave her a little nudge.

"Rumor has it you and someone else might be doing something about that."

Before Rebecca could reply, April called out for everyone to come over to watch. Just as well; she didn't want to talk about Boyd and Tulsa.

The dancers grouped around the monitor and watched the production, the WCBT's previous performance of *La Bayadère* from five years earlier. April wanted the new corps members and company apprentices to have a perfect sense of the uniformity required, how crucial it was for all twenty-four dancers to be in perfect synchronicity during the Kingdom of the Shades scene. One by one the Shades, dance spirits of the afterworld, descended an upstage ramp, amid ghostly light. Dressed in white tutus, each Shade took an arabesque pose with a demi plié that brought the back leg even higher, followed by a demi-plié step back, stretching in a graceful cambré—an arch back—left arm overhead. They straightened, took a few steps forward, and another Shade joined the line of dancers. Together they repeated the movements, with a new Shade following. The ramp zigzagged back and forth four times so that at one point twenty-four dancers, six rows of four, all struck the same arabesque pose at once, the same arched cambré back. The sight of the whole corps moving in tandem was gorgeous, ethereal, soul-stirring.

This scene was the corps de ballet's moment of glory, a classic among the entire repertoire of classics. The rest of the time, it often seemed, the corps dancers merely served as elegant background scenery. But that was the plight of a corps dancer in story ballets, and the WCBT audiences loved their *Giselle* and *Swan Lake* and *Coppélia*. They were moneymakers. The principals, as well, loved them.

Final casting for the principal and soloist roles in *La Bayadère* had not yet been announced. The list would go up after the current production's closing performance, that night. There was speculation, of course. Dena had been in rehearsal, learning the repertoire for Nikiya, the female lead, but that was no guarantee. Anders commonly tested out four or five dancers for a lead role but cast only three of them in performances. There was, however, a sense that even if Dena didn't get cast this time, it would happen soon. She was being groomed for principal, anyone could see that.

Except that something was up with Dena of late.

"Isn't Dena performing tonight?" a few people had asked Rebecca upon seeing the day's revised rehearsal schedule. She'd had to tell them she was equally clueless. She knew Dena would rather crawl across broken glass than give up any of her roles or performances, and she'd already given up Sunday's. She'd called Dena after her doctor's appointment, left a message on her cell phone, her home phone. No reply.

April clapped her hands. "Okay, girls. Let's try it again, with better synchronicity."

Their work recommenced, uninterrupted until ten minutes later, when Anders stepped into the studio. Every dancer noticed. Spines straightened, chins lifted, bellies were sucked in. Energy suffused the dancers' every step. Anders watched as he stood next to April, the two of them murmuring from time to time.

The hairs on the back of Rebecca's neck rose. He was watching her.

A jolt of sensual self-awareness shot through her, a near-forgotten feeling. It was a shock to have it return, like some exotic little creature presumed extinct, only there it was now, vibrant and trembling before her, within her. This man, settling his attention on her with interest.

She was quick to understand, however, that this was not about her, but Dena. When April cued the accompanist to stop the music and called for the dancers to take a five-minute break, Rebecca began walking in their direction even before April had time to motion for her to join them. April looked surprised. Anders didn't.

She and Anders stepped to the side of the room, away from April and the dancers. He came straight to the point, which, as expected, involved Dena. "I'm concerned," he said. "She left a message following her doctor's appointment, but it was rather evasively worded, and I learned nothing new. I think she deliberately left something out." He hesitated. "Can you offer me any clearer details about your sister's condition?"

"I can't," she admitted.

"You can't, or you won't?"

"I can't. She hasn't told me anything yet."

He studied her suspiciously. "I don't believe you."

"Anders. Not all sisters instantly confide in each other."

When he realized she was telling the truth, he sighed, shook his head. "She's trying to pass this off as inconsequential."

"I agree."

"A balance issue is not inconsequential." He fixed his gaze on her, expression fierce, but she knew he wasn't expecting a response. This wasn't a dialogue, it was Anders seeing past her, deeply engrossed in his own thinking. She could almost feel his mind working, analyzing, proposing, rejecting.

"So," he said finally, his attention returning to her.

"So," she echoed.

"I need your help."

A question seemed to pass between them.

Where are your priorities here, Rebecca?

And now he held her gaze in the way he used to, intent on her alone, as though she were a fascinating, complicated puzzle he was determined to solve. With that, it all came back in a rush: the infatuation, the all-consuming desire to please him, obtain and sustain his attention. It both appalled and reassured her how quickly these feelings aligned themselves within her, reshaping her in a matter of seconds.

"Maybe I can find out something for you," she said, trying to keep her tone casual.

He rewarded her with several beats more of his attention. "I would appreciate that. Come find me when you have news."

"I will."

At lunch break, she stepped outside, where the afternoon sun blazed down on the slow-moving traffic and grand, neoclassical structures that comprised the Civic Center. She tried contacting Dena again. No answer. A texted "Where r u?" produced no response. She called their mother, who knew nothing about the results of the appointment either. After finishing the conversation, Rebecca paced, frustrated, watching the eternal line of cars and impatient drivers make their stop-and-go way down the streets. The next call she was reluctant to make. She'd never gotten along well with her father, particularly after the divorce and his remarriage, where, even more insulting, he appeared to be genuinely happy. Today, however, she needed answers. She punched in his number, half-hoping he'd be out.

He was in.

"Well," Conrad said, "it's a day for hearing from my daughters."

Her next breezy words caught in her throat. If Dena had called him so soon, Anders had been right; it was something bad.

"How's Janey?" she asked. Janey was The Other Wife, the woman he'd left Isabelle for.

"She's good. Thanks for asking."

"Um, so, Dena told you the results of her doctor visit?"

"She did. You?"

"Well, I'm her sister." She spoke in a confident, *we both know what happened, after all* fashion. He bought it.

"Whew. Bad news," he said.

"I had trouble taking it all in," Rebecca lied.

"It certainly was a lot to take in."

"And here's a problem. Anders is worried, but Dena's not telling him anything."

"That doesn't surprise me," he said. "She's in shock, it needs to settle into place. And it's nothing but bad news for the man. She told me he won't let her perform until it's all cleared up. Well. *That's* going to be a while."

She stuttered out a vague sort of reply, her mind swirling with the ugly possibilities.

"The brain tumor has to come out," her father was now saying.

"The brain tumor..." Her breath left her in one cold whoosh.

"She hates that word too. Fine, the acoustic neuroma."

What on earth was an acoustic neuroma?

He hesitated. "Just what did she tell you, Rebecca?"

Manipulating words to get an answer she was seeking was one thing, but lying directly to her father was another. "We... we haven't talked."

"But you told me you had."

"Well, yesterday," Rebecca admitted. "And the night she fell. I know plenty, Dad."

"No, you don't." His voice grew cold. "Christ. You tricked me into telling you what might have been confidential."

"Dad…" she tried, then fell silent.

He drew in a breath with an audible hiss. "This is so like something your mother might have done, it just chills me."

That hurt more than it should have.

After an awkward, joyless conclusion to the call, Rebecca walked slowly back into the building, dazed over the shock of what she'd just learned. One thought, however, cut through her fog: Anders must know. Immediately.

Ben answered her tentative knock on Anders' closed door. He smiled at her and glanced over his shoulder at Anders, sitting at his desk, phone to his ear. Anders cast the two of them an irritated glance before gesturing to Rebecca with his chin for her to take a seat. Ben gave her arm a quick squeeze—code that the irritation was with the caller and not her. Ben was good in that way. She took a seat in one of the two chairs facing the desk, as Ben returned his attention to Anders and the laptop, perched on the corner of Anders' desk.

Anders was in discussion with someone over logistics for the company's summer tour in London. Ben, consulting the laptop, called out numbers to him: costs, theater seat counts. Anders, eyes on his own monitor, repeated the numbers to his caller, adding on his own demands and expectations. Sometimes the caller's response satisfied him, other times he rolled his eyes with impatience and began to argue.

As Rebecca waited, she surveyed the photos on the wall behind Anders' desk, headshots of the company's esteemed principal dancers through the years. There was Katrina, Javier, and further down, Ben, from his own tenure that had ended ten years ago. Back then, he'd looked a lot like Boyd: same thick gold hair, pleasing facial symmetry, a brilliant, confident smile. Now, at thirty-five, Ben's face was leaner and his hair was thinner, darker, short, receding at the temples. "God, just shoot me if that's what my hair ends up looking like, too," Boyd had once said, which had revealed more about Boyd than maybe she'd wanted to know.

She wondered how she would have liked the younger Ben. Would he have been just another handsome, talented, self-absorbed dancer? No matter; life had forced him to accept the constraints of a career-ending back injury in his twenties, and shift to administration, take on the challenge of being Anders' assistant. Baptism by fire. The Ben who sat before her exuded quiet competence, patience and compassion. She couldn't imagine the same kind of changes ever coming over Boyd.

Anders argued with his caller for another five minutes before they came to an agreement. Finally he hung up the phone and regarded Rebecca expectantly.

"Yes…?"

"It's news on Dena."

"And?"

She hesitated. "It appears that she has an acoustic neuroma."

"A what?" Ben asked, puzzled.

"A brain tumor," Anders told him. His eyes flickered shut for an instant as he released a heavy sigh. "I was wondering if that were a possibility." He glanced over at Rebecca. "Benign, yes?"

"Yes."

"A brain tumor," Ben said in a hushed voice. "Oh, shit."

Anders rubbed his temples. "Christ. *For helvede*," he muttered, followed by more curse words in Danish. "What are they saying for treatment?" he asked Rebecca.

"I think surgical removal."

He nodded. "Soon, I imagine. Perversely, I hope so. For her sake and ours. She can't have balance issues and dance." More dark Danish words. He looked at Ben and the two of them exchanged a mournful glance.

"No Nikiya for her," he said to Anders.

"No," Anders admitted. He glanced over at Rebecca abruptly, as if surprised to see her still there, privy to casting news. "Thank you, Rebecca," he said in a more brisk tone. "We need to know these things. I won't mention to Dena that I know, however. I'll let her tell me the news when she's ready."

"That would be better," Rebecca admitted.

Oh, God. Her poor sister. Only now was the bad news fully sinking in.

Anders studied her a moment longer before he turned back to Ben and the computer screens. Her cue to disappear.

Late afternoon, April was rehearsing the *Spirit Hour* cast to help out Laurel, Dena's understudy, whose substitution for the program's final performance had become official. Today Laurel seemed more confident on the stage, eager to take a second stab at performing it. The female corps dancers, having run through their passages without a hitch, now stood on the periphery as Laurel and Nicholas worked on one of the trickier passages. Mid-rehearsal, Anders and Ben stepped into view. Anders gestured for April to keep the rehearsal going.

This time his eyes did not seek out Rebecca, which was likely a good thing. He had a no-nonsense, dispassionate expression on his face as he watched Laurel and Nicholas. She recognized it as the look of a man unafraid to make unpopular decisions.

He stayed only three minutes. A frown creased his brow and he leaned in toward Ben to murmur something. Ben listened, nodded, his expression revealing nothing.

Anders left. Ben waited for a pause in the rehearsal to signal for April's attention. April stopped the accompanist and in the silence that followed, the two ballet masters conversed in low tones. Rebecca and Pam exchanged puzzled looks.

"Dancers, ten-minute break," April called out. "Laurel and Nicholas, come here, please."

The news became clear fast: Anders had bumped Laurel from the role. Katrina, the principal who'd performed the same role in the first cast, would step in to take Dena's place for the night's performance. April dismissed Laurel, and the rest of the dancers settled into stretch poses on the stage floor until Katrina arrived, five minutes later, cool and composed, ready to step right into action.

After rehearsal, the corps dancers congregated in the women's lounge to commiserate with Laurel. The WCBT was a close-knit company in that way. Although petty competitions did exist, along with social delineation between the ranks, for the most part the company members tried to support one another. Among the corps females, this was doubly true.

Laurel sat huddled on a bench, eyes red, chin trembling. "He didn't even give me a real chance," she said. "I was nervous the other day. I was so hyped to do it tonight. It would have been great, I'm sure of it."

Charlotte, a DBD and one of Rebecca's housemates, had a murderous expression on her face. "That asshole. He couldn't even break the news to her. One word to Ben, and off he waltzes, to destroy the next person's day."

Pam shot her a warning glance. Charlotte stopped talking, but her eyes still shone with rage. Laurel's peers, the younger corps members, comforted her, told her there was always the next time. Rebecca didn't have the heart to tell them there probably wouldn't be a next time.

"Wait till Boyd hears about this," she heard Charlotte mutter to one of the other DBDs. Charlotte glanced up and met Rebecca's eyes. Her gaze darkened. "What did Anders want with you earlier?"

Rebecca frowned. Although they all lived in the same house, she and Charlotte were on less friendly terms than Rebecca was with Pam and the other two roommates. Charlotte was more Boyd's friend, and shared Boyd's zeal in their mutual hatred of Anders, particularly after he'd dropped Charlotte's best friend, Courtney, from the company roster three years ago.

"He's concerned about Dena and wanted to know what was up with her."

"…and?" Charlotte prodded.

"And I told him I knew as much as he did. Which wasn't much."

She wasn't about to share anything further. Not even with Pam. This was between her and Anders and Ben. Just like it used to be.

And yet, whatever elation that thought produced, it was overshadowed by the pain of Dena's news and the way Rebecca had recaptured Anders' attention with it. And how, in return, he'd recaptured her loyalty.

She'd lost something. The not-caring, the workaday happiness she'd found in the corps, in her life with Boyd, with Pam.

In the course of just a few days, it all seemed to be slipping away.

Chapter 5 – Dena

Sweat poured down Dena's back and crept into her eyes, making them sting. Her lungs ached. Her quads and calf muscles burned. She turned the notch on the step machine one level higher. Another. Another.

Three weeks since the diagnosis of her acoustic neuroma. Three days since *La Bayadère* closed and the company's season ended. Two days until her surgery.

The other dancers on this Monday, the first official day of layoff, were probably sleeping in. Not her. Not after being sidelined through *La Bayadère*. Instead, she was at her neighborhood gym, climbing the step machine. None of the stage's glamour in this small, enclosed space, with its green industrial carpet, dank, briny odor, and middle-aged ex-jocks comprising its membership. But it was walking distance from her apartment, a bargain price, and today it was a place of comfort. Here she wasn't a sidelined dancer, she was simply another exerciser.

Being sidelined was agony. Watching *La Bayadère* from the audience as her comrades danced had been agony as well, but she'd done it for Lana, who'd been the soloist chosen to play the lead for one performance. She'd been a gorgeous Nikiya. Which hadn't prevented Dena from crying through most of the production.

Rebecca, as per normal, had been gorgeous too, but Dena had a bone to pick with her sister. Thanks to her, the other dancers had found out about Dena's medical condition long before she herself had felt ready to share the information. Rebecca, who'd promised to keep quiet about it, had tried to explain, but Dena had cut her off with a shaky, indignant "save it for later." Since then, they'd avoided each other.

Cardio work complete, she slung a towel around her sweaty neck and headed, still panting, over to the mats, the exercise balls. For the next thirty minutes she focused on crunches, plank pose, core muscle work, willing darker thoughts away. With her surgery looming, however, serenity didn't stand a chance.

She'd taken care of preoperative business, the blood work, questionnaires, insurance forms, paperwork, authorizations. She'd learned that risks during a craniotomy included "general difficulties, such as bleeding, infection, stroke, paralysis, coma and death." She hadn't known whether to laugh or freak out over the last two, so she did a little of both. She was to arrive at six o'clock in the morning the day of the surgery and they would pump her with antibiotics, a drug to prevent seizures, and other, more complicated, scary drugs. Her neurotologist explained that with the approach they'd use—trans-labyrinthine, or translab for short—the incision would go behind her ear and only a patch of her long brown hair would have to be shaved. It could have been a lot worse.

"Worse" was the fact that the translab procedure would sacrifice her hearing in her left ear, reducing it from compromised to nonexistent. She'd inquired about alternate procedures, but was told that the odds of facial nerve damage—and thus facial paralysis—would become higher. She needed an unharmed facial nerve; without it, she would no longer be able to emote on that side, crucial for any performer. Therefore, translab it would be. She hadn't told Anders about her imminent partial deafness, but she had a hunch he knew already. For someone handed such shocking, unexpected news, he'd been surprisingly calm and informed about the diagnosis and anticipated recovery time.

In a few days she would get her skull cut open. Thinking about it made her queasy with dread, light-headed with fear. Or, better put, light-headed because a large tumor was pressing against her brain stem that, if not removed, would eventually kill her.

She redoubled her efforts on her abs, holding the next plank pose for a full three minutes. Her arms shook; her core muscles screamed in protest.

There. That gave her something different to think about.

Thirty minutes later, she stepped outside onto Castro Street. The day was cool and overcast, dampness lingering from a morning shower, but it hadn't dampened the spirits of the pedestrians. Here in the Castro, not much did. It was an endless parade of Interestings, dressed in all colors of the rainbow, so to speak. Men holding hands, others strutting in their skimpy gym shorts and close-fitting tee shirts that showed off their admittedly gorgeous physiques. A tall woman with cascading black curls and a half Mohawk strode past, chin held high. She wore high-heeled combat boots, velvet leggings, a full-length crimson cape, and clutched an iron staff. Very regal. Very weird. Two approaching businessmen shot her a look of mild curiosity before returning to their own conversation.

Dena headed over to her friend Celia's coffee shop, two blocks away. Celia made her own scones; today it was a treat she'd allow herself. Celia, who knew about the upcoming surgery, would probably insist.

When Dena entered the shop, redolent of cinnamon and coffee,

Celia was talking to a slender woman in jeans and a hoodie whose back was to the door. She laughed when she saw Dena. She pointed and the other person swung around.

Surprise. It was Rebecca.

Shit.

"That's sisterly intuition for you," Celia called out as Dena approached. "I told Rebecca I hadn't seen you, and she told me she had a hunch you'd stop by here this morning."

"Crazy, isn't it?" Rebecca said, beaming at Celia who beamed right back.

Celia might have known about the surgery, but Dena hadn't told her about Rebecca's big mouth and Dena's subsequent avoidance of her. She swallowed a sigh and smiled at Celia.

"Well, all I can say is that I hope my sister didn't intuit my intentions further and take the last scone."

"No, sirree. I wouldn't let my favorite customer suffer in that way," Celia said. "I made sure there were plenty today. Just in case you stopped by."

"Baker's intuition," Dena said.

Celia nodded. "That and, well, I know what's coming up later this week."

Her eyes met Dena's.

"Yeah," Dena said softly. "That."

"So, Deen," Rebecca said in a carefully bright voice. "I was wondering if maybe this was a good time to chat?"

She couldn't avoid her sister forever. In reply, she offered Rebecca a resigned nod.

"Looks like that'll be scones for two," Celia announced. "Today they're on me, ballet chicks. Happy season's end to you. I hope you both gain ten pounds."

They all laughed. Celia, blonde and pink-cheeked, weighed close to two hundred pounds, but her comfort with herself and her body was palpable. She liked hearing Dena's stories about the dance world, and in turn, offered her support whenever Dena needed it.

The espresso bean grinder's noisy whir, followed by the hiss of milk being steamed made it easy to avoid conversation with Rebecca for a while longer. Five minutes later, though, they sat across from each other, each fortified by a scone and a steaming latte.

"So…" Rebecca began, and smiled.

Dena offered her a stiff nod.

"An eventful week."

"Yes," Dena said.

"Ready for a family dinner tomorrow night?"

"It'll be… interesting."

As if her life weren't surreal enough right now, they'd all agreed to a family dinner, the four of them, the night before the surgery. It would be the first time they'd been together as a family since the divorce. Isabelle, who'd moved back out to the Bay Area after the divorce, lived in Los Gatos, fifty miles south, with Dan, her partner of two years. She'd be coming up to spend the next two weeks with Dena, helping out.

Rebecca dipped a corner of her scone into her latte before taking a bite of it. "When's Dad arriving from Chicago?"

"Tomorrow afternoon."

"And Mom?"

"She'll drive up before rush hour."

"What's that going to be like, having Mom as a roommate again?"

Dena shrugged. "I'll manage. It was either that or spend the time, post-op, in boring Los Gatos."

She loved San Francisco and her apartment, a two-bedroom unit in the Castro that she and Lana had snatched up three years earlier. It was on the second and top floor, with a skylight in the kitchen that lightened up the entire room. Big picture windows in the living room overlooked the city's hills. Just being there made her feel happy, grounded, secure about her place in the world.

"Did Lana leave town already, or is she just staying at Gil's?" Rebecca asked.

"She flew out yesterday."

"It's not like she's been there in the apartment much lately, anyway, huh? I noticed her room looked pretty empty, when I peeked in, last month."

Dena frowned. "What were you doing in there?"

"Just being nosy."

"No kidding."

"Why doesn't she just move in with Gil officially and save rent money?"

"She says her family would disapprove."

"They're engaged, though. What, is she going to keep that up until they get married?"

"At least through the summer and into the fall, she's saying."

"That's nice for you."

"It is," Dena admitted. "I don't look forward to trying to find and test out a new roommate. It's going to be tricky."

"Yeah, I'd guess. You're not exactly the easiest person to get along with."

Dena scowled at Rebecca. "Speak for yourself."

"Hey, I'm the one with four housemates. We get along fine. Well, mostly." She took another coffee-dipped bite of scone before speaking again.

"In fact, that brings us to how the truth about your condition slipped out. Look, I told Pam, okay? She's my best friend and she knew I was upset about the thing you weren't telling people. She steered me into the kitchen when the others were in the living room, and she all but guessed it. She said 'cancer' and I said no, not really, and she asked what that meant and I said not all tumors were cancerous and she said omigod, Dena has a brain tumor." Rebecca spoke rapidly, staring at her scone plate. Finally she looked up.

"I told her not to tell anyone and she swore she wouldn't. And I don't think she did."

"Then how did the other dancers find out?" Dena asked.

"There's so many of us in that house. I assumed everyone was in the living room watching the movie and couldn't hear us, but if someone had gotten up to use the bathroom, and was being super quiet, they could have snuck up and eavesdropped."

"That's sleazy."

"I agree."

"Who did it? Charlotte?"

"Maybe. I honestly don't know how to read her."

"I don't trust her. She's always hated me."

"To be honest, I'm not sure how much she likes me, either," Rebecca confessed. "Although sometimes she'll act all chummy, inviting me to confide in her. Like when we found out Laurel got bumped from your role. She wanted me to tell her what Anders and I had been talking about earlier. And I was like, oh, please. If I can't tell Pam what I found out, I'm not about to tell *you.*" Rebecca scrunched up her face at the thought.

Dena's hand, en route to her coffee cup, stopped. "Wait. What did you 'find out' while talking to Anders?"

A look of unease flashed across Rebecca's face and was gone so fast, Dena decided she'd imagined it. When Rebecca spoke, it was in the condescending, big sister tone Dena knew so well.

"You're squishing together two events," she told Dena. "I spoke to Anders during rehearsal before lunch, and ninety minutes later, Dad shared the diagnosis with me. And I *still* can't believe you told him before you told me." She allowed a note of injury to creep into her voice.

"Sorry. I was freaked out. No offense, it's just that Dad's the one I turn to when something bad is happening. He makes it seem less insurmountable. You and Mom make it feel, well, worse." She took in Rebecca's hurt expression. "I didn't mean for that to sound the way it did. But Dad and me, we get along in the way you and Mom do."

"Mom and I don't always get along. We argue plenty."

"Yes, but in a different way than she and I argue."

"Kind of like the way Dad and I argue," Rebecca said dryly.

"Right. Like that."

"I need water," Rebecca said, rising. "Do you want a glass?"

"Sure."

She watched Rebecca make her way over to the condiments counter. A tall, good-looking guy mixing half-and-half into his coffee made a comment, to which her sister replied with a lilting laugh and response that charmed him. His eyes remained locked on her as she poured two waters.

Rebecca, the charmer.

Rebecca the manipulator, Conrad would have grumbled. "She tricked the news out of me," he'd told Dena the afternoon of her diagnosis, when he'd called her back to apologize. At the time she hadn't been too bothered; it had meant one less person to break the news to. And she'd taken it as proof that Rebecca genuinely cared, so desperate to know what was up.

What did you 'find out' by talking to Anders?

Dena's question had rattled Rebecca, if only for an instant. The smooth, better-worded reply had followed too quickly. As if Rebecca were trying to hide something.

Rebecca hadn't found out anything by talking to Anders. Instead, though, maybe she'd found out something, from an unsuspecting Conrad, and run right in there to tell Anders.

No, impossible, Dena told herself. Too mercenary. Sisters didn't do that to sisters. Family came first; case in point was this family dinner they'd all agreed to.

And yet.

If Anders had known about the acoustic neuroma before Dena went in to tell him, it would explain why he'd been so calm about the news, so prepared for discussion about it.

The instant the thought arose, she knew it to be the truth.

She clutched at her coffee cup, a sick feeling washing over her.

Rebecca returned to the table, smiling to herself, but stopped short when she saw Dena's expression. "Hey, are you okay? You look faint. Here, drink this water."

Dena ignored the proffered glass. "Tell me this, and please don't lie to me."

"What?" Rebecca set down the glasses hastily and lowered herself to sitting.

"I need to know. Did you go and speak with Anders a second time that day, and tell him about my acoustic neuroma?"

Rebecca's eyes darted about, as if she were internally assessing which story would serve her best.

"Don't lie," Dena warned. "I'll find out the truth anyway."

"Okay." Rebecca's shoulders sagged. "Yes."

"So, like, right after you got the information from Dad?"

Rebecca kept her gaze downward. "Yes."

The enormity of her sister's betrayal made it difficult to speak. "Why?" Dena managed.

Rebecca looked back up. "Anders needed to know."

"I told him!"

"Not till late afternoon. He needed answers sooner. He singled me out during rehearsal and asked for help with precisely that. It was for him."

Rebecca didn't sound apologetic in the least. A righteous spark now lit her eyes.

"Oh, my God," Dena said slowly. "This means nothing to you."

"It does! It's just that he's our *boss,* Dena. Telling me he needed my help."

"And you value your relationship with your boss above all. Above your relationship with your own sister."

Here Rebecca seemed to falter. "Look. You don't understand. It's complicated."

"Then explain to me! Give me one good reason why you ran in there and told Anders the news so fast. Why you didn't give my own feelings on the matter a second thought."

Rebecca's expression twisted with regret, sorrow and some other indefinable emotion. "I can't," she said finally.

Outrage propelled Dena to her feet. "I cannot believe you," she said, voice shaking. "And that you lied about it five minutes ago. And that you can't even justify your actions to me, now."

"No, I can't."

"No good reason beyond your own self-interest, then. Making yourself look good for the boss." Dena hastily grabbed at her bag, at the remains of her scone. Celia, from behind the counter, glanced over at them in alarm. "Well, thanks, sis. So glad we could have this heart-to-heart just before I undergo major surgery. You really do have the gift of timing, you know that?"

Rebecca looked stricken. "Dena, I'm so sorry."

It was as if every ounce of Dena's carefully stockpiled serenity, wisdom and patience had been blasted away, leaving behind only unhinged rage. "Bullshit," she spat. "And for the record? I think you're despicable."

"I think I am, too," Rebecca whispered, which only enraged Dena further.

"Spare me the pity-party theatrics. And don't bother trying to communicate with me before my surgery. I think you've done enough harm."

"But what about our family dinner?" Rebecca protested.

"Screw the family dinner. It's cancelled."

She made her phone calls that night. Rebecca would not be joining them for dinner on Tuesday night, Dena informed Conrad and Isabelle respectively. In fact, she herself didn't want to go out on a group dinner. What had they been thinking, this faux cheery event, this misguided attempt at normalcy? There was no normal. There was no cohesive family unit.

The whole family loyalty thing was a joke. She told them to ask Rebecca why.

The morning of her surgery, she rose early, unable to sleep. She was allowed no food or drink, so she merely waited for the sun to rise, for her mother to wake. She'd drive Dena to the hospital and Conrad would meet them there. Rebecca had called Isabelle the night before, offering to drive, begging to be a part of the morning. Dena's response to the relayed query had been a decisive "no."

At the hospital, Dena completed the admission process and all too quickly was called in, to have vital signs checked and answer yet more questions. She then followed the nurse to a second room, where she was instructed to change into a hospital gown and "relax" on the gurney. Next she was taken into the operating room holding area. Her parents were there, trying to act casual, as if this sort of thing happened every day.

The operating room nurse breezed in, followed by the

anesthesiologist, who set up the IV, chatting in an easy tone, telling her he'd been to the ballet with his wife, but it had been a contemporary dance night and he wasn't sure how to comment on what he saw, except that it had all seemed very well done and his wife had been impressed. While he was talking, the chief resident came in, followed by her neurotologist, who would remove the tumor once the neurosurgeon had made the opening.

"Okay, confirming with you that the tumor is on the left side," he said, a Sharpie pen in hand, and when she quavered "yes," he made a mark, bizarrely, on that side of her neck. Was there a risk that he, or the neurosurgeon might be that absentminded or confused, to not otherwise know?

"Just procedure," he assured her, taking in her unease. He then explained to her and her parents how the neurosurgeon's work would commence the procedure. He'd drill through Dena's skull, the mastoid bone, navigate through the brain tissue to expose the area around the tumor, before turning the work over to the neurotologist.

Visualizing the high, whining sound of a drill as it chipped a hole in her skull made panic bubble up from within her. As if on cue, the anesthesiologist suggested a mild sedative to help relax her. Yes, she told him. Please. Quick.

Her neurosurgeon arrived, and her parents prepared to leave. Dena had been holding her father's hand, but the sedative had already begun to work its magic and she released it easily, offering her mother a drunken wave.

They wheeled her into the operating room. Lots of lights and activity, but she was getting even more dopey. A crowd had assembled, all in their little greenish scrub outfits that, she decided, could work for ballet dancers as well. Stretchy, roomy, great for pliés and grand battements. And the overhead lights, the blue-green hue that the lights cast on the whole room, made it feel like a set for some neoclassic ballet choreographed by Anders. Blue and green gels over the lights. She liked that thought. She liked the warm feeling the anesthesiologist's sedative had produced.

One of the nurses tucked an errant strand of Dena's hair off her face and smiled at her, a mixture of sympathy and brisk confidence. "There's nothing more you have to do," she said, which comforted Dena, or maybe it was just the drug. She wanted to thank the nurse but words weren't coming out of her mouth anymore and when the anesthesiologist approached her and told her it would all be over in the blink of an eye, she was grateful he didn't seem to expect a reply either. Because the clouds came in an instant later and engulfed it all.

Chapter 6 – Rebecca

The surgery was to have taken five to six hours; at three o'clock it had been seven.

Rebecca, in the surgery department's waiting room with her parents since lunchtime, felt a sick anxiousness building in her stomach. Her father had been checking at the nurse's station for updates. She assessed him as he stood there, his returned presence in her life always a bit of a shock, this handsome, charismatic, too-busy father she'd both loved and feared as a child. He'd retained his athletic good looks, although his dark hair was now threaded with grey and little wrinkles appeared on his forehead and around his eyes. He still commanded attention wherever he went, however. He was a lot like Anders in that way.

Prior to Rebecca's arrival had come the news that the neurosurgeon had finished with his entry work and Dena's neurotologist had taken over. At one o'clock, the nurse at the desk had informed Conrad the surgery was going as expected. Shortly after two o'clock, news of "a bit of a delay." But since then, nothing. Only the soft whoosh of cold re-circulating air through the room's vents and the nurses' low, assured voices as they talked with patients and each other.

"No news is not bad news," the nurse at the desk assured Conrad. "They're just busy with her."

Rebecca left the waiting room to get some fresh air and check her phone for messages. Boyd had called, saying that he and the girls had arrived in Tulsa and their hotel rooms were fantastic, that Rebecca would have loved it. The three of them had adjoining rooms, one for him, one for Pam and her new Oregon friend. Unless things got, you know, friendly in a different way with him and the Oregon friend.

He liked to do this to her, hint to Rebecca that the women were always looking his way and it was only his loyalty to her that kept him from responding. That was his way of retaliating for her lack of cooperation. He'd wanted her to drop the studying for her biology final so she could spend time with him. He'd badgered her about joining him in Tulsa for the week, even as she protested that, biology final aside, Dena's surgery was taking place and she had to stay local.

"She's not even talking to you," he'd pointed out.

He had a point there. Which Rebecca knew she deserved. She should have supported her sister over Anders; what the hell had she been thinking? But that was what Anders did to her. When he fixed his gaze on her, something in her went a little crazy, sending more sensible priorities askew.

She texted Boyd a reply, sipped water from the drinking fountain and returned to the waiting room. Her mother met her inquiring glance with a shake of her head.

No news.

Fear began to curdle the contents of her stomach. What if something were going wrong, catastrophically wrong?

"Stop thinking the worst," her father said, as if reading her mind. "She'll be fine." He sounded impatient. She knew that meant he was worried as well.

Her mother sat there reading, looking as composed and beautiful as ever. Relatives were always telling Rebecca she was a carbon copy of her mother in her younger years. Isabelle did not appear to be mirroring Rebecca's anxiety at the moment, but Rebecca observed how the magazine she was reading remained on the same page over the next fifteen minutes.

Four o'clock. No news.

Four-thirty.

Among the many worrisome aspects of the delay was a personal problem: her biology final was in a few hours. She wanted to kick herself for her stupidity in not seeing this one coming, this conflict on the day of Dena's surgery, the bind it put her in now. She'd planned to be here for Dena when she came out of anesthesia in the early afternoon, before returning home to study for the last few hours. But this delay was throwing a wrench into all of that. Now, she couldn't imagine leaving the hospital to go study, much less take the biology exam.

She voiced her concerns to Isabelle, sitting next to her as Conrad paced.

"Call your teacher and explain," she told Rebecca.

"I think I will. I'll be right back."

She slipped outside to a courtyard on the ground floor to make the call. The wind had picked up, even within this enclosed space. Misha answered his office phone and she told him she had a conflict regarding the day's final.

Silence greeted her words.

"Hello? Misha?"

"A conflict," he said in a flat voice. "Imagine that. Wait, let me guess. It's a sick relative."

How could he have known?

"Which means you have to leave town, oh, about right now," he continued. "Or you're calling from out of town."

It dawned on her that he thought she was making it up.

"No, not in the least. I'm in a hospital, in San Francisco." The wind buffeted against her, chilly and fog-laced. "My sister's in surgery."

"Emergency surgery?"

"No, scheduled. But it's gone overtime."

"The time to reschedule this final was before today. Further, I will not discuss this over the phone. I made my rules clear to you students at the beginning of the year and it's spelled out on the syllabus. No phoned or emailed excuses. Either you make alternate arrangements to take the final early or you show up on the assigned day. No show, you get a zero."

"But I have a legitimate issue! And I'm *not* out of town, whooping it up, if that's what you're implying."

"You're really in San Francisco?"

"Yes!"

"Then come discuss this issue in person. I'm here for the next forty minutes."

"Look. I can't do that today."

Misha's voice grew harsh. "Then you get an F on the final."

"You, you..." she started, but before an obscenity could slip out, she hung up. "You bastard!" she screeched at the now-silent phone.

Which to choose, the class she dared not fail, or support for the sister who wanted nothing to do with her?

Back upstairs in the waiting room, she tried to keep her voice steady as she reported the news to her parents. Conrad eyed her irritably. "He'll listen if you go in? So go in, right now. Just do it, instead of fussing about it."

"Fine, fine." She glared at her father. "I'll go."

She drove to the college, shaking with rage and anxiety. Traffic at this time of day was unbearable, a snarled mass of congestion. But Misha was still in his office. "It would have been nice if you'd just *listened* to why I couldn't come in, or take the test," she burst out the moment he looked up and saw her.

Misha looked equally irate. "Look. You were the third student this week to try this on me. The previous call was just an hour before yours. Another sick relative story, one he couldn't substantiate. I get stories like this every term. That's why I have to draw a hard line."

"I was seriously calling from a hospital."

"Okay, that part is legitimate. That you were where you said you were, and you actually showed up to discuss it works in your favor now. But you said this was a family member's scheduled surgery. Unless we're talking a triple bypass, it's still not a valid excuse to present, three hours before a final."

Hot tears collected beneath the surface, which she successfully blinked away.

"No. Not triple bypass. But brain surgery, to remove a tumor. On my little sister."

His resolute expression evaporated. "A craniotomy?"

"Yes."

"Your sister has a brain tumor? Oh, God. I'm sorry. What kind of tumor?"

"It's called an acoustic neuroma. It's when—"

"Yes. I know what an acoustic neuroma is. Where is she? If it's San Francisco, I'm guessing UCSF?"

She nodded.

"And do you know if the procedure is translab or retrosigmoid?"

"I... I don't know."

"Do you know who the surgeons are? She's probably got both a neurosurgeon and neurotologist."

"I don't know."

He frowned. "Rebecca. What do you know?"

The tears rose higher, like a giant wave. "I know that I'm scared," she managed, before the wave crested and she doubled over, weeping into her hands.

Like that, Misha's attitude shifted, turning him from stern teacher back into sweetheart guy, moving to sit next to her, procuring her Kleenex. She mopped her face, gulped in air to calm down.

"I'm sorry," Misha said once she'd composed herself. "I wish you'd told me all this straight out."

"I tried. I called."

"You did, but why wait till today, in the middle of it, to call? Why didn't you tell me about this earlier? We could have set you up for the test on an earlier day."

"I wanted the time to prepare. And I *was* prepared. She was supposed to be done by two o'clock, which gave me a few extra hours to prep even more. I was thinking, 'where's the conflict there?'"

He looked shocked. "She's not a pot roast, Rebecca. These things don't work that predictably. A craniotomy is serious business."

"Yes. As I was trying to explain to you. And you made me leave the hospital in order to drive through city traffic and explain it in person."

He winced. "Okay. My bad. You're absolutely right, the final should be secondary to something this serious. Don't worry, we'll work something out for you."

She felt too rattled to return to traffic immediately. Misha fetched her a Diet Coke and listened as she talked, letting her worries and thoughts spill out without regard to social convention. She talked about her rivalry-but-not with Dena, the way her own support now seemed tainted because of her loyalty toward their artistic director, who was her boss, after all. She admitted she'd thought Dena's surgery would be quick, a best-case scenario, because of the way Dena herself was. Her stubbornness, her strength of will, defined her and lent the impression that Dena would somehow, even under anesthesia, push her way through this latest obstacle and leap up from the operating table, demanding a quicker finish so she could rest up and get right back to what she preferred.

Misha chuckled. "Sounds like my younger brother."

"Strong willed?"

"Oh, boy, and how. Great guy, very charismatic. Tremendously talented, but he's always been determined to do things his own way. Could have been a world-class concert pianist. But he didn't like following someone else's rules, so he's just sort of blazed his own trail through life. And gotten by." The mirth left his expression. "Guess I'm lucky he never had interest in trying to become a doctor."

Something puzzling about him became clear. "You tried, didn't you?" she asked. "That's why you sound so knowledgeable in the classroom and about my sister's procedure. You went to medical school."

"Wow." He looked startled. "I'm that transparent, huh?"

She liked this guy; he was a real person. "No, not at all. It's just that I understand sibling rivalry."

"Well, you hit the nail on the head," he said with a gloomy nod. "Our dad was a surgeon. Guess I felt competitive there, too."

"You said 'was.' Is he retired?"

"No. He died four years ago. Cancer. I was in my second year of medical school at the time, hating it. Failing it, in truth. My dad saw what was going on and told me to get out, that being a doctor had been his path and not mine. That it would only make me bitter if I kept trying to compete, with him and David both."

She thought of her own hypercritical father. "Ouch. That wasn't very kind."

"No, actually, it was. Oh, I was defensive and hurt at the time, particularly when he told me he thought I'd do better as a teacher. That seemed so second-place." He studied his hands. "In the end, though, he did me a huge service. It all worked out. But it sure wasn't easy, that year." He raised his gaze to meet hers. "Remember the stuff you were saying to me when you came into my office last time? About not knowing what comes next after the thing you've prepped for all your life has fallen through?"

"How could I forget?"

"Well. Suffice to say, I get it."

He did.

"Thank you for telling me that story," she said softly.

He mock-winced. "My grand over-sharing? Some teacher I am."

"No, no. You're a better teacher this way. Compassion motivates people, not just stern discipline."

"Stern discipline, as in threatening to flunk you without hesitation?"

She laughed. "Would you have, really?"

"The good news is that I don't have to ponder that. You are officially excused for the next twenty-four hours. But that's all." He wagged a reproving finger at her as he rose. "Friday afternoon, grades are due in. You have until Friday morning to take it, got it?"

"Got it."

"I kind of need to get moving here." He motioned toward the door. "Are you okay to drive now? If not, I can give you a lift."

She rose as well. "No thanks, I'll be fine. I feel much better."

They walked out of the room and down the hallway together. "Hey," she said, "I forgot to ask about your night at the ballet. How did you like it?"

"Oh, Rebecca." His footsteps slowed. "You were stunning. So beautiful. I mean," he added hastily, "the *production* was stunning. And beautiful. The sets, the costumes. All the dancers." He still sounded flustered.

"You're right," she said, pretending to not notice. "It really was a gorgeous production. I was just a small part of it. One of the herd."

A pang cut through her. "I'm sure you couldn't even tell which dancer I was."

"Oh, but I did. At least in that Kingdom of the Shades scene."

"Impossible. There were twenty-four of us, all dressed alike, all moving alike."

"You were the fourth one in line to come out. And in the front row when all of you were dancing together."

She regarded him in astonishment. "You *did* see me."

He smiled back. "I have good powers of observation."

"Spoken like a true biologist."

"I can admit to that," he said as he held the building door open for her.

Out in the parking lot, she turned to him. "Thanks for everything. I really appreciate it." She wanted to say more—thank him for letting her share her worries, share his own vulnerabilities—but the mood between them had returned to business.

"No problem," he said. "Study. Take care. And call me tomorrow to confirm your test time availability."

"I will. Thanks."

Calmer now, she drove back to the hospital, parked and made her way through the corridors. Their waiting room had emptied out. Aside from an elderly couple in a far corner, her parents were the only two left in the seating area. The clock read 6:15pm.

At the doorway, she hesitated. Her father's expression was unreadable but there was raw fear in Isabelle's beautiful brown eyes.

Terror clutched at her gut.

"Was there bad news?" she cried, rushing toward them.

They looked startled. "No news," Conrad said. "Which means no bad news."

Isabelle tried to smile at Rebecca. "How did your talk with your teacher go?"

"Good. He's letting me take the final the day after tomorrow. But there's no news at all about Dena?"

"No," Isabelle and Conrad said at the same time.

She sank down on the seat next to her mother, her legs curiously weak.

Silence once again fell over the room. Thirty more minutes passed and then Conrad sprang up. Rebecca hadn't even seen Dena's surgeon, the neurotologist, until her father was there in front of him, asking how it went. The surgeon was smiling, but it was a professional, unreadable kind of smile, as he spoke.

Dena was all right. In stable condition. The surgery, however, had proved much trickier than expected. The tumor had been vascular, not cystic. "Very bloody, very complicated to extract," the surgeon said. "I've done hundreds of these procedures, but this one kept me... challenged."

Rebecca and Isabelle had joined Conrad. "But the tumor's out now?" Isabelle asked.

"It is."

"And Dena's all right?"

"Yes, she's in recovery, coming out of the anesthesia. Then she'll be transferred to the ICU, as planned. She'll be feeling kind of puny over the next few days and she'll have a heck of a headache. But all that's to be expected."

"So it's good news," Isabelle said in a shaking voice.

Except for one thing. The facial nerve had to be clipped.

"It was unavoidable," the surgeon said. "Vascular tumors are so much trickier. Embedded. Like I said, this was one of the trickiest in all my years of experience. The facial nerve had already been crushed and compromised. But the clipped nerve has been grafted and should regenerate."

"A nerve, that's secondary," Conrad said. "The important thing is that she's fine. The tumor's fully out."

"Yes, and yes."

Conrad continued on with questions and took in responses, but the last bit of the news had stunned Rebecca into silence.

They'd clipped Dena's facial nerve. Instant paralysis on the left side of her face. Months of recovery time required, not weeks. In worst cases, the paralysis was permanent.

Her throat closed up. Oh, dear God. Her poor little sister.

Nothing would ever be the same.

Chapter 7 – Dena

"It will be over in the blink of an eye," they'd told Dena.

She blinked.

Well. They'd been right.

First thoughts: a blanket of warmth, of sleep, lifting bit by bit. A room. A clock that read eight o'clock. Twelve hours had come and gone, just like that. More awareness drifted in. A nurse came to check on her, asked her if she could wiggle her fingers, her toes. Yes, and yes. Eyes flickering shut again, even as awareness grew. Sounds, beeps, her own breath. Sore throat. Very sore.

Footsteps, later. The nurse returned. She shone a light in Dena's eyes and asked her what her name was, and did she know where she was?

Her "UCSF Hospital" reply degenerated into a rasped "Sss fff h'spital," but the nurse seemed satisfied. Movement beneath her; they were wheeling her into a different room.

Aware of parents, of Rebecca. A clock that blinked 9:00pm. Shut her eyes and when she opened them again, Rebecca was gone. A different nurse approached with the same interrogation routine. Yes, Dena told her. She recognized her visitors. Mom and Dad.

Shut her eyes. Opened them and now her parents, too, were preparing to leave.

"We'll let you rest, honey," her father said.

"Wait," she slurred. "Jsst got here."

Except she saw, to her confusion, that the clock now blinked 10:30pm.

Too tiring to ponder.

She was in the ICU. Tubes and wires everywhere: in her nose for oxygen, IVs taped to her arm, a pulse oxymeter on her finger, wires snaking off her chest. Bed positioned at an incline, more sitting than lying down.

Relief took hold; it was over. The terrible thing was gone.

All too soon, another sensation: headache pain. First just an ominous pressing sensation but as the anesthesia wore off further, it morphed into explosions of pain, a battlefield, a war raging, nerves screaming in agony every time she made the slightest move of her head. She shut her eyes, willing it all to go away.

The room was awash in a ghostly half-light. She dozed and woke, now after mere minutes. The headache grew worse. Whimpers of pain brought on the nurse, who set up a morphine drip. Her headache started to ease.

Without warning, the nausea hit. Heaves arose from within her and now she was throwing up, her head exploding with each heave.

Recovery had just taken a turn for the worse.

The nurse hurried in, tried to help, dabbing Dena's lips ineffectually with a damp washcloth. The nausea faded, only to return ten minutes later. Round two.

Round three.

Round four.

Thus passed the single worst night of her life. She hadn't imagined this kind of pain and misery coexisted on earth, compounded by drug-addled confusion and anxiety. "More morphine?" the nurse asked, noting her pain.

But what if the morphine was what was making her so sick? The thought took hold; she was allergic to morphine. She would die from the pain or die from the reaction.

"No," she croaked.

"All right," the nurse said, far too cheerfully, and returned to her nearby seat and desk.

Heaving and throwing up, head exploding. A moment's escape into sleep only to be woken by the nurse, shining a bright light into her eyes, asking her more questions.

Did she still know where she was?

In hell, she wanted to say, but pushed out another "hospital." She became aware of the sour, rank smell of her body, this unnatural perspiration, unwashed-smelling, like she'd been living off the streets. It frightened her. She did not smell like herself. It was as if an alien had come and stripped her of her body, her life, half her brain. Only a tiny part remained, a lucid, trapped, terrified nub that could only cower in the dim recesses of her mind.

She must have finally slept deeper, because when she opened her eyes next, the room was bright with filtered sunshine, and her neurotologist had come in.

Their eyes met and relief washed over his features.

"Oh, pretty," he said softly.

She didn't feel pretty. She felt, in truth, pretty fucked up.

"Do you know," he continued, "this is one of the best moments in my line of work. Especially after a tricky surgery like yours. If for some reason I weren't allowed this exchange, seeing you recognize me, I would lose so much. So. Thank you, Dena."

It seemed kind of him to say, so she made a mumbled sound of accord and shifted her head up and down, a mistake that sent an explosion of pain through her head. She winced, squeezed her eyes shut.

"Yes," he said, his voice rich with sympathy. "There's that too. Unfortunately, that's your side of the equation. The first few days are a little rough. They'll pass, though." She must have dozed, soothed by the cadence and assurance in his voice, something about the nerve and regeneration—or maybe it had been a complaint, the nerve of her generation, I mean, really—and only woke when the words stopped.

Her eyes fluttered back open. He smiled at her and patted her hand. "We'll talk more about it later. For now, just rest."

"Okay," she mumbled, and let sleep claim her before he could say anything more.

She slept, or as well as one could in the ICU, plagued by beeps, machine readings and nurse interruptions. The sunlight had shifted, creating new shadows when she woke later, her mind processing impressions more clearly now. She heard the sound of conversation on the other side of the room, where a curtain separated her from a nearby patient. She took greater note of the wires and IVs connecting her to drips and machines. Shifting her legs, she felt the uncomfortable presence of a catheter.

But she'd stopped throwing up. Maybe she was over the worst, she told herself.

Then her family arrived.

Everyone's reaction was wrong. Her mother acted too bubbly, her father too brisk. She wanted to tell them to cut the act, the PR smiles, and just react normally.

Rebecca, who came in a few minutes later, gave her just that. The shock on her face, the low "oh, God," told Dena all she needed to know.

The four of them engaged in a stilted sort of conversation. Dena mostly listened, having mumbled that it hurt to talk and it hurt to nod. They seemed to understand, and kept the conversation light, chatty. At least her parents did. Rebecca, meanwhile, looked worried. Dena finally met her gaze.

"What's up?" she asked Rebecca, who hesitated before she spoke.

"I'm so sorry, Deen. About the clipped nerve."

"The... what?"

Rebecca looked uneasy. So did her parents.

"The facial nerve."

"What're you saying?" She could hardly get the words out.

"Deen," Rebecca said. "The facial nerve was clipped. You didn't know?"

Her world upended, spilling out every other thought. "What do you mean?" she cried, which she instantly regretted. Fireworks of pain. And the realization, only now, that the left side of her face felt heavy, numb, particularly around and inside her mouth, like when you were at the dentist's, numbed up for a filling.

Her father took her hand. "Sweetie. It was a very vascular tumor. It was tough to get out, all embedded in... well, whatever it gets embedded in. Very bloody. They had to clip the nerve to get it out. But they grafted the nerve back. It will regenerate, they say."

They cut her facial nerve and the surgeon didn't tell her? Or had he, and she'd been too fogged to process it?

He had. She remembered now. Not "the nerve of your generation" after all.

The news sent shock waves through her system that, instead of subsiding, grew bigger, crashing into her mind over and over.

They cut her facial nerve.

"Oh, Dena," Rebecca began, voice quavering, and stopped short, eyes wide with chagrin.

Rebecca, the deliverer of betrayal and bad news, over and over.

A wail tore out of Dena, producing a tsunami of pain from all directions.

Rebecca reached over to touch her, but right then, Rebecca seemed more like a demon than a sister.

All rational thoughts fled her mind, replaced by panicky, terror-laced ones.

"Get out of here," she shrilled—worse pain yet—pulling back from Rebecca's touch. "You want to hurt me! You're trying to kill me! You did all of this!"

She could hardly breathe. Her heart began to pound double-time, eliciting all sorts of beeps and alarms from the machine, which terrified her even more.

She heard the sound of running feet, nurses' voices.

"What's going on here? What are you doing to agitate her?"

Everyone began talking at once.

"I was just…" Rebecca tried.

"Unfortunately she just learned," Conrad began.

"She gets this way," Isabelle cut in. "Highly emotional, and—"

"Out, all of you," one nurse ordered. "There should only be two of you here at a time, anyway." Another nurse hurried over to Dena's side and made an adjustment to the machine above her IV drip. A moment later a golden warmth spread through her, blanketing the rage and terror, rendering it docile, manageable. The stridency in the voices receded, the pain lessened.

Clipped nerve? Destroyed career? No matter. Not in this fuzzy place of comfort.

She hoped they kept her here forever.

Forever didn't last nearly long enough.

The nurse woke her. Unfathomably, she wanted Dena to try to walk.

Her goal, she informed Dena, was to promote movement and cognition, all of which would get Dena out of the ICU quicker.

"Who wants to stay in the ICU where you can't get any real sleep?" she asked Dena. "Who wants to have a catheter in if you can help it? First things first—let's get it out. And I'll bet you'd feel much better with a sponge bath and a change of sheets."

"I can't," she moaned. "Moving hurts too much."

"I'll bet you can," she said, ignoring the second part of Dena's reply.

The nurse reminded Dena of April at the WCBT: cordial enough, but brisk and businesslike. Not wanting to be your friend so much as the one who helped you move up to the next level.

"And there you go," the nurse exclaimed, all but yanking Dena from her safe perch.

Left with no other choice, Dena slid her legs the rest of the way to the floor and took shaky, careful steps, clinging to the nurse. En route to the bathroom, she caught a glimpse of herself in a mirror. She looked both absurd and horrifying, like someone dressed for Halloween. A turban of sorts encased her head, a mix of white cotton gauze and an Ace bandage. She had a black eye and her face looked swollen. The left side where the incision was appeared even lumpier. No wonder her family had acted strangely upon seeing her.

The nurse had been right about the sponge bath, although even afterward, the stench of unwellness still clung to her skin. But that, and more efficient pain and anti-nausea medication, made her feel better. Finally the nurse left her alone and she was allowed to sleep again, dozing even through a second visit from her parents. She could still hear them, however, conversing with the nurse.

"Your daughter is just so lovely," the nurse was saying, which made Dena smile inside. "What a beautiful, porcelain complexion, and those graceful arms. I hear she's a professional ballet dancer."

"She is." Conrad sounded proud. "A soloist. With the West Coast Ballet Theatre."

"Wow. What an honor to be taking care of her. I'll have to ask for her autograph before she leaves the ICU."

"She'd love that," Isabelle said.

"And someone mentioned there being a second dance daughter, with the same company. Will we get the chance to meet her, too?"

There was a pause. "Oh, she's not going to be visiting in the ICU anymore," Isabelle said. "Other things to do, and such."

The pleased feeling evaporated.

The nurse and her parents chatted a few minutes more until the nurse completed her task in the room and slipped out. Silence filled the room.

"That sounded kind of crass," Conrad said to Isabelle a moment later.

"What did?" Isabelle asked.

"Rebecca having 'other' things to do."

"Well, what did you want me to say? The truth?"

When Conrad spoke again, he sounded irritable. "Oh, whatever."

"No, not 'whatever.' Don't play me out to be the villain here."

"Oh, so I am?"

The tension-laced exchange tore Dena from her doze and she stirred uncomfortably. The conversation stopped and sleep reclaimed her, delivering her back to a place of sweeter oblivion.

Night settled in. The medications, while more effective, made the room spin all around her. The spinning settled her in all the wrong places. Several times she woke feeling like she was suspended on the wall. She was sure of it; it filled her with unspeakable terror. She lay there, afraid to make even the slightest move, affixing all her muscles against the bed to keep from spilling out. When she tried to explain this to the night nurse, she nodded.

"It's the antiseizure medication. That, and all your other

medications are just doing their thing. Don't worry. You're fine. I'm right here."

Bad dreams haunted her, waking her with a start. Every time she'd close her eyes again, the nightmares would envelope her, vague but terrifying scenarios that would dissipate the instant she woke. Rebecca was in one of them. She approached Dena with her hands behind her back. She was smiling at Dena, which made it all the more terrifying. Something was behind Rebecca's back. A knife, a club. She was going to attack Dena. Isabelle had been wrong; Rebecca had been simply lying in wait.

Panic sent her heart banging against her chest. Alarms wailed out, confirming Rebecca's illicit presence, the imminent threat.

She awoke with a gasp, eyes flying open in terror. Shards of pain tore through her head.

The nurse hurried over, glanced at the flashing on the monitor screen, and laid a reassuring hand on Dena's shoulder. "It was only a bad dream. You're fine."

"My sister was hiding something from me," she mumbled to the nurse. "Something scary."

"You just relax and go back to sleep."

"Tell her to stay away."

"I will. You're safe, don't worry."

Friday morning brought with it a certain level of euphoria, if only because it meant she'd survived a second terrible night. The nausea, too, had dissipated, enough for her to eat some actual food, indulge in liquids beyond ice chips. The pain radiating through her skull whenever she moved, however, was still fierce, even with pain medication.

A CT scan ruled out bleeding from the brain, and spinal fluid leakage. That part, at least, was good news. "Mere headache pain," the chief resident assured her, beaming, during morning rounds. How uncomplicated and manageable he made it sound.

But even he couldn't put a positive spin on the side effects of her facial paralysis, notably her compromised left eye. She couldn't blink her eye fully, nor did the eye self-lubricate any more. Which made it feel horribly dry, scratchy. "We'll want to watch that closely," the chief resident told her, breezy attitude now gone. "Your cornea isn't getting the protection it needs. We'll have an ophthalmologist check in on it."

The nurse administered thick, viscous drops and ointments that blurred her vision. The ophthalmologist, a kindly man with a prematurely grey thatch of hair, stopped by an hour later while her father was visiting. The examination lasted a minute, after which he seconded the chief resident's opinion.

"Your unprotected cornea puts it at risk of ulceration. Options for us to consider here include placing a gold weight in your eyelid to help it close. Or a tarsorrhaphy—a procedure in which we'd stitch your eyelid partially shut, in the corner, better protecting the cornea."

Both ideas horrified her. Even Conrad winced. "Does she need to decide right now?" he asked the ophthalmologist.

"No, it's just something to think about. We'll stay with ointment and drops for her now." He turned to Dena. "The nurses will teach you how to tape your eye shut at night. At your post-op appointment in a few weeks, your blink reflex will be reassessed and at that time, you'll need to make a decision on more permanent protective measures."

Behind him, the physical therapist appeared at the door. "Shall I come back in a half hour?" she called out. The ophthalmologist turned and smiled at her.

"I think we're done here. Unless Dena and her dad have any further questions for me."

They didn't. He left, and the physical therapist approached. She was short with curly black hair and exuded energy. She introduced herself as Ellen. "Ready to practice walking?" she asked.

"I suppose I should try," Dena mumbled.

Ellen turned to Conrad. "Dad, this task is between us girls. Why don't you get a cup of coffee and meet us back here in twenty minutes or so?"

It was a command, not a request. He nodded meekly and left.

Ellen helped her to standing, presented her with a walker, and together they made their way out of the room and down the antiseptic-smelling hall. They moved at a slow pace, as her brain factored in the changes from nerve-squashing tumor, to no tumor.

Walking proved to be no easy feat. Every time she tried to let go of the walker, the world tilted on her. It didn't help that the ointment in her left eye had rendered everything foggy, distorted. But she kept moving doggedly forward.

To her left, she noticed the railings along the wall. They reminded her of a ballet barre.

Hey.

"Can I try walking, just holding on to that?" she asked Ellen.

"Of course. That would be great! I didn't want to rush you if you didn't feel ready."

Simply gripping the round, cool metal of the bar calmed and soothed her. The dancer in her woke: her abdominals engaged and pulled in; her spine straightened; her chin rose a notch. The dizziness, too, she now saw from a dancer's perspective. When you moved across the floor in chaîné turns—that moving "chain" of lightning quick revolutions en pointe—the dizziness could all but knock you down unless you focused your gaze on a fixed spot, coming back to it again and again as you turned. Even when spotting, you got dizzy, particularly after a set of thirty-two chaîné turns across the floor. She remembered how, as a student, she'd try to act nonchalant at the end and walk normally, even though she was dizzy enough to tip over. And if she didn't feel dizzy at all, well, it was a sign she should have pushed herself harder, moved faster, gotten another half-dozen turns in during those sixteen counts of music.

That dizziness was identical to this feeling right now, she realized. And she'd had eighteen years of practice in walking gracefully through dizziness.

She began to walk, first clutching the railing, then loosening her grip. A minute later, she dropped her grip entirely.

"Dena, my goodness," Ellen stuttered from behind her. "That's some impressive work."

"Thank you," she said, concentrating on her task.

She knew pain. All dancers did. It was a given in the professional dance world that one part of your body or another would be aching, strained, throbbing, compromised or otherwise injured. Granted, she'd never considered pain like this. But something inside her, the tiniest flicker of optimism, rose up from the ashes.

She'd get through this and find her way back home.

Chapter 8 – Rebecca

Even though Rebecca had a key for Dena's apartment, she always knocked on the door as a courtesy, giving Dena or Lana the chance to answer the door before she let herself in. Today, she could hear a low murmur of conversation going on within. No one answered her knock, so she rummaged around in her bag for her keys.

It was Thursday; Dena had come home from the hospital on Sunday. Conrad had left town once he felt satisfied that Dena had settled in at her apartment with Isabelle at the helm. He'd pulled Rebecca aside before leaving and told her she should continue to stay out of the way, keep her visits to Dena regular but short, and if Dena didn't want to see her, Rebecca should slip away without fuss.

"Don't you go upsetting her again," had been Conrad's farewell words to Rebecca. Not *I love you,* or *good luck with your upcoming tour, honey.* Just a warning in his voice, his eyes, followed by a "goodbye, now," and a brisk, crushing hug that felt more punitive than affectionate.

Just as she found the keys, she heard the brisk *tap, tap* of footsteps inside. A moment later, the door swung open to reveal Isabelle, flushed and beaming.

"Well, hello, other daughter," she sang out.

"Um, hello, Mom." Rebecca studied her quizzically. She looked beautiful, if overdressed, in a cream silk blouse, dress shoes and navy leggings. Over Isabelle's shoulder she caught sight of Dena sitting in the living room. She, too, looked animated, listening to something or someone with great interest. The smell of fresh coffee wafted through the air.

"We have a visitor," Isabelle announced. "Your boss is here."

"My boss?" Rebecca stuttered. "Anders?"

"Well, who else?"

What the hell? Impossible. Rebecca stepped inside. And yet the unmistakable timbre of Anders' voice dispelled all doubt. A wild rush of elation replaced her confusion. Her crush—here! The day exploded into sunshine.

He sat on the couch, one arm slung over the back cushions, in vacation attire: a faded tee shirt and jeans with a hole in one knee. A three-day growth covered his jaw. He exuded relaxation and pure feral sexiness. At times like this it seemed like he was only in his thirties, much closer to Rebecca's age than her mother's. (He was, in truth, fifty to Isabelle's fifty-three, but Rebecca always tried to avoid the comparison. Too close to home.)

Dena sat in the easy chair across from the couch. Her long brown hair had been brushed into a ponytail. She'd abandoned her bathrobe in favor of pink sweatpants and a matching zip-up sweatshirt but she still looked like a post-op patient with her bandages, bruises and facial swelling. The big, turban-style bandaging was gone, but Rebecca knew she still had staples in at the incision site, behind her ear. From this angle her facial paralysis was hidden. Dena looked over, saw Rebecca, and immediately her smile cooled.

"Hi there," she said. "Anders came to visit."

Anders glanced over at Rebecca and offered her a preoccupied greeting. Isabelle returned to her spot next to Anders on the couch, angling herself toward him. "What were we talking about?" she asked.

He smiled at her. "Villas in France."

"That's right." Isabelle settled herself in more comfortably. "And you are not allowed to leave until you write down the name of that villa you stayed in."

"You have my word."

Rebecca took a seat and listened as Isabelle quizzed Anders about traveling in France, memorable towns throughout Europe, and oh, did he still own that beautiful Russian Hill property here in San Francisco?

"I do," he said. "And you— still choosing to not grace the city with your full-time presence?"

"Los Gatos works for Dan and myself. It lacks San Francisco's energy, of course, but it's beautiful and peaceful."

"It suits you well, I can tell. There are roses in your cheeks."

"Oh, that's from seeing you, here, today!"

Rebecca resisted the urge to roll her eyes. Years back, new to the company, she'd enjoyed the way her mother and Anders were so friendly with each other, as if that somehow bought her more clout, but now she longed to tell her mother to act her age and stop flirting.

She met Dena's eyes, hoping for some "that's Mom for you" commiseration, but Dena only gazed back at her, expressionless.

No sisterly connection, then.

There hadn't been, since the ICU incident.

How to explain to Dena, her banishment from the ICU by their parents, the way she hadn't been allowed to return, much less talk about why, until Conrad deemed it "safer"? The look on Dena's face when she finally did show up, two days later, had made her feel just terrible.

You've hurt me in the worst of ways. That was the message Dena's body language told her, even as Dena herself had been cordial, composed. She'd listened to Rebecca's apology but offered nothing in return beyond an "ah" that didn't require nodding or speaking too much. The paralyzed and thus expressionless face on one side made it hard to read what was going on inside Dena. When she kept the emoting side of her face solemn all nonverbal communication ceased. It was disorienting, upsetting. Overnight her sister had become a stranger.

Isabelle rose, announcing she was off to find paper and pen, write down all these impossibly wonderful recommendations Anders was making that she'd never remember, and he was doing it just to challenge her feeble, aging brain. Her overblown gaiety made Anders burst into laughter, an equally excessive reaction, Rebecca decided, to a quip that wasn't even particularly funny. Anders watched Isabelle glide away into the kitchen. He was still smiling as his gaze landed on Rebecca. He seemed much more off guard and relaxed than he was during the season, on the job.

His gaze grew thoughtful.

An electric current tore through her, down one side of her body and up the other. Her heart began to hammer so loudly she was afraid he might hear it. But she kept her expression composed, matter of fact. Neither of them said a word. He kept his eyes on her for a moment longer before shifting his attention to Dena.

"Dena," he called out. "What are you working on?"

Dena paused to consider this. "Floor stretching. Barre, this morning and yesterday. Pliés, tendus and dégagés. I'll add rond de jambe today."

"I think he means your physical therapy exercises," Rebecca offered.

Dena didn't respond, or even look Rebecca's way. Neither did Anders.

"Dena knows what I meant," he said. He rose, walked over to her, offered Dena his hand. "Come show me."

Conrad had bought and set up a portable barre for Dena before leaving, which stood alongside the wall that led into the kitchen. Beneath it, a vinyl runner mat over the carpet simulated the smooth veneer of a dance studio floor. Anders directed Dena to the spot now. He stood and studied her movements as she warmed up with a few pliés and tendus. With one hand still on the barre, her foot then traced a slow half-circle on the floor, a set of eight careful ronds de jambe, continuing on to a few ronds de jambe en l'air and one final grand rond de jambe.

"Good, good," Anders said. "Try a développé à la seconde now."

Dena's body responded obediently, the toe tracing a path from ankle to knee, before developing out to the side and up.

Some dancers had the ability, the right hips and hyperextended legs, to extend their leg high, close to a 180-degree split, particularly the Russian-trained dancers, the Vaganova Academy and Bolshoi school graduates. It was a bit of a circus trick, a huge audience pleaser. Dena could do it; she'd always been able to surpass Rebecca's extension, even when just a student. The leg rose now to its full extension, inches from her head. It was hypnotic to observe.

As if hypnotized herself, Dena let go of the barre, raised both arms to high fifth, and held the pose in perfect steadiness.

And like that, the soloist was back, in top form, pure art in motion.

She looked so beautiful. Rebecca felt her throat tighten.

The spell broke a moment later when Dena wobbled and grabbed at the barre. "The dizziness is still affecting me," she said, half-laughing, bringing her leg down.

"A bit, perhaps, but otherwise, wonderful!" Anders told her.

"Thank you," she told him, beaming.

But only half her face could beam. What was once a beautiful smile now became a crooked smirk, a grotesque caricature of a symmetrical face.

And she knew it. A stricken look crossed her emoting side and an instant later, the expression fell slack, neutral once again on both sides.

"Your développé looked absolutely splendid," Anders said, as if he hadn't noticed her facial asymmetry. "You've lost nothing. Keep it up."

Dena seemed more subdued now. She gave him a solemn nod. "I will. Thank you."

Isabelle returned to the room and handed Anders paper and pen. After he'd jotted down his recommendations, he looked at his watch.

"It's time for me to take my leave," he said, handing the pen and paper back to Isabelle. He leaned over and gave Dena a kiss on the cheek. Rebecca trailed Isabelle as she walked Anders to the door.

At the door, he took one of Isabelle's hands in both of his and brought it to his lips. "Stay as beautiful as you are, dear Isabelle," he said.

This time Rebecca couldn't refrain from rolling her eyes. To her horror, Anders caught her in the act.

"Rebecca," he said sternly.

She gulped. "Yes, sir?"

"Walk me out to my car, please."

"Yes, sir." Her legs shook as she followed him out.

Outside, the May afternoon was overcast, with a fog-laced breeze that made it feel more like March. "Where are you parked?" Rebecca asked. He gestured to the other end of the block, near a pair of leafy, low-hanging trees.

They walked without speaking. "Dena's got a challenge there," he said finally.

So. He wasn't going to berate her. Her shoulders relaxed. "Yes," she said. "The surgery was a lot trickier than they'd expected."

"Then again, it was a craniotomy. And it's only been a week."

"Yes."

They arrived at his car, a sporty silver Lexus, his only nod to ostentation. He turned to her. "Your mother tells me she's staying with Dena, looking after her, into next week," he said.

"Yes."

"Do they require your presence?"

His question mystified her. "Well, I stop in. But the truth is, I don't think Dena wants me around her right now. In fact, she seems almost disturbed by my presence."

"At times like this, a mother can often provide the best support. You're her peer. You have what she's temporarily lost."

"Why do you ask?"

"I'm going to Carmel on Saturday." He paused to let that sink in. "I'd like you to join me."

She could hardly process it all. Four years of nothing, and now this.

"Anders. To... sketch?" she stammered.

"Of course."

"But ... Boyd." She regretted the words even as they slipped out.

He looked both amused and impatient. "Apparently I need to remind you, Miss Lindgren, that sketching is an artistic endeavor and nothing more."

A hot blush crept up her neck. "I was merely saying," she began in what she hoped was a dignified tone, "that I would have to cancel my plans with him."

"I happen to know he left San Francisco."

"Maybe I was going to leave San Francisco myself and visit him."

"Ah."

"But those plans weren't set in stone."

"Ah."

She paused, but only for an instant. Her heart sang, her pulse pounded.

"Yes," she told him. "I believe I can make this weekend work."

"Good. Saturday morning, early. Six o'clock? I want to catch the morning light."

"All right."

"I'll have Ben pick you up at your place."

"I'll be ready."

He slid into his car without another word, started it up and drove off. She walked back to Dena's apartment in a daze.

Carmel, again. At last.

Ben arrived early on Saturday, amid a chilly, dense fog that rendered the morning sleepy, dreamlike. She lived with Pam and three other females in a restored Victorian just off Alamo Square. It had been a great find, but the catch was that it took so many of them, all DBDs, of course, to make it affordable. Pam would be moving out at the end of the month; Rebecca couldn't imagine what the environment would be like without her. That morning, it was just Rebecca and Charlotte in the house. Rebecca made sure to meet Ben at the door and slip out quietly. Always this subterfuge, at Anders' insistence. Ben never seemed to mind.

And, in truth, Rebecca felt more comfortable with him than she did with Anders. Ben was fifteen years Anders' junior and nine years older than Rebecca, much like a protective older brother to her. Ben had been in her home, Anders hadn't. Ben had been inside Anders' home, Rebecca hadn't. Ben was their intermediary in personal matters. That had been one of the stipulations, that first meeting in private with Anders, all those years back. It was all about discretion. Only Ben could know.

Traffic was light and the drive to Ben's place, where Anders was waiting, took less than fifteen minutes, even with a stop for coffee. Anders got out of his car as Ben pulled up in the tiny driveway. Anders offered a neutral "good morning" to both of them as Rebecca switched passenger seats.

The Lexus was warm and inviting inside, plush leather, still sporting its new-car smell. "You're not going to ask me to stop for anything, are you?" Anders asked, settling himself back in. "Ben took care of you?"

Rebecca held up her coffee cup. "He did, thank you."

He nodded; he'd expected no less.

The drive out of the city and down Highway 101 proceeded in a quiet, meditative fashion. An hour past San Jose, Anders took a side highway connecting them to the coast. Fields of artichokes and strawberries were soon replaced by Monterey pines and cypresses, the latter arched into tortured shapes from the winds that blew from the Pacific Ocean.

Carmel, nestled against the Pacific Coast, was tiny and quaint. Folksy architecture mingled with shaggy cypress trees, and narrow streets that curved and wound, sometimes around enormous trees right in the road. The houses were snug, miniaturized, many English cottage-style, a few with thatched roofs like something out of a Brothers Grimm fairytale book.

Nothing had changed in four years. Same bumpy little gravel drive where Anders parked his car. Same sleepy little cottage, half-hidden by trees and bushes. Once inside, he opened the curtains, exposing windows and the enclosed backyard. He moved around the chilly room, turning on the heat, putting on water for tea, telling her to make herself comfortable.

Same bedroom dominated by an oversized bed with a downy crimson comforter and pillows. Same closet with a few items of clothing in it. She chose the woman's robe, shut the door, and began to undress. Her hands were icy; she was nervous, as if she were doing this for the first time. He had an artist's loft in San Francisco. Several other times it had been there.

She drew a deep breath, put on the robe, and left the bedroom. Already the living room had started to warm up. Anders had brought out a half-dozen soft blankets, in colors of nature. Deep green of the cypresses. Blue-green like the sea, another the color of light through ice, that palest blue possible. Pumpkin. Coral. Soft yellow like butter, so alluring she was unable to resist burying her face in it, inhaling its light lavender scent. It was as satisfying a prospect as gorging on pastries, wrapping her body with these blankets.

Anders smiled at her reaction. "Let's start there. You and the blankets."

And there it was, their most intimate shared act.

He sketched her.

Sometimes charcoals, other times pastels. Ideas. Portraits. Glimpses. Nudes, always. Sometimes just a part of her body. Hand against abdomen. The small of her back. Her full backside. Never her face or its distinguishing characteristics. He was good about protecting her identity. The first time, over six years ago, he'd shown her his sketchbooks beforehand. Ben had been the one to bring her there. He'd been Rebecca's chaperone, so she wouldn't feel threatened, boxed in. The three of them had met in Anders' San Francisco artist's loft that first time, sipping San Pellegrinos, her leafing through his artwork, both intimidated and intrigued, until she agreed to pose. Ben had left and it was just her and Anders, and items of clothing that she peeled away as she became more comfortable. He'd busy himself with something else each time she disrobed. It was not intended to be a striptease. It was not, as he told her more than once, a sexual experience in the least. It was his craft, his attempt at a different kind of art. Capturing sensuality. Putting it to paper instead of movement.

She discovered she enjoyed herself as his model. She became comfortable, utterly trusting, cast under the same spell he seemed to be under. Nude, she moved according to his direction, sometimes slow, sustained movements like twists, head angles, bending, arching back, and other times he'd have her reclining on an armchair, or a pile of pillows on the platform, hair spilling down her back, or over her face, or draped over her arms. They worked in silence for hours at a time. He'd always tell her to take a break after an hour, during which time he'd continue working. She'd don a robe, get a drink, look over his shoulder.

Sometimes she'd recognize herself in the sketches. Other times what she saw was shadows and angles and this wondrous luminosity he'd somehow managed to conjure up, even with just charcoals and white sketch paper. Sensuality. The beauty of her dancer's body. She loved these glimpses of herself through his eyes. She loved them more than her real self. These were pure, organic, untainted by thought or desire or ambition or disappointment or physical limitations. The same feeling coursed through her as she watched Anders watch her, when she was back in pose. He'd study her, really look at her, before shifting his gaze to his pad, his easel. He had no other agenda at times like that. He was immersed in his craft that, miraculously, he found through gazing at her. It was like a gift that kept giving.

Even though five years had passed, they quickly found their groove and by noon, it was as if there hadn't been the long break. Over dinner that night, at a tiny Italian restaurant they both enjoyed, she summoned the courage to ask him if it was different for him now, five years later. If she was different. Meaning less compelling.

He regarded her from over his glass of wine. "You're older. Your body reflects a few changes. But you're no less beautiful. There's a new depth to it. A maturity. You're like your mother—yours is the kind of beauty that will only deepen with age."

His response thrilled her. Only the reference to her mother kept her feet on the ground. She wanted it to be just the two of them there. No Isabelle, no Dena, no company members or administrators. He must have felt the same; he'd turned off his cell phone. So had she. This was no time for a call from Boyd, wanting to know how much she missed him.

The wine loosened her further, bringing back old feelings. The hunger for him to not just see her, sketch her, but to touch her. Make love to her. Her dream of many, many years.

Really, since she was twenty. That first night, at a function while they were on tour, she'd thought they were headed in that direction. She'd seen the look in his eye, after all, and when Ben had knocked at her hotel door that night, late, telling her Anders wanted a word, she'd assumed that meant only one thing. Once in Anders' room, alone with him, she'd accepted a drink and they'd talked.

The prospective sketching came up. He asked her if she thought she might have a problem with nudity around him. The suggestion of it, the invitation, made her dizzy with pleasurable anticipation. She cleared her throat and told him no, she would have no problem with that. Then she waited, heart thumping, for the seduction to proceed further.

It never did. Instead, after twenty more minutes of conversation, he consulted his watch and told her that Ben would be back shortly to escort her back to her room.

"You don't want anything more from me?" she asked in disbelief.

This made him smile. "Of course I do. I'm a man. But you're a young girl, not to mention one of my dancers. I know not to get myself in trouble. Nor you."

"I'm twenty-one."

"You are not. You just turned twenty."

She'd forgotten that, as her employer, he had access to the truth.

"Well, I'm mature!"

"I agree. I wouldn't allow you to be here with me, like this, if I didn't think you were."

He didn't bring her down to Carmel to sketch her until a year later. It was here, late in the evening, that she decided to offer more to him. She'd just turned twenty-one; she felt invincible as she emerged from the bedroom naked.

"Anders," she said in the most seductive voice she could muster, "I want you to make love to me."

He smiled in a benign fashion, as if she'd just performed a charade. "Rebecca. Fetch yourself a blanket. You look cold, dear."

His amusement, far from the arousal she'd anticipated, stung. She retreated into the bedroom, feeling young and stupid and ashamed until he coaxed her back out with the offer of a brandy and a *Casablanca* rerun on PBS.

But she was twenty-six now.

Only she had a boyfriend now.

After dinner they went back to the cottage. He poured them both a Courvoisier, slipped a vintage jazz CD into the player, and they sat on the couch in the semi-darkness, listening to the music. She rested her thigh against his. He shifted, not away from her, but more into her, so that the pressure increased. She could feel the chemistry between them building, but understood that she'd have to be the one to make the move. He was not a director who seduced his dancers, nor allowed himself to be seduced. She believed what he'd told her, years back, about never getting personally involved with his dancers. Or anyone, it would seem. Divorced, never remarried, he appeared almost monk-like in his devotion to his job. She'd observed him fielding unwanted attention in her years with the company, from dancers, WCBT administrators and patrons alike. Each time something tight in her would ease as the woman—and occasionally man—abandoned his or her efforts finally and walked away in frustration.

"I think I'll just slip into something comfortable," she said now, rising from the couch. He offered no comment. She wasn't sure if that was a positive sign or not.

In the bedroom, she studied her reflection in the mirror and asked herself what the hell came next. There was Boyd to think about. Her own pride. The fact that relations between her and Anders, after four years of increasing distance, were once again ideal, and to disturb that perfect balance in any sort of way could ruin it.

Just leave it alone, a voice inside her said. *Content yourself with what you have.*

That, from the twenty-six-year-old.

Do it. It's now or never. And never is a long, long time.

That, from the twenty-one-year-old, banished to the back of her mind, determined to have one last say.

She took off her clothes and watched the way her chest moved in and out, her breath rapid and shallow. The risk she was taking both unnerved and delighted her. It was as if someone had flung open a skylight inside her. The new view was astonishing. The possibilities right then seemed endless. And terrifying.

Just this one night, she promised herself, and those were the very words she used on Anders as he regarded her, from the couch, a minute later. She stood in the door archway, the very same one she'd leaned against those five years ago, pleading with him to make love to her.

He said nothing. His eyes were fixed on her, in a different way now, and the thrill it produced washed over her like a wave, a slow delicious ache. Until he frowned.

"You were mistaken," he said. A flash of terror overcame her, that he was going to reject her again, and what a fool she'd just made of herself. But she said nothing, did nothing.

"You said you were going to slip into something comfortable," he continued. "I do not see how this qualifies as slipping into something."

Something inside her relaxed. "So, if I'd told you I was going to slip out of something uncomfortable, I'd be covered?"

"No. You would not be covered. Because here you are, uncovered."

She began to walk toward him. "Just this one night," she repeated, both to him and herself.

Still sitting, he held out his hands as if he were her dance partner, ready to take her into an overhead lift, and all she needed to do was draw close, press her hips into his hands, and trust him to do the rest. So she did.

Chapter 9 – Dena

The doctor, an oculoplastic surgeon, was another addition to Dena's vocabulary of specialists and procedures. He was not as likeable as her neurotologist or the neurosurgeon who'd cut her head open. Now that it was safely in the past, she took a lurid sort of pleasure in telling it how it was. A hole drilled in her skull; what a racket *that* must have been. And now, little cracks and pops as the bone parts fused back together. Just like Rice Krispies in milk. Her neurotologist liked to exchange playful banter, but this Dr. Vanderhaven was humorless. Tall and spare, he was set in his opinion of what must come next for Dena's eye: a tarsorrhaphy. Which meant stitching the corner of Dena's eyelid shut for an undetermined amount of time.

He spoke in the most annoying fashion, peppering his speech with little sayings that clearly had meaning to him, but went over her head. "If it walks like a duck, quacks like a duck, looks like a duck, it must be a duck," he'd said first. And: "You can't squeeze blood out of a turnip." On his wall, in framed needlepoint, was an equally obscure one: "All the flowers of tomorrow are in the seeds of yesterday."

Even her father, who'd flown in to join her for the consultation, was having a hard time dealing with Dr. Vanderhaven, there in the examining room.

"We're thinking she might prefer a gold weight," Conrad said. "More comfortable, better looking."

Dr. Vanderhaven shook his head. "No. The horse is out of the barn."

Conrad lost his patience. "Look, would you please speak in English, for chrissakes? We're discussing my daughter's eye here, not some barnyard animal."

The doctor took an injured tone when he spoke again. "Her blink reflex is still ineffective. The cornea is dry. Dangerously so. If not treated aggressively, the dryness could cause ulcerations, irreversible damage. She could go blind in that eye."

"Ah. So the horse is her cornea."

Dr. Vanderhaven ignored Conrad's sarcasm. "A tarsorrhaphy is the right way to go."

She took stock of the situation. Life these days was one long battle with residual headaches, distorted visual perception, partial deafness, overwhelming fatigue midway through even the calmest of days. Three weeks post-op felt like three months, if the slowness of her recovery was any indication. Maybe the doctor had a point. With a tarsorrhaphy, she'd have less eye maintenance to worry about. A longing engulfed her to have a knowledgeable advocate, there alongside her father, counseling them over what to do.

But she didn't have that. Therefore, she decided—which was to say, she gave in to the doctor's strong opinion—that a tarsorrhaphy it would be. In two weeks' time.

June twenty-third. Which, ironically, had been a day on her calendar for almost a year, when the dates for the company's London tour had been settled. She'd been excited beyond measure. Opening night in Covent Garden. Twelve performances and two thrilling weeks in London. Now, on that day, she'd be having her eye stitched partially shut while Rebecca and the others took to the stage, lived the glamour.

At least the tarsorrhaphy would give her something else to think about.

The other dancers returned from layoff. Lana took one look at Dena's still bandaged, compromised face and burst into tears. Sylvie, when the three of them met up for lunch the following week, acted all breezy and nonchalant, as if she'd been coached.

"There's our wounded compatriot!" she sang out when Lana and Dena entered Celia's café that chilly, fog-laced afternoon. "I'm surprised I haven't seen you in the studios!"

Right.

"Ha, ha," Dena said, aiming for the verbal equivalent of a smile. "Not up to that just yet!"

Sylvie rose from her chair in the corner and hurried over to give Dena a hug. She caught a whiff of Sylvie's expensive floral scent and the softness of her pink cashmere sweater, before Sylvie released her, beamed at her, and led her by the arm, as if she were blind, over to the corner table that looked out onto the street activity.

"How are you *doing?*" Sylvie exclaimed, answering her own question before Dena could. "You look great. So thin! But, wow, you've still got some bruising. And... stuff."

She was nervous, Dena could tell. She herself felt nervous, too. This was her first time out socially. Walks she'd taken with Rebecca or her mother didn't count.

"Yes. Lots of stuff." Dena settled into the seat across from Sylvie. "And you, welcome back to San Francisco!"

"Great to be back." Sylvie beamed, tossing her long russet hair over one shoulder. Her smooth, pale skin looked particularly unblemished and dewy fresh. "Although I'm sore as anything from rehearsals. How'd I get in such bad shape in only three weeks' time?"

"Tell me about it," Lana said, taking the seat next to Dena. "Back home I'd told myself I was working out, but once back here, rehearsing, the real truth came out."

"Still," Dena said, "it's not a bad feeling."

"True." Lana nodded. "Actually, it feels great to be back, working hard again."

"I can imagine," Dena said, and somewhere in her foggy brain, envy throbbed.

Sylvie popped up from her seat. "I'm starved. Let's order and catch up afterward."

What to eat was a decision few dancers took lightly. You had to choose your calories carefully. Dena had lost weight in the weeks since the surgery. Post-craniotomy rehab aside, there'd been challenges; eating with a half-numb mouth, after all, was no fun. An odd metallic taste seemed to permanently reside in her mouth. The risk of biting her left cheek, the left side of her tongue, was omnipresent, as was having food or drink dribble out of that side unnoticed. Coffees were definitely harder now. For now, she settled on a large green smoothie she could drink through a straw.

Sylvie ordered a mixed green salad with chicken breast and two hard boiled eggs. Lana ordered like she hadn't eaten in days. It was a bit of a joke between the three of them, how much Lana could get away with eating and never having it show on her frame. Junk, too, like potato chips, potato salad, chocolate chip cookies. She and Sylvie watched in fascination, ten minutes later, as Lana dug into her mayonnaise-laden potato salad with a thick-cut potato chip, making satisfying *mmm* sounds as she crunched it all down and reached for two more chips.

She let Sylvie and Lana do most of the talking. Even just sitting quietly, trying to engage, was exhausting. Her head pounded. Her brain and mind seemed to be working independent of each other, the words of her friends going in one ear and out the other as she struggled to appear normal, relaxed, just another dancer returning from layoff, catching up with friends. Her gaze drifted out the window, to the street scene outside. It was still foggy, windy. She watched a young, dark-haired woman cross the street, the determined tilt of the woman's chin, as if daring the traffic or the wind to challenge her. She paused in front of Celia's shop, gave her jacket a little shake, and entered. She called out a greeting to Celia, who appeared and greeted her cheerily. A regular, then.

Lana had finished her meal, but was still looking around hungrily. "I think I'm going to get one of Celia's cookies. One for either of you?"

She and Sylvie both declined. Silence fell over the table once Lana left.

"So," Dena said, to fill the awkwardness. "Tell me how are rehearsals going."

Sylvie flashed her a bright smile. "Great. Hard on the body, of course. Dancing *Spirit Hour* is a bitch. But you remember."

"I do."

Sylvie had been cast in Dena's place for the tour performances. It was only fair; Sylvie, like Dena, had learned and rehearsed the part last fall, but only Dena and Katrina had been cast. Sylvie, like Dena, was slim yet muscled, and petite. They often were paired with the same partners, as well.

"Nicholas is such a fabulous partner," Sylvie added. "He's really making it easier for me than it might have otherwise been."

Great. Now Nicholas wasn't just her ex-lover but her ex-partner. Dena swallowed her jealousy. "Nicholas is good. One of the best."

"He is. In dance, I mean."

"Yes. That's what I meant, too."

Because dance was what they'd been talking about.

Right?

Sylvie looked down at her plate, suddenly interested in the remaining lettuce leaves, eating them slowly, as if they were something to be savored. Dena, tired of trying to focus on conversing—had it always been so difficult with Sylvie?—glanced over to the counter, where Lana was standing politely behind the dark-haired woman, who was still monopolizing Celia's attention.

The woman turned to survey the room. Dena saw the way her gaze landed on Sylvie and her, before she turned back to Celia, who nodded and said something. Dena could only imagine the dialogue.

Who's the one with the messed-up face there?

Oh, that's Dena. She's a really good dancer. Or used to be. Such a shame, huh? Let's not be so obvious that we're staring at the wreckage of her face, though, okay?

Good idea!

Especially because Lana, behind you there, is her roommate.

Even more of a good idea!

But Lana was friendly, sociable, and a moment later had joined their conversation. The woman asked her a question and now it was Lana's turn to glance Dena's way and turn back to say something in response. They chatted for a minute longer, before the woman said her goodbyes and left with her cup of coffee. A minute later Lana, cookie in hand, returned to their table.

"Who was that?" Dena gestured to the front door where the woman had exited.

"Her name is Tatum Monroe. Apparently she's a social media guru, runs her own consultancy, and is a fairly well-known blogger, if you're into that sort of thing."

"Nope," Dena and Sylvie both said.

"She likes the arts. She recognized us as Ballet Theatre dancers."

"I saw her trying not to stare at me," Dena said.

"Actually, she knew who you were."

"Right. That's what she told you."

"No, she guessed your name. She's seen you perform, in fact. Thought you were sublime. Her words, not mine."

A little bubble of pleasure rose in Dena. "Oh," she said. "Okay."

"She wanted to come over and introduce herself, but I told her you were newly post-op and probably not up to it just yet."

She was four weeks post-op, but that was beside the point. "Thanks." She shot Lana a grateful look. "That was the right thing to say."

"Did she recognize me?" Sylvie asked.

Lana chuckled. "She thought maybe you were a corps dancer."

Sylvie drew back in indignation. "She did *not*."

"Well, she didn't recognize you from sight, but when I told her you were a soloist, new this year, she figured out who you were."

"So, she knew my name? Like she knew Dena's?"

"Yes, Sylvie, she knew your name." Lana's amused gaze caught Dena's and for a moment, things felt almost normal again, the two of them chuckling over Sylvie, who sometimes got too caught up in looks and rankings and being noticed.

Talk drifted to the upcoming London tour. Sylvie was excited, she announced. Super excited. She wanted to make sightseeing plans with Lana right then and there, seemingly unaware of how Dena might be feeling. Which was: crappy. Fatigued and left out and crappy.

Lana gave Sylvie's foot a little nudge, and finally Sylvie shot Dena an apologetic look.

"You'll be getting *such* a good rest during that time, Dena," she said. "Really, I'm kind of jealous. My left hip joint is already aching, and that tendonitis I had three years ago started flaring up. My doctor's saying I should take three months off, that it would do wonders for my body, and I told him not a chance. But you—all this is going to be great preemptive care for your body."

"She's right!" Lana beamed at Dena.

"You're both right!" Dena nodded vigorously, which made her head pound worse. But she couldn't beam back at them. She knew how horrible her face looked with one half broadly smiling, the other half deadened and expressionless. She looked like a Halloween mask.

"And when we regroup again, in August," Sylvie continued. "You'll be ready to dance by then, right? Because that... stuff, it's going to heal in—what did you say, back in May? Twelve weeks or so?"

"Well, unfortunately longer, because they had to clip my facial nerve," Dena said. "Probably more like five or six months." Which would put them around November. *Nutcracker* rehearsal time.

"Perfect," Lana said. "You'll be good to go for performing in December."

"You think?" Dena clung to the conviction in Lana's eyes.

"I do." Lana made a fist and pounded it on the table for emphasis.

"I do too," Sylvie said.

Dena offered them a broad smile before she remembered how it looked. "Thanks, you guys. I appreciate the support."

From Lana, another nod of affirmation. From Sylvie, something less assured. She was still nervous about how Dena looked.

She shouldn't have smiled. It was too soon to expose how dismal things really were in her recuperation.

No further socializing or meeting people until she looked better, she vowed.

Because Rebecca had the unerring ability these days to do precisely the thing guaranteed to bother or upset Dena, it shouldn't have come as a surprise that she violated Dena's new mandate—one that, admittedly, Rebecca couldn't have known.

It was twilight. Lana was long gone, Dena having insisted that Lana should spend all her free time over at Gil's, just like before the surgery. Besides, she reassured Lana, Rebecca was coming over. And sure enough, around six-thirty, Dena heard the quick knock, the musical jingle of Rebecca's keys at the door.

"Come in," Dena called from her bedroom where she'd been resting.

She heard Rebecca enter the apartment. "Dena?" she called out a moment later. She sounded hesitant.

Dena rose and went into the living room where she spied Rebecca, still at the door, sort of behind it as if she needed its wooden protection.

"Hey," Dena said.

"Hey." Rebecca smiled uncertainly. "Look. Um, I brought someone with me. Someone who wants to meet you."

She thought surely she'd misheard Rebecca. "You what?"

"I brought someone." By then, she'd stepped in, and gestured to her side. A moment later, a guy appeared. A stranger. A good-looking one, with dark hair and eyes, broad shoulders, whose presence immediately filled the room.

Dena felt almost faint with outrage. She ignored the guy and directed her response to Rebecca alone. "You brought a guy here. To meet me. You keep sinking lower and lower in my book, you know that? Is that your goal?"

The guy took another step in, hands up, guilty expression, as if he'd been caught stealing. "Look, I'm so sorry. Blame me. I asked to meet you. She thought you might be hesitant. But I thought, stupidly, I see now, that maybe you'd like to meet *me.*"

She stared at him blankly, wondering why he'd thought that.

"You see," he said, his expression earnest, "I speak medical."

Which was funny, unexpectedly so, even to him, you could tell.

All three of them began to chuckle, which replaced the sibling chilliness that had filled the room.

"Hi, I'm Dena," she said, and he strode over to shake her hand.

"I'm Misha. I teach the biology class Rebecca finished last spring."

She studied him as he explained how he and Rebecca had bumped into each other near Union Square. He looked a bit like Gil, Lana's fiancé, undoubtedly the best-looking guy on the company's administrative side, with his dark hair, chiseled jaw and movie star smile. Misha had the jaw, his hair the same glossy black color, although Misha's tousled, longer hair and unshaven chin looked more like an oversight than a fashion statement. And, unlike Gil, he seemed utterly unaware of his looks, his bookish charisma.

"Talk came up about you," he was saying, "and since I'd offered Rebecca a ride here, I thought, well, hey, let's stop in and chat with you directly. I'm so sorry. Really."

"It's all right," Dena said. "Welcome. Please. Have a seat."

While Rebecca excused herself to make a quick phone call, Dena joined him on the couch and answered his questions. She marveled at the freedom of not having to explain what a cranial nerve was, or a trans-labyrinth procedure, or a BAHA implant, which could potentially recoup some hearing on her deaf side. They discussed consequences of a clipped nerve, the wait-and-see nature of determining the graft's success.

"A clipped nerve is lousy luck," he said. "Some tumors are in such a risky position, it's a toss-up whether to keep part of it in there or sacrifice the nerve. Having part of the tumor still in there isn't the perfect solution, either. Even though acoustic neuromas are slow growing, it would still be there, with the risk of a future craniotomy to remove more of it. So, at least your odds of that are pretty much nonexistent."

Dena told him about having decided on the tarsorrhaphy.

He wrinkled his nose. "Ugh, that's no fun. Are you sure the gold weight in the eyelid wouldn't be a better fit for you?"

"I don't know." A dazed, trapped feeling crept over her. "The doctor intimidated me. I just sort of gave in to what he recommended."

"Then I'm sure it was the right thing to do for right now," he said. "Don't worry. It's wholly reversible."

He spoke calmly, with confidence. Her trapped feeling eased. "Want to be my medical advocate in the future?" she said, only half-joking.

He grinned at her. "Sure, I'll take that job."

She liked this guy. A whole lot.

Rebecca returned to the room. "Sorry for disappearing like that."

"No problem!" Misha fell silent but his eyes followed her as she picked up a magazine from the adjacent armchair, tossed it on the coffee table and sat in the chair. His expression—indeed, his whole demeanor—had grown soft, helpless, and Dena instantly understood how it would be.

Disappointment rose in her and evaporated just as quickly. In truth it made things easier. She would be the little sister and Misha would be her friend and it was what she needed more than anything.

Life didn't often hand you gifts like this, while you were thus hobbled and compromised. She'd be a fool not to take it just because the gift had a crush on her beautiful, un-hobbled sister.

He turned down their offer to join them for dinner. Five minutes later he rose, apologizing to Dena again for showing up at her door unannounced.

"It was no problem at all," Dena said, and she meant it.

"Wait," Rebecca said. "Don't leave until I jot down the name of that place in Sonoma we were talking about."

"All right," he said, smiling at Rebecca, but when she disappeared into the kitchen for paper and pen, his smile, just as warm, shifted to Dena.

"Rebecca mentioned the dance company's upcoming London tour," he said.

"Yeah."

"That's got to be tough for you, sidelined like this."

"It is," Dena admitted. "And to make matters worse, that's my surgery day for the tarsorrhaphy."

"Oh, wow, insult atop injury," he said, and the sympathy in his voice made her throat tighten. "I imagine someone's got you covered there, for transportation and post-op help?"

"My dad's spending a few days with me here."

"Think you'd like company after he leaves?"

His suggestion was like a ray of sunshine piercing the dark cloud of gloom enveloping her at the thought of a London-less and tarsorrhaphy-laden week.

"I would like that so much," she confessed.

"That would be around the last week of June?"

"Exactly."

He nodded. "Easy to make happen. Do you like Thai food?"

"I do. I love it."

"Oh, good, me too." He smiled. Not Gil's million-dollar Hollywood smile, but a sincere, lovely, nice-guy smile. "I'll plan to bring over takeout and we'll make an evening of it. Early, though, if that's okay, because I've got a commute down the coast to Moss Beach."

"Early is great. I go to bed way early these days. Seems like I could sleep most of the day."

He nodded. "Sounds like a body trying to recover from a craniotomy."

She smiled, caught herself too late about her frozen face, and

115

realized what the hell, it didn't matter. This guy wasn't fazed by brain tumors or the sight of her facial paralysis. He was attracted to her sister. She could just be herself.

Rebecca returned to the room and Misha's attention shifted to her and their discussion, giving Dena the chance to process what had just transpired.

Really, it was strange. As a dancer, you met so few people outside the dance world. She wouldn't have thought she'd want, or need, such a person in her life.

She did.

Chapter 10 – Rebecca

Somewhere over the Atlantic, around 35,000 feet, Rebecca tried to break up with Boyd. In light of the Carmel weekend, the escalation of her Anders infatuation, it seemed only appropriate. But to her dismay, Boyd wouldn't take her words seriously. Instead he chuckled.

"Don't be so jealous," he told her as he flipped his tray table to its closed position in the seat before him. "Nothing happened on the Tulsa trip. Pam's friend from Oregon didn't mean anything to me. We were all just having fun."

His reply rendered her mute with confusion. Was he thinking she'd been keeping him at arms' length since his return because of mere jealous feelings? Boyd, interpreting her silence as acquiescence, gave her a friendly pat on the thigh before reclining his seat back and propping his pillow up against her shoulder. "Wake me when we're in London," he said, and in a matter of minutes he was asleep, the weight of his head pressing into her.

Her adrenaline, activated by the gravity of her decision and attempts to implement it, subsided. Soothed by the steady low rumble of the plane's engines, the whir of circulating canned air, she, too, grew sleepy, compliant, accepting of how things were.

Transatlantic jet lag from the West Coast, as per normal, hit hard. At their London hotel a few hours later, the bleary-eyed dancers assembled in a large meeting room, where continental breakfast had been laid out. Even though it was June, heat pumped out of the radiators, rendering the room overwarm, sleep-inducing. It felt like 2:00am, mostly because it *was* 2:00am, at least in their bodies. Locally, it was late morning, ten o'clock. But the tea, doused with milk and sugar, was fragrant, hot and comforting. Anders moved briskly among them like a man with no need to ever sleep. An entourage followed him; he appeared to be conducting two interviews and a meeting with a theater contact and a hotel contact, all at the same time.

Ben detached himself from the entourage to make announcements to the fifty-one dancers present.

"Okay, gang, you have today to relax, let your body catch up. Get daylight on your face, resist the urge to go sleep if you can. And don't stay out late tonight, no matter what your body's saying, or you'll regret it. Try to get up at the local time tomorrow." He consulted his clipboard. "Jenny's here for massage therapy but she has limited time slots. Wardrobe wants each of you to check in some time tomorrow at the theater. Company class will be at three o'clock on the stage, dress rehearsal at five. Rick will be our stage manager here, as well, and told me to remind you to be sure to sign in, or he'll hunt you down. And plan to stay as late as needed for lighting, staging, whatever arises. This will be our only dress rehearsal with the orchestra."

Next, Lucinda, the company's public relations director, tall, blonde and imposing, took a moment to speak with them.

"Remember," she began, and here she paused to glance around at them, expression solemn, as if what she were about to impart was crucial, never-before-heard wisdom, instead of the same speech as last year. "Wherever you are, be aware that you are ambassadors of the company, and should exercise discretion in behavior and comportment. Particularly when taking photos of yourself. I know some of you like to share them via social media these days. Try and stick to the neutral ones, like you standing in front of the theater, or Leicester Square or Hyde Park. Backstage at the theater, no. Dressing rooms, really, please don't. During performances, absolutely not."

One of the younger corps dancers raised her hand. "But why?" she asked when Lucinda nodded at her.

"Because we have a *mystique* to maintain."

"Yes, but, sometimes that mystique makes us seem, um, out of touch? Aloof. Like what we do and how we act is some stuffy high art that the mainstream can't relate to."

Lucinda's eyes bulged. Her mouth opened and shut without a sound coming out. It was hard not to giggle at it all. The DBDs were careful not to look at one another.

"This *is* high art. One of the highest," Lucinda said in a hushed, scandalized voice. "And there are things that we, as ballet dancers, do not reveal or expose."

No one remarked aloud on the fact that Lucinda, a lifelong administrator, clearly born and bred for the job, had no ballet experience whatsoever. She was not one of those administrators with whom you could banter or tease in a good-natured fashion. Only Anders and Ben were allowed to do that with her. But she was not someone you could brush off, either. Lucinda had power in the company. Even the DBDs honored that.

Which didn't stop the group of them from having a good laugh over Lucinda's words in the hotel elevator an hour later. Rooms had been assigned, bags flung into their respective quarters, and now they were headed out to take in London. "To *expose* ourselves to the public," Joe, the most senior of the DBDs, said.

"Quick, let me get my camera out," Boyd said, and they all laughed.

The elevator was slow-moving, but they didn't care, even when, with a wheeze, it stopped on the sixth floor. The doors slid open to reveal Anders and Katrina standing there, murmuring to each other. To the DBDs' dismay, the two of them stepped in.

Instant buzzkill.

Anders and Katrina didn't notice the awkward silence. Anders, without greeting any of them, punched the button for the lobby and kept up his conversation with Katrina.

"I've discussed this with Leonard. *You* define the pace, dear girl. His job is to keep the music at your tempo. Tomorrow night is your time to establish what you need. If they start to rush you, simply cue the stage manager. I've told Rick to keep an eye on you there, especially during the Grand Pas, and he'll cue Leonard if need be. That's what tomorrow's dress rehearsal is for—to work with the conductor on what feels lagging, what feels rushed. Opening night, it's too late."

He had no elevator etiquette voice; he spoke as though he and Katrina were still in an airy hallway and they were the only two around. No DBD spoke; it would have been impossible to speak over him, anyway.

It was rude in so many ways. For the first time since Anders had singled her out to talk, back in the spring, irritation and resentment sprang up in Rebecca's mind. She saw the other DBDs exchanging charged looks and knew they were all thinking the same thing.

Asshole.

He simply didn't care about other people. Not those outside his charmed circle.

The elevator stopped on the third floor, where more people were waiting to get on. Not dancers, but three heavyset adults.

Anders looked around irritably as if aware of the DBDs' presence for the first time. He seemed to single out Boyd to blame for the fact of their presence. "For God's sake, man," he said to Boyd, "move two steps back. Can't you see others need to get in? What are you, furniture?"

The air in the elevator seemed to chill by ten degrees. Boyd's nostrils flared, but he took two exaggeratedly small steps back, which elicited further shifting and soft grumbling from the others. Anders, for his part, slipped his arm protectively around Katrina's waist and moved them both to the side, right up against Rebecca. His glance flickered over her, acknowledging not so much her, but the parameters of her body, to make sure he had room to take another step back, if needed.

It was needed. The three people stepped in, squishing everyone tighter. Now Anders was as close to Rebecca as he'd been that night in Carmel.

That magical, dream-come-true, over-too-fast night in Carmel.

He did not acknowledge her. Instead he continued chatting with Katrina about costumes and what would be required from her for tomorrow's press visit and photo shoot. He was so close, Rebecca could feel the heat rising off his body, the brush of his shirt against hers, the taut muscles beneath. His hand was resting on the small of Katrina's back now, fingers splayed as if to protect maximum surface space from the potential hazards of the ox-like presence of the corps dancers.

Those hands, large, strong and decisive. They'd held charcoals and pencils and transposed her image onto paper. They'd run down the length of her naked body as she'd lain there, trembling with a still-baffling need to possess, be possessed. Those hands, their firm pressure, that had left her and her body far too soon, leaving behind their imprint, if only in her mind, where the ache, the sick longing, never abated.

She felt faint. It was hard to breathe.

She looked over at Boyd and the others.

They were having a hard time, too.

A miserable eternity later, the elevator shuddered to a stop on the lobby level and disgorged its passengers. Even after Anders and Katrina had departed, their presence seemed to remain, subduing the DBDs as if a spectral chaperone now accompanied them.

Quieter now, the group of them headed for the nearest Underground station, to take the Tube to the West End. Rebecca found herself stumbling, lagging behind the others. Jet lag, she told herself. Only jet lag. Because there was nothing between her and Anders anymore. Some little seed of hope which had been germinating—it had been when the company was on tour, six years earlier, that he'd invited her to his suite, after all—had been stomped on. Not by some tormented *I can't do this, I must be strong* attitude on his part, but by his chilling, utter indifference.

Because one night had meant one night.

An approaching train rushed out of the tunnel and into the station with a clatter and squeal of brakes, followed by the pneumatic hiss of opening doors. The DBDs boarded the crowded car and found standing space in the back, where they huddled and talked.

Boyd, too, was having trouble letting go of the memory of Anders.

"Calling me furniture," he fumed. "And the look he gave me."

The train clacked through a dark tunnel that curved, jostling them around. "He's an asshole," Charlotte said, securing her grip on the overhead rail. "What would you expect?"

"He would have never taken that tone with one of the principals or soloists. I'll bet he speaks kinder to his dogs."

"He doesn't have dogs," Joe said.

"There, you see? They ran away. Or died from emotional neglect."

"You can't let the guy poison you," Joe said. "Look where we are. London!"

As if on cue, the train slowed and a minute later stopped at the next station. The doors opened, and even though little room remained, more and more passengers pushed their way in. It became comical, the number of people crowding in, including a busker who, cheerfully oblivious to the space constraints, began to play his guitar, enthusiasm superseding talent, as he sang "With a Little Help From my Friends" in a loud Bob Dylan-esque fashion. It was impossible to talk seriously anymore, and so very easy to relax. After all, like Joe said, they were in London.

London!

They left the Underground station and there it was. The spires of Westminster Abbey beckoned and the House of Parliament towered over the banks of the Thames River. Hearing Big Ben gong the hour made them all laugh, giddy as elementary school students on a field trip. They walked and walked, pointing out signs and majestic buildings amid an endless sprawl of shops and people and interesting things to see. They passed the Freed's retail store on St. Martin's Lane, which caught the DBD females' attention. A tour had been set up for them for the next day, at the Freed manufacturing facility, where pointe shoes were hand-made to each dancer's personal specification, crafted by a dedicated maker. Tomorrow, the DBD females joked, they would finally meet their maker.

From time to time, they saw some of the other WCBT dancers, in clusters, walking, pausing to gaze around, point out items of interest to one another. The youngest company members were all one noisy, happy crowd. The principals, in smaller groups, appeared more sedate. Katrina and Javier drew their usual attention, in the midst of their own private entourage. They'd brought a nanny to watch their son, whose birth almost two years earlier had been the source of much speculation. Were they a couple or not? Was the rumor that he was gay merely a rumor? Impossible to know; they kept their personal lives personal and their professional lives above reproach. All three of them were visually arresting: Javier's Cuban good looks and blonde, Dutch-born Katrina's pale purity had produced a gorgeous child.

They spied Lana, Sylvie and Nicholas in Piccadilly Circus, and then again in Trafalgar Square less than thirty minutes later. Both times, the other DBDs shifted their gaze elsewhere, but Lana and Rebecca made eye contact and exchanged friendly smiles. The second time Rebecca snuck over to Lana while the others were preoccupied. Lana met her midway.

"You're thinking of her, too, aren't you?" Rebecca asked.

"I am," Lana said. "I'm thinking of how she must be feeling right now, alone in that apartment, knowing we're all here."

"Probably feeling crappy," Rebecca said. "And tomorrow's that eye procedure for her."

"I know. I set up a flower delivery for the day after tomorrow. Something cheery, to take away a little of the sting."

"That was smart of you. And kind."

"It's just that I feel bad," Lana said. "I wish there was something more I could do."

"Me too," Rebecca said sadly.

How nice to speak candidly about Dena with someone who cared. While the DBDs had initially listened and offered sympathy, now, with Pam gone, Rebecca felt as though the others had grown impatient. DBDs didn't support Privileged Ones. Period.

Pam wouldn't have seen it that way.

She missed Pam.

She missed Dena.

She told herself it was Pam she was missing the most, two nights later, as the dancers prepped for their first performance. She sat before the mirror in the theater dressing room she shared with five other corps dancers, and her gaze fell on her good luck talisman.

Every dancer had a little something, the first thing they unpacked from their theater trunk, the last thing they put away. A special charm bracelet or coffee mug; a knickknack, a framed photo. Pam's Special Thing had been a rhinestone-studded hair clasp gifted by Darci Kistler two decades earlier. Rebecca's was a delicate, pint-sized porcelain doll, whose elaborate crimson and gold costume made her look like one of the visiting princesses from *Swan Lake*. The year Dena was ten, she'd saved every penny for who knew how long to buy the doll for Rebecca for Christmas. Seeing Rebecca's delight, her reassurance that yes, she loved it, Dena had burst into tears. "I just wasn't sure," she'd said in a wobbly voice as Rebecca hugged her in response. "I wanted it to be special." And it had been, from that moment on. The doll had seen the teenaged Rebecca through it all: the audition with the WCBT ballet school; the grueling training years; the heady, early corps de ballet years; the later, less fruitful ones.

It sat there now, propped against the mirror on Rebecca's dressing table. She touched the doll's tiny slippered foot like she did every night before performing. With her index finger she tenderly stroked the doll's pert little nose, her pink cheeks. A good luck ritual, but more. A connection to family. To the sisters she and Dena had once been to each other. Tonight the sense of nostalgia and sorrow it conjured made Rebecca's eyes sting, rising tears she irritably dashed away a moment later.

Showtime. Time to push sentiment aside and go perform.

Lights, curtain, action.

She took in the familiarity of it all. The company's transported marley floor all laid out, the sidelight booms and overhead fixtures set to each ballet's specifications, exactly the same lighting as on their California stage. The cool whoosh of air that always filled the warm stage the moment the heavy velvet curtains rose, separating performer from audience. You and the movements you'd learned and rehearsed over and over and over until it had all become as familiar as walking. From the orchestra pit, the familiar music, courtesy of the company's orchestra and conductor, transported to London as well. Behind the scenes, the same production and lighting crew, attuned to every cue, every movement onstage and off. This collaborative world all of them helped to create nightly. San Francisco or London, it didn't matter.

When not dancing, she remained in the wings to watch the others.

She watched Sylvie perform with Nicholas. Onstage Sylvie was beautiful and smiling, a perfect fit in Dena's *Spirit Hour* costume, in perfect synch with her new partner. Offstage, she was a bitch, snapping at Nicholas, or anyone in her way. "Where's the fucking Vaseline?" she snarled one night. "God *damn* it, I keep it back here for *me*." Rebecca watched her face contort with rage, followed by a swift mule-lick of her teeth in the seconds before her next cue so her lips didn't stick to her teeth in a too-dry mouth. Not so pretty a face.

Watching Katrina dance the second night, all beauty and grace, supple extensions and airy leaps with feather-soft landings, Rebecca felt an old despair resurface, that she could never be half as good. None of the females could compete with Katrina, not even Dena. Years back, this had stung horribly. Now the despair in Rebecca was less, more like a gentle, melancholic tug, that left more room for admiring. She wondered if the male dancers watching Javier felt the same way, as he executed flawless quadruple and quintuple pirouettes, powerful leaps, double tours en l'air, sweat flying off him as he whipped through his revolutions, forever at the top of his game.

Watching as Lana's costume tore, another night, exposing her backside while she danced.

Admiring Lana's skilled improvisation until her exit offstage, where Betty, the wardrobe mistress, repaired it in the forty-second pause Lana had before going back on.

This view from the periphery, a simultaneous glimpse of onstage drama and offstage reality. A corps dancer's perspective. Amazing how much you saw when your world existed here, outside the limelight.

One night, post-performance, Rebecca and Boyd slipped away from the other DBDs in the crowded hotel bar and found a quiet, empty lounge area on the mezzanine level. Tensions between them had eased, as if Anders' dual snub in the elevator had realigned them, brought out the return of Boyd's earlier, more romantic persona.

Alone now, the two of them sipped pints of lager and talked. Boyd brought up Tulsa, as he frequently did. This time his monologue featured the River Parks area, which had twenty-six miles of paved trails alongside the Arkansas River, dotted with fountains, sculptures, performing venues, playgrounds. "Pammy thought you would love it, really love it," he told her.

Why not consider this new job, this easier path? Soloist work was infinitely more interesting than corps work. These daily glimpses of Anders and his disinterest were exhausting, debilitating. Really, what was keeping her here? Even Dena wanted her gone. All four of the emails Rebecca had sent since leaving San Francisco had gone unanswered.

"Maybe I'll have to check out the River Parks area for myself," she said in a soft voice.

He glanced over at her in surprise and set down his lager. "Really? You're still considering it?"

"I am. I mean, what is it that's here for me, anyway?"

"Exactly. Except me, of course." He chuckled, leaned in and planted a kiss on her lips.

Boyd was the way to go, she told herself as she kissed him back, then kissed him a second time with more fervor.

There. That was how you set yourself back on track.

Anders liked to teach company class daily while they were on tour. In some ways, it was their most intimate, get-along time together as a company. Here was when he relaxed his guard, lost his aloof nature and became sociable, almost chatty, telling them he loved them all, how he'd been bursting with pride watching them perform the previous night. Today, however, he was impatient with them during center work, when the adagio he'd just set for them stymied them. They were onstage, where company class usually took place during performance seasons. They'd all marked the adagio, split into two groups, as per normal, but eight counts into the first group's turn, he stopped them.

"No, dammit." He pounded his fist on a nearby metal fold-out chair. "Slow. Sustained. But with intensity. With energy. The body is slow but it doesn't *look* slow. It's vibrating with energy, with restraint. It's the tip of the iceberg beneath which lies a volcano."

This brought a stirring, a few chuckles, as they pondered the unlikely nature of that, wondering if it was merely one of his infrequent slipups in English. When he'd slipped up in the past, he'd scowl and let out a torrent of Danish or German words, a rant sometimes continuing for up to a full minute. Now, however, he chose to maintain his temper. Instead, he looked around the stage and when he saw Rebecca in the periphery, he motioned for her.

"Rebecca. With group one. Here, in front of me."

There was a collective pause, an inhale of affront from the dancers standing in the front. Company class, whether onstage or in the studio, had an etiquette and hierarchy, just like all classes did: barre always first, rond de jambe after pliés and tendus, never before, an adagio in the center always before pirouettes, before grand allegro. The higher your rank, the better spot you could stake out in front of the mirror. Front row center was for the principals, the senior soloists. Not left-in-the-dust corps dancers, relegated, more often than not, to group two. But here Anders was, motioning for Katrina and Javier to make room for Rebecca, pointing to the spot right in front of him. She crept over to it, feeling the reproof shot her way by the others. Once Rebecca was in place, Anders cued the accompanist, who recommenced the music, a gorgeous Debussy-esque ballad.

She knew, of course, what Anders was seeking: the way she moved for him when modeling. Easy enough done, particularly when his gaze remained on her.

The adagio began with a slow port de bras before the leg developpéd à la seconde and moved around to the back, to a penché arabesque. Her leg went up, up behind her, nearly 180 degrees—when was the last time her extension had been so high, her balance so solid? Fingers grazed the floor before her head and chest rose back up. She moved in a promenade, arms slowly rising to high fifth, leg behind her in a high attitude derrière. The music pounded, seeping inside her, doubling her energy. The movements continued ever so slowly, feline and sensual.

He kept watching her. She noticed; they all did. A dancer always focuses on their own placement and technique, observing themselves in the mirror, but concurrently they sense who has the teacher's attention. Anders was particularly bad about focusing only on one or two favored dancers, a practice Rebecca, like all the DBDs, had always resented. It hurt to never be watched, knowing you were dancing for yourself alone. Working on one's technique in class was crucial, but so was being noticed. In the end, that was what marked them all as performers. The hunger to please an audience was always there.

The adagio ended with arms in second, wafting down to a low fifth, feet neatly tucked into their own tight fifth position. As the last piano note echoed through the space, she stood there in a daze, trying to catch her breath, regain her bearings.

"Was that a mark, just for Rebecca, or an adagio for all of us?" one of the principals in the first group called out in a petulant voice.

Anders didn't respond to the question. "Lovely," he murmured, still looking at her. "Simply lovely, Rebecca."

"Thank you," she murmured, heart now hammering for a different reason.

Anders stirred from his reverie, clapped his hands twice. "Second group, where are you? Why are you keeping me waiting? First group, move!"

Boyd and the other DBDs were looking at her strangely. Boyd's face held a stricken expression, as if he'd just caught sight of something baffling, troubling, that he couldn't quite decipher. She averted her gaze and moved to the side so the second group— including all the DBDs, of course—could take their places.

Class ended thirty minutes later. She collected her dance bag, water and towel, and made her way over to her friends.

Joe, always the kindest of the DBDs, smiled broadly and held out an arm. "You did us proud, there, Beck," he said, giving her a hug.

She smiled and thanked him. The others were less enthusiastic in their praise. Boyd remained silent until the others had walked on and it was just the two of them.

"What?" she asked, feeling her back muscles clench with unease.

"Something's changed," he said slowly.

For a wild moment she considered confessing everything to Boyd. In the same breath, she brushed it off as impossible. She could never tell a soul about her and Anders; that was the mandate she'd agreed to. Her guilt now was her burden to bear.

She remained silent. He shook his head. "It's just, I guess… Having Pam gone feels all wrong. We don't feel like the same group anymore."

That was all he'd picked up, in the end.

"You're right," she said. "But maybe it was just time for everything to change."

He nodded. Thinking, surely, of Tulsa.

Tulsa was no longer the change she had in mind.

Chapter 11 – Dena

Rebecca, upon her return from London, recoiled visibly when she saw Dena's eyelid partially sewn shut. She stood there in the hallway of Dena's apartment, her beautiful brown eyes wide with uncertainty. Travel cases and bags of food lined the hall behind her, in preparation for the next morning's departure for Tahoe and the annual vacation with Conrad and his wife Janey.

"Oh, wow. That… thing," Rebecca began. "It looks painful."

"It's called a tarsorrhaphy," she informed Rebecca testily.

"A what?"

"Tarsorrhaphy. Tar—*sore*—heffy."

"Oh. Okay." Rebecca looked terrified, which made Dena feel even worse, which made her narrow her eyes at her sister, which was easy since one of the eyes had been stitched half shut.

Janey had had a similar reaction when Dena saw her the previous afternoon. But coming from Janey, it had been more tolerable. Her sweet, freckled face and kind blue eyes had conveyed such genuine empathy, Dena had vowed to hover close to her and avoid Rebecca during their six days together.

Misha had been right. The tarsorrhaphy had been a mistake. A colossal, breathtakingly big one. Tight, made-to-last stitches that hurt, worsening through the procedure day and the next. Her eye had swollen nearly shut, in spite of constant cold compresses, along with mega-doses of ointment and Advil. Over two weeks later, it still felt horrible.

She could hardly bear it, this new reality of having a third of her eyelid—hardly just a "corner"—sewn shut, knowing it would remain so for several months. At least until she got her blink reflex back, Dr. Vanderhaven had told her, sternly, as if this had all been her fault in the first place.

"Is that Rebecca I hear?" Janey called out from the kitchen, where she was frying onions.

"It is," Rebecca called out in a friendly tone, composure reinstated.

Janey emerged, smiling, to give Rebecca a hug. Just having her in the room made Dena feel better. Janey was everything Isabelle wasn't: easygoing, soothing, utterly unconcerned about how she looked or dressed. Her shoulder-length sandy hair had been pulled back into an untidy ponytail and her turquoise blue top clashed with her green sweatpants, but Dena adored her for it all.

"How was your tour?" Janey asked Rebecca. "You must still be exhausted."

"I am," Rebecca said. "On top of that, I had to help my best friend and now-former housemate relocate to Portland. We drove up and I flew back this afternoon."

"Wow, you're doing double duty these days!"

"Yeah. But at least I got to spend time with my friend."

The sizzling sounds in the kitchen grew louder. Janey excused herself and left the living room just as Conrad came in.

If Janey was the soother of the group, Conrad and Rebecca were the arguers.

Conrad, still in business attire, his white shirtsleeves rolled up, greeted Rebecca with a brisk hug. "How was your tour?" he asked

Rebecca in a distracted fashion, as if he knew the answer already.

"It was fine. But I'm really tired," Rebecca said. "If it's okay with you, I'm going to bail on dinner and just go home and rest."

"How can you still be tired? You've been back for five days. We specifically delayed this vacation so you could have rebound time. Besides, I was in Taipei and Janey's on Chicago time. Do you see us complaining?"

"It's because I just spent three of those five days helping Pam move up to Oregon, Dad."

"Well, that was your choice, sweetie, wasn't it? You knew this was the plan. I'm footing the bill for five nights in a luxury resort and the one thing I ask is that we eat dinners together."

"Fine, I promise to eat by your side the other nights."

Dena sighed inwardly and took a seat on the couch. Rebecca always insisted on butting heads with Conrad. It was like a script they followed every time. Why couldn't Rebecca just clam up, do as their father asked, and afterward reap the considerable benefits?

"Why are you being so difficult?" Conrad was saying now.

"I'm not!"

"Well, you're not trying to be part of the solution here. And you certainly aren't taking into account poor Dena. You've been back from London for almost a week and this is the first time you've stopped to see her? What kind of sisterly support is that?"

"I was helping someone else!"

Conrad turned to Dena. "What do you think—should we give her the gold medal for most supportive friend? To someone who doesn't even live locally anymore?"

Rebecca had grown very still. "I don't have to go on this trip," she said to their father.

This was not part of the script.

Conrad frowned. "What are you saying?"

"You call this trip a gift to us. I am not required to accept it. In fact, I'm thinking it's best that I don't."

Confusion clogged Dena's mind. What was Rebecca saying? Of course she had to go. She surely wanted to go. Nice meals, a fancy hotel, massages, hot tubs, pampering. And besides. They went as sisters. No matter how distant they'd grown during the season, once a year, in July, they had this week together.

"Rebecca," she said. "You have to go."

Rebecca's gaze swung around to Dena. "No, I don't."

"But it wouldn't be the same!"

Rebecca glanced at Conrad, then back at her, her expression one of chilly unfamiliarity.

Janey came out from the kitchen, her face creased in concern. "Rebecca," she said. "Honey. You wouldn't let us down like that, would you?"

"This is not about letting anyone down. This is self-preservation. I won't go just to be a punching bag."

"Who's punching you?" Conrad looked mystified.

Rebecca made an impatient sound. "Really, Dad?"

"Really."

All the spirit seemed to fizzle out of her. "Forget it," she said dully. "You three go and enjoy yourself and each other's company. You'll do just fine, without me."

"No!" Janey exclaimed. "It would be all wrong. Rebecca, please!"

Dena exchanged uneasy looks with Conrad. *Were* they too hard on Rebecca?

"All right, sweetie, you've made your point," Conrad said in a more cajoling tone. "I'm sorry if you think we're hard on you. I'm just trying to look after your wounded sister at the same time. Of course we want your company."

"Definitely!" Dena chimed in.

Conrad reached over and gave Rebecca's shoulders a rubdown. "What you need is a couple of days of mandatory relaxation, in a beautiful environment."

"Rebecca?" Dena asked uncertainly. "Please?"

Rebecca stepped clear of Conrad's shoulder rub and gave them all an even, assessing look. "Fine. I'll cooperate with the trip," she said. "But I'm going home right now because I'm tired—and I don't care if the rest of you are full of energy or bothered by the fact that I'm not. Enjoy your dinner. You can pick me up tomorrow morning. Hopefully I'll be less tired then."

At ten o'clock the next morning, Dena sensed they were all holding their breath as Rebecca joined them in the car. But once she saw the treats in the back seat—croissants, raspberry Danish and rich caffe lattes from the city's best bakery—she smiled, and the air grew less tense.

Normally Rebecca was the chatty one when the two of them were paired up in the back seat on these trips, but this time Rebecca remained silent. Which felt fine at first. Dena didn't particularly want to hear about London or the tour again; Lana had already updated her on the company's adventures and successes. It had been painful to listen to. She sensed Rebecca knew this. And yet, unless Dena herself made overtures, they were going to be acting like polite strangers for the next five days.

"So, Pam's gone," she said, and Rebecca nodded sadly.

"Yeah."

"I'm sorry you've lost your closest friend to Oregon."

"Me too. I'll miss her."

"Who's moving into the house, in her place?" Dena asked.

"Steph."

Steph was a corps dancer, but Dena's age group, not Rebecca's.

She and Steph had even trained in the same group, in the WCBT ballet school. She was a good dancer, maybe even exceptional. "I didn't realize you were friends with her," Dena said.

"She's more Charlotte's friend than mine."

"You know, I thought maybe Anders was going to promote her, a year or two ago."

"She thought so, too. We all did. But these things happen."

Like they had four and a half years ago. To Rebecca.

Awkward.

But to her relief, Rebecca didn't comment on that, and instead shifted the topic.

"Did you meet up with Misha while we were gone?" she asked Dena.

"I did."

"Was it okay?"

"Yes."

In truth, more than okay. Each visit had raised her spirits like nothing else. And he'd appeared to be enjoying himself each time, too. Between them had sprung an intimacy aided by two factors: she was the little sister and not the object of his crush; he was a medical person, un-repelled by her facial paralysis. The tarsorrhaphy had fascinated him. He'd kept staring until she'd growled "enough already," which had made them both laugh afterward and her marvel that they already felt this comfortable with each other. She could say anything she wanted, express exactly how she felt. She didn't have to disguise her facial paralysis from him. It literally didn't matter with him.

"What did you guys do?" Rebecca asked.

"He brought over Thai takeout, and we watched Monty Python."

"You love Monty Python."

"So does he, it turns out."

"Was he just saying that to be nice?"

"Hardly. He's got more skits memorized than me."

"Are you going to see him again?"

"That's none of your business," she snapped, forgetting that this was supposed to have been a uniting, placating sort of conversation.

Rebecca looked wounded. "Sorry. It's just that I introduced you to the guy, after all. I wanted to make sure that hadn't been a mistake."

"It hadn't been."

"Fine. I'm glad."

"Thank you. For the introduction, I mean."

"You're welcome."

Tahoe was pines, blue skies, cool temperatures at night, sun, fragrant nature and mountain scenery by day. Their suite of rooms was on the concierge level, with staff who doted on them and their every request. Lazy mornings, good meals, hot tub soaks and massages all helped them relax. Even Rebecca and Conrad started getting along.

Their routine included meeting at noon for lunch together and an afternoon's exploration of the area, sometimes a drive along the lake's periphery, other times a walk. Dena resisted Conrad's suggestion that she wasn't up for a real hike. She'd been giving herself daily barre, an adagio and petit allegro inside her apartment— anything was possible when you were desperate enough—but cardio was equally important.

Today the trail they'd chosen started off gently but became steeper. Dena grew winded, in a good way. Janey, however, wasn't in as good of shape. Neither was Conrad. They began to lag behind. Conrad extended a hand to Janey, who was now breathing heavily.

"Ready to turn back?" Dena heard him ask her. Dena turned to look at them. Janey was nodding, too winded to speak.

"Girls?" Conrad called out, and Rebecca turned around now too. "We've had enough."

"I'd like to keep walking," Dena said.

He looked worried. "Are you sure you're not overdoing it? I think you should stop now."

"I really want to keep going," she said.

"Rebecca," he commanded. "Keep a close eye on her."

"I will."

"Don't you go making any assumptions."

"Dad," Rebecca said. "I've got it. I'll keep her safe."

Conrad hesitated, which made Rebecca bunch her fists in defensiveness.

"Dad," Dena said. "I'm a big girl. I'll be fine, whether Rebecca's with me or not. I'm so much better than I was, just a few weeks ago."

"All right. But don't overly tax yourself."

"I won't."

It was the first time she and Rebecca had gone off for a walk alone, just the two of them. There was an awkwardness to it. Closeness didn't return just because you were both happy exercising. But at least it was a start.

They made their way steadily uphill, alongside the creek with its little cascades and rocky outcroppings. The overhead sun filtered through the trees and beamed down on them. It was peaceful, only the sound of birds and gurgling water disrupting the silence. They paused thirty minutes later at a vista point to enjoy the broad expanse of summer alpine scenery.

"This is great," Rebecca said, not winded in the least.

"It is," Dena agreed, slower to catch her breath. "I like Janey so much," she continued a moment later. "But…"

Rebecca waited expectantly. "Yes?" she prompted.

"She can't exercise for shit."

Rebecca snorted with laughter. "No kidding."

They both dissolved into snickers.

Rebecca seemed to relax her guard. "I thought it was just me, being exercise-manic in the way Dad hates."

"I knew that couldn't be the case with me," Dena said. "I'm a recovering post-craniotomy patient and even I have tons more stamina than her."

"I've been losing my mind at the gentle pace we've been taking," Rebecca said. "Since the first day we arrived. The first hour. I'm just not wired for 'gentle exercise.'"

"I'm with you there."

Finally something they could agree on.

"Well, we both know I can't say this around Dad, because he hates it when we're obsessed with dance during vacations. But I'd give anything for a good, comprehensive barre workout."

"Why didn't you say so?" Dena said.

"Because, well, you know." She gestured toward Dena. "It wouldn't be fair on you."

The chilly feeling returned. Because one of them was 100 percent in shape and the other was severely compromised. A competitive feeling stirred within her.

"Do you not realize that I've been working out two times a day for, like, a month now?" Dena asked.

"Really? Would you be interested…?"

"Of course. Why would I not be?"

Rebecca glanced at her watch. "Anyway, we'd better head back, or Dad will get worried."

They descended the trail in silence, alone with their own thoughts. As they reached the trail entrance at the parking lot, however, Rebecca stopped.

"So. If I can find the right space, for a barre, are you in?"

"I've already researched it. They'll unlock the fitness room an hour before the first exercise class of the day. And to answer your question, yes, I'm in."

"Tomorrow morning?" Rebecca asked.

"Seven o'clock. I'll be there."

The fitness room was perfect, with a mirror along one wall and in the corner, exercise balls and stationary bikes. At 7:05am, she and Rebecca wheeled out two of the stationary bikes to the center, using the handlebars as their own barre.

They'd both brought the basics: for Dena it was a pair of leather slippers, leotard, cutoff tights, her favorite barre sweater. She never traveled away from home without these things, along with a ballet barre CD. It took little room in the bag; what self-respecting dancer *wouldn't* have packed it, just in case?

Over the tinny music coming from Dena's portable CD player, they took turns calling out the combinations for pliés, tendus, dégagés, ronds de jambe.

Dena watched Rebecca closely, critically. She took in the practiced movement of Rebecca's legs, her powerfully arched feet and pointed toes, all utilizing the kind of energy put forth by someone who'd been dancing and performing recently. Were Rebecca's ronds de jambe more articulated? Her port de bras movements more flowing? She could still match Rebecca, she decided each time.

Barre lasted forty-five minutes. Afterward, in the center, Rebecca set a placement exercise for them, and after that, Dena followed with an adagio.

"How was that?" Rebecca asked, once they'd danced the adagio twice. "Are we done?"

"Why are you assuming I want to stop before petit allegro?"

Rebecca eyed her anxiously. "I don't think you're up to moving around so fast, with such feet-intensive work. I mean, no offense. Sometimes even I trip during petit allegro."

"That's because you're a klutz. And we're doing a petit allegro."

She took a step in front of Rebecca and called out the combination, incorporating glissades, jetés, assemblés, with échappés and entrechats quatre and brisés to finish the sixteen counts.

"That's too much for you," Rebecca said.

"No, it's not!"

They did it together four times. Dena's energy soared, even as she fought for breath afterward. "Now everything with beats," she said, still breathing heavily.

Rebecca, panting, stared at her in astonishment. "No way," she said. "Too much."

Oh, the thrill of the challenge. Dena's energy tripled. "What, can't do it?" she taunted.

"This is about what you can do, Deen, not me."

"Bullshit. I'm up to it. Are you?"

Rebecca's eyes narrowed. "Of course I am."

Music, cue, and they were off. It became a contest of sorts. Two sets. Two more sets, starting on the left. More. Rebecca dropped off midway. Dena kept going.

Biggest high ever. Best she'd felt since the surgery. Riding that high. It was like that bad performing night, pre-diagnosis, where she'd pulled the energy from who knew where, and kept going and going.

Until she peaked and crashed.

It happened within the span of an instant. She stumbled and dropped to her hands and knees, unable to reorient, feeling like she was either going to pass out or throw up.

"Dena?" Rebecca said. "Deen?"

The world had gone fuzzy, with blackness around the periphery.

She was only vaguely aware of Rebecca's voice, right in her ear, and then here was Rebecca, on the ground too, curving her body protectively around Dena's.

"Relax against me," she heard Rebecca command.

The blackness subsided. She was okay. She'd be okay.

But instead of having a relaxing moment, she began to cry.

And cry, and cry.

This terrible situation. This terrible world of hers, with her fucking infirmity. She couldn't believe how bad it felt, right then, as if a delayed load of self-pity and sorrow, a boatload of it, had been dumped on her.

Rebecca gathered Dena closer as Dena cried, giving in to the tears, to everything. Just when she thought she was done crying, another fresh bout of grief would come over her, and another. But through it, Rebecca didn't let her go.

Eventually the tears subsided, and with it, the intensity of feelings. She struggled to upright herself, regain some dignity, and Rebecca released her hold. Dena swiped at the wet side of her face. Tears no longer came out of her paralyzed side, which made her feel robbed, somehow.

"Can you get me my eyedrops?" she mumbled to Rebecca.

"Sure. Where are they?"

"Right there in my dance bag. In the top pocket."

Rebecca fetched her the eyedrops and watched as Dena inserted drops into the scratchy, dry, compromised side.

"That thing with your eyelid," Rebecca said.

"The tarsorrhaphy."

"Yeah. Is it as bad as it looks?"

"Yes."

"Oh. I'm sorry. I'm so sorry, Deen. For everything."

Dena studied her sister; Rebecca's eyes were red, teary. So she'd been crying right along with Dena. Not for her, but with her.

Which made all the difference in the world.

"Thank you," she told Rebecca.

A light tap at the door interrupted them; a woman's face appeared in the window. Rebecca motioned her in.

The woman poked her head into the room. "Is it okay if we come in and set up for the step class?" she asked.

"Sure," Rebecca said. "We were just finishing our workout. Help yourself."

She and Dena stuffed their dance bags and headed out. In the weight room, however, Rebecca came to a stop. She looked worried.

"Dad's going to take one look at you and be all over me."

"No, he won't."

"You just don't know."

"We'll explain."

"Doesn't matter. It'll be all my fault. He'll have a shout-fest, like he always does with me."

"Look," Dena said. "Leave Dad to me."

"Really?"

"Really."

Rebecca's relief was evident. "Thank you. I'd appreciate that."

"You're welcome."

The closeness they'd shared was fading. Back to being polite.

Or maybe not. Because as they were leaving the building, Rebecca spoke again. "You kicked my ass today. Fine. I know for a fact you can't do it again, tomorrow morning."

"Go ahead and tell yourself that," Dena scoffed.

"You can't."

"I can."

"Is it a bet?" Rebecca challenged.

"Hell, yeah."

"Fine. You're on."

Dena noticed Rebecca's grin as they walked and realized it had been a trick, to reignite Dena's spirits.

Oh, clever Rebecca.

It had worked. And tomorrow, she promised herself, she'd kick Rebecca's ass again, and have the last laugh.

September

Chapter 12 – Rebecca

She was the only ballet dancer in her college aesthetics class, and quite likely the only professional ballet dancer the rest of the students had ever met. The way the boisterous, outspoken, outnumbering males (eighteen to two) smiled at her gave Rebecca the uneasy impression that they were just waiting for her to reveal her academic ineptitude. Which she, as a result, half-expected too. Constant focus on body work, attacking lengthy combinations and passages physically instead of just mentally analyzing them tended to do that to a person. *Don't think, dear. Just dance,* Balanchine had famously told his dancers.

Tonight, in aesthetics class, one of the students was arguing his support for organismic theory, citing passages from the writings of someone named Kurt Goldstein. When Rebecca timidly asked what organismic theory was, he smiled at her in a pitying way before expounding at great length about how society was like a living human body or biological organism, more than just the sum of its parts. Both had a gradual process of development from a simple to complex state, with differentiation in functions and integration in structure.

Nell, the teacher and the only other female, told the student to find a way to connect the topic to aesthetics and he went quiet.

Rebecca's brain began to whir. A ballet, from its inception in the choreographer's mind to the collaborative effort required by groups and teams to rehearse, present and perform it, all matched organismic theory. Galvanized, she waved her hand and Nell motioned for her to speak. But in her excitement to share her thoughts, Rebecca's words came out wrong. Instead of "this grand organismic society of dancers," out came "grand orgasmic society of dancers."

The explosion of laughter in the room nearly shook the windowpanes. It went on and on.

"I want to see this society," one of the older men roared out.

"There's your representative," another crowed, and pointed to Rebecca.

All eyes fell upon her, making her conscious of her skimpy attire. It was a warm September evening and she'd dressed accordingly in a pale, clingy spaghetti strap top and short shorts. Had she not said a word, her scantily clad state would have gone unnoticed. Now, flushed pink, giggling out of sheer embarrassment—it was either that or cry—she saw how she met her classmates' preconceived notion of a ballet dancer: a pretty, giggling, empty-headed girl who frequently mistook organisms for orgasms.

"No, no," she protested. "Ballet dancers aren't ..." She waved her hands.

"Aren't what? Orgasmic?"

Renewed howls of laughter greeted this comment.

Nell made a half-hearted effort to quiet the students down, but she, too, couldn't stop laughing. The apologetic glance she sent Rebecca's way a minute later was laced with a certain cynicism, even disappointment, a *thanks for making females in academics look bad.*

She didn't bother sharing the story with Boyd, who already resented the way her coursework and meet-ups with Dena claimed all her attention and free hours. She did, however, tell Joe late the next afternoon as they were leaving the main rehearsal studio together, following *Fractal Analysis* rehearsal, a classical-meets-contemporary ballet scored to Haydn and Shostakovich, chock full of contrasting flow and stasis, interpersonal tensions and synergies. Joe, hearing the story, laughed and laughed. From him, it was okay. Joe, as a ballet dancer and as a gay male, had endured his share of ribbing in his life. And he, too, had taken and completed the same college degree program.

"Why'd you choose the class?" he asked her as they strolled down the hallway, passing the three smaller studios, where rehearsals hadn't yet ended.

"I thought it would be easy, relaxing. I wanted something moderate since I'm taking kinesiology too. Philosophy that deals with the principles of beauty and artistic taste? A no-brainer, I'd thought. Except that now they think I'm brainless."

He chuckled to himself. "I'm sure they can't get enough of you in that class."

"It's not the kind of attention I want, or need. God. I'm going to keep my mouth shut for the rest of the semester."

He was still chuckling as they approached the call board, a blackboard-sized bulletin board with notices and rehearsal sheets tacked up. Wardrobe had its own section to notify dancers of costume fittings. PR, too: notices for publicity photo shoots or interviews. But September was, first and foremost, rehearsal season for the repertoire the company would perform throughout the spring season. Choreographers and stagers had been showing up, from their various corners of the world, to teach the dancers the movements, the crucial nuances of the ballets they'd choreographed, or were representing. Most of them, after a few intensive weeks, departed, leaving rehearsals for the répétiteur and three ballet masters to run.

The next day's rehearsal schedule had been posted. *Arpeggio* was back, slated for Program IV in March. Created by Lexie, the company's choreographer-in-residence, it was a playful, neoclassical ballet that featured eight dancers, highlighting three pas de deux couples. Soloists' work. The ballet had special meaning for Rebecca: the last time it had been performed was four and a half years earlier, when she and Dena had both been cast in it. Corps dancers being tested for something bigger.

Joe seemed to be remembering the same thing. "You and Dena. You tore up the stage, you two, way back then."

"Yeah," she said softly. "Talk about a lifetime ago."

She studied the names posted for rehearsing. Lana. No surprise; she'd been cast along with Dena and Rebecca last time. Sylvie, in the role that would have been Dena's, had she not been sidelined. How she hated seeing Sylvie replace her sister. Partnered up with Dena's beloved Nicholas, to boot.

Boyd came up behind them and spied the *Arpeggio* rehearsal sheet as well. "Oh, that one," he said and gave a dismissive sniff. "You know, Lexie had picked me, too, to rehearse one of the soloist roles, last time. I was doing great, until Gunst came sniffing around and got me bumped. Why should he have had say over the choreographer?"

"Because when you're the resident choreographer, you kind of tend to listen to the artistic director's suggestions," Joe said.

"It's bullshit," Boyd muttered. "The choreographer liked me. Friggin' Gunst."

The three of them studied the other rehearsal sheets. Each of the four studios had their lists of what was being rehearsed and when. Plenty of corps rehearsal time for herself, Rebecca noted: Balanchine's *Scotch Symphony*; a new staging of *Carnival of the Animals*. But a fifth list made her pause in confusion.

SF Arts Commission reception, Atherton-Sykes Gallery, 7p-10p
Kessler, L

Devries, K

Lindgren, R

"You, Katrina and Lana," Joe said, pointing at the list. "What's that all about?"

"I'd guess it's one of those networking events," Rebecca said. Pleased anticipation began to bubble up within her. Six years ago, once the sketching had started, so had the invitations to functions like these. But once he'd promoted Dena, the invitations had stopped.

"A harem," Boyd said in distaste. "That's what Gunst wants to bring."

Rebecca feigned annoyance. "What if I'm not free? I count on evenings for class or homework in the fall."

"Well, the boss has spoken," Joe said. "Do homework later."

"Or skip it entirely," Boyd said.

A nearby studio door opened and Ben appeared, along with one of the visiting choreographers. When Javier, behind them, claimed the choreographer's attention, Ben wandered over to the call board, taking note of the announcement as well.

"Well, Miss Lindgren. It appears you've been summoned once again." Ben spoke in a serious tone but his eyes danced. "I believe I am to escort you."

As he'd always done. Anders had surely instructed him, back then, much in the way he'd instructed her ("a black sheath dress, not too short, sleeveless, hair down, please").

"I would be much obliged, kind sir," she told him, smiling.

"Six-thirty, your place?"

"I look forward to it."

She did. And not just because it meant she'd have an entire evening of Anders' company, which, she knew, would be sporadic at best. Ben had become a closer friend since Carmel. The weekend's dreamy magic had been brutally cut off when Anders made an abrupt shift in plans halfway home, dropping her off at an anonymous strip mall in San Mateo, so that he could turn around and head south, back to Palo Alto, to meet someone who'd just called. He waved aside Rebecca's dismay, all but shooing her out of his car, with an assurance that Ben would pick her up within thirty minutes. "You'll be fine, dear," Anders said, preoccupied, consulting his watch. "Have Ben get you a bite to eat; I forgot to get you lunch, didn't I?"

Worse, it was one of those crappy, tired-looking malls, no recognizable venue besides a dollar store, signs painted on the other windows advertising food and retail in Spanish, along with an internationally understandable "Bail Bonds," the guttural drone of highway traffic one block away. She'd stood there, shivering in the settling fog, all good spirits fizzling out of her. Ben, showing up right on time, was all sympathy, and insisted on taking her out for a nice dinner, an upscale Mexican restaurant with platters of succulent seafood and overpriced premium margaritas. When she balked over the prices, Ben shook his head.

"It's on Anders. He owes you this," he added, a hardness creeping into his voice that surprised her. But then he turned playful, cracking jokes, making her laugh, cajoling her into more margaritas. It was the perfect antidote to the harshness of Anders' drop-off. A shuddery half-sob slipped out of her, the sound a kid makes after a good cry. To her embarrassment, Ben heard.

He waited until the waiter had cleared their plates and departed before saying anything. "Hey." He touched her hand. "Know that I'm here for you, Beck. Now, and always."

It had been the kindest thing she'd heard from a man in a long time. Maybe ever.

She watched him now as he walked back to the visiting choreographer. She could feel Boyd, in turn, studying her. "What?"

she asked in exasperation. "What did I do wrong now?"

"Nothing," he said, but he didn't look convinced.

Joe gave Boyd a nudge. "Don't sweat it. I say the rest of us have our own party tomorrow night, at the girls' place. Free of any ass-kissing or surface talk with strangers."

"Free of pandering to the enemy," Boyd agreed, with one last frown cast her way.

Pandering to the enemy the next night had its perks: great food and beverage; glamorous people; a beautiful venue, like an art museum, with an elegant high-ceilinged lobby, glittering with reflected glass, track lighting. Original artwork abounded. She felt Ben's reassuring touch on the small of her back as he guided her through the crowds. She remained by his side as he chatted with the others. He'd assured her he welcomed her company, but she sensed he was doing it so she wouldn't have to stand alone and feel conspicuous.

She saw a familiar face in the crowd: an attractive woman in a black and ivory dress, with regal bearing that spoke of lifelong professional ballet training. The next time she and Ben were alone, she directed his attention to the woman.

"Isn't that Alice, who used to work in development under Gil? Who danced in the company with you, years back?"

"It is." Ben smiled. "Let's go talk to her."

She could feel a current of recognition pass through the WCBT employees present at the sight of Alice. She'd been one of them for many years, after all. After injury had ended her performing career, she'd worked her way up the ladder in development to the role of Gil's associate, only to defect to the San Francisco Symphony's development team five years ago. Which, of course, hadn't endeared her to Gil and Anders.

Katrina had also spied Alice and gone to join her. The two of them were immersed in a parenting conversation by the time Rebecca and Ben arrived.

"… probably just more teething," Alice was saying. "He's cranky and inconsolable, drooling like mad, keeps shoving his fists into his mouth. We all slept horribly last night. You?"

"Dario's tantrums have gotten worse. Unbelievably disruptive."

"Oh, you poor thing."

Alice's eyes lit up in pleasure when she saw Ben. She squeezed his arm and gave him a kiss on the cheek. She smiled at Rebecca as well.

"Hello there, elder Lindgren. It's Rebecca, right?"

Rebecca nodded, pleased to be recognized, and offered Alice a shy smile.

"It's been a while since I've seen you at one of these functions."

"Five years," Rebecca agreed. "You were still working with us here."

"Ah, the good old days." Alice paused, and her eyes grew alert over the approach of someone behind Rebecca. A moment later she felt a presence by her side, palpable, electric, which meant it could only be one person.

The warm, confidential mood had evaporated. "Anders," Alice said, in a friendly, polite voice. "So good to see you."

"Hello, my dear." Anders scrutinized Alice. "You're looking fit. No husband tonight? There… still is a husband, yes?"

In response, Alice smiled extra sweetly. "Yes, there still is, Anders, unless he's decided to leave me since this morning. And no, he's not here. He's looking after our son. Besides, Andy Redgrave told me he'd be happy to play chaperone tonight. He even had his car and driver pick me up and deliver me here. Isn't that sweet?"

Touché. Of course Anders wouldn't find this sweet; Andy Redgrave's family foundation pumped millions into the California arts, with the symphony receiving a million dollars annually to the

WCBT's $250,000. Andy Redgrave was the friend everyone wanted.

Anders frowned at her. "Which means it's your intention to monopolize Andy's attention all evening."

"Anders, observe. Gil's already claimed it." She gestured to the corner of the room, where Gil, Lana and Andy stood talking. "And besides, here's what I think. You still haven't forgiven me for switching to the symphony's development team."

"You took *our* funding with you."

"Nonsense. I took my skills with me. The Redgrave Foundation hasn't changed its funding with either the symphony or the ballet since I went over there. Check your books."

"Gil mentioned there might be changes for next year," Anders said.

"Yes, that's a possibility for us, too."

"What are your negotiations with him regarding that? I would like to know."

"Sorry," Alice said. "That's classified."

"You know far too much about the West Coast Ballet Theatre, which gives you an unfair advantage."

"That's how life goes sometimes."

"Really," Anders said, "I must insist."

He was using his authoritarian voice, the one that made all the dancers quake and hasten to accommodate his wishes. Rebecca grew still, trying to shrink herself down. She sensed Katrina, on the other side of Anders, was doing the same. It was the safest defense.

Alice was not quaking. Instead, she cocked her head as if he'd spoken in Danish and she was puzzling over the translation. "Darling Anders. I don't work for you anymore. Or for the West Coast Ballet Theatre. I'm curious about what purpose you think trying to intimidate me will serve."

No one spoke in such a fashion to Anders Gunst. No one.

Rebecca was afraid to draw a breath. Even Ben looked uncertain.

Fury and disapproval radiated from Anders, but when he spoke, his voice matched Alice's silken tone. "Intimidate you? Nonsense. I was merely posing a question. You're a resilient girl—I think you can handle it."

It was Alice's turn to stiffen in defensiveness. You could almost see her mind churning, trying to find the best comeback.

"Has it never struck you as an anomaly"—she addressed the group as a whole, but clearly the barb was directed toward Anders— "that men and women in their twenties and thirties get referred to as 'boys' and 'girls' in the ballet world? Women who are mothers, even, like Katrina here."

Rebecca felt the sudden, shocking pressure of Anders' hand, sliding possessively around her waist. The warmth and firmness of his touch all but stole her breath. He pulled her and Katrina on his other side closer, sort of corralling them in. It was like that moment in the London elevator, except that this time she, too, was deemed someone to be protected. Cherished.

"My girls have no complaints," he said to Alice. "Do you, girls?"

As if.

"No," she and Katrina chimed, obediently, together, like well-rehearsed school children.

Alice shot them both a *how could you?* look, not unlike the one Rebecca's aesthetics teacher had given her.

Anders chuckled as though he'd won a high stakes bet. "My beautiful girls. Really, Alice, do you see a more beautiful pair of girls in the room right now?"

Alice smiled back at him.

"I will agree with you, that these two *women* outshine all the other women in the room. Ballet dancers certainly are adept at presenting beauty and grace in an elegant package. What do you think, Ben?"

She turned to Ben, who'd been watching the interaction like a spectator at a table tennis match.

He laughed out loud. "I think I am simply enjoying the mix of beauty, intelligence and wit this little circle is providing me."

"That's a coward's answer," Alice scoffed.

"It's a diplomat's answer," Ben replied. "One my employer will not hold against me tomorrow morning when you are long gone, tucked safely away in your symphony administrator's office."

This time Anders laughed too, in genuine amusement, which dispelled the tension.

"All right, boys," Alice said. "I need to go network." She leaned in toward Anders, laid her hand on his chest, and kissed his cheek. "Goodbye, then, sweetheart."

Rebecca watched her stroll away with a growing sense of admiration. Calling Anders a boy, and sweetheart, and getting away with it. Challenging the man in a discussion.

Impressive.

It was close to midnight when Ben dropped her off at the house. She crept inside, sleepy, wanting to be alone, process the night, the conversations. But Boyd and Joe were still there in the living room, watching television with the others. Boyd sprang up when he saw Rebecca and followed her into the kitchen, quizzing her about the night.

She offered him a generic recap, but he looked unsatisfied.

"What aren't you telling me?" he asked afterward.

"What do you mean?"

"Just be honest with me."

This baffled her. "I am. I was."

He hesitated. Now he looked nervous, which made her feel nervous. Had he learned something about her and Anders? Dread clutched at her chest and squeezed.

"Is something going on between you and Ben?" he asked.

Her breath came out in one great exhale of relief. "Boyd! Hardly. He's an administrator. Besides that, he knows we're a couple. Ben would never cross either of those lines."

"No. I wouldn't have thought he would. But you two seem… close." Unease battled with suspicion, creasing his brow. "And I heard you spent time together, maybe even the night. Back in May."

Holy shit. She'd been spied on.

"Sure." She spoke rapidly, eyes trained on the refrigerator. "I told you about that. A couple days down south, in Carmel."

"You told me about a day in Carmel. You never mentioned it was a male you'd gone with."

"That's because it was such a nonissue. Ben and I are good friends. We're very comfortable with each other." This, at least, was wholly true. "And can you name anyone who's more trustworthy, aside from maybe Joe?"

"No," he admitted.

She yanked open the refrigerator to grab a mineral water, pausing to cool her hot face, collect her thoughts. As Charlotte had been the only other housemate still in town that weekend, that meant she'd made note of Rebecca's movements and reported them to Boyd. She'd had a hunch Charlotte was not her friend, but this confirmed it. A chill passed through her; thank God for Anders' suspicion of such a thing, his insistence on using Ben as the middleman.

Boyd, satisfied with her reply, asked if Anders had been his usual arrogant self at the function.

"Yes," she said. "You would have liked the way Alice handled him, though. Remember her? Former soloist, worked with Gil in development?"

Boyd nodded.

"Anders was hassling her and she threw it right back in his face. It was fun to watch."

"Wish I'd been there." His reply sounded guarded.

In response, she took a long pull of her mineral water, the gurgle of it the only sound in the room until the refrigerator compressor kicked on, producing a low hum. A safe, reassuring sound, and it meant all was running smoothly and there was no reason for concern.

An illusion she would allow herself to sustain a little bit longer.

Chapter 13 – Dena

Trader Joe's on a Sunday afternoon was maybe not the best time for a weekly stock-up, but the time worked for Rebecca, and was something the two sisters could do together agreeably. Even enjoyably. Like most Sunday afternoons, the place was overcrowded with shoppers and activity, a savory herb smell arising from the nearby sampling table. Dena was doubly grateful for Rebecca's company; stores and crowds were exhausting to navigate since the craniotomy. But Trader Joe's had her favorite cracked wheat sourdough bread, cheeses, cheap dried apricots and bagged almonds.

Over the buzz of conversation around them, Dena told Rebecca about her meet-up with Lana the previous day. "We went to my gym and gave ourselves a barre, there in the aerobics room. She told me my extensions still look great."

"I agree," Rebecca said, weaving their shopping cart around the crowds.

"I asked her if she thought I was ready for company class, and she said yes."

Rebecca stopped the cart and reached over for a box of crackers. "Ah," she said, although she seemed more intent on examining the box's label.

"So," Dena said, less confident. "Maybe next week I'll give it a try."

Rebecca didn't reply.

"What do you think?" Dena persisted.

Rebecca met her gaze with reluctance. "Honestly? I don't think you're ready, Deen."

Her good mood subsided. "Oh, and you're a better judge than Lana, who's a rank above you to begin with."

Rebecca didn't take the bait.

"I'm going crazy," Dena fretted. "I need to go back to company class. I'm physically much stronger than I was that week in Tahoe. My stamina's better. I'm less dizzy. I'm ready."

"It's more," Rebecca said. "Watch it!" she exclaimed, pulling Dena away from stepping back into someone wheeling a cart past on Dena's left.

"Thanks," Dena said, chagrined. "Didn't notice." Noisy places were awful with her single-sided deafness. Full hearing meant you knew which direction a voice was coming from. With this, you had no clue, and so she was constantly bumping into people on her deaf side.

"You're thinking that problem is going to arise." Dena gestured in the direction of the person who'd passed. "But just for the record, it's tons easier for me in a studio. One entire wall is mirrored, for starters."

"It's not the partial deafness that's got me worrying for you," Rebecca said.

"What, then?"

Rebecca waited until a cluster of shoppers had cleared their aisle before speaking. "Dena. You may feel physically ready. But you don't look ready."

Because of the way her face looked.

The insinuation felt like a kick in the stomach. "Lana didn't say anything about that," Dena quavered.

"No, I don't imagine she would. She's too nice."

"Unlike you."

Rebecca flinched but held her ground. "I'm your sister."

"If I keep my right side neutral, it matches the paralyzed side."

"It's the eye, Deen. That thing's a liability."

The *clang, clang* of a bell at the nearby checkout stand rang through her head and made it ache horribly. Suddenly all the stimulus and extra effort on her part to function in the busy outside world hit her. She just wanted to get out of there and go home. Even talking felt like too much.

Particularly talking with her sister.

So much for agreeable Sunday afternoons together.

Need encouragement, she texted Misha the next day.

Will bring a pint of it over at 4p, he texted back, which made her smile.

This, too, had become a welcome new routine in her life. One or two afternoons a week, Misha stopped by, sometimes staying for just an hour, other times, the entire evening. Sometimes they hung out in the apartment and he made them dinner, some lengthy, complicated recipe the scientist in him was eager to experiment with. Other times they walked her neighborhood, window shopped, dropped into a restaurant for Thai or Chinese takeout—she still didn't like eating out in public with her facial paralysis issues—and bringing it back to the apartment to nibble on while watching a movie. She treasured these meet-ups. They made her feel human again.

Misha showed up promptly at four o'clock and held up a brown paper bag. When she inspected the contents, she laughed. It was a pint of Ben & Jerry's Cherry Garcia ice cream.

"I can't keep eating stuff like this when I'm not dancing all day," she told him, even as she headed to the kitchen for bowls and spoons. "It's making me gain weight."

"It's therapy," he called out. "Cold ice cream makes even numb cheeks tingle."

"Nothing makes numb cheeks tingle."

Only half her mouth could chew and taste and feel still, but the sweetness and texture of the ice cream on her right side was nice, and she could trust Misha not to laugh or look appalled when surplus dribbled out of the left side of her mouth. When this happened, which it regularly did, he would simply hand her a napkin from a nearby pile and gesture to the spot, never breaking the flow of their conversation. She'd learned never to attempt eating without that pile of napkins close by.

"Your cheek will tingle at some point," Misha told her, digging into his own bowl of Cherry Garcia. "One day you'll wake up, annoyed by little prickles of sensation."

"It's been five months of waiting."

"Nerve regeneration takes a long, long time. Don't lose faith yet, Dena. Things are happening."

"You're wrong, they're not." She stared gloomily at her bowl.

"You don't know that for sure."

"Well, you don't know yours for sure, either. The odds of it working are low; we both know that. More likely than not, I'll have to go for that second surgery."

He nodded, looking more serious. "The hypoglossal-facial nerve graft."

"Yeah. That."

She knew it by its easier name, the 12/7 nerve graft. Misha had given her the rundown in layman's language. Basically they'd cut her open below the ear, expose the nonfunctioning facial nerve, and further down her neck, expose the hypoglossal nerve—the twelfth or "tongue nerve," Misha had called it—and cut that nerve, too. They'd reattach the portion of the twelfth nerve coming from her brain to the stump of the facial nerve, and once again, she'd just have to be patient and wait and wait, to the tune of twelve to eighteen months, and hope for it to take. It was all too depressing to consider.

"How's your ballet rehab going?" Misha asked.

She immediately felt less gloomy. "It's going great. I'm so ready to get back to company class. But Rebecca rained on my parade yesterday."

"Uh-oh. How?"

"She nixed my idea of returning soon. Told me she was 'worried,' because of how I look. How my eye looks."

She expected Misha to roll his eyes, agree with her that Rebecca was too looks-oriented, and if Dena's body was ready, that was all that mattered. But to her dismay, Misha nodded.

"She's right. That tarsorrhaphy looks awful. And it's making you feel awful, I can tell. You should consider getting it reversed."

She wasn't sure if Misha's blunt assessment made her feel better or worse. "My doctor wants to give it six months. For my own good, he says."

He moved his chair closer to her, leaned in. "Look at me," he said.

She raised her eyes. He reached out, cradled her face in his hands, peering into her eyes in a way that produced a flutter that shot straight through her, like nothing she'd felt since Nicholas, three years earlier.

"Blink," he said.

She blinked, but more in surprise than in response.

"What?" she stuttered.

"That's it. Just blink again."

She blinked. Up close, she saw how his brown eyes were shot through with specks of gold and his skin was unblemished, even this close, except for the shadow of beard stubble. She'd never been in this kind of setup without having the guy kiss her. Except there was no desire in Misha's eyes. Only curiosity, satisfaction.

He nodded, released his hold. "There's some blink reflex. Granted, nothing like the other side. But I'm going to argue that you don't need that tarsorrhaphy. I think you could get by with a gold weight."

Hope rose in her, and fell just as quickly. "Try telling that to my doctor."

"I will," he said. "When's your next appointment?"

The hope sprang back. "Coincidentally, at the end of this week. Friday at three o'clock."

"Perfect. What's your doctor's name?"

"Vanderhaven."

"Ophthalmologist or oculoplastic surgeon?"

Only Misha could have known enough to ask that question.

"Oculoplastic surgeon."

"I'm going with you. Together we'll get this whole issue straightened."

"You don't know this guy. He's tough."

"I can be tough, too. Just ask your sister."

On Friday afternoon, Misha met her outside the clinic just before her appointment.

"Are you sure about this?" she asked.

"Absolutely."

In silence they entered the building, took the elevator two levels up and headed to the office midway down the hushed carpeted halls.

He took a seat and leafed through a magazine, relaxed, as she signed in and took the seat next to him. Five minutes later, the door leading to the examining rooms opened.

"Dena Lindgren?" the nurse called out.

"That was fast," she murmured to him as they rose.

"They knew I was here," he murmured back. "They know authority when they see it."

She laughed, and something in her relaxed.

In the little examining room Misha prowled around, examining items on the stainless steel counters, the jars with cotton balls and Q-Tips, the medical knickknacks, the posters on the wall displaying extreme close-ups of eyeballs and various veins and nerves.

They didn't talk. With Misha engrossed, Dena tried to take deep breaths to control her rising anxiety. Now that she saw her condition through not just Rebecca's eyes but Misha's, she was certain the tarsorrhaphy was indeed unacceptable. But Dr. Vanderhaven liked things just as they were.

A knock sounded at the door and Dr. Vanderhaven entered without waiting for a reply. He stopped short when he saw Misha, standing by the counter, one elbow resting comfortably on it, as if to demonstrate partial ownership. Dr. Vanderhaven looked at Dena and back at Misha.

"Well, hello," he said finally, in that humorless, coldly efficient way of his.

"I brought a friend—" Dena began, but Misha had already stepped over to him, shaking the doctor's hand, introducing himself.

"Dena has mixed feelings about the tarsorrhaphy, and I'm inclined to concur," he said.

Dr. Vanderhaven looked confused. "I'm sorry, back up, please?"

Misha explained.

The doctor's *I still don't get it* expression that followed managed to incorporate both disdain and incredulity. Dena's toes curled in her shoes. Dr. Vanderhaven was going to be an asshole.

"Forgive me," he said to Misha. "*Who* are you, and remind me again of your authority here?" *You loser,* his gaze seemed to say.

Dena winced. Poor Misha.

But Misha only chuckled. "I'm a failed medical student, of course. And hell hath no fury like a failed medical student who's defending a patient in need of a different treatment."

"The patient needs the tarsorrhaphy."

"She does not. It's a hindrance. Dena's a professional ballet dancer. The tarsorrhaphy was an inappropriate choice from the start."

"It's the safest."

"It's cosmetically displeasing, it restricts peripheral vision, and further, does nothing to improve active eyelid closure."

Dr. Vanderhaven tightened his lips. "No. End of issue."

He reminded Dena of Anders, which made her resistance wilt away. "Misha," she murmured. "It's okay."

Misha ignored her words as he stabbed a finger at Dr. Vanderhaven. "If you won't listen to reason, we'll find another oculoplastic surgeon who will address this logic."

"This *is* logical."

"Her blink reflex is strong enough to support the gold weight alternative."

Neither of them were paying any attention to her at this point. The two of them had grown more heated, which proved Dr. Vanderhaven wasn't emotionless after all, merely humorless. They argued, tossing unfamiliar words back and forth, like a verbal game of dodgeball, phrases like "resultant paralytic lagophthalmos" and the risks of "superficial punctuate keratopathy."

"You have no experience with this matter whatsoever," Dr. Vanderhaven thundered.

"I know people with experience in this matter," Misha thundered right back. "And I've spoken with them at length. Dena and I will go there. In fact, I see little point in continuing this discussion. Please see to it that her records are transferred in a timely manner when you get a call from Dr. Darvish's office."

Dr. Vanderhaven hesitated. "Dr. Darvish is far too busy to take this on."

"Not for Dr. Lavigne's son. They were medical school friends. Good friends."

"Dr. Lavigne…"

"My father. Deceased now. But his fellow surgeons remember him well. They'd be only too happy to help."

"Your father was a surgeon?"

Misha nodded.

"Fine," he snapped, not conceding to Misha so much as deferring to a fellow surgeon, or the thought of losing a patient to one. "We'll reverse the tarsorrhaphy. But if I observe excessive drying at her follow-up, with the gold weight in place, the tarsorrhaphy will go back."

He glared at Misha, who smiled right back at him, now the picture of innocence. Dena could barely contain her jubilation.

A cancellation in Dr. Vanderhaven's overbooked schedule allowed the procedure to take place the following week. The entire procedure only took twenty minutes. The first few days post-op brought pain, bruising, swelling, and required careful surveillance and eyedrops, but each day yielded improvement. Miraculously, the gold weight inserted into her eyelid did its job. She could blink. One week post-op. Misha studied her successful blink and smiled at her, well pleased with himself. She reached over and squeezed his hand in equal parts pleasure and gratitude. To the casual observer, they might have looked like lovers, gazing into each other's eyes with such intensity, such affection.

"You're taping it at night, just like before?"

"Most definitely. And when I lie down for a rest."

"Good." He smiled at her. "So. How are you going to celebrate?"

"By going right back to company class. As soon as possible."

The following Wednesday she made her triumphant return to company class. The first person she encountered, surely a good omen, was Nicholas. His shock at the sight of her was instantly replaced by a broad smile, his arms open wide. The comfort of it, when she went to him and hugged him, made her chest tighten, her face contort, and she was glad it was buried in Nicholas's sweatshirt so no one could see the asymmetrical distortion.

"I've missed you, Deen," he murmured. "I can't wait to partner up with you again. *Spirit Hour* just didn't feel right without you. You and I, we get in that groove when we work together, you know?" He angled his head to meet her eyes, and she nodded, careful not to try and smile.

He noticed that. He peered closer at her face.

"Holy shit, you've got a black eye," he said, taking a step back.

Lana and several others had come up behind him, exclaiming in delight when they saw her. Rebecca stood in the periphery, eyeing her in a worried way. Dena looked at all of them and a rush of self-consciousness came over her.

"I've got more than a black eye," she admitted. "I've got lots of stuff still. I'm a recovery in progress."

Half the group fell silent, but the more sociable ones—and thank God for them, she'd never been so grateful for their chatty, outgoing natures—exclaimed about the bruising still around her eye. She told them about the tarsorrhaphy, the facial paralysis and everyone took a collective step back in horror at the thought of it, at the concept of not being able to blink, smile, grimace, yawn or emote in any way on the left side.

Rebecca had been right to insist she wait. Dena tried to keep her expression neutral, so that both sides were equally expressionless, but she fooled no one. Not in this looks-conscious world. They all asked the same question: when would the facial paralysis disappear, so she could smile, and thus perform, again? She didn't know who knew about her left-sided deafness. She wasn't offering up the information. She felt enough like a freak already.

She only did the first half of class, the barre, placement and adagio, with Lana and Rebecca hovering protectively nearby. The rest of class, the pirouettes, petit allegro and grand allegro, she sat out to watch. She'd forgotten how fast, how relentless the class pace was. Her brain wouldn't have been able to retain the combinations that Curtis, the ballet master teaching class, was throwing at them. Even the corps dancers and apprentices looked like superstars to her.

But something else was concerning her. Sylvie had greeted Dena, giving her a swift "I'm so happy to see you back here" hug, before hurrying to her place at the barre right behind Nicholas. But thereafter, she'd avoided eye contact. It was distressing. She finally sought out Sylvie after class, grabbing at her arm to keep Sylvie from leaping away. She saw the panic in Sylvie's eyes.

"What is it?" Dena asked quietly. "And don't say nothing."

Sylvie looked down. She drew a deep breath and looked back up. "Okay. Here it is. Nicholas and I, well, we got together one night on tour. You know how these things happen."

"Yes," Dena said, dying inside, remembering all too well the night she and Nicholas had hooked up, the magic of it, the way her world had seemed charmed beyond measure.

Sylvie tried to maintain a solemn expression, but her euphoria, the sexual satiation that seemed to ooze from her, spoke louder. "I know you two were involved once. I feel terrible. If you're not okay with it, Deen, I'll end it. I value our friendship that much."

Yes, end it, Dena wanted to say. *I don't need this loss too. Not right now. Not when I can't just get up and focus on my dance instead.*

"Don't be silly," she said instead. "It was just some fun we had, a few years ago."

A lie; it had been the greatest romance of her life so far, with nothing even coming close since then.

But the relief on Sylvie's face was genuine. "That's what he said too," she told Dena.

Which hurt.

Sylvie seemed anxious to leave after that, edging away from Dena, saying she needed to get going, to stop by Wardrobe for measurements before rehearsal. Dena watched her grab her dance bag and scurry away. She sighed, retrieved her own dance bag and towel.

Rebecca stood waiting by the studio door, her expression stricken, as if she'd intuited what Sylvie had just told her. But she smiled as Dena approached.

"Hey. Let's go celebrate your return."

Dena studied Rebecca suspiciously. "Don't you have rehearsal in twenty minutes?"

"Yes, but that's enough time to go have a sparkling apple juice toast down in the café."

"I think I'll just go home."

"Dena. You have to celebrate the little steps. *We* have to celebrate them."

Dena stopped. "You were right, by the way. About it being too soon for me to come back here and be around the other dancers."

"Well, it's not too soon anymore. C'mon. To the café."

"All right," Dena relented, and the two of them left the room together.

When was the last time she and Rebecca had left company class together, walking down the hall side by side like this?

Years.

"Hey," Rebecca said softly.

"Yeah?"

"Welcome back, sis."

Chapter 14 – Rebecca

Nutcracker was making its way onto the rehearsal schedules, and one thing a corps female could count on was a part in either "Land of Snow" or "Waltz of the Flowers," if not both. Flakes, as they affectionately (or not) called the former, was energetic, seven minutes of near constant movement. Twenty dancers ran on, leapt, spun, swooped. They formed geometric patterns in the center of the stage, moving like a human kaleidoscope. They shot down the diagonal in a single file line of grand jeté leaps. They ran off, replaced by pas de deux vignettes from the Snow Queen and King, and ran back on once the royalty had departed. Midway, movements became quicker, patterns more whirly, like the increasingly heavy snow falling and swirling around them. Anders had re-choreographed Flakes eight years earlier, deciding to go for more snow and more controlled chaos. A hundred pounds of paper snow bits per performance? Let's make it two hundred pounds. Let's make the movements and turns faster, really spinning. It was madness. Exhausting. The critics had loved it. Audiences, too.

The choreography was harder on the body than the brain. It took them only two rehearsals with April to set the entire piece. Today they ran through the whole piece for the first time.

"But this doesn't seem all that challenging," one of the new corps dancers said afterward to another member of the ensemble. "I mean, tiring, sure, but not complicated."

The older dancers, overhearing, chuckled over the comment.

"Wait till the snow gets added," Rebecca told her, and everyone nodded in agreement.

Oh, the snow. The challenge of dancing onstage under an onslaught of little papery bits, the risks as it accumulated on the stage. Invariably, among the twenty of them, there were a few skids and near falls. Foot traction aside, there was the nuisance factor, as well. If you were sweaty (and you were always sweaty), it clung to your skin. Someone always ended up inhaling bits of the bitter, flame-retardant flavored stuff, gagging and hacking backstage to get it back out. The snow clung to false eyelashes and you had to keep dancing, blinking like a madman, and hope it didn't affect your vision. Later, back in the dressing rooms, it became a contest to see who had the most original location for the snow bits: your hair, inside your ear; pasted to your neck; tucked deep into your bodice; inside your tights (how??).

This was Rebecca's tenth year of dancing *Nutcracker* as a professional, counting her apprentice year. She'd always been deemed a reliable dancer, one blessed with relatively few injuries, and had been cast for all thirty performances, each year. Which meant that, by the end of this year's Nut run, she'd have performed Flakes 300 times.

There was something kind of horrifying about that.

Or was it just sad?

Flakes was the last rehearsal of the day. Rebecca, intent on untying her pointe shoe ribbons to ease off the shoes, didn't notice Steph, the newest DBD and housemate, approach until she stood over Rebecca. Her pale cheeks—everything about Steph was pale, her blonde hair and brows, her milky skin, even her blue eyes—seemed even more devoid of color than usual.

"Congratulations," she said to Rebecca, sounding neither warm nor hostile.

Rebecca regarded her in confusion.

"The rehearsal sheet's up. You're slated to rehearse Arabian for *Nutcracker*."

"I... *what?*"

Steph offered her a faint smile.

"You didn't see it coming? Really?"

Rebecca scrambled up from the floor, ignoring her half-taken-off pointe shoes and clop-clopped her way out into the hall, loose ribbons trailing behind her. Other dancers had congregated around the call board, scanning the rehearsal sheets for their own names.

There she was. And not even third cast status, but second cast.

Arabian Dance, with Jimmy, a newly promoted soloist. Slow-moving, sensuous, sinuous, partnered work. A coveted role, usually reserved for the soloists.

Anders was letting her give it a try.

She could feel the gape-jawed silence of Boyd and Charlotte behind her. Joe let out a little "Whoa. Beck!"

Steph was conspicuously silent. With reason. Two years earlier, she'd been the corps dancer singled out for soloist roles like this, right alongside Jimmy. Now her name appeared only on the Flakes and Waltz of the Flowers rehearsal lists.

"Well. Proof yet again," she said in a flat voice to Charlotte. "This is it. He's officially stopped noticing me."

"Don't let it get you down," Charlotte soothed in a low voice. "That choice is bullshit."

Rebecca pivoted around and met their scowls.

"Nice job," said Charlotte. "What did you have to do for it?"

Her face grew hot. "Nothing. I kept my head down and danced."

Boyd studied her, his expression sour. Only Joe seemed genuinely happy for her.

"It's just a rehearsal," Rebecca said to all of them. "Not casting."

"That's true," Boyd said. "I wouldn't go holding my breath."

"I'm not. Like I told you. I'm just keeping my head down and working hard."

Oh, the elation, though.

She fretted about how Dena might respond to the news, but Dena was surprisingly supportive, if not terribly interested. She was more concerned about neatening the apartment for Misha's imminent arrival; the three of them were going out to eat together. It had been Rebecca's idea, an opportunity to help smooth over any awkwardness Dena might still be feeling around Misha. Rebecca, after helping Dena neaten, wandered over to the dining table and peered inside a white Macy's bag.

"What's this?" she asked, pushing the white tissue aside to reveal several new sweaters in autumn colors. She examined a label on the top one: 100 percent cashmere. Nice.

"Mom was here," Dena said. "She'd bought some things for me."

"Wow. That was generous of her. The blouse you're wearing, did she get you that too?"

Dena fingered the sleeve of the silken V-neck blouse and nodded.

"It looks good on you."

"Thank you. I used to borrow dress shirts from Lana, but all her things are at Gil's now."

"She never spends the night here anymore, does she?" Rebecca asked.

"No," Dena admitted. "She shouldn't even be paying rent. Gil did something tricky—he sent the landlord a check to cover Lana's rent until the end of the year. Then he tried to soften the charity by telling me I was helping them out of a bind, that Lana needed the psychological impact of having somewhere else to go."

Rebecca chuckled. "Did you buy it?"

"I did. I felt so noble, until I realized it had all been about their helping me."

"That's Gil for you."

Dena chuckled too. "It is." But any mirth faded from her voice with her next words.

"Mom's offering to help me out in January." She didn't look happy.

"Help you, how?" Rebecca asked.

"She's offering to pay Lana's half of the rent in exchange for coming up whenever she feels like it. Basically renting the second room."

Rebecca winced. Dena and Isabelle had fought endlessly back when the three of them had shared an apartment, in the ballet school years.

Dena took in Rebecca's reaction and nodded gloomily. "I don't know if I'm ready for that. I mean, Mom's been really helpful and sweet since my surgery"—she gestured to the Macy's bag—"but I'm afraid things will shift and she'll start nitpicking again and getting on my nerves."

"Well, consider interviewing for another roommate."

Dena looked even gloomier. "The thing is, I don't know if I'm ready for that, either."

"Look, that's months away. Maybe something will come up. At least Mom can be your backup plan."

"Misha told me he should be paying part of the rent. Or at least for the times he's spent the night."

Dena sounded so matter-of-fact, Rebecca thought she'd misheard.

"Spending the night?" she repeated, stunned when Dena nodded. "Are you trying to tell me you two are...?"

Dena seemed more outraged than flustered by the insinuation. "Are we what? Sleeping together? Get your mind out of the gutter, Rebecca. God. We're *friends.*"

"Oh, okay, right. Sorry." She took in her sister's glare, her unexplained anger, and offered a helpless shrug. "I'm surprised, that's all. I thought this dinner together tonight, the three of us, was something to help the two of you feel more comfortable around each other."

Dena shot her a look of disbelief. "Becca, we achieved 'comfortable' our first evening together, months back. He's been coming over here twice a week since then. We spend all evening together."

"Oh," was all she could manage.

"I told him to consider this his home base in the city, especially since Lana's never here. And in turn, he's contributed all these nice touches. You mean you haven't noticed that, either? The Cuisinart in the kitchen. All the spices in the cabinet. The new utensils. That higher quality frying pan."

"I thought that was Lana."

"Why would she do that if she never ate here?"

"Good point."

"Sheesh." Dena shook her head. "You are so caught up in your own world. Buildings could catch on fire around you and you wouldn't notice."

Dena might have had a point, because the next day Boyd had to be the one to inform her of the bad news. It was during lunch break and Rebecca had tucked herself away to study, paging through Kant's *Critique of Judgment* to complete her analysis and summary of the book's second section for aesthetics class. Boyd's news, however, made all other thoughts fall away.

Joe had ruptured his Achilles tendon during a rehearsal mid-morning. "It was loud," Boyd reported, face grim. "He landed wrong on a double tour and that was it. Everyone heard it snap."

Rebecca stared up at Boyd, aghast. She knew what such an injury spelled: a long, slow rehab. He'd be out for months, minimum, not even taking barre. It would be a year before he could consider performing again. Maybe in your early twenties you could stand a chance at a comeback. But Joe was over thirty.

She scrambled to her feet. "Where is he right now?"

"Lorraine took him to the hospital."

"Oh, God. I need to see him." She glanced down at her textbook and notes and hesitated.

Boyd noticed, and snorted. "Priorities, huh?"

She ignored him and sifted through her bag for her phone. Yes. Priorities.

By the time she got a hold of him, Joe had left the hospital and was back at his apartment. She begged off the last hour of rehearsal so she could stop by his place and squeeze in a visit before her class that night.

He answered her knock and let her in. In his sweats and his favorite frayed red sweatshirt, he looked fine, aside from a foot in a splint and crutches. Relaxed. Calm.

For a reason. He told her, right up front, that he'd decided to quit dancing.

"Joe!" she cried. "You can't mean that!"

"I do." He crutched his way back to the couch and sank down with a sigh, propping his injured foot high up on a pillow stack. "Look. I've had a half-dozen surgeries in the past twelve years. The dislocated shoulder, the ACL tear, and now this. I'm thirty-one and in constant pain. I'm tired, and I'm not getting the roles anyway. It's time to stop this insanity."

She made them cups of tea and they sipped as he recounted the drama. The WCBT had in-house medical personnel for this very reason. Lorraine, their physical therapist, had assessed him and whisked him to the hospital, where a company-affiliated orthopedic surgeon was able to see him within two hours.

"Gunst showed up, there at the hospital, while I was waiting. He sat and waited with me. Can you imagine anything stranger? It was like he'd become Ben for the afternoon, genuinely caring about my welfare. We talked about Denmark and the Chesapeake Bay, growing up in those two places, and their similarities. Crabbing. Fishing. Childhood memories. Our families. Not one word about dance. It was surreal."

He accepted another cup of tea. Afterward, he watched the steam rise in curls from his mug. "It made me think... I don't know," he said. "Thinking is the wrong word. I understood. I understood right then and there, that it was done. Everything. The ballet career, the vendetta against him. The resistance to all the things I didn't like, or thought were unfair. This fighting attitude. All of it just poofed away. Call it endorphins or something. Point being, I knew I was done. And I was instantly at peace with the decision." A single tear rolled out of his eyes.

"Surgery is the day after tomorrow. I told Gunst that once things were stable, I wanted to go home, back to Maryland, for the bulk of the rehab. If I'm going to be sidelined through the next several months, might as well be with family. And he was totally supportive. He's going to keep me on the roster, through the end of my contract, if need be, so that I can draw insurance and union benefits. I can live there the whole time if I want."

A sob rose up from deep in her chest and burst out. And another.

"Aww, Beck," he said, and leaned over to envelope her in a hug. "Don't cry for me."

"I'm being selfish," she sobbed into his shoulder. "I'm crying for *me*. You're my family. I can't bear to think of you being gone. First Pam and now you."

"Cheer up, Toots. You're getting a second chance. That's just how these things go. Nothing either of us can do to change it."

Boyd came over to the DBD house ninety minutes later, with plans. She was back at her desk, cramming, desperate to finish the aesthetics assignment before class. Boyd didn't seem to notice her distraction. The plan was to gather at Joe's, he said. Everyone was in on it. They'd bring over dinner, cheer Joe up, remind themselves that they were a team, all of them, even now.

"Did you hear what Joe's thinking, because of Gunst sweet-talking him?" Boyd demanded. "He's leaving! Saying he's ready to give up the fight. We're all going over there and persuading him not to."

"I'm sorry, I can't join you," she told him tersely. "Joe knows it."

"Why the hell not?"

"I've got class in forty minutes."

Boyd looked incredulous. "Tell me you're kidding."

"Nope." She offered him a brittle smile.

"*The class. The classes,*" he mimicked in a high, mincing tone. "That's all that matters."

She told herself not to blow up at him. "Tonight, yes."

"Because Tulsa sure doesn't."

She fell silent.

"Because you've never really considered Tulsa. You were just stringing me along there."

She glanced at her watch and rose from the desk. "I'm running late. We can talk about Tulsa later," she said as she began to shove the books into her backpack.

"I want to talk about Tulsa now. And how you're making me look bad, telling them 'I've got this great partner who would work out great, only she's too busy to give you the time of day.'"

"I've got bigger things on my mind!"

"Then fuck it," he said in a low, vicious tone. "To hell with you. Maybe I'll ask Steph to go with me. She's a much better dancer than you, anyway. Why you're getting all this attention right now is beyond me. And to think you're throwing my efforts to help you better yourself right back in my face."

He was only trying to hurt her, she told herself. He was hurting as badly as she over Joe and his news. "I'm leaving," she told him, closing her mind and her ears to the continued ranting that followed her down the hallway.

She ached for Joe, and all of them, on the way to class. Because it was an omnipresent threat to every last one of them. When you're left behind in the corps for so many years, you understand that eventually, something's going to give. No, she didn't want to go to Tulsa. She would not go to Tulsa. Her career would end here. When Anders let her go, that would be it.

No matter what Boyd said, she knew beyond a doubt that the classes mattered. Because one day, something would have to come after ballet.

Just ask Joe.

Chapter 15 – Dena

Dena encountered Tatum Monroe a second time when she entered Celia's coffee shop one early November afternoon just as Tatum was leaving. Her eyes, an arresting amber color, angled like a cat's, widened with delight at the sight of Dena.

"I literally just now gave Celia my card to hand over to you when she saw you next," Tatum exclaimed. Celia, behind the counter, held up a business card and nodded.

Energy seemed to radiate from Tatum as she walked with Dena back to the counter. Last time, her hair had been tucked away, but today she wore it loose, an extravagance of black waves, so shiny and dark, they seemed to impart a violet sheen. It reinforced the impression, along with the eyes, that Tatum was part exotic animal, something on the savannah, studying Dena with such interest. She told Dena how much she loved coming to the city, from her home base in the South Bay, to see live theater and dance. "Too expensive to do all the time," she said, "but I love it whenever I do go. And that's where I saw *you*." She gave Dena's arm a pat. "You are a sublime dancer. A nymph. No, not a nymph, that's too wimpy. A goddess. Really," she added when Dena began to laugh in protest. She turned to Celia. "This is one divine dancer. Do you have any idea how good she is?"

"I had a hunch," Celia said, grinning.

Dena invited Tatum to join her for a few minutes at her table. "I hear you're a social media consultant," she told Tatum. "I have to be honest, I don't have a clue about what that entails."

Tatum elaborated. She'd trained as a journalist in college, she told Dena, and worked slavishly as a freelance writer for a few years, but soon found more lucrative earnings in social media avenues, like building and maintaining websites, managing freelance online marketing projects for small businesses and startups. "As for my blog, I created it as a diversion, a fun, pressure-free way for me to keep writing regularly," she said. "I'm thrilled that so many people are reading it. And it's a great advertising tool for my social media services."

"Wow. That's all pretty cool."

"It is." Tatum's cat eyes gleamed. "These are crazy, exciting times for the social media community. It's the final frontier. It's more global and pervasive than anything we could have imagined, thirty years ago. And it's only going to get bigger and more relevant. Which brings us to why I wanted to touch base with you," she said, eyes settling on Dena. "You have a Facebook account, I saw."

"I do," she said, mystified. "I don't post often, though."

"No Twitter?"

Dena shook her head. "I wouldn't know what to do with it. Social media just isn't my thing—I'm too much of an introvert."

"I'm watching several ballet dancers around the world experiment with social media and garner lots of attention. They have websites, blogs, fan pages; they're taking pictures and posting them online, shots backstage and behind-the-scenes. People are eating it up."

"Our public relations person has a problem with that much sharing," Dena said. "There might even be a company rule against it."

"If there is, I'll bet you that rule will change. Soon."

In response, Dena shrugged and broke off another piece of her muffin to nibble on.

"Dancers are finding their voices in the online world," Tatum continued. "And it's a win-win situation. It gives them much more power and control over their destiny, while concurrently bringing transparency and accountability into the ballet world. The way the New York City Ballet fired eleven corps dancers in spring of 2009? Just dropped them. God. Utterly callous. Twenty years earlier, the company would have been able to keep it all hush-hush. But because of social media, the rest of us found out."

"Yeah, that was crappy for the dancers," Dena said.

"And then Peter Martins went and hired new corps dancers."

"That's just how it goes. He was within his rights."

Tatum leaned back in her seat and folded her arms. "Wow. You're more matter of fact about this than I expected."

"Well, it was horrible, and I felt terrible for the fired dancers," Dena said. "But that's the professional dance world. There's not the same kind of safety you find in other occupations. We know that. And every year the company training schools produce top-notch talent. The artistic director has to find the best of them a place in the company or lose them. Truth is, they're cheaper than senior corps dancers, too."

Tatum didn't look convinced. "I'll tell you what. I wish I'd had the platform and social media pull, back then, that I have right now. I would have made sure the whole online world knew what had been going on, as it was happening."

A calculating, scheming look had come into Tatum's eyes.

So let's target the newly disabled dancer, set her up as a social media puppet, so when her artistic director tries to get rid of her, we'll let everyone know. Expose the big bad wolf in action.

Dena rose from her seat in alarm at the thought. Tatum looked up, startled.

"I have a hunch about where you're going with this," Dena said. "And I have to say, I'm not interested. You picked the wrong dancer."

"Wait ..." Tatum began, but Dena kept talking.

"You're sniffing around for scandal within the ballet world so you can be the one to break the news and spread it."

"No, that's not it." Tatum waved her hands. "Dena. Please sit back down."

Tatum looked genuinely distressed; Dena sank back to her seat.

"I'm not trying to set you up in any way, Dena. I swear. Honestly, I wasn't even thinking of any connection between the New York City Ballet firings and you. It was just a ballet story I remember from last year."

Dena remained wary. "Tell me, then, what's prompting you to make this offer to me? I just don't buy the coincidence of it all."

Tatum studied her hands before she spoke again.

"Okay. Brutal honesty?" She looked up.

Dena nodded.

"That day in June when I came here and saw you and your two dancer friends, it was so clear you'd been through something major and traumatic, and that you had a long recuperation ahead of you. It just made my heart twist. I looked at the other two, who, frankly, seemed a little oblivious to your pain, your challenges, more concerned with how *they* looked."

She could tell Tatum was telling the truth because the glib expression had disappeared. She looked almost sorrowful now. "And, okay, back to the City Ballet dancers, the sense of injustice. Seeing you, I felt so... indignant. How unfair it all was for you and your career. And I told myself right then, that if I could help you in any way, I would. So, fast-forward to last month, when I took on a client, an operatic tenor who has to take a year off singing for vocal cord surgery and rehab. He was frantic to do something professionally proactive during his downtime, so now he's blogging, posting pics on a new social media site called Instagram, involving himself in Twitter and Facebook. He's got a great looking website now, too, if I don't say so myself. He says all of it has really cheered him up *and* increased his fan base tenfold."

Her gaze settled on Dena. "I could help you in this way. I'd love to do it. And I'll bet the diversion would help you, too."

The suspicious thing in Dena relented. "Okay, that all makes sense. And I appreciate the offer. It's really generous of you. But we're not talking a year off for me. It's been five months already, I'm back in company class, ramping up more each day. Pretty soon, things will get even busier. *Nutcracker* and all."

"Oh, wow, you'll get a part?"

"I'm not sure. I need to discuss my ideas with our artistic director. None of the Act Two dances, of course. That would be too much. But the dancing doll in the Act One party scene is a small but fun role. She's expressionless, so my facial paralysis wouldn't work against me."

"Well!" Tatum said in a bright voice that didn't match the skepticism in her eyes. "I'll cross my fingers for you!"

"Thanks!" Dena kept her voice just as bright. "Appreciate it!"

Tatum rose. "Anyway, let's leave it at this. Know that I'd love to work with you. I come to the city a few times a month. Maybe we can meet up again, after the New Year?"

"I'll have to wait and see—I won't always have this kind of flexible free time. Because I think they'll definitely be rehearsing me in January, even if I'm not getting cast. I'll need to pour all my energy into that."

"Well, hang on to my card. I'd love to stay in touch."

Dena picked up the card and gave it a little wave. "Got it. Will do."

She didn't let Tatum's invitation and its unsettling implications rest long in her mind. Not when she was making her way back into the swing of things. She treasured every minute of company class. She arrived thirty minutes early to give herself a comprehensive warm-up. Fifteen minutes into barre, past pliés, tendus, and dégagés, she was well into the groove, sweat collecting as she worked her muscles to their maximum efficiency. She could feel the perspiration trickle down her back, her chest, pool around her waistband and saturate her tights and leotard. Even being sweaty felt good, a gift handed down from up above. A grace. An honor, to be a dancer, immersed in the craft.

Yes, there were challenges. The single-sided deafness, resisting the urge to smile, or even emote, because of how it clashed with her face's frozen side. Quick-to-rise fatigue and brain fog. Trying to keep up with the others in petit allegro. The pain of cramping calves and the frustration of lower leg extensions, but pushing herself brought pleasure. That familiar pinch in the arched back when her leg stretched ever higher behind her for a sustained arabesque. The stretching of the obliques, the abs, during a cambré and full port de bras. The golden light that flooded her heart and seemed to whisper, *you're home again.*

Until casting for *Nutcracker* became evident.

Thirty performances, three casts, using over a hundred dancers. The rehearsal sheets crowded the call board, spilling over onto the adjacent wall. But Dena's name showed up on no rehearsal list. Therefore, no chance at being cast.

"Please, Anders," she begged when she met with him to discuss it. "Physically, I'm up to speed for *something.*"

Anders, from behind his desk, sighed and rubbed his face. "Dena. I love your positive attitude. It's an inspiration to all of us. But you are not 'up to speed,' darling girl. You've improved dramatically from the first month, but you are not a hundred percent. Not even eighty."

"I can do it," she insisted. "The smallest dancing role. Like the dancing doll in Act One."

"Yes, you could, and no, I won't cast you there."

"A party guest, then. A maid."

He shook his head. "I'm not putting you in roles better suited for corps dancers. I won't compromise your talent, your rank. Besides, in regards to the party scene, dear girl, it's mugging. Pure and simple. It's not dance, it's acting. It's mime."

Which one could not do with a half-paralyzed face.

No *Nutcracker*, then. She could hardly process the thought. What was she supposed to do with herself through it all? "Maybe I should just leave town for the month," she burst out, surprising herself.

Anders looked startled as well. *No, no*, Dena hoped he'd say. *You need to stay. We need you close.*

"Do you have plans?" he asked instead.

What had prompted her to voice such a dramatic, half-baked idea? To the artistic director, no less. "Oh, my father has always wanted me to come out and visit for the holidays," she improvised. "I've never had the chance. Obviously. But now…"

He nodded, smiling. "I can't think of a better solution. For him and you both."

Well, shit.

"Okay, then!" She angled the expressionless side of her face his way so he couldn't see her dismay. "That's what I'll do!"

Conrad, at the least, was thrilled by her idea, eager to have her spend the month with him and Janey in Chicago. "Come even earlier," he urged. "Spend Thanksgiving with us here. That's never happened before."

Of course not—no ballet dancer had time off during the Thanksgiving holiday weekend, much less time before and after Christmas Day. If you were a ballet dancer, you were married to *Nutcracker* through the month of December.

It wasn't the solution her dancer's soul craved. But it was the only way out. Because, overnight, being around the studios had become intolerable. In that purpose-driven environment, ramping up for the performance run, there was no place for a sidelined dancer.

Sylvie was rehearsing Snow Queen in Cast III. Even bigger, Lana got second cast Sugar Plum Fairy. Rebecca got Arabian in the same cast.

It was time to go.

The Monday before Thanksgiving, she and Lana packed up their belongings, preparing the apartment for visitors. Conrad had found renters, friends of Janey's parents, eager to sublet the apartment for three weeks in December, who hadn't flinched at Conrad's proposal that they simply pay the month's rent. For Lana, this was the final move-out. It would be official after this: no longer roommates.

Lana, to Dena's frustration, wouldn't accept any of the subletters' money, even though she'd already paid December rent. It meant Dena pocketed an extra $1500. Which pissed her off, somehow, even as she knew—they both knew—how much she needed it for January rent.

Lana wanted to chat, as they neatened the living room together. Wedding chat. Dena tried to appear engaged and interested.

"You don't mind that Sylvie took your place as bridesmaid?" Lana asked.

"Of course not. I hope you don't mind that I didn't feel up to the occasion."

"But you're still coming to the wedding, right? I mean, Chicago and Kansas City are an easy day trip by car."

"I'll do my best."

"Did I tell you about that change on the cake order that we made?"

"Um, I'm not sure."

"When Gil heard I was dancing Sugar Plum Fairy, he called them and sent them on a search for sugar plums. Actual sugar plums. And he said that instead of a bride and groom, there should be a Sugar Plum Fairy and her cavalier. Of course I said no way. But it turns out they've got a border icing that's called 'sugar plum.' That's the color. So, when we heard that, we agreed, oh, definitely. No one else is going to make the connection, but it'll make me smile!"

Dena had no response for this.

"Anyway." Lana's voice grew less confident. "I'm rambling. Sorry."

"It's okay. It's your wedding we're talking about, after all, right?"

"That's true!" she said, and a moment later she launched into a new story, this one about the menu for the rehearsal dinner. They were going to do barbeque. Kansas City barbeque.

"Gil's been giving Nicholas trouble for never having eaten real barbeque before," Lana said. "He's only had California barbeque. Which is so not the real deal."

This got Dena's attention. "You mean Nicholas is flying out for your wedding, too?"

"Well, yes. With Sylvie in it, and all, and the way Nicholas gets along well with... everyone."

Lana's words trailed off.

"Like Gil." Dena kept her voice normal.

"Well, yeah."

"From all that double dating the four of you have been doing."

Lana looked guarded. "Oh, Sylvie told you about that?"

"No, she and I haven't talked much lately."

"Then how did you find out?"

"You just confirmed it."

In the silence that followed, Lana's eyes grew bright with tears.

"This is harder than you think, Dena, being on the other side of your infirmity. Always saying the wrong thing, doing the wrong thing. I can't even talk about rehearsals around you anymore, or anything unrelated to company class, because I know it hurts you. I try to keep pace with you in class so you don't feel left out. I practically try to screw up during pirouettes or grand allegro so you can see that we all have bad days."

"Bad *days?*"

"Bad spells. Mine's waiting somewhere in the future. I know it is. And I wish it could be now so that we could commiserate together. But it's not, and I can't, and you're pushing me away, no matter what I talk about, and I'm so sad about this all."

"Well, sorry." Dena didn't know what else to say. Neither did Lana.

They finished quickly after that. Lana loaded her boxes in Gil's car and within fifteen minutes, she was ready to go.

"Happy Thanksgiving." Lana looked miserable. "Call me in December. Or text me. Please."

"I'll try," Dena said. "And you, have fun with the Nut run. Be a good Sugar Plum Fairy. You deserve the honor."

"Thanks."

They exchanged a hug, which felt more awkward than comforting, and then Lana was off.

Misha had offered to drive Dena to the airport on Tuesday. Late morning, all packed to go, she gazed around at the emptier apartment, the sofa, armchairs and tables foreign looking without her personal knickknacks and favorite throws draped over the sofa back. All valuables, including Misha's recent additions, had been locked into the back hall closet for the duration of her absence.

Leaving. Giving up, if just temporarily.

For a month she'd forget the West Coast Ballet Theatre, forget the dancers, leave that world behind. Come back after the New Year, and leap into it all.

A new year. A new chance.

Chapter 16 – Rebecca

"Ready to do this Nut thing?" Jimmy, Rebecca's Arabian Dance partner murmured as they stood waiting in the cool darkness of the upstage left wing.

It was the second night of *Nutcracker*, although opening night for their cast. Nerves gripped Rebecca's insides, but excitement did too. "Ready." She squeezed his hand. "Merde."

"Merde," he whispered back.

Spanish Dance ended onstage, amid a torrent of applause. While the performers took their bows, Jimmy placed one hand on her right hip, the other under her left thigh. Once the orchestra commenced Arabian's familiar brooding melody—one Tchaikovsky had plucked from a Georgian lullaby and not Arabian at all—he hoisted her overhead. Her right foot tucked into a neat passé position, toe to knee. He strode onstage and she sailed above him like a ship, holding a long, diaphanous scarf aloft that unfurled and undulated behind them.

Arabian Dance. Four minutes of slow, sinuous extensions, lifts, lunges, entangling and disentangling. Pure sensuality. Performing this dance was such a different onstage experience from any other. Never speeding, never stopping, just one languorous movement into the next. She felt more keenly aware of the blinding stage lights, the audience, the dancers watching from the wings, the stage manager at his monitor, the screen's ghostly glow. Her feet reveled in the subversive joy of performing in leather slippers and not pointe shoes. Her body felt liberated, too: the costume, with its chiffon harem pants and glittery, wispy top, exposed her midriff. Jimmy's hands were firm and sure against her bare skin. At one point he met her eyes, his freckled, all-American face turned exotic, beautiful, with tan Pan-Cake foundation and bold eyeliner strokes. His expression was serious, regal, but his eyes danced.

Six weeks earlier, Jimmy had been a good sport about losing one partner and gaining her. Ben had told Jimmy not to worry, that Rebecca was a quick study. She already knew the part, after all, from understudying it years earlier. Back then, she'd zealously attended every rehearsal, taking notes, observing the way the three different couples who would go on to be cast approached the serpentine poses and passages differently. Jimmy was brilliant, one of Anders' finds two years back, a farm boy from Texas who'd turned down an all-expenses paid basketball scholarship to pursue ballet instead. He had it all: musicality, great physique, feline grace, big jumps, effortless turns, beautifully articulated feet. Twenty years old, newly promoted to soloist, he was still wide-eyed about this new world of his and how easy (to him) it all was. "Wow," he'd said to Rebecca after their first run-thru with Ben. "That was fun! You dance like you're much younger."

Ben had burst into laughter. "Never underestimate the allure and talent of an older woman, my man," he'd said, clapping Jimmy on the back. She'd laughed, too, but it was still a jolt. When she'd joined the company as an apprentice, Jimmy had been ten.

Oh, God, she was getting old.

Except she had to admit, it *was* fun. Huge fun. Working with a talented younger dancer, one clearly on the rise, carried with it a certain dazzle factor. No jaded, snippy pessimism, no bitter acknowledgement of thwarted dreams. Seen through Jimmy's eyes, *Nutcracker* became a fresh thing again, a delight. Magical, even, hearing the orchestra commence Tchaikovsky's jaunty overture before the curtain came up on the 19th century family Christmas Eve party scene. Magical, seen through the eyes of the youngest performers from the ballet school. Pre- and post-battle scene, you'd see them lined up in the hallway in their neat rows of twelve, little tin soldiers and mice, herded by volunteer parents who kept watch over them at all times. They'd flatten themselves against the walls whenever a company member passed by. One look at their painted faces, their thrilled, awed expressions, brought a tightening to Rebecca's throat. It made her, if only for a moment, believe in magic again, in the power of dreams.

Eventually, of course, the thrill of the production would fade against the reality and exhausting nature of a thirty-performance run in twenty days. Dancing multiple roles each night, her energy would decline, slowly but surely. Her hair would grow dull and grimy, caked with ultra-hold hair spray, sweat, foundation that had crept into the hairline, oily makeup remover that clung even after showering. Soon she would wake every morning wondering what was going to hurt the most with her first few steps: throbbing toes, inflamed knee joints, ankles, hips. It wasn't just her; past the mid-run mark, rehearsal sheets and casting sheets would be revised hourly to accommodate new injuries, new substitutions right and left.

But for now, the magic.

She called Dena mid-run to see how she was coping. Dena seemed cheerful, even bubbly. Conrad and Janey were treating her to meals out, shows, day spa visits, she reported. She felt so pampered, so physically relaxed.

"I can't imagine," Rebecca said. "I literally can't." She stretched on the couch, shifting her weight off her throbbing right hip before repositioning the frozen gel pack on her left knee.

"It's been so decadent," Dena said. "The weight gain is not the best, but that will change, once I'm back home and taking daily company class again. And, hopefully... Well, you know."

Being rehearsed.

Dena's goal. Her greatest hope.

"We saw a Nut performance," she told Rebecca.

"Amateur or professional?"

"Professional. The Joffrey."

"Good?"

"Yeah."

"What was it like, sitting in the audience?"

"Hard. Emotional."

"Hang in there, Deen. You won't be sidelined forever."

"I have to tell you," Dena said, "watching them made me even hungrier to get back to work. I literally dream about it, every night."

"Well, I think you need to be patient a little longer."

"Except that, maybe something's about to change," Dena said.

This puzzled Rebecca. "Um, like what?"

Dena hesitated, but when she finally spoke, the words came out in a rush. "Okay. Here it is. Sylvie called to talk. She thinks Anders might be making a decision about something. See, she overheard Anders and Lucinda in a private discussion."

"I think that's called eavesdropping."

"Whatever. She heard Lucinda tell him, 'we'll make it official in January.' And Anders said, 'If the time is right, I'll tell her the news. She'll be pleased.'"

There was an expectant pause.

"All right," Rebecca said, mystified. "And this means...?"

"That maybe he's decided to put me on the rehearsal schedule once we start back up."

Rebecca's heart sank. "Oh, Deen. That's a pretty far stretch. He could have been talking about anything. Anyone."

"We know it's a female, and I'm ninety-nine percent certain it's a company member."

"Okay, that narrows it down to thirty of us. And, what's more, it could be about anything. The number of pointe shoes we're allotted. Or whether Mimi gets opening night of *Giselle* over Katrina."

"Fine." Dena sounded angry. "Sorry I said anything. Drop it."

"It's just that—" Rebecca began, but Dena cut her off.

"I said drop it."

The silence between them felt cool and brooding, like it had been last spring.

But at least this time Dena made an effort to maintain the alliance. "How's the Nut run going?" she asked, more polite than curious.

"Oh, same old, same old. Everyone's getting really tired."

"Becca." Dena sounded strained. "What if he keeps me sidelined the whole season?"

How could she respond to that?

"Has anything changed?" she asked Dena. "The muscles on your face?"

"No," Dena admitted, her voice flat with discouragement.

"Well, that doesn't matter," Rebecca said briskly. "Because remember the words Sylvie overheard. They could have been about you."

They weren't. Rebecca knew this, somehow. But Dena needed that dream. And sure enough, by the time they bade each other goodbye, the lilt was back to her voice.

"Time to go take a walk before it gets too dark," Dena said. "I need my twice-daily exercise."

"Go for it. Love you, sis," Rebecca said, surprising herself. She hadn't said that in years and yet it had flowed out effortlessly.

"Love you too," Dena said. "Can't wait to come back."

The mystery surrounding Anders' announcement revealed itself three days after Christmas, on the company's closing performance. Rebecca had returned backstage to retrieve a forgotten sweater and observed Anders murmuring something to Lana on the opposite wing. Lana gasped, took a step back, and her hand flew to her mouth. The way he smiled at her, a fatherly pride sort of smile, told the story.

He'd promoted Lana to principal. Rebecca was sure of it.

This was Dena's "Anders has good news for someone."

Oh, the mixed feelings right then. The sweetness of watching Lana, almost clumsy in her shock, react to the news. The sorrow of how this would hurt Dena. In-house promotions to principal were few and far between. Dena was screwed.

"Thank you, *thank* you!" Lana was saying, half-crying. She gave him a hug, a sweetly awkward thing, before dashing off, never even registering Rebecca's presence in the shadowy half-light.

Anders had keener powers of observation. She stood there in silence as he approached her. He was wearing a suit and tie, which always made him look more desirable, more inaccessible.

"You heard," he said.

"No. But I can guess."

"And?" He raised one eyebrow.

"You promoted her."

"I did." He sounded calm, matter-of-fact.

Anders never got sucked into the emotional angle of promotions and their repercussions amid the dancers. He'd shown no emotion, those years back, when he'd informed Rebecca that he was choosing to promote Dena over her. "It's Dena's time," was all he'd said in explanation, and she'd been too stricken with shock to even respond.

"Dena's going to be disappointed," she said now, which was the understatement of the century.

"These things happen."

What a cop-out. Was Dena going to take comfort in a platitude any more than she had?

"Yeah, well, I'll let you be the one to tell that to my little sister."

In the silence that greeted her retort, she wondered if she'd finally overstepped her boundaries. He was the artistic director, after all. Their intimacy had been on a personal level alone. But he said nothing. Instead he kept his eyes on her with that steady gaze of his, which overtook her indignation and, no surprise, became its own reward.

"You did well tonight," he said.

She gave him a dignified nod. "Thank you."

"Do you have plans right now?"

Boyd and the DBDs were meeting up back at the house. Boyd was expecting her presence, her compliance, now that Arabian was over and "you're back where you belong, with us." He'd said that. Not in a harsh, punitive way, but more like an affirmation. A dreary one.

"Not important plans," she admitted, which she immediately regretted when she saw the corners of Anders' eyes crinkle in amusement.

"Come join my group for a glass of champagne across the street at L'Orange."

She pretended to waver. But Anders was leaving the next day for Paris and a rendezvous with his ex-wife—they'd married young, divorced young, stayed on good terms. After tonight, she wouldn't see him for two whole weeks. "All right," she said finally.

"I'll have Ben walk over with you. Shall I tell him twenty minutes?"

"Yes. I'll be ready."

The holiday season was still in full swing at L'Orange. Tiny LED lights twinkled and intertwined along the stairway curving up to the second level. Wreaths decked the taupe walls of the private alcove Anders had reserved for his group. Tonight a surplus of Beautiful Women graced the room as well. They glided about like swans, sporting long, silken evening attire, toned and bejeweled bodies, with impeccable makeup and coiffures. They hovered around Anders, hung onto his every word, took turns laying a hand on his arm, his shoulder, as if to establish proprietorship.

Rebecca abandoned her efforts to compete and sought out Ben instead, but a trio of the Beautiful Women soon descended upon him as well. A tall, striking blonde named Petra, in particular, seemed very interested in getting to know Ben better. Ben without Rebecca nearby.

He grabbed at her arm as she turned to leave the group. "I'm here if you need me," he murmured. "Just give me a nudge and I'm yours."

Anders noticed her finally and beckoned her over with a smile. He kept talking to his guests, now a pair of silver-haired donors, but as she approached he placed his hand on her back, drawing her in, which, predictably, made her go dopey with pleasure. Once he finished his conversation with the donors, he dropped his hand and turned to her.

"I didn't want to forget to tell you something."

"What is it?" she asked, as her heart began to race. Had the plans for Paris fallen through? No meet-up with the ex-wife? Instead... Carmel?

Oh, please, oh please.

"I was going to call—" he began, but another couple approached to congratulate him on the performance run, and they had that Old Money look about them, so he chatted politely, while she stood there, thoughts ricocheting about. Finally he returned his attention to her.

"Where were we?" he asked.

"Something you wanted to tell me." She tried to sound casual. "You were going to call someone?"

"That's right." He smiled. "I was going to call your mother and wish her happy holidays, but I never got around to it. I leave tomorrow and it'll be a whirlwind. Wish her a Happy New Year for me, will you?"

That was it? That was the only reason he'd signaled for her to join him? To talk about her *mother?* She wanted to cry in disappointment. Instead she tried to smile.

"Of course I will," she said in a high, unsteady voice.

He tilted his head as he studied her. "You don't seem like yourself."

"I am," she said. It's just…"

"Yes?"

It's just that I was hoping we could talk more. Be alone. Replay Carmel. Throw all caution to the wind. Instead, she only said, "I suppose I'm just very tired."

"Of course you are, poor girl. You look exhausted. A bit manic."

His attention got diverted even as they were speaking. She stood by his side for several minutes more before she gave up and slipped away.

Ben sought her out twenty minutes later. "Anders says you look exhausted and that I am to take you home."

"No, thank you," she said stiffly. "I'll get myself a taxi."

"Beck. Let me drive you. I'll enjoy your company."

"What about *Petra?*" The snippy, jealous tone that slipped out appalled her.

Ben remained unfazed. "She's leaving too."

"Well, then, okay. Thank you."

In the car, they were both silent for the first five minutes, as scenery shot past.

"I'm sorry if I messed up things between you and that Petra woman," she said finally.

"You didn't," he said, and out of the corner of her eye she saw him grin. "Truth be told, I have an invitation to join her, after I drop you off."

"Oh," she said, wondering why she found the idea so objectionable. "That's great!"

He offered no comment, and they drove the rest of the way in silence.

Approaching her house, she groaned aloud at the sight of Boyd's car parked on the street a few houses away. "Oh, God. I'm not ready for him. For them."

"Okay," Ben said. "We don't stop."

They trundled past the house. Ben found a parking space at the end of the block and slid his car efficiently into it. He cut the engine, the lights, and the two of them sat there.

"How's Dena been doing?" he asked, and she shared the details she knew.

"I'm glad she took advantage of the chance to get away," he said.

"It was a nice change for her. But she's hungry to get back." She hesitated. "Can I ask you something in confidence?"

"Sure. Try me."

"Dena is hoping Anders might be ready to rehearse her when we all return in January."

He pondered this. "And what's your take on that?"

"I worry he won't consider rehearsing her for some time to come."

He didn't respond immediately. Ahead of them, a traffic light turned green but no car went through. It was a cold, damp night; the windows were starting to fog up.

"Regrettably, I think you might be right," he said.

So. Dena would come back to not one but two pieces of disappointing news. A sense of vicarious despair settled in, weighing her down.

Ben glanced at her. "You're fading. Let's get you inside."

They walked toward the house. "Got New Year's Eve plans with the gang?" Ben asked.

"Boyd wants everyone to join him back in L.A. He leaves tomorrow. I'll drive down on New Year's Eve day."

"You don't sound excited."

Something gloomy in her stirred. "Frankly, I'm not. Pam canceled. Seeing her was what I was most looking forward to." Except that things had changed there, too. Pam had embraced her new life and new friends so intensely. She had a boyfriend, a new support group. The DBD world was history. The cancellation was proof.

"That's quite a drive for a party with friends who all live locally," Ben said.

"I know, right? All of us driving to L.A. and back, just because Boyd's home base is there. I'm not even sure if it's worth it to go." She realized only after speaking the words how little she wanted to go.

"Then don't."

She shook her head. "I'm trying to keep the peace. Boyd's counting on me."

"Yeah, I get it. Alice invited me to a dinner party at their place. There will be spouses and toddlers. I'll be the only non-parent there. And did I mention that small children scare me?"

"Take your own advice. Don't go."

He chuckled. "I will take the 'she's counting on me' defense, as well."

"Keeping the peace is worth something."

"It is."

"Stable relationships are, too."

"Agreed."

Her gloom increased as they approached the house. When they stopped at the base of the stairs, she turned to look at Ben. "Thanks for the drive and the walk to the door."

"My pleasure."

"Have fun with that woman."

He chuckled, but didn't reply. Nor did he make a move to leave. "Hey," he said softly. "Want a little gift?"

She regarded him curiously. "Okay."

"Can you keep this just between us?"

"Of course." The gloomy spirits hesitated, like thieves approaching a house they realize is occupied.

He leaned in and tucked a hand around her neck as if he were preparing to kiss her. But his lips stopped at her ear.

"Anders liked you in Arabian," he murmured. "He liked your work with Jimmy. He told me to talk to Lexie after the layoff and see about having you join Jimmy on the rehearsal schedule."

"For, for *Arpeggio?*" she stammered.

"Shh." He glanced up at the door of the house, but of course no one had heard. He straightened, his eyes full of mirth. "Yes, indeed," he said. "You heard me right."

The news seemed to work its way from her mind to her face and through her body, like a warm, buttery heat. "Oh, *Ben,*" she breathed, and looked up to meet his smiling face.

"Merry Christmas, Becca," he said.

She flung herself at him in pure glee and hugged him tightly. He hugged her back just as fiercely.

A shout of laughter from inside the house a moment later made them break apart. "Okay, now," Ben said. "Be sad. Go in there tired and gloomy."

She grinned at him. "I am so miserable and bereft of any good news," she said in a monotone, and let her shoulders mock-droop.

"Perfect."

The world paused for a moment as they stood there, smiling at each other. Happiness coursed through her, but not just because of the good news. It was because she could be fully herself with Ben, and not hide Anders stuff, or Dena stuff, or who she was at her core, and sometimes the relief of sharing your deepest self with another human being became the biggest gift of all.

"See you next year," Ben said finally, reaching out to give her fingers one last squeeze, before heading back to the street, his car, his other life.

Tucking her gift close to her heart, she drew a deep breath and returned, as well, to her other life.

January 2011

Chapter 17 – Dena

January wasn't supposed to have turned out this way. There she'd been, throughout the cold, rainy month of December in Chicago, counting the days to her return to San Francisco, to the company, the prospect of dance a shining beacon of hope piercing the foggy gloom of her mind. But this disappointment, this crappy despair?

Dena sat clutching the steering wheel of her Honda Civic as she drove southbound on Highway One in a light rain. The windshield wipers softly swooshed back and forth as the raindrops momentarily blotted out the scenery. San Francisco's ordered city environment was long gone, buildings and neighborhoods replaced by the broad expanse of the Pacific Ocean to her right, cliffs to her left. Past the town of Pacifica, the highway narrowed and began twisting, hugging the coastline, ascending steeply. There was a perilous nature to it, driving on the slim ribbon of asphalt, feeling like you could hurl yourself and your car over the steep precipice if you failed to follow the road's sharp curves. So easy to end it all, if you really wanted to.

What had been the proverbial last straw? So many options to consider. Struggling in company class, overlooked by all, except Rebecca and Lana. Her sister, so busy, happily rehearsing a soloist role, among others. Sylvie and Nicholas, in love. Lana, newly married, newly promoted. Lexie, her favorite choreographer, who'd promised in late October to try and get her on a rehearsal schedule for *Arpeggio*, but now he only shook his head. "It breaks my heart," he told her. "You're one of my favorites. But it would only be raising false hopes. Anders isn't considering you for casting right now."

Maybe it was the follow-up neurotologist appointment; he'd been disappointed by the lack of result from the facial nerve graft and agreed that the second surgery, the 12/7 nerve graft, might be required. How soon could it be? she'd asked. Next month? Next week? But he'd told her no, no, they wouldn't even consider surgery until a full year had passed, to give the original nerve graft every chance. "Aside from that, though," he'd told her, "your recovery has been wonderful. Exemplary." Not until she was home, resting, too fatigued to do anything more, did it sink in what her doctor was saying. She'd "recovered" from her craniotomy and tumor removal. Recovery did not mean going back to the Dena she'd been, pre-acoustic neuroma. That was no longer a possibility.

This compromised state was the new normal. This was it.

The shock of that realization was like running a marathon and you think you see the finish line and as you approach it, gasping, happy, drained, you see that it's a detour sign instead, and that the other finish line, the real one, is miles and miles away, too far to even see.

What was going to happen to her dance career, her world? What if Anders dropped her from the company roster? Her contract was up for renewal in the spring; he had the legal right. She'd never once seriously pondered a life outside ballet. She hadn't needed to. Even now, the thought simply couldn't plant itself in her brain. Call it denial, call it foggy brain syndrome. She couldn't ponder such a monstrous, terrifying concept.

She didn't know what was supposed to happen next. She only knew she couldn't continue to show up at daily company class, now onstage at the theater because it was performing season, and if she'd thought it had been hard to keep her spirits up last fall, it was nothing like now, with everyone else so happily immersed in performing regularly once again.

She'd skipped company class the next morning, and the next, and no one besides Rebecca seemed to notice. The company was running Program I by night and deep into rehearsals for future programs by day. She passed hour after hour in the winter dimness of her living room, brooding, until she couldn't take the toxicity of her thoughts any longer. So she fled. Left a brief, terse phone message for Rebecca that she was taking the car and getting away from it all.

Past Devil's Slide on Highway One, the road grew less perilous as steep cliff-sides gave way to flatter land, farmland, grazing land, along the San Mateo County coast. Her plans had been to go to Half Moon Bay, a coastal community that had a historic downtown, shops, a harbor, nearby walking beaches. A sign for Moss Beach, however, distracted her first.

Misha's town. His childhood home, still owned by the family. His mother, he'd told Dena, was renting an apartment in Phoenix, close to Misha's sister, where she could enjoy sun, heat and grandchildren, but no one in the family could decide whether to sell or just rent out the Moss Beach home they all loved. In the interim, Misha was living there.

She didn't expect Misha to be there on a weekday, but there was still a certain comfort in stopping in Moss Beach, knowing it was his territory. She drove past the tiny town center, little more than a post office, gas station and store, and took the right turn toward the Moss Beach Roadhouse, a clapboard two-story structure built in the 1920s that Misha told her had once been a Prohibition-era speakeasy. High on a cliff above a secluded beach, it was easy to visualize how it had been, with Canadian rumrunners setting anchor under the safety of the dark, the fog, unloading crates of whiskey to men who whisked it up in car trunks to San Francisco. The place was secluded and tricky to find, all right. By the time she'd arrived at the restaurant's parking lot, she was shaking from the stress of so much unfamiliar driving, eager to get out of the car and stay out of it. Below the parking lot, down on the beach, she could hear the Pacific Ocean as it crashed and wheezed.

The rain had abated. It was more like a mist now, obscuring the view much beyond the coastline, but Dena liked it that way. Sleepy, overcast, soft grey. The restaurant wasn't crowded; it was late for lunch and she got a prime table, right against the windows overlooking the ocean. She decided to order a big, heavy lunch, a gesture of both defiance and defeat. The seven pounds she'd gained over the fall months had morphed into ten through December, which, on her small-boned frame, showed. She didn't even look like a dancer anymore. She looked like anybody else. The thought cut her unexpectedly.

She wasn't "just like anybody else." It was worse.

Without ballet, she was a nobody.

Her waitress came over and introduced herself as Alison. She looked to be in her thirties, with a weathered face and merry eyes, whose contagious good spirits prompted Dena to accept her suggestion of starting with a glass of white wine. Once she'd returned with the wine and taken Dena's order, Alison lingered to chat with her about the restaurant, the neighborhood. She told Dena she'd worked here at the Roadhouse for years, that there were a good number of regulars in addition to the tourists, and that it was a fun job, particularly since she'd grown up nearby.

"I have a friend who grew up in this area, too," Dena said. "His name is Misha Lavigne."

Alison smiled. "Sure, I know Misha. I went to school with his older sister. Misha's a nice guy." The smile broadened. "David's even nicer."

Dena eyed her uncertainly. "His younger brother?"

She nodded. "He's a lot of fun." Her smile seemed to harbor private amusement.

"I've never been to his home," Dena said, "but I know it's close. Misha said it was an older Craftsman style house, white, two story?"

"Yep, that's it. Two blocks over, toward the marine sanctuary trail."

Another customer waved for Alison's attention. She excused herself and hurried away.

Her meal of Dungeness crab cakes and fries arrived and she wolfed it down, dipping it all in the rich, savory aioli that accompanied it. She could feel her waist expand by the moment. What the hell. She wouldn't be in a unitard any time soon. Resignation grew, and became almost comfortable. She accepted Alison's offer of another glass of wine, which made her relax more, more, until a pleasing fog seemed to settle over her brain, her body.

Too much so. Having wine at lunch had been a mistake, she realized in retrospect. Once she'd paid the bill, all she wanted to do was sleep, one of the marathon naps she'd seemed to require since the surgery. Deep, like middle-of-the-night sleep. Fully staged, orchestrated dreams. She'd wake feeling drugged, in a stupor that could last hours.

Knowing she couldn't nap, she decided to walk around, pass by Misha's street, ward off this sleepiness. Her regret over this whole game plan was morphing into something huge and unforgiving. She should have known the sleepiness, the mental fog, would strike sooner or later. Leaving San Francisco, her energy had seemed boundless, like in her pre-acoustic neuroma days, but the adrenaline required to get her this far was long gone and in its place was this semi-invalid's lack of energy. Why oh why hadn't she considered that part of the equation?

She found Misha's street. She saw his car first, before the house. A wave of shock passed over her, one of both relief and jittery nervousness. She stood there, wavering, not knowing what came next. She couldn't very well walk up to his door and knock, admit she'd come down to Moss Beach and now she was here. She would have seemed like a stalker.

To her stunned surprise, the front door opened and Misha stepped outside. He looked around, as if expecting her. When he saw her, he smiled and gave a little wave.

It was surreal.

He walked toward her. She approached, on legs that now felt wooden.

"Alison from the Roadhouse called," he was saying. "She wanted to make sure I knew you were around. She said you were acting sort of bewildered when you left."

More likely Alison had called to warn Misha of the potential psychopath, to whom she'd given directions to Misha's place. But Dena could formulate no reply for Misha. She could only gape at him, mute.

He held out a hand. "You look like someone who needs some refuge."

She looked at him, his hand, and her whole body began to shake. Tears began to build behind her right eye, the only one that could still shed tears. Warning alarms wailed in her head; she'd never cried in front of Misha before. Never. Ranted, yes. Sulked and whined, yes. But she still had her pride, and crying would be unspeakably undignified, not to mention ugly.

She burst into tears.

She covered her weeping, distorted face with her hands, which Misha gently pried off a moment later, before enfolding her in a full body hug.

This, too, was not Something They Did. Quick hugs, sure. Never prolonged hip-to-hip contact. Until now.

This was turning out to be a day of firsts.

"Let's go inside," he urged.

"I can't. I shouldn't," she sobbed. "I'll get sleepier and I still have to drive back to the city and I have to go back there to that life without dance and *I just don't think I can.*"

The last words rose to a near shriek. Her knees buckled. She would have slid to the ground if he hadn't been holding her.

"Dena." Misha pulled back but kept his hands anchored to her shoulders as he met her eyes. "Then you don't go back. You stay right here."

"I can't!"

"Um, and why would that be?" He looked at her, all calm and expectant, which made the worst of her panic subside.

"I'm barging in on your space. Without an invitation."

"Okay. First, this is a four bedroom house. I think I can accommodate a visitor. Or four. Secondly, if I'd thought you'd had any interest in coming down to tiny little Moss Beach, doing nothing but gazing out at the ocean, I would have invited you a long time ago."

He had a point. And this was Misha, after all. Her tension began to ebb.

He slung an arm around her shoulders and began to walk her toward the front door. "C'mon, let's go inside. There are three spare rooms for you to pick from, for a nap. You'll be like Goldilocks. And it's like I knew you were coming—I've had some beef and stock bones simmering since this morning. I had this crazy urge for French onion soup for dinner tonight, even as I was thinking, what a waste, going through the whole process for just one person. You like French onion soup?"

"I love French onion soup," she sniffed.

"Well, it's our lucky day. I'm following the recipe and it serves eight. We are guaranteed leftovers through tomorrow night, too, so you'd better plan to stay through the weekend."

She began to smile. "Only if it helps you out."

"Like you can't imagine. Wasted homemade French onion soup is a crime against humanity. So is wasting a perfect opportunity for a marathon nap."

"Okay, then. All right. Guess I have to do my part."

Hours later, she felt like a different person. With the soup still simmering, imparting a heavenly aroma, she and Misha relaxed in a living room that breathed *family*. A stable, established, well-off family. Dena sensed the Lavignes had been wealthy, yet not ostentatious. The furniture looked beautiful, well-constructed, but lived in. On cherry wood tables sat framed photos, ceramic and glass accessories, some homemade, some fine art. In the corner of the room, a grandfather clock ticked. She wanted to stay in this space, this bubble of security, forever.

They talked. She told him she'd lost all optimism about keeping up with her career, with ballet. He told her he understood; he'd gone through a similar roller coaster when struggling with the decision whether or not to stay in medical school. Sometimes you just had to let go of trying so hard, and see where life landed you, they agreed. Sometimes, watching stupid movies that made you laugh and forget your own life was the best therapy. A theory they tested out that evening. It worked.

The next morning, Saturday, Misha had to leave. He was part of a field research project, he explained, that couldn't be missed. She assured him she'd be fine, that solitude in a quiet place was precisely what she wanted and needed. In his absence she made herself a second cup of tea. She took a walk in the nearby marine sanctuary, forested with eucalyptus and cypress trees. A thick blanket of coastal fog made everything feel sleepy and manageable. Ocean waves grumbled in the distance. She walked slowly, without aim, without a goal, until hunger sent her back to the house. The only sound as she ate some of the French onion soup—even better the next day as a leftover—was the peaceful *tick-tick* of the kitchen clock on the wall. When sleepiness rolled over her again, she slipped back into the bedroom for a nap.

More deep sleep. More blissed-out oblivion.

She woke at a stirring sound by the doorway and for a long moment she thought maybe she was dreaming. A man—he was young, maybe her age—was leaning against the door frame, arms folded, watching her with a polite, bemused smile on his face. She sensed she should be feeling fear, except that he didn't look like he wanted to attack her. He was actually rather good looking, with longish dark blonde hair, wavy and streaked with gold. He had beautiful eyes, like Misha's, although they were blue to Misha's brown. He was oddly like a negative image of Misha, pale hair and eyes, face and arms tanned where Misha's was not, but the same facial structure.

"Who are you?" she slurred.

"Who am I? As that's my bed, the bigger question should be, who are *you*?"

"I'm Misha's friend."

"Why aren't you sleeping in Misha's bedroom, then?" he asked.

A flush of defensiveness pierced her fuzzy state. "Because we're not that kind of friends."

"Poor Misha."

She pushed herself up to sitting. "You're Misha's brother, aren't you? David."

"I am."

It was sinking in just how embarrassed she should be feeling, to have been caught sleeping. And her left eye was still taped shut. She tried to get out of the bed. God, it was *his* bed.

He raised both hands. "Don't get up. Please. I'm sorry, I shouldn't have barged in on a sleeping woman. I just... wasn't expecting you."

"Why didn't Misha warn you? Or warn me, for that matter?"

Then again, it wasn't as if this had been a planned visit.

"Don't blame Misha. I've been gone for months. Spending a year in Europe. I wasn't supposed to be back for another month. But I lost my free rent in Rome. So, *ciao, Italia*, hello California."

"I'll get out of your room. I'm sorry."

"No, no. I'm leaving," he said. "I really just came to dump off stuff, raid the fridge, and then I'm off to Santa Cruz to visit friends. Sleep. You're still zonked." He began to shut the door. "Tell Misha I'll call him."

As she was debating whether to get off the bed and act more socially correct, the door re-opened and he popped his head in again. "Mind if I play some music? I'm having snacky pangs for some Beethoven."

The strangest request. Still groggy with sleep, she could only nod. And a few minutes later she heard the music.

Piano music; Misha's brother, playing the piano, astoundingly well.

She fell asleep again, immersed in the music, and it was as if someone had handed her a beloved, familiar blanket to wrap around herself as she slept.

Misha was astonished, upon his return, to hear of David's abrupt arrival and departure. He strode into the kitchen and Dena heard him heave an exaggerated sigh. "He's been here, all right," he said, and she joined him in the kitchen. He gestured to the sink, where the French onion soup pot now sat, crusted and empty, along with a dirty bowl and spoon. A yellow sticky note posted above the sink had *Yum!* scrawled across with a smiley face.

"I'm guessing that wasn't you who finished off the soup?" Misha asked.

Her eyes bulged. "God, no. There was tons!"

"Did you at least get a serving before he got to it?"

She began to laugh. "I did. It was delicious."

He scowled. "At least one of us got seconds."

"Does he do that often?"

"All the time."

"I guess he thinks you're a good cook."

"And I guess we're having something else for dinner."

"I make a great plate of scrambled eggs," she offered, and he smiled at her.

"You are my guest this weekend, and you are not allowed to cook. Pour yourself a glass of wine and keep me company, though, as I prep something."

Misha shared more details about his brother as he fried up a half dozen chicken tenders, set them aside and fried up shallots, garlic and mushrooms in the drippings. He added Marsala wine, chicken broth and a knob of butter, and set it to simmer on the back burner.

"David is… I don't know what he is. A slacker. A genius. Both. He's very, very talented, both academically and musically." He grabbed a pair of Roma tomatoes and began to chop them. "But he lacks the drive to see anything through. I should be grateful he didn't decide to follow me in the medical sciences. He probably would have breezed through medical school, just to show me how easy it was, before flitting off to India to go 'find himself' or something."

"I heard him play the piano. It was amazing. I thought it was a professional recording, it was so good."

"He's got a huge talent on the piano. He turned down a place at Juilliard in favor of going to UC Santa Barbara instead. Top reason? Because UC Santa Barbara is a better party school. It broke my mom's heart. Being a concert pianist had always been her dream, but she had to settle for teaching the piano. David could have gone all the way." He scraped the tomatoes into a side bowl and began to chop fresh basil. "At least that was how it looked, back when he was fifteen. He just seemed to have this golden patina shining over him."

"Rebecca was like that. Things seemed to come to her so effortlessly."

He nodded. "Rebecca's really something. Talented, beautiful *and* bright."

Her and her big mouth, bringing up Rebecca.

He filled a pot with water for pasta and set it on the burner. He added the basil to the tomatoes and gave the sauce in the pan a stir, before topping off his wine glass and Dena's.

"Thank you for doing all of this,"she said, gesturing to the food, the living room. "Letting me stay here like this."

"My pleasure. I've mooched off you at your own place, so it's a pleasure to reciprocate."

"Can I… stay a little bit longer?"

She watched for any guarded look that might arise, but Misha only smiled.

"Dena, you can stay as long as you want."

His words and smile were music to her heart.

Sunday morning passed in the same comfortable daze as Saturday. By now she'd successfully eluded any direct contact with Rebecca, at first inadvertently, now deliberately. She didn't want to talk to her happy, busy sister. She knew it was a childish thing, taking her pain and anger out on Rebecca, but it was the only weapon she had. And she was hurting. So she used it.

Three calls received, two messages left, no actual conversation exchanged, culminating in a series of increasingly terse texts.

Rebecca: "i want the car."

Dena: "u cant have it. leave me alone."

Rebecca: "where r u???"

Dena: "im safe and u cant find me."

Rebecca: "WHAT IS UR PROBLEM???"

No reply required, she decided.

A few minutes later, the trill of her phone announced a call. She saw, to her surprise, that it was coming from Boyd. Goaded by suspicion, curiosity, she took the call.

"Is Rebecca right there?" she said, interrupting his greeting.

"No," he said in surprise. "I'm alone, and I'm in the guys' dressing room. Why would she be?"

"Never mind. Hi. What do you want?"

He explained. She had trouble figuring it out. He seemed to feel that Rebecca was carrying on with Ben behind his back, which made no sense to her.

"She's always been friends with him, since I joined the company," Dena said. "Nothing's changed, one way or the other."

"They spent New Year's Eve together. She canceled on us because she said she wanted to stay home and just chill, but what does she do? Joins Ben for a party."

"It sounded like it was just a little dinner party at Alice Willoughby's. Katrina and her little son were there, too."

"Oh, right. Her good friends, Alice and Katrina," Boyd said. "Couldn't wait to spend time with them. And, coincidentally, spend all evening with Ben."

"There were toddlers running around. It was hardly a romantic setup."

"Fine, so explain Carmel," he said. "Back in May. Right after our season ended. One weekend they went away together, alone."

She searched her memory. "Okay, well, I remember her going away for the weekend in May. It was two weeks after my surgery. But wait, Ben didn't go away with her."

"Yes he did. Charlotte told me she saw Rebecca leave with Ben early Saturday and return with him on Sunday night."

"Look. I remember," she said. "That was the Saturday Ben came to visit me. Anders had come during the week that had just finished. Rebecca can vouch for that—she was here too."

The pause that followed lasted so long, she thought they'd been disconnected.

"Boyd? Are you there?"

"I am. Sorry. Was just… figuring out things." Another long pause. "You say that Anders came by, and the three of you visited."

"Four. My mom was there, too."

"How was Rebecca acting?"

"God, I don't know. I was a little preoccupied by my own stuff at the time. But, I seem to remember she seemed subdued. Deferential to Anders, of course. Very attentive."

"And she went away the following weekend."

"Yes. And Ben dropped by my place that afternoon. So that shoots down your suspicion."

"Right," he said, sounding a little dazed. "Absolutely right. I appreciate the insight."

A flicker of uneasiness crossed over her after they'd ended the call. Something hadn't seemed right, there.

It was too hard to think about.

Let Rebecca and her boyfriend figure it out.

Chapter 18 – Rebecca

Sunday was the final performance of *Sea to Shining Sea,* in which Rebecca and Boyd both had small parts. It featured a set rich with imaginative detail and whimsy, alongside a darker undertone that hinted at pathos. Dun-colored ships, oversized pink seashells, and superimposed images on the backdrop gave the ballet a cinematic quality. The choreography was sweetly classical, but with an edge, lush phrasing punctuated by propulsive runs across the stage and back.

Through the performance, Boyd acted oddly. He danced well enough, his leaps, tours and pirouettes clean and brisk, but whenever offstage, he moved with a preoccupied heaviness that Rebecca initially took to be fatigue. They were all tired after a week of performing by night and six hours of rehearsing for future programs by day. Today's matinee performance ended Program I's run. The next program, commencing in eleven days, was *Giselle,* rife with busy, anonymous ensemble work—she was, yet again, a Wili and a villager—that would both exhaust and frustrate her. Beyond that, however, lay Program III, and IV with the golden allure of *Arpeggio.*

Post-performance found her back at the house, slumped on the couch, soaking her ankles in a bucket of ice water. She checked her phone for the third time that day; still no real message from Dena or clue on her whereabouts. She sighed. Dena was toying with her, spoiling for a fight, for whatever reason.

She heard someone enter the house. A moment later, Boyd appeared in the living room entryway. "You're early," she said in surprise. "I thought the plan was to meet for dinner out."

"It was. But I wanted to talk first."

Unease passed over her, like a breeze from an open window.

She patted the spot next to her. "Have a seat. Talk away."

He looked around, cocked his head at the sound of voices coming from the kitchen. "I'd rather we do this in private," he said.

The breeze turned into a gale. "Oh. Oh, okay," she managed. "My room. Let me just finish icing my ankles here."

"Fine. I'll go say hi to Charlotte and Steph."

He disappeared into the kitchen. She sat there, heart thumping madly against her chest, sensing that whatever he wanted to discuss was not a good thing. In a dazed, mechanical fashion, she pulled her feet from the water, dried them off and hobbled to the bedroom. A minute later he joined her.

"So," she said as she sank to her bed, trying to sound confident, curious. "What gives?"

He remained standing. "Well, I talked to Dena."

She leaned forward in confusion. "I'm sorry. My *sister*, Dena?"

He rolled his eyes. "Do we know another?"

"You're saying that Dena called you?"

"No. I called her."

"When? Why?"

"At the theater, before the performance. I had a question."

"She took your call and not mine?!"

"Evidently."

This was getting stranger and stranger. "But what would you need to discuss with her that you wouldn't with me?"

A hard look came into his eyes. "I have discussed the issue with you. Multiple times. And I've found your answers unsatisfactory."

Queasiness overtook her. "Boyd. What are you going on about?"

"You and Ben."

"I told you! There's nothing between Ben and me!"

"I believe you now. Particularly after talking to Dena."

"Why?" she cried. "What did she say?"

He drew a deep breath. "That Carmel weekend, back last May. You were not with Ben."

"I was. I have witnesses—he picked me up, he dropped me off."

"And the middle part, Beck. What about that? As in, Saturday afternoon, when, lo and behold, Ben was over at Dena's, visiting her, checking up on her." He nodded at her dumfounded expression. "That Ben. Such a solicitous one. Helping out both the Lindgren girls. Only, why would Ben need to help you out? Unless, it was to help out someone else in the process. Now, who could that be?"

Words failed her. They were unnecessary at this point, anyway.

"You were with Anders." He stated it as a fact, but she saw in his eyes how badly he wanted her to deny it.

"Look," she tried. "It's not what you think. It was... well, something I do for him, that I used to do for him, years back, before I was even friends with you. A service of sorts."

He stared at her in horrified fascination. "Oh God. You clean his house."

In spite of the grim situation, she laughed. "Please. Do I look like a cleaning lady type?"

"No," he admitted. "And besides, you're a slob."

"Not as much as you are." She wanted more than anything to keep it on this lighter level, cheerfully debating who was the bigger slob, easing the conversation toward a new topic.

But Boyd did not desire a topic change. "Why did you go away with Anders for the weekend?" His voice was low, menacing. She rose, as if to sidle away, but he gripped her arms, forcing her to meet his gaze.

The truth burst out. "I'm his artist's model, okay? He sketches me. That's all he wants me for."

Both his jaw and hands went slack. "Artist's model?! He *sketches?*"

"Yes. And why not? Why shouldn't he have a hobby?" She strode over to her mirrored chest of drawers, grabbed at a brush and began to vigorously brush her hair. The clenched feeling inside her eased a little. Okay, so the secret was out; Anders would be furious if he knew. But maybe she could leave it at that with Boyd. She offered him the most comprehensive yet innocuous details that she could. He was calm until he figured out the unclothed part.

"Jesus Christ. You were naked for the man? And you don't consider that to be something you'd tell your boyfriend?"

"It was not a sexual experience! It was art. Sketching."

He asked a few more questions and she replied in a careful fashion, as if this were a job interview. They were both sitting on the bed now, side by side, looking straight ahead, both enveloped by their own gloom, by the awful facts before them.

"And in all those years, the guy never made a pass at you. Never took it further. That's what you're telling me?"

She hesitated, which gave him his answer.

At first he seemed more dazed than angry. "Why?" he asked in a strangled voice. "To hurt me? To get back at me for being the better dancer, the one who's going somewhere? *Why?*"

Once honesty had taken hold, it seemed incapable of stopping. A part of her stood there and watched, helpless, as she destroyed their relationship further. "Because I'm in love with him," she whispered.

He sprang up, lunged away from her, shaking with wrath.

"You are the most cold-hearted, faithless woman I've ever been with. Had a relationship with. That you could have *done* that, had those feelings, and never told me. It makes me sick. It makes me want to puke."

"Boyd," she began, "please…"

But the protest remained lodged in her throat. What could she say, anyway? She was the villain in every way here.

"You're pathetic. Just pathetic." Boyd stood there, hands balled. "When I think of how we befriended you, how Pam took you under her wing, when all along, you were…" He couldn't even finish his words. Without another glance, he turned and strode out of the room. She heard him stomp down the hall, into the kitchen, and recount what had just transpired. A feminine cry of dismay, of indignation followed. More female voices, joining theirs in the kitchen. More indignation.

"I knew she was no good for you," she heard Charlotte say.

"What a treacherous bitch she turned out to be," someone else said.

"You can do so much better, Boyd," Steph said. "Drop her, totally."

"Can we kick her out?" one of them asked.

"I think we should try. Laurel would totally take her room."

"Let's make it happen."

"I'll bet she's listening. Let's talk about this somewhere else."

"Yeah, let's. C'mon, Boyd. We'll buy you a beer. Dinner. Anything you need."

"Thanks, you guys. I love you."

"We love you, too."

"You're what matters. Not *her*."

"Oh, *totally* not her!"

The sound of heavy footsteps replaced conversation, and within five minutes the group of them left, slamming the front door with a thud that echoed through the house. Rebecca sat in silence for another ten minutes, unmoving.

What had just happened? How had everything gone so wrong, so fast?

Why had Dena told Boyd about Anders and that weekend?

Her little sister had screwed her, and screwed her good.

She snatched up her phone from the dresser table. Enough of texting; she wanted real answers from her sister. But when her call rolled over to voice mail she could only leave a message.

"You know, thanks for returning my calls and messages. And for ratting me out to Boyd; we broke up because of it. Was this your way to get back at me? Have you been hatching your revenge since you found out I told Anders about your acoustic neuroma? I guess you've been chuckling to yourself over the past twenty-four hours, watching texts and voice mails from me accrue. And then, to top it off, you take Boyd's call!"

An unhinged sob rose in her throat.

"Do normal sisters do this shit to sisters, Dena? I really want to know. Because it seems to me you're being spiteful and cruel, and what's more you're enjoying it! And if you don't respond to this message, well, I'll know that's the case."

She hung up and strode into the empty kitchen. She raided the refrigerator, drinking milk from the carton and forking her way through someone's leftover Chinese takeout noodles. What the hell, her roommates had declared war on her; might as well give them more ammunition. She paced the house, too agitated to sit, too exhausted to go out. Twenty minutes later she checked her phone. No reply from Dena.

She poured herself a glass of red wine and returned to her bedroom. The others came back an hour later and ignored her for the rest of the night. It had never been stronger, this sense that she was surrounded by enemies, and that she needed to find another place to live. Fast.

This was confirmed by a note on the kitchen counter the next morning. *Rebecca,* it read, *this is your thirty-day eviction notice, that we hope you'll accept quietly and not contest. The rest of us don't consider having you here to be a livable, workable situation. We will notify the landlord and we suggest you do the same. PS: leave earlier if you can. Laurel wants your room.*

It was official. She was out.

And still no response from Dena.

Monday afternoons were, like last semester, lightly scheduled in anticipation of a business management course set to start right after the *Giselle* run. To avoid the DBD house, she went over to Dena's. Dena still wasn't home, nor had she communicated, even after Rebecca's most recent snarled message, which ended with, "you bitch, if you value our relationship in any way, you'd better respond."

No response. Aggravated beyond measure, and now worried, she called their mother to see if Dena had communicated with her over the past few days.

She hadn't. "Is this something I should be concerned about?" Isabelle asked.

"Oh, no, nothing to fret about. She's just off somewhere relaxing, and wants to be mysterious about where!"

"Well, when you speak with her, tell her I'd like to come up and spend the night sometime soon. Did you hear I'm her new part-time roommate?"

"I did. What fun!" she lied.

"I know! Just like old times!"

Just what Dena wanted.

"Yeah! Anyway, I'll be sure and give her the message. Bye, Mom!"

"Bye, sweetie!"

To pacify her rage and growing worry, she sat on the couch, pulled a half dozen new pairs of pointe shoes from her dance bag. She spent the next hour sewing ribbons onto the shoes. As she was finishing up the sixth pair, she heard a jingling sound outside the door, of keys being jostled, fitted into the lock.

Finally.

But to her surprise, it wasn't Dena who stepped into the room, but Misha. He seemed just as shocked to see her.

"Why are you here?" she demanded.

"Why are *you?*" he challenged back.

"I'm waiting for my sister to come back and explain what the hell is up. Is she okay?"

"She's fine. I'm here to pick up a few things for her. She's not coming back today."

"How do you know?"

He looked insecure, but only for a moment. "Because she's staying with me."

What in the hell was the world coming to?

"Can you please explain to me what Dena is doing there with you?" she burst out.

"Nothing. Relaxing."

Her worry evaporated, replaced by fury.

"I have been trying and trying to get in touch with her. I was getting freakin' *worried.* And what's more, I've had errands to run for four days now. She knows I count on the car on Sunday or Monday afternoons. You call her, right now, and tell her she needs to come back here and turn the car over."

Misha's face turned stubborn. "I'll do no such thing, Rebecca. Dena's in pain. She came to Moss Beach for comfort, refuge. I won't ask her to leave before she's ready to."

She shoved the pointe shoes violently aside and rose. "Look. I am having a very bad week and I have things to do, which require the use of the car that belongs to both myself and Dena."

He shook his head. "I'm not sending her home just because it would be convenient to you."

She didn't know whether to scream or cry. She drew in a slow breath, like you were supposed to do when you wanted to hit someone or something, counting to five before speaking.

"You know, I get that you're her new best friend, her 'better than any sister' advocate, and that it far exceeds any sort of friendship you and I have forged. But that it should translate into ganging up against me? That's cold. Seriously. And for the record, Dena's not the only one in pain. My boyfriend just broke up with me, largely because of something Dena said to him over the phone. But I can't jump in a car and drive away, outrun my sorrows, because my sister has kidnapped the car and plans to stay hidden away for who knows how long. She's not even using it, either, is she? It's just sitting there, while she kicks back, taking one day at a time, unconcerned about the rest of the world."

He hesitated, clearly torn.

"Are you going to Moss Beach right now?" she asked.

"I am."

"Fine. I'll go with you. Once there, I'll take the car and leave. If my sister doesn't want to come out and acknowledge me, fine. She can stay there. You drive back to San Francisco every day she can carpool with you. When her highness is all done with her down time."

He gave a low, despairing groan of capitulation. "Do you really need the car?"

What she really needed to do was confront her sister and give her a vicious shake, but she'd settle for getting possession of the car.

"I do," she replied.

"Fine. But let it be known that I deeply oppose the idea."

"Your opposition has been noted."

"We leave in five minutes."

"I'm ready now."

"I'm not." He pulled a handwritten list from his pocket.

Rebecca collected her spread-out belongings and used the bathroom. Five minutes later, they were in his car, driving in silence out of San Francisco, down the coast, as the late afternoon sun glittered over the Pacific Ocean.

Once in Moss Beach, they trundled down a narrow road, winding, curving, before he pulled into a driveway, next to the silver Civic. "Wait here," he said. "Don't come in with me, please. I'll tell her what's up."

The magnitude of her actions had begun to sink in during the ride, but it was too late to change anything.

This was going to end badly. For all of them.

Chapter 19 – Dena

When Misha told her Rebecca had returned with him, Dena had thought it was a joke. That was the kind of spectacularly inappropriate setup only Rebecca would consider dumping on her, like the time she'd brought Misha over to meet Dena, four weeks post-op, never mind that all of that had turned out great. Misha would never do that to her, she told herself. Then she glanced out the window and saw Rebecca descend from the passenger side of Misha's car.

Apparently he would.

She couldn't believe how much it hurt. She'd never felt so ashamed of her second class status next to Rebecca, than she did right then, listening to Misha's explanation of why he'd chosen to support Rebecca over her. "She was demanding a ride and accusing me of playing favorites," he said. "I'm so sorry, Deen, but I felt stuck. She really seemed to need the car. She says you should stay here, though. Please stay." His eyes implored.

With the bubble of security and sanctuary now shattered? Feeling so grubby and plain and disfigured next to her beautiful, healthy sister with her excellent powers of persuasion?

Forget it.

Her single-sided deafness worked in her favor on the drive back to San Francisco. With her good ear facing the passenger window, she could block out any attempts at apology from the driver's side. But Rebecca, ironically, didn't seem to have any interest in apologizing. Instead, the longer they drove, the more she realized that Rebecca was angry at *her*. As if Dena had wronged her by having an emotional breakdown, fleeing the city and the WCBT in order to self-repair in a quiet place. The car, okay. She should have communicated with Rebecca about the car.

It had been her plan to call, once Misha came back with her phone cable and she'd recharged her dead phone. Which reminded her that she now had the charger cable from the things Misha had brought. She pulled it from her bag and plugged it into the car's connector. She fished out the dead phone and hooked it up to recharge.

A few more minutes passed in a brooding silence. Finally Dena spoke.

"What are you acting so miffed about, already?" she demanded, shifting in the seat to face Rebecca. "And don't go telling me this is about your all-consuming need for the car. We both know you could have lived without it for another few days. Did you just feel the need to show off how you have Misha wrapped around your little finger?"

Rebecca ignored the accusation. "Please tell me, precisely, what you said to Boyd when you took his call on Sunday." Her words sounded clipped, biting, well-rehearsed.

"God, is that what your rage is about? Misha said you told him Boyd broke up with you, and that you're trying to pin it on something I said. Hardly. I *saved* you. Boyd thought you and Ben were illicitly involved and I assured him you weren't. I told him I knew for a fact that Ben didn't go whisking you away to Carmel for a romantic weekend. I can't believe you're glaring at me now when it seems like you should be thanking me. Besides, give me a break—

you and Boyd weren't in love. It was a convenience thing, being a couple instead of being alone."

"You're saying you didn't tell Boyd who I'd gone off with?"

"Correct. How would I have known that?" Dena checked her phone battery. Still showing up as red. In another two minutes, though, she'd have enough battery power to access her voice mail.

From the corner of her eye, she saw Rebecca regarding her actions in curiosity, then, in concern.

"What is it?" Dena said in exasperation. "Do you have a problem with me charging my phone?"

"Your battery's that low?"

"It was dead. I'd left my charger at the apartment. Which was the main reason Misha swung by the apartment for me. And I was going to call you, by the way. Tell you that I'd have the car back for you by tomorrow. You didn't have to hijack my life in the process."

Rebecca seemed even more worried now. "How long has your phone battery been dead?"

"I don't know. A day?"

"Specifically, what time? Sunday afternoon?"

"I don't know. I suppose so. Sometime after Boyd called."

"Oh, shit," Rebecca said in a low voice. She took her foot off the gas pedal and the car began to slow down.

"What, is there a problem with the car? Are you going to blame that on me, too?"

"You didn't get my messages," Rebecca said in a flat voice.

"I did. I responded. Except for not saying where I was."

"The messages after you talked to Boyd."

"There were none. Or, wait. Maybe I'll see them now." She glanced down at her phone, finally charged enough so she could turn it on again.

Plink. Plink. Plink. Plink.

Four texts and three phone messages.

By now, Rebecca had eased the car into a nearby turnout and cut the engine. "Look," she said, and now she sounded desperate. "I didn't know why you weren't calling me back when it was clear I was upset and needed to talk to you. I kind of raged at you on the last two messages. Said... things."

"Like what?"

Rebecca shot Dena a pleading look. "Things like, 'I think you're a bitch' and 'I think you're enjoying my pain.' And worse."

Dena studied her phone. The cheery icon that informed her she had messages now resembled a little bomb. She had a sudden, panicked urge to fling the phone out the window before the phone itself detonated.

"I'm so sorry," Rebecca said. "I misinterpreted things on every level. I thought you told Boyd something you didn't. I thought you were messing with me by not returning the last half dozen calls and texts. I ruined your getaway for nothing. Please let me drive you back to Misha's."

"It doesn't work that way. You can't undo what you did."

"How can I make it up to you?"

Dena considered this. "You can give me a better explanation. Tell me what happened between you and Boyd."

"He asked who I was in Carmel with. He didn't like the answer."

"Who were you with?" Dena asked.

"None of your business." Rebecca's tone grew sharp again.

"Um, apparently it is very much my business. You made it my business. If you were sneaking away with someone else and didn't want your boyfriend to know, you should have notified me on what story you wanted me to tell."

"I was not sneaking away, and it was not a romantic rendezvous. Well. Mostly not."

"What is that supposed to mean?"

"Forget it. Drop it. I'm sorry, okay? I'm so sorry I ruined things for you at Misha's. Please don't blame him for any of it. It was totally me. I was being a bitch."

"Trust me. I believe you."

They didn't talk again until they were approaching the outskirts of San Francisco. Dena gestured to a retail strip off the highway.

"Mind if we stop for groceries?"

"No problem."

Inside the store, as they wheeled a cart down the aisles, Dena recommenced her interrogation. "So Boyd broke up with you because of who you were with." She reached over and picked out a loaf of whole grain bread.

"Please let's just drop it."

"If you answer my questions, I'll let you take my phone and delete the messages you don't want me to hear."

"You've got a deal," Rebecca said without hesitation.

"Okay. Who were you with?"

Rebecca sighed. "I was with a man."

"I could have guessed that part."

"Someone I've known for a spell. Since... taking college classes. Someone I met on campus."

It sounded like a lie in the making. No wonder it had aroused Boyd's suspicion.

"A classmate?"

"No," Rebecca said. "More like an instructor."

Dena stopped the cart at the refrigerated section. "So how did you help him?"

Rebecca took her time selecting a trio of yogurt cups before she spoke. "He's an artist. I was his model. I posed for him."

"In the nude?"

She hesitated. "Yes."

Maybe Rebecca was telling the truth after all, Dena decided. No one could have made up such a story on the spot, nor conjured up the pink blush now staining Rebecca's cheeks.

They wheeled the cart to the produce section, where Dena picked out broccoli and a half dozen apples from a pyramid. Rebecca glanced at her watch. "Wow, it's late. Almost dinner time."

"Do you want a drop off at your house?" Dena asked.

"Ugh." Rebecca squeezed her eyes shut. "No, I don't want to go there. I've got a situation there. But... wait." Her eyes flew open and she turned to Dena. "Actually, wow, it frees me to offer *you* a solution."

"To what? What are we talking about?" Dena placed the bagged apples in the cart.

"The roommate thing."

"Please explain."

"I'm being evicted."

"What the hell?" Dena gaped at her. "What did you do?"

"Boyd told my roommates about our breakup," Rebecca said as she pushed the cart to the next aisle. "They adore him, and despise me for hurting him."

"What, precisely, hurt him so bad?"

"Well... Carmel."

"But you were trying to tell me the Carmel weekend was not a romantic escape."

"Yeah, well, the artist's model thing, the nude posing, really freaked him out. He saw it as a betrayal. He told the others, and now, they want to skin me alive," Rebecca said. "They want me out, and fast. They think they're being extra mean, telling me in writing that 'this is your thirty-day notice but please leave earlier if you can.' But now I realize that note frees me of any rent liability. If I act fast enough, I can even get out of paying February rent there."

She turned toward Dena, her eyes bright with excitement. "And Mom's no problem for me—she and I have always gotten along great. Have Mom still pay a share of the rent, and I'll cover your half, and you'll be rent-free, Deen!"

Two feelings coursed through Dena. One, a staggering sense of relief. Rebecca's offer would save her. They could make it happen. Rebecca was right; being around Isabelle would be manageable if Rebecca were there, too.

But why would Rebecca's friends and roommates evict her for simply spending a weekend posing for some guy in Carmel? No dancer was that shocked by nudity. Females thought nothing about being topless around the male dancers. A fast change backstage with only your tights keeping you from full nudity was no big deal. For the better part of their work day, the dancers were more unclothed than clothed. Why the fuss over Rebecca getting nude for an artist?

She'd slept with the guy. That was the only explanation.

Even then, an eviction still seemed excessive. But Rebecca was beaming at her, and she was right, this was a solution to a big problem.

"Okay," Dena said. "That would really help me. Are you sure, though?"

"Positive."

"It won't be all that comfortable whenever Mom comes up to spend a few nights. Three of us in that small space."

"It'll work. Don't you worry. This will be my apology for today's gaffe."

"Thank you. I appreciate it."

"No problem. Glad to help. Sorry again about today."

Back at the apartment, Dena put away the groceries and listened as Rebecca argued with Charlotte over the phone.

"Fine, I'm out," Rebecca snarled. "I'll empty my room tomorrow. That gives you three days of January to make the change happen. Your note absolves me of any rent obligations for February."

She listened with impatience to Charlotte's response. "You leave Anders out of this," she said a minute later. "And I don't care what you think of me."

An uneasy feeling passed over Dena. She wanted to believe Rebecca. But her story, and her roommates' response, simply didn't add up. Particularly since Rebecca's story about the Carmel weekend and the guy had nothing to do with Ben.

Rebecca hung up with a sigh. "Good riddance, but it's done. I'm out. I will officially pay your half of the rent in February."

"Thank you. Really. That's huge."

"I'm glad to help. See? I told you I'd make it up to you."

The uneasy feeling remained.

"Tell me something, though," she said to Rebecca.

"Sure." Rebecca began putting cans from the grocery bag in the side cupboard.

"What did Anders have to do with that?"

"With what?"

"You told Charlotte 'leave him out of this.'"

Rebecca's hands faltered, but her voice didn't. "Oh, that. Charlotte's such a fool. She's thinking that if Anders hears I'm in disgrace with my group of friends—correction, *ex*-friends—that it will affect casting preferences. Like, he'll pull me from *Arpeggio* rehearsals. As if!"

"And how did Ben come into the equation? Because that was Boyd's first suspicion, the reason he called me."

Rebecca kept her focus directed on the cans, arranging them in neat rows with the labels facing forward. "It's because Ben dropped me off and picked me up at the rendezvous location."

"So Ben knows the guy."

"Sure. Well, I asked for his help, with transportation. So I introduced them."

She was lying again.

A great wave of sadness came over Dena. What kind of sisters hid so much of themselves behind a mask? Was it a performer's flaw, because you spent so much of your time faking it, smiling, affecting an emotion other than the one you were feeling? Sustaining the illusion became more important than sustaining integrity.

She waited a full minute before speaking again, so that Rebecca could be lulled into thinking she was off the hook. When Rebecca wandered over to the couch, Dena joined her.

"You know, you haven't been fully honest with me for a long time," Dena began, "and you don't see how that's affecting our relationship. You seem to want to think that things turned chilly because we're different ranks in the company, with different friends. I know your friends hate me, and that I don't have many friends. I've made my peace with that. But you've been hiding something from me for so long, you don't even realize it. That it defines you. That it defines *us.*"

Rebecca's mouth opened and shut without a word.

Dena continued. "Back in the ICU, after my craniotomy, I had this terrible nightmare. That you were hiding something from me, behind your back. Oh, it doesn't sound scary in the least now, but that night, I was rigid in terror over it. I've always told myself it was a dream, nothing more. But now I'm thinking it's one of those things that was meant to float up in a dream, the way your psyche offers you answers you might not otherwise figure out."

Rebecca sat there, frozen in silence.

"You're hiding something," Dena repeated.

"No, I'm not."

"I'm done believing your words. And for the record, the ease in which you lie, to your *sister*, is kind of fucked up."

Rebecca rose, agitated. Dena did too.

"What are you not telling me?" Dena said.

"Nothing!"

"Liar!"

They stood there, like boxers in a ring, both of them ready to fight and defend, to the bitter end. Dena was not going to let this one go. And Rebecca knew this. She stood there, tense and contracted, wrapping her arms around her body as if to physically protect herself from what Dena was seeking. Her eyes, however, glittered with defiance. A *you can't make me tell you* look that used to enrage Dena, years back, during their childhood scuffles.

Something rose up within Dena, violent and powerful. She lunged toward Rebecca, who tried to duck out of her way, but Dena caught her arm.

A superhuman strength had come over her, the inertia that had fogged her all month long evaporating as she twisted Rebecca's arm behind her back and frog-marched her, like a cop in a crime detective show, to the mirror in the living room.

"Stop it, you're hurting my arm," Rebecca cried.

"Look at yourself," Dena shouted, meeting Rebecca's eyes in the mirror. "Stop lying! Stop hiding the truth from me. You look yourself in the eyes and *tell me who you were with in Carmel.*"

"I can't!" Terror now filled Rebecca's eyes.

Dena gave Rebecca's arm another twist, and Rebecca emitted a shriek.

"Why can't you tell me?" Dena shouted.

The shriek rose to a scream. "It's *complicated!* Ow, ow, you're hurting me!"

The answers came, all at once. Dena dropped her hands.

Flashback to the meet-up at Celia's coffee shop, back in May, days before the craniotomy. Dena, shaking with rage, demanding to know why Rebecca had run and told Anders about the acoustic neuroma diagnosis, and then gone on to lie about it.

And you value your relationship with your boss above all? she'd asked Rebecca. *Even above your relationship with your own sister?*

You don't understand, Rebecca had said. *It's complicated.*

"It's Anders," Dena said now. "You went away with Anders. He was the one you posed naked for. He was the one you slept with. Ben was involved because Ben always supports Anders. And you."

"I… No, it's not…" Rebecca began, but Dena cut her off.

"Oh, stop already. Can't you see when enough is enough?" She gestured violently to Rebecca's reflection in the mirror. "Look at you. Look at your eyes."

Rebecca was close to crying. Dena had never seen her look so wrecked. So scared.

Dena softened her tone. "There's so much fear in you, Becca. I'm your sister. Why can't you trust me with the truth?"

"I do!"

"Maybe most of the time. But not this. You are so wired to evade this truth that you don't see how sad it is that you're lying to the people closest to you."

Rebecca's beautiful eyes filled with tears. "Because he said no one could know. Ever!"

She angrily brushed away the tears and pivoted away from Dena.

"Becca. It's time to open up. Otherwise it'll forever separate us. Is that what you want?"

"No."

They stood there in silence until Rebecca exhaled, a soft sound of defeat. "Do you have any booze, at least? Because if I'm going to talk, I'll need a stiff drink."

"Will wine do?" Dena asked.

"Yes."

"I'll go get it."

Dena fetched them both drinks and joined Rebecca back on the couch. Rebecca took a sip of the wine. After a second sip, she set the glass down, leaned against the cushions, shut her eyes and spoke.

"I'm his artist's model. I have been since I was twenty. I was his muse, his special thing. Never sex, back then. It was bigger than sex. More sacred. Pure. He loved to look at me and sketch me. And that meant everything to me. Because, of course I was in love with him. How could I not be? Being his artist's model was the best thing I could hope for with him, and it was enough. Ben knew; no one else could. That was the rule. And then, overnight, Anders lost all interest in me. For the next four years, nada. When he started noticing me again, just last spring, it was—I don't know how to explain. Like one of those deserts that only gets rain once a decade, and right afterwards everything explodes into bloom."

She sat back up and met Dena's eyes.

"He asked me to find out what was wrong with you. I did, and told him the news about your acoustic neuroma. I would have done anything to have him keep looking at me in that way. I was a little crazed. More than a little. I betrayed you without a second thought. I did the same to Boyd. In Carmel that night, I begged Anders to make love to me. He didn't seduce me; it was the other way around. I can hate myself for what I did, except that it all seemed so beyond my abilities to resist. That's the power he has over me."

In silence they both sat, looking at the coffee table, their two half-full glasses of wine.

"What happened when I got promoted?" Dena asked.

"That's when it all stopped."

"Oh, my God," Dena half-whispered. "You must have hated me."

"I couldn't hate you. I loved you. I was so proud of you. You got the promotion, not me, but you were my sister, after all."

She paused, and a look of astonishment came over her face.

"I'm lying. Because I'm trying to be nice, act like a sister should act. But you know what, Dena? You want to know the whole truth?" She turned to Dena, eyes glittering again. "I got so tired of being proud of you, of being your sister. After a while, I did hate you. I fucking *hated* you. That ineffable thing you had when you danced. I could train for a dozen more years and never have what you had. I'd watch you, I'd watch Anders watch you, and I hated you as much as I loved you. In fact, the feeling was almost the same. Both were like fire inside me."

Silence fell, but the terrible words seemed to linger in the air, like cigar smoke. Dena watched the rapid rise and fall of Rebecca's chest. There'd been no histrionics attached to her words, no attempts to soften their impact. It was, in truth, damned scary, like having your best friend calmly admit to having once committed a murder. A little voice inside Dena whispered, *careful what you ask for.*

Rebecca's expression and shoulders relaxed, as if the thing that had possessed her while she spoke had gone away.

"Do you hate me now?" Dena asked, almost fearing the answer. But to her relief, Rebecca only shook her head.

"No," she said, and this time Dena didn't have to wonder if Rebecca was telling the truth. "I love you. But it's dawning on me what a complicated love it can be."

"It's *complicated*," Dena mimicked in a high voice, before she could censor the reply for appropriateness. Rebecca looked at her, startled, and began to laugh.

"*Touché*, little sister," she said, "you can be a bitch, too," which made Dena laugh too.

"Sisters and artistic directors," Dena said. "Damn. Those relationships are *complicated.*"

"And mothers, and roommates," Rebecca added, which made them laugh harder.

They sipped their wine and chuckled to themselves for a moment longer.

"You know, I always thought it was Mom who had the crush on Anders," Dena said. "The way she'd light up like a Christmas tree whenever the two of them talked. Guess I was way off the mark there."

"Speaking of Mom," Rebecca said. "She told me to tell you that she wanted to come up and visit sometime soon, to test out her new drop-in-anytime status."

"Oh, boy," Dena said.

"Ready for it all to happen, sis?"

"I am."

"Good. Because it all starts now."

Chapter 20 – Rebecca

"Done," Rebecca said, dumping an oversized duffel bag, straining with too many clothes, onto the floor of the living room.

"Done," Dena agreed, setting down a cardboard box of books next to it.

They stood there, panting, gazing around at the boxes, bulging laundry baskets and filled paper bags that constituted Rebecca's home life, now crowding Dena's living room. A queen-sized mattress, frame and box spring, a microwave, a small television, a tub chair. The DBD house had come with its own dense oak dining table and chairs, heavy, unmovable couch and love seat from the original owners who'd rejected the furniture themselves, leaving it behind for tenants. It had made for a quick move-out, assisted by a morning U-Haul rental while the other occupants had been attending company class.

Rebecca glanced at her watch. "I need to run if I'm going to drop off that truck and warm up before the first rehearsal. Are you okay with this mess? I'll move things around tonight."

"No problem. I'm feeling pretty wiped out. I'm going to go rest once I've had lunch."

"You were Power Woman, back there at the house," Rebecca said, sizing her up. "I knew you were strong, but I think you're stronger than me."

"Of course I am. Just because you're taller and older doesn't mean a thing."

"You scared the shit out of me last night."

Dena chuckled. "You kind of riled me up. How's your shoulder?"

Rebecca reached up and massaged her right deltoid. "It's sore. You could have torn a ligament."

"Sorry. I wasn't thinking."

"That's an understatement. You were possessed." Rebecca collected her jacket, her overstuffed dance bag. "All right, I'm off."

"Work hard."

"You know, we can leave for company class together each morning, now."

Dena shook her head. "Not me."

"You prefer going separate, huh?"

"I'm not going to company class, Becca."

Rebecca's heart sank. "Deen." She tried to sound stern and big-sisterly. "You need to get back to company class."

The sternness had no impact.

"Look. It might be over for me," Dena said. "All of it. But I'm not going there right now. Let's leave it at that. Please."

Both of them fell silent. Outside the sun had broken through the clouds. From the big window, they could see hills and cityscape roofs and yards and people walking.

"Just remember this," Rebecca said finally, trying not to sound as helpless as she felt. "I'm here for you. Whatever I can do to help you, I'll do. I swear."

"Thank you. Now go." Dena gestured toward the door. "You're late and I'm sick of you."

Rebecca chuckled. "Okay. See you this evening."

The day's first rehearsal took place onstage, in the half-lit theater. The company was fine-tuning *Giselle*, the classic 1841 story ballet about a village girl betrayed by love who dies and becomes a Wili, one of the vengeful maiden spirits who dance men to death, but who insists on protecting her own beloved when he visits her grave. Today's rehearsal, the Act II scene in the moonlit forest, consisted of standing on the sidelines with the other twenty-three Wilis, all of them perfectly still, on one foot, the other tucked behind, arms curled in a low fifth position, gazes down. Basically, they were scenery, in their diaphanous white tulle rehearsal tutus, as two soloists, assistants to Myrtha, Queen of the Wilis, rehearsed their solo variations. For forty-five minutes, April, Anders and the lighting director stood downstage center and watched the soloists, starting and stopping them as needed. During these passages, the corps ensemble of Wilis held their poses, shifting only two times. And that was it: stand, stand, stand, shift; stand, stand, stand, shift. Easy, apprentice-level stuff, cramping muscles aside.

Easy to space off, affording Rebecca the opportunity to ponder how badly she'd screwed up her life in the course of forty-eight hours. Not to mention the shock of having revealed so much to Dena the previous night. Then concern over Dena herself. And Boyd. God, how she'd hurt him. He had every right to despise her.

Twenty-three other Wilis shifted.

Whoops.

"Rebecca! Don't be late," April called out in exasperation.

"Sorry," Rebecca squeaked out.

Anders, standing next to April, glanced over at her. "She didn't take my class this morning," he observed, loud enough for all to hear. "And look what it does to a dancer."

Shit. Who would have guessed Anders would be teaching company class today?

The reproof in his voice, however, was tempered by the little crinkle in the corner of his eyes that signified amusement, tolerance. Nearby, she saw Charlotte cast her a dark glance. For an instant, their eyes met.

Pure hatred. Scorn. And something worse, glinting in Charlotte's eye.

You'll pay for how you hurt Boyd, the look said. *We'll get even.*

A chill crept over Rebecca. Anders would tear her to bits if he knew she'd violated the "tell no one" pact. But that wasn't her greatest concern just then. Charlotte's malevolence was more dangerous. It hit her, deep in her belly, how vulnerable she was, how vulnerable she'd just made both herself and Anders.

She would have to watch her back.

Arpeggio rehearsals were the bright spot in her life. "Welcome back," Lexie had told her three weeks earlier, at her first rehearsal. "Do you remember your part?" He'd grinned at her assurance of "every last bit," his blue eyes merry, boyish, a sharp contrast to his mane of wild grey hair that made him look like a mad scientist. "Oh, you'll do *splendidly,*" he'd said.

She loved being back in the world of *Arpeggio.* She loved working with Jimmy again, being included in this elite group. Lana was in the same cast, as was Nicholas, and they treated her as an equal. Sylvie was in their cast, in Dena's old role. Which of course made her miss Dena's presence all the more.

Lana voiced the same sentiment, when the second cast dancers were given a break and stretched out on the floor in the corner. Lana lay on her belly, legs behind her in a frog pose. Jimmy did a set of push-ups. Nicholas massaged Sylvie's shoulders. "I miss having Dena in on the action," Lana said to Rebecca. "Do you remember that afternoon, five years ago, when we did the photo shoot with the trio of us?"

Rebecca, stretched in the splits, began to laugh. "And the way Dena was so energized, she leapt right over the guy taping cables to the floor?"

"Omigod, she was so funny. So full of energy."

"Okay," Nicholas said, "that explains why she almost flew out of my grasp on our opening night."

"No, that was your sweaty hands," Lana said. "I remember the way her eyes bulged when she realized you couldn't maintain your grip."

"Oh, that was horrible." Nicholas buried his head in his hands. "It was like seeing your life pass before your eyes. I don't know why I didn't think of keeping talcum powder backstage before then, but I sure as hell remember to do it now."

"And thank goodness for that!" Sylvie said, as if to inject herself into the memory of a performance she hadn't even been around for.

Jimmy, having completed his push-ups, rolled onto his back, using Rebecca's thigh as a pillow. She gave his chest an affectionate pat.

Lana turned to Rebecca. "How's Dena?" she asked. "I miss seeing her."

"Recovering from a bout of flu," she lied. "A good time to baby herself, since she's not required in rehearsals," she added, trying to make that sound like an appealing thing.

Nicholas nodded in understanding, but Lana seemed to catch the subtext. She looked troubled, Dena had likely been ignoring Lana's calls and texts, too.

"You know, you should invite her to come attend rehearsals with us," she told Rebecca.

Jimmy glanced over at Lana. "Hey, we can do that?"

"Why not?" Lana said.

"I don't think we can," Sylvie said. "Don't you remember when I had my visitors and tried to slip my cousin in for the day? Ben got all preachy on me."

"That's different," Lana said. "She wasn't a company member."

Sylvie shrugged. "In the end, is it worth sticking your neck out for?"

God, how she hated Sylvie.

"Oh," Lana said in a subdued tone. "I guess I didn't think it through."

"All right," Lexie called out. "Let's run this section through with my second cast now. First cast, take a break."

Jimmy rose and helped Rebecca to her feet. Lana touched Rebecca's shoulder as the others made their way back to center. "Tell her I care, okay? That I want to support her, any way I can."

"I will," Rebecca promised.

Once all of them had taken their places, Lexie cued the accompanist. He watched the dancers, coffee in one hand, moving the other fingers to the Mendelssohn score, like a conductor, his eyes glued on them, calling out the occasional directive, and, from time to time, a breezy comment that had them chuckling.

Runs, brisk pas de basque steps, chaîné turns and partnered overhead lifts, everything quick, finely articulated. Whimsy, when Jimmy launched himself horizontally through the air to be caught by the other male dancers. Adorable, when Lana, in a partnered lift, extended her legs into a 180 degree split and quickly brought in her feet to touch in center, like a crab's claw closing and opening. It was a ballet they all enjoyed being in. But you couldn't let your focus drift in an *Arpeggio* rehearsal. Lexie might have acted casual, but his eyes were sharp, his brain moved fast, and the intricate steps and passages even faster. Your mind and body had to be 100 percent present.

Lana was right. Dena belonged here too.

Maybe a newly promoted principal couldn't risk sticking her neck out, but a ninth year corps dancer could, she decided in bed that night. Particularly one who'd become closer friends with the artistic director's second-in-command. And the opportunity came the very next day, when Ben taught the women's company class. Once a week the company split up according to gender and either Ben or April would take the women and focus on pointe work while Anders or Curtis, the third ballet master, taught the men and had them focus on jumps. When Ben's class ended, as the other women trailed off in groups of two and three to grab a snack before rehearsals started, she lingered to chat.

"Seems like I haven't talked to you in a while," Ben said. "How are things?"

"Good. *Arpeggio* is buckets of fun."

He smiled. "I thought you'd enjoy it."

"I do."

"So. Where's Dena these days?"

"She's out with the flu."

"For over a week? That doesn't sound like her."

"I think getting over a flu is harder when you're still dealing with post-craniotomy stuff."

"That's true. I tend to forget she's still dealing with that. She doesn't let her infirmity show, if she can help it."

"Ben?" She hesitated, then spoke her next words in a rush before she could lose nerve. "What would you think about Dena attending *Arpeggio* rehearsals?"

He regarded her quizzically. "Well, she's not on the schedule."

"I know. I'm proposing something off the schedule."

"We ask you dancers to follow what's on the rehearsal grid for a reason. If everyone started attending rehearsals for ballets they weren't in, it would defeat the purpose of the grid. It's like the military. It works because everyone stays right on plan."

"But Anders isn't putting her on anywhere. It's like he's forgotten all about her."

"This is a crazy time of the year for the artistic director. You know that."

Time for honesty. Ben was as trustworthy as it got.

"Ben." She waited to speak again until he looked up at her. "Dena's not coming to class because she's given up all hope. That's the real reason. And I'm scared for her. Not dancing is destroying something in her. Being back in a rehearsal environment could make all the difference."

He said nothing. She watched him move about, pick up his clipboard, grab his sweatshirt from a nearby folding chair.

"You have a point," he said finally. "But rules are rules."

She made the puppiest-looking puppy dog eyes she could muster.

"Ben? Please, can you consider making an exception this one time? As a favor to me?"

He met her eyes. She held his gaze. When he began to smile, she knew she'd convinced him.

"You did help me out, as a personal favor, on New Year's Eve," he said.

"I did. Toddlers, little kids, married couples, terrifying domesticity. I did it for you."

He chuckled and tossed his sweatshirt at her. She caught it and wrapped it around her neck like a scarf.

"All right," he said. "I'll take it up with Lexie."

"Thank you, Ben. Thank you so much."

"Anything for you, Beck."

That night she returned to the apartment to find Dena stretched out on the couch, in the same robe, lounge pants and pajama top she'd been wearing when Rebecca left at nine o'clock. She still hadn't brushed her hair. She was surfing the channels on TV without paying attention to any of them.

"Guess what?" Rebecca said. "You might be able to attend a rehearsal!"

"Doing what?" Dena asked, but she looked like she didn't care.

"Well, shadowing. Like the understudies do."

"Okay. That's good to know."

"Just 'good to know'?" She stood before Dena, frowning, hands on hips.

"Don't act so surprised, Becca. You know how things are. I'm not even sure if I can have a dance career anymore."

"Lana wants you there, too. It was her idea, actually."

"Be sure and tell her thank you for me."

She sighed and joined Dena on the couch.

"Dena. What would help?"

"Nothing."

"I'm not going to let that be your attitude," Rebecca said. "How about taking one of my classes with me? I'm starting one up right after the *Giselle* run. Fundamentals of Business Management.'"

"No, thank you."

"Knitting? Learning sign language? Cooking class?"

Dena scowled at her. "Are you crazy? Why would I do that to myself?"

"Here's why. You would do that in order to save yourself from slipping into an abyss. You've got to occupy your mind with something else."

Something akin to animation washed over Dena's emoting side. Rebecca instantly seized on it. "You've got an idea. Tell me. Please."

"What the hell," Dena said, "since we're grasping at straws, and you're going to keep badgering me until I produce something. It's just that, back in June, I met this blogger. Well, she's a social media consultant mostly. Her name is Tatum Monroe. She saw me and Lana and Sylvie at Celia's and talked to Lana for a few minutes. Apparently she knew who I was. I saw her at Celia's again in early November. She offered her services to me, completely free of charge, said she'd set me up with a website and blog. Urged me to do the whole social media thing."

"Was she legit?"

"Yes. Celia says she makes good money, and has a huge social network."

"Why the offer to help you?"

"She seemed very sympathetic about my being sidelined. She thought I might want some diversion."

"What did you tell her?"

"I told her no thanks. I told her I thought I'd be rehearsing by now, and wouldn't have the time." At her words, the flush of animation on her face faded.

"And she's offering this free."

"Yeah."

"Wow. Take her up on it."

"I don't know," Dena said. Her shoulders rose and fell. "It all seems like just too much work."

Rebecca rose. "Well, I'm all for it. But it's your choice, of course. Think about it while I go get some food started. Pasta okay?"

"Sure."

Five minutes later, Dena joined her in the kitchen as she was chopping cucumbers for a salad.

"Will you help me?" she asked.

Joy and relief welled up in Rebecca, but she kept her tone casual. "Of course I will."

"I'm not even sure how to start."

"We just call her. Tonight. I'll set up the first meeting with the three of us there. It'll give me the chance to confirm she's cool, and genuinely wants to help you."

"You're busy. Crazy busy," Dena said. "Why would you do all that?"

She wanted to hug her little sister. She wanted to give her a good shake. She set down her chopping knife and turned to Dena.

"Because this is what sisters do for each other."

Dena drew in a slow breath and exhaled before speaking again.

"Okay. I'll try."

Chapter 21 – Dena

Misha had invited Dena down to Moss Beach for another weekend visit, an apology and thank-you-for-forgiving-me combined. They'd timed it to fall on the first weekend of *Giselle* so she could be far away from the excitement she was excluded from anyway. But when she arrived on a drizzly Saturday afternoon, Misha greeted her not with a welcome, but with a worried look.

"My brother just pulled a Rebecca," he said, holding the door open for her.

"What is that supposed to mean?" She stepped in, set down her overnight bag on the foyer table and regarded him in confusion.

He looked gloomy as he took her coat. "He's here. Showed up unexpectedly. Yesterday I let it slip that I'd invited you for the weekend, and now, here he is."

Before he could elaborate further, she saw his brother, loping down the steps from the second level, his smile the same as the one in the family portrait hanging on the wall.

Misha sighed. "Dena, this is my brother. David, meet Dena."

Misha's brother looked the same as she'd remembered from her sleep-stupor perspective: careless good looks and blonde curls like someone out of a children's Bible, although one look at his smile, the glint of mischief in his blue eyes, you knew he was no angel. "Nice to meet you, in a more official capacity," he said.

"Nice to meet you, too," she said.

David turned to Misha. "Okay, let's see if I remember all the things I'm not supposed to talk about. One,"—he held up a finger—"having seen Dena sound asleep on my bed, and the potentially inappropriate feelings that arose at the sight." A second finger shot up. "Two, that her ballet career might be on the bust. Three, that she's hot. Four, that she has half a paralyzed face. Five, that she's got an incredible dancer's body." A sidelong glance her way, as if to confirm, made him grin. "Six, that she's hot. Oh, wait. That was number three. How about that she's got this gorgeous hair that looks like something from a shampoo commercial, and I've got this frantic urge to bury my hands in her hair, get them all tangled in it, which you and I didn't discuss, Mish, as being appropriate or not, but I'm thinking it's probably inappropriate?"

"Way inappropriate," Misha agreed.

"Duly noted," David said, and offered Dena a wolfish grin.

Misha looked at her, his expression such a mix of chagrin, apology, and aggravation, that she had to chuckle. "Well," she said to Misha. "This time it's your problem and not mine."

"Dena," David said, beaming as though she'd offered him high praise, "you will quickly come to see that I am the life of the party and not the problem."

"Please start by helping me in the kitchen," Misha told him. "We've got a tea to serve our guest. If you insist on staying, you're going to work."

"Yes, big brother. Anything you say."

"Anything I can do to help?" Dena asked Misha.

"Not a thing. I'm spoiling you this weekend. Have a seat."

Dena settled herself on the living room couch. Outside, the light drizzle that had accompanied her drive was turning into a full-fledged rain, pattering softly against the roof and windows. Music played softly from the speakers, something piano and Mozart-ish. When the two brothers returned with trays bearing tea, cups and shortbread cookies, Dena commented on it.

"It is indeed Mozart," David said with a pleased smile. "His piano concertos. Great stuff, lots of little surprises planted within the music. Mozart was fun that way, testing the boundaries of his time, what a classical composition should or shouldn't sound like. Big fun to play."

"I enjoyed hearing you play the piano, that last time," she offered shyly, as she accepted a cup and saucer from Misha.

"My Beethoven day. His piano sonatas are fun stuff, too. A little more tempestuous. Misha said it had been rude of me to play the piano while you were resting, but I told him ballet dancers liked hearing live piano music. Was I right?"

She loved hearing live piano music on a daily basis, in company class and rehearsals. Thinking about it shot a pang through her. But only a tiny one; she'd found refuge since her last Moss Beach visit in numbness. No strong feelings meant no crushing despair. "You're right," she told David. "They do." She smiled gratefully at Misha as he poured her tea and nudged the sugar bowl her way.

"I dated a ballet dancer once," David said. "One time I was asking her which composer she liked the most, and she couldn't answer that. Not even what era of classical music she preferred. Which was weird. I would have figured all ballet dancers would be totally into classical music."

"Some of us more so than others."

"You?" David asked, reaching over to snag two more shortbread fingers. "And please don't tell me you're not into it, or my illusion of you will be crushed."

"Very into it," she assured him. "I've always been affected by music. From my earliest years, even before I'd started ballet."

A memory came back to her. Lying in bed one night, five years old, unable to sleep. Her parents had some music playing in the living room, the soundtrack to *Out of Africa,* which was stirring her so deeply that she started to cry. She lay there in bed, weeping, wondering how her parents could listen to it so casually—they were chatting and rustling newspapers—while inside her, it felt like someone had cut open her chest, pulled out her beating heart and set it there on a table, exposed and vulnerable. She began to sob louder, which made the conversation in the living room stop, and a moment later, her parents appeared at her doorway. She tried to explain, between hiccuppy sobs, how the music made her feel. They looked baffled.

"I'll find better music for you, okay, sweetie?" her father said. "I know just the thing."

He put on Prokofiev's *Peter and the Wolf,* with its simplistic melodies and cartoonish villain motifs, and she felt like calling out that no, it was all wrong, that she *wanted* the heart-pulled-out-and-beating feeling.

She heard them talk again, once they thought she'd fallen asleep. "What was that about?" her mother asked.

"Just Dena being Dena," her father said. "The music stirred her."

"I don't know, Conrad. That was too much. Do you think Dena might be... autistic?" She sounded scared.

"Oh, I wouldn't say that," Conrad replied. "I bet she'll become a musician, though. A classical musician. One ballet dancer daughter, one violinist. Wouldn't that be great?"

She found herself telling David and Misha the story.

David grinned. "*Out of Africa,* huh?"

"Okay, so they weren't the most sophisticated music listeners, my parents."

"No, it's great. John Barry has a great classical touch that appeals to the mainstream."

She shifted the subject to him, asking about his piano-playing youth. The two brothers argued about how it had been, David being shuttled to and from San Francisco in his early teens to be tutored at the Conservatory of Music, the sacrifices the others in the family had made.

"What made you stop?" Dena asked.

David inspected the last bit of shortbread on his plate as he pondered this. "Frankly, I got bored with the practice part of it by the time I was seventeen. I mean, six hours a day, every day, for the rest of my life? You try and ease up, take a break from it, and it shows. And maybe this is what you face, too. Ninety-five percent practice time to five percent performing."

"That about covers it," Dena admitted.

David popped the shortbread into his mouth. "Way too much work," he said between chews. "Not for me. I don't want to be a slave to my craft and the demands of the classical music world. I want to play what I want, when I want."

"You want to be irresponsible and party," Misha said.

"Hey. I'm a free spirit. What can I say? And I've yet to get arrested or threatened by creditors, so I must be doing something right."

"You owe me five hundred dollars still," Misha said.

"Not to worry. You'll get it back. Eventually."

"When are you going to go back and finish that last year of college?"

"Big brother, I am learning from the great institution that is called life. There will be plenty of time for the other. Some day."

A timer in the kitchen sounded and Misha excused himself to check on something simmering. The moment he left the room, David leaned in.

"So… you," he said, studying her intently.

"What about me?"

"Misha says your recuperation is going slower than you'd hoped. That they're not letting you dance."

"He's correct. And it may be that I have to make the decision… to quit dance."

Such a comfort, the numbness.

"And you'd really do that?"

"If it's what made the most sense, I would."

David looked skeptical. "I don't buy that you'd just walk away from your dance career."

"Sorry," she said. "It's the reality of things."

"What would you do?" he persisted.

"I don't have a clue."

"You seem pretty calm about it."

"I've had eight months to consider it."

He shook his head. "There's no way. You wouldn't. You *couldn't*."

Before the agitation could arise in her and ruin her nice, relaxed feeling, she rose. "I'll just go see if Misha needs a hand in the kitchen."

"He doesn't."

She went to the kitchen anyway. Misha was adding a cup of wine to something in a Dutch oven that smelled like roasting meat. "You all right out there?" he asked her, glancing over in the direction of the living room.

"I'm fine. Just wanted to see if you needed any help."

"Nope, I'm ready to stick this beef back in the oven and come back out."

She yawned, as a wave of sleepiness and fatigue crested over her. Misha noticed. "It's that time of day."

"It is."

"Do you want to take a rest?"

"That might be a good idea."

"Okay. Let me show you to your room."

In the living room, she flashed David a look of apology. "Forgive me, I need to go rest for a while."

"Rest away, milady. Any chance it will be in my bedroom again?"

"No!" Misha said, louder than necessary, which David seemed to find amusing.

"We're putting you in my sister's old room," Misha told her. "It's on the second level. It's a little chillier and has some storage boxes in it, but I put flannel sheets on the bed. I think you'll be comfortable up there."

"It sounds perfect," she assured Misha.

She followed Misha upstairs, the sleepiness descending over her like a heavy wool blanket that someone had dropped on her shoulders. The room was sweetly girlish, rose-colored walls and a white-painted headboard that matched the vanity table across the tiny room. Within minutes of settling into the room's feather bed, sleep claimed her.

At some point, the music began, David's piano playing once again piercing her dreams. Waking, she lay there listening for several minutes, awash in a pleasant optimism, before she rose, made herself presentable and padded downstairs to the music's source. It was coming from the family room, where a lamp in the corner had been turned on to ward off the approaching winter darkness. Delicious cooking smells wafted from the kitchen: Misha's braised beef in wine.

David looked up from behind the piano as she entered the room. "Hi there. Misha had to run over to Half Moon Bay for some stuff. I'm to cater to your needs. Do you want me to talk or play music?"

"Play music, definitely."

"A tribute to my musical chops and not a ding on my conversational skills, right?"

She laughed, taking a seat on the couch. "Correct."

He played. Chopin, she recognized, with a pang. The accompanists for company class favored Chopin, or Chopin-esque pieces, for the adagios. Fauré triggered a similar memory. Debussy's *Clair de Lune*. Other pieces and composers, she couldn't name. Then, as if he'd figured out what produced the maximum reaction in her, he switched back to Chopin.

Just like that night in her childhood, the music slipped past her defenses and produced a deep contraction inside her, equal parts pain and pleasure. It went deeper still, until the tears began to rise, and she could only sit there, crying, trying to display only her expressionless left side so he wouldn't notice.

She'd been numb and it had felt good. Okay, not good. But safe. Manageable.

He kept playing, soulful, stirring pieces that seemed chosen for their ability to pierce her heart deeper, deeper. She was crying audibly now, and he stopped and regarded her impassively. It couldn't have been more awkward. She worked to compose herself and only then did she look up and meet his eyes.

"Well," he said, "I think it's safe to say that dance is not done with you yet."

She stared at him in disbelief. "You did this on purpose. Tried to provoke a reaction."

"I suppose I did."

What a horrible, disreputable person he was. No wonder Misha had seemed anxious about having him around this weekend. "That was a pretty shitty thing to do."

"Not at all," he replied. "I was just helping you see where you stand with your art. You need it. It nourishes you. That's not going to go away just because you're sidelined for a year or two."

"*Two* years?" She wasn't sure which appalled her more, his words or his casual attitude.

"Whatever. Point being, you're still a dancer. It couldn't be more obvious. That gorgeous body of yours, the way it moves. The way you're sitting there now, all swept away by the music. You're a dancer. You can't not be one. Ever."

The truth of this, the twin emotions of fragile hope and crushing despair, crashed into her. He was right. And right then, the truth hurt. Now that the numbness was gone, it all hurt.

The tears rose up again and spilled out.

She heard Misha come in through the front door. David looked anxious.

"Look, Dena. I just want to make sure you're looking at the issue clearly."

Misha came into the room and saw Dena's distraught expression. He stopped in his tracks and swung around to glare at David. "This is entertaining her? This is making sure she's enjoying herself here? Dammit, I ask you to do this one thing and you—"

"It's okay, Misha," Dena interrupted. "It's nothing. He was playing his music for me. It made me sentimental, that's all."

Misha turned back toward Dena. "That's all? Because frankly, you look upset."

"That's all it was."

She stayed close to Misha after that, keeping a wary distance from David. As Misha sent him off to set the dining room table with the family china, she remained with Misha in the kitchen, chopping parsley and garlic, grating lemon zest for something Misha called a gremolata.

"Am I allowed back in the kitchen?" David called out when he'd finished setting the table. "Tell Dena I'll play nice."

Which of course made them laugh.

Dinner was luxurious, memorable. A caesar salad with dressing made from scratch, long planks of romaine dripping with savory egg, oil, anchovy, lemon and parmesan goodness. Braised beef, topped with a rich wine reduction and a sprinkling of the gremolata, which was astonishing. A bottle of fine red wine and au gratin potatoes completed the perfection. David had seconds, thirds, perfectly willing to accept a distant ranking in the family culinary skills department.

True to his word, David remained on good behavior. The background music he'd chosen, while still classical, was lighter, more relaxing than the music he'd played on the piano. After dinner they gravitated back to the living room. David put more wood in the fireplace as Misha proposed a movie.

David wrinkled his nose. "A movie, how prosaic. We've got a fire, this beautiful woman, a little more wine. What movie could compete with that?"

"Dena?" Misha asked.

"Indulge me one last time with the music," David begged Dena. "Trust me."

She chose the music option, curious, in spite of herself, to see how he planned to provoke or impress her with Misha right there.

He rose and went to his iPod, docked in the living room's stereo system. "Hmm," he said as he scrolled through his music. "All right. I think I'll play Mahler, who doesn't particularly qualify as light in anyone's book. But the slow movements from his symphonies can be just incredible. This one is the *Andante Moderato* from his sixth symphony. It's uplifting. Way uplifting. We won't have you listen to the rest of the symphony—it's brutally tragic, dark, driving."

"How astute of you to eliminate that part," Misha said.

"So, the Andante is in the key of E-flat major," David continued on cheerily, "which makes for a far cry in mood and theme from the other three movements, in A-minor. And *my* take is that it's all the more gorgeous and heartfelt because of what surrounds it. Life can be like that, you know? The sweetest sweetness is that which follows the most bitter."

"Enough philosophizing," Misha said. "We want to listen to music, not your voice."

David chuckled but said no more. The music began and he sat back down, across from Misha. The two brothers conversed in low tones about family-related issues, as she focused on the music.

David had offered the perfect description. The music, pastoral and calming for the first dozen minutes, grew in intensity, imparting a soaring quality that did just as David had said. It lifted her up, higher, higher. Now the lulled feeling gave way to one of urgency, so sweetly urgent, nearly ecstatic. And in that moment as she sat there, listening to the music, something was handed back to her, something deeply personal and grounded in the timeless. In this near-mystical moment, ballet called her back.

How simple it all was. She was alive and breathing, the music was radiating through her core, and right beside it, a natural byproduct of it, was her dance. Everything else faded to insignificance. Nothing existed beyond this, the music calling her name, promising it would be there, always, and that, for her, to dance was to breathe.

Tears slipped out again, flowing down her right cheek, but this time they didn't bring pain, only peace.

Two minutes later, the music ended but the exalted feeling remained. "Okay," Misha said. "Enough? Movie now?" Both brothers looked inquiringly at her.

"Um, maybe more of David's music?"

David laughed out loud. Misha frowned at him.

"The lady has spoken," David said, rising, returning to his iPod.

David was smart; he knew how to work his brother, as well, who favored the blues. He interspersed that with jazz, African music, sultry Brazilian ballads. Dena could feel Misha casting her concerned glances from time to time. With good reason: the music was continuing to work its spell on her. Once again it opened something inside her, like David's playing had done, but in a more sensuous fashion, like her blouse was being unbuttoned, one button at a time, exposing more and more of her. David saw this; he'd likely planned it. Misha glanced from Dena to David and his worried look deepened.

David seemed to be enjoying himself enormously. During lapses in conversation, his gaze would swing over to settle on Dena, not flirtatious so much as intimate, openly approving. It was the most effective come-on she'd ever experienced, reawakening all sorts of sensitive nerves, ones that had not been crushed, clipped or otherwise damaged.

She drank in the attention; it had been so long since anyone had made her feel so desirable, as a woman and not a patient. She'd already decided she wouldn't act on David's unspoken invitation. He was the wrong brother. If anything, it made her crush on Misha— time to call it what it was—deepen. Meeting David's eyes the next time, she saw that he understood all this. Misha alone hadn't picked up on her decision, and she sensed his unease, his discomfort, in the way he'd nudged himself closer to her, their thighs mere inches apart now, his arm resting on the couch cushion just above her shoulders. And that was all right, too, that she and David were letting Misha remain unaware of their intentions, or lack thereof.

It was, in fact, kind of fun.

Chapter 22 – Rebecca

Few things in the world of personal relationships are as uncomfortable as breaking up and having to encounter your ex in the workplace on a daily—make that hourly, nights included—basis. Topping the list of beyond-uncomfortable would be having aforementioned ex run his hands over your body, encircle your waist with his arm, plant his hand on your inner thigh before lifting you, catching you in a fish dive, holding your body close before releasing you. Both of you are skimpily clad, sweaty, panting. His breath is warm and audible in your ear. Skin slides against skin, your sweat intermingling. There is no place to hide, physically or figuratively.

How was it possible, Rebecca kept asking herself, that Anders, after three years of never pairing her up with Boyd, had now placed them together to rehearse? *Songs of Yesterday* featured, in addition to a principal couple, a corps ensemble of eight females and four males. It was a plum role for the four females who paired up with the males in two sections, almost demi-soloist work. She couldn't decide if it had been generosity on Anders' part, or his idea of humor.

Boyd himself knew better than to complain or make trouble. It was the best role he'd been given to rehearse in the past two seasons. Further, he was days away from having the signed Tulsa contracts in hand. Until then he had to play the game carefully, not allow any of his hatred toward Anders or Rebecca to show. Making Rebecca look bad in *Songs* would only make him look bad. And he still wanted to look good.

Ego, in the end, trumped retaliation.

She was four courses away from obtaining her degree. Two of them, within her program, she could take after season's end and complete with relative ease. She'd fretted over the third class, an outside business course that covered fundamentals of management. At first glance the students had seemed far more advanced than she, more focused on careers, some already in professional jobs, looking to enhance their business skills. She dreaded a repeat of the condescending vibe of the aesthetics class, but to her relief, that didn't prove to be the case. She was further aided by the second week's assignment, to bring in a cited example of a business being run well, from periodicals or newspapers, and be prepared to discuss why it worked. She found a recent *San Francisco Chronicle* article that had featured the West Coast Ballet Theatre.

The article elaborated on the company's success, the fact that subscriptions and single ticket sales were up, a staggering feat, given the poor economy. It praised executive director Charlie Stanton's guidance, the board of trustees, a healthy endowment, but focused on Anders, his engaged style, smart programming choices, his finger ever on the pulse of what audiences were seeking.

How odd, to be sitting in this college classroom, with all these smart, driven people, professionals and pre-professionals alike, discussing Anders and the working side of ballet. How thrilling and energizing.

At her teacher's prompting, she explained more about how the company was set up, as an association, with both the executive and artistic director reporting to the board of trustees. And how crucial the trustees were. Their biggest job: to help bring in money, either by raising it or extending their own. Many of the trustees regularly underwrote some of the WCBT's operating expenses. Andy Redgrave and his foundation, for example, had contributed $300,000 to increase the company's marketing budget for the spring season, while another had underwritten last summer's London tour. And for every story ballet, over a dozen couples or individuals had contributed over $100,000 each. You saw them referenced in the program, that *these performances of* Giselle *are made possible by This Super Rich Couple, and the Generous Billionaire Foundation, and John & John Johnson.* Often, it added close to a million dollars to each ballet's budget. A ballet company couldn't thrive without this kind of support. She hadn't fully appreciated that before.

In the classroom, the other students listened with interest to her explanation of how the WCBT's endowment foundation operated, as a separate nonprofit, with its own board of directors that managed its funds and distributed four percent of its earnings annually to the ballet association.

"How did they manage during our last economic downturn?" one of the students asked. "I heard how arts organizations across the country were taking big hits right and left."

"We did fine," she told him. "The board of directors and company administrators handled it smoothly."

The truth, yes, but sugarcoated. It had been hell for the administrators and management team. She'd learned from recent research that the company's $50 million endowment had dropped fifteen percent in value by December 2008. It crept its way back up, regaining much of its worth by the following December, but by then, ticket sales and contributions had dropped. Through all that and the following year, WCBT administrators had scrambled, crunched numbers, made cut after cut to balance their $30 million budget.

But, to Anders' eternal credit, no programing was cut, no dancer lost their job, and they still managed to tour internationally.

How humbling, to think she'd known him through those crisis years and never seen the worry on his face. She remembered he'd been in meetings a lot, more impatient and snappish. But that had been her DBD phase, with all of them believing he was simply a cold, unfeeling bastard at heart. In truth, he'd been holding the artistic side of the company together through bravado, bluster, assurances to the board of trustees that he'd produce value content and bring ticket sales back up, fill the house for the performances, likely staking his own job on the claim.

She wanted to talk to Anders about this, pick his brain, tell him how she now understood and admired decisions he'd made. She wanted to ask him, "What does it feel like to be at the helm of such an astonishing organization? Do you lie awake at night, sleepless with worry about things? Have you ever pondered failure, or is that not in your vocabulary?"

The next day, she tried. He was in his office toward the end of lunch break. His door was cracked open, his secretary gone. She tapped at his door and poked her head in. He was standing behind his desk, engrossed in reading a report.

"Anders. Can I have a minute of your time?"

He glanced up, saw her there, and returned his attention to the document. "Why?" he asked.

She stepped into the room. "I'm in a business class and I've been researching the inner workings of our company. I have to say, I've found it to be endlessly fascinating. So many layers upon layers, and the company's success points to excellent choices made, right and left." For a moment she felt like Alice Willoughby, intelligent and informed, having a discourse with Anders, meeting as equals to discuss his executive skills.

Anders said nothing. Her confidence faltered.

Go, her instincts shouted. *Leave.* Already she could tell that today there would be no indulgent glances, no looks of amused tolerance, like during the *Giselle* rehearsal when she'd missed her cue.

"Anyway," she continued on bravely, "with all I've learned, it made me wonder what it's been like for you, being this company's artistic director over the past ten years. Has it been ... hard?"

He frowned. "What, precisely, are you trying to ask me?"

"Just, what it's like. Shifting your energies, your mind, from an artistic point of view to a business one, on a daily basis. Were you always this way, so focused and guided, both artistically and strategically inclined?"

"I don't think about it," he said. "I just do my work."

"Oh, surely you've given it some thought. Twenty-two years ago, you were an internationally acclaimed principal dancer, and now you're an internationally acclaimed artistic director. Keeping the company afloat while other dance companies, large and small, are failing."

"Well, it sounds like you've given it enough thought for the both of us," he said, eyes still fixed to his report.

Frustration exploded inside her. "I wish you'd give me a straight answer. Why do you have to be this way?"

This got his attention. He raised his eyes and cast her an aggrieved glance. "No. The question is, why do *you* have to be this way?"

"I just wanted to discuss something intelligent with you. Use my mind a little more."

"I don't pay you for your *mind.* I pay you to dance. You want to analyze something, analyze the choreography. The music. And leave me out of it. Why are you thinking it's all right to bother me with this nattering, anyway?"

You are no Alice Willoughby, his angry expression told her.

The office door opened wider and Ben entered, a sheaf of papers in hand. "What took so long?" Anders snapped. "We have work to finish."

"Sorry." Ben glanced from Anders to her.

"Get her out of here." Anders gestured toward her irritably. "She wants to chitchat."

"Thank you," she retorted, stung, "but I know how to leave an office all on my own. I'm going to college, after all."

Ben laughed. Even Anders chuckled, humor restored now that the problem was leaving.

She did not laugh. She strode out, fuming, eyes on the carpet as she headed toward the elevator. The *ping* as the elevator doors opened made her quicken her steps.

"Hold the elevator," she called out to the person who'd just stepped in. She sped up and dashed in just as the doors started to close, only to discover Boyd, of all people, already in the elevator.

Great. This, now, too.

They were the only two in the elevator and she could feel him study her. "Cozying up to Anders in his office?" he asked.

"Fuck off," she spat, too angry to worry about tiptoeing around his still wounded ego.

"God. What's your problem?"

She ignored him.

"Seriously," he said in a less snide tone. "What did he do to piss you off?"

"He mocked me, okay? He belittled me and chased me out of his office."

"Oh." Boyd seemed to respect her rage more than her deference. "Asshole," he added a moment later.

"Totally."

They said no more as the elevator carried them down to the lobby level, but she took a certain comfort in the fact that over this, at least, they could still feel allied.

On the ground floor, she motioned for Boyd to step out first. "There you are," she heard a female voice say, and she stepped out to see Charlotte striding toward Boyd. "I was looking for you," she said to him in a cozy tone that faded when she saw Rebecca.

"What's going on?" she asked Boyd, as she sent one last poison glare Rebecca's way.

"Nothing. Nothing at all," Boyd said, ignoring Rebecca once again.

The three of them were all headed to the same place: studio two for the upcoming *Songs* rehearsal. Rebecca lingered by the elevator, pretending to adjust the contents of her dance bag; she wasn't about to tag along or trail behind them. Their voices soon receded but she could still hear Charlotte's indignant, "Don't tell me you're going to be *friends* with that bitch now," and Boyd's soothing, "It's nothing, Char. Don't worry."

So much for feeling allied again.

But in rehearsal, fifteen minutes later, Boyd seemed to behave more respectfully toward her. By the time Ben, running the rehearsal, stopped the accompanist to work with the four corps couples in the center, Boyd was acting almost agreeable.

"Guys, you need to get much more air beneath your partners here," Ben said. It was the sisonne section, a rapid pair of low partnered lifts, angled to the right, to the left, then lifting the female overhead for the third one that she would then hold, frozen, legs in a split.

The four couples tried it again for Ben. He shook his head.

"More. Here, let me show you what I mean." He strode over to Rebecca and Boyd. "May I use you?" he asked Rebecca. She could hear Charlotte's snort of laughter over his choice of words, from where she stood in the periphery, as one of the non-partnered females.

Ignoring her, Rebecca nodded.

He gripped her hips in an exaggerated fashion, clamped onto them. She demi-pliéd in preparation, sprang up and he pushed her into the overhead lift. She shot straight up; it had never felt so effortless on her part. Ben set her down but kept his hands on her hips as he discussed what the male's intention should be, just before the lift. "Like you're riding a Harley-Davidson," he quipped, making little revving motions with his hands against Rebecca's hips, which made everyone laugh. She relaxed into his touch, into the comfort of his nearness, this protective force in her life. He was so not-Anders, so not-Boyd. He made her feel good.

Boyd watched them closely. Something flickered behind his eyes—suspicion? calculation?—or perhaps not, because when it came time for the couples to try it again, he flashed her a professional smile and said, "I think I'm up to the task here," and there was no more chilly distance. It was, in truth, their best rehearsal yet, his behavior civil, even thoughtful. That he left immediately afterward, joining Charlotte, who'd scurried over to him to whisper something in his ear that made them both laugh, mattered little to her. Let them have their gossiping, she decided. They seemed to need it.

The next *Songs* rehearsal went even better between her and Boyd. Gone, the disdain, the physical recoiling from her. He began leaving his hands on Rebecca's hips, the way Ben had, while the dancers were paused, getting feedback, or discussing the steps. The physical closeness, the remembered intimacy of Boyd's touch, seemed to break down a defensive barrier inside her. Boyd, too, grew friendlier, even a touch flirtatious. Like the old, pre-dating days.

Rehearsals ended for the day. She changed in the women's lounge adjacent to the big studio and, upon her departure, was surprised to see him in the hallway, lingering. Together they walked down the narrow hall, chatting. No one else was around. Around the corner, by the stairwell, he paused. To her confusion, he nudged her closer to the wall, his hands falling on her hips.

In the distance came the sound of voices, footsteps, from the far end of the corridor. He took a step closer. "How about a little review work on the art of partnering?" he whispered.

She met his eyes, now dark with desire, and an instant later his mouth clamped down onto hers. His hands went to her shoulders, fingers hooking the spaghetti straps of her shirt, sliding them down. The shirt slid as well, making it easy for Boyd to dip his hand in and scoop out her right breast, fondle it, right there in public. She tried to protest, but his lips still covered hers, his tongue hungrily probing her mouth.

A dizzying sense of confusion came over her, shock over the desire he'd ignited.

He gave a low chuckle. "Someone's been feeling lonely," he murmured between kisses. "Whatever shall we do about it?" The fingers of his other hand reached down, flicked open the top button of her jeans and unzipped her fly. His boldness unnerved her even as it excited her.

"It's me you want right now, isn't it, Beck?" His breath had grown ragged. "Just me."

"Yes," she heard herself gasp out.

"I thought so." His hips pressed into hers. The sound of voices, footsteps, grew louder.

"Someone's coming," she tried to say, but Boyd kept kissing her, fondling her. Which began to feel not sexy but tawdry. They were in public, after all. She tried to push him off, but he seemed oblivious to the reality that people were approaching.

The voices from around the corner grew more distinct and she recognized Charlotte's. Her insides seized up. A moment later, three people swung around into view just as she succeeded in pushing Boyd away. She yanked at her clothes, desperate to cover herself, knowing it was only contributing to the entertainment.

"Oh," Charlotte trilled. "We're not interrupting you two, are we?"

The other two, male corps dancers and lethal gossipers, stood there, taking in everything with bug-eyed mirth, mouths in perfect Os.

"Nah," Boyd said to Charlotte. "Nothing important." He turned back to Rebecca and held one hand up, pure pantomimed rejection, like something out of a story ballet. "I changed my mind about your offer. Don't want it. You're used goods now."

She couldn't even defend herself, protest that the offer had not been hers. Not with the breath knocked out of her. The five of them stood there, a tableau of frozen figures, until Boyd lurched toward Charlotte and the two of them hurried away, snickering, in the direction from which Charlotte had come. The two gossipers moved next, on toward the stairs as Rebecca finished rearranging her clothes with shaking hands, overcome with shame and fury and hurt. How deeply Boyd and Charlotte must hate her, to have done this. Charlotte had likely hatched the whole thing in rehearsal when Ben had asked Rebecca "may I use you?"

"Used goods," she heard Ernesto, one of the dancers, say in the stairwell. "Ouch. That's harsh."

"He got her good. Did you see her face?"

"Yes, and his," Ernesto added.

"Dang. And they call *us* drama queens."

Their laughter echoed even as their voices and footsteps receded.

Used goods. Whom to despise more, Boyd and Charlotte, or herself?

Right then, a toss-up.

Chapter 23 – Dena

Three weeks into Tatum's social media campaign, Dena was ready to say it had failed. Simply another example of the nothing-is-working phenomenon at play in her life. Like the grafted facial nerve, still inactive, despite the acupuncture, physical therapy, massage therapy, facial stimulator therapy, and Misha telling her to hang in there, don't lose hope just yet. Like her return to company class, to the studios, where nothing much could happen, because she was sidelined. But she did it all anyway: the therapies, company class, the blog Tatum had helped her set up alongside the website. She posted diligently twice a week, alternating "how to" pieces about ballet with her own personal musings. She tweeted a half-dozen times daily. She snapped ballet-related photos to post daily on Instagram, focusing on artful arrangements of old, used pointe shoes, which the company females discarded by the dozens each week. On her Facebook fan page, at least, traffic had started picking up, a growing number of fans who posed ballet-related questions, which she sensed Tatum and the dance bloggers in her network had helped generate.

It wasn't bad. That was what Tatum kept telling her.

"Don't get discouraged," she told Dena over the phone one afternoon. "It's early. It takes a month, at the very least, before results start showing up. But trust me, they will. In the meantime, did you look into discussion forums like we talked about?"

"I did. A ballet-related one, and the other for acoustic neuroma patients."

"And?"

Dena stretched out on her sofa, tucking a decorative pillow behind her head. "I'm enjoying it. Especially the acoustic neuroma forum. It's such a rare, weird thing, having an acoustic neuroma. It's tough to explain how much the fatigue and brain fog, even after the craniotomy, can wreck your routine. Your life. All of us have pretty much been derailed by it. Some people have to deal with facial paralysis, partial deafness, some don't. Some have tinnitus that didn't get better after going deaf, it only got worse. Can you just imagine? This ringing in the ear on the deaf side that turns into a scream by late in the day."

"God, that sounds horrible."

"It does. It makes me realize I could have had it much worse."

"Do the other posters know you're a professional ballet dancer?"

"Yes, and want to hear something funny? They keep asking if I'm the dancer who played Natalie Portman's double in *Black Swan*. They're convinced I'm just being shy, or humble, when I tell them no, it wasn't me, it was Sarah Lane. Some of the Facebook fans are speculating about the same thing. They've even asked me about the rumor over at the ballet forum."

Tatum began to laugh. "I noticed that too. How do you respond?"

"I tell the truth, and say that I have no idea how the rumor got started. Was it you?"

"I would love to say it was. What a clever marketing idea. But, no, it wasn't."

"How should I handle this? I feel bad about it. Sarah Lane shouldn't be upstaged a second time."

"Just continue with what you're doing. Let people know it's a mistake, that you don't know how the rumor got started. Get indignant about it, say you'll get to the bottom of the mystery." She chuckled again. "It's brilliant. It's generating a buzz about who Dena Lindgren is, and why everyone's talking about her, even as Dena herself is trying to push the credit in the direction of Sarah Lane. Nothing fuels a buzz better than protestations of innocence."

"All right, that's what I'll do."

"How are things going for you, work-wise?" Tatum asked.

Dena sighed. "I'm climbing the walls. I really do need this social media diversion."

"Well, it's been a delight to work with you and help you brand yourself. I'm only sorry it's all come at such a price to you. Really, I wish you'd let me write a piece about everything, your struggles, the way ballet is so caught up in image that they can't tolerate facial asymmetry on a dancer who is otherwise dying to dance again."

"Nope. Do not."

"How about something subtler? The wounded heroine fighting fierce odds sells so well these days. My readers would eat it up. So would my dance blogger buddies."

"I'm sorry, Tatum, but it's still a no."

And yet, something inside Dena hesitated. While it was important to adhere to the code of company conduct and etiquette, there was this to honor: the frustration and loneliness she suffered as she worked and sweated and struggled her way back into the company. Returning to daily class a second time had not been the return of the hero she'd been last September. Now she was just a sidelined dancer who would continue to be sidelined through the season, until her next surgery and beyond. Around the others, she felt invisible.

Rebecca saw her, at least. As did Lexie, Lana, Nicholas, the four of them, welcoming her into *Arpeggio* rehearsals. But Sylvie, unlike the others, seemed uncomfortable with the setup. Even a little hurtful. Like the "I don't think my understudy needs an understudy" line. That was what Sylvie had said, a sort of jokey aside, in rehearsal the first day, with Dena tucked in back with the understudies. No one had laughed at Sylvie's comment. Rebecca had looked furious, Sylvie's understudy confused. Lana and Nicholas had frowned. Sylvie, subdued, had apologized to Dena, who'd brushed it off with a wave and a crooked smile, waiting until rehearsal's end to lock herself in a bathroom stall and cry. Afterward, she'd gone up to the fitness room and fiercely worked out for two more hours.

Dena rose to a sitting position on the couch. "You know, what's been the toughest thing lately, is the humbling nature of it all. It's given my ego the most unbelievable, undignified whack."

"Oh, Dena, I can only imagine."

"But I have to say, as hard and unchanging as things seem these days, they're much better, compared to how I felt a few weeks back. Yes, the situation is still crappy. No, there's no certainty and stability I can count on anymore, beside the fact that I know I'm a dancer who needs to keep dancing. It's that I've stopped clinging to the hope that something magical is going to happen and put everything back in its right place and I can be 'me' again. That story is just a pretty illusion." She shut her eyes, in order to better access the strange, new thoughts that had been percolating through her lately. "All this energy I've been wasting, supporting an illusion that the fantastic seasons I've had should be the lone definition of success. What a heavy load, to keep trying to compete with that other Dena. She's gone. She's dead. And realizing that doesn't even make me sad anymore. Truth is, it makes me feel healthier inside than I have in a long time."

Silence greeted her words, and she began to laugh out of

embarrassment. "Tatum? Did I put you to sleep with my babbling?"

"Wow," Tatum said in a hushed voice. "Repeat everything you just said. It was amazing."

"I don't think I can," Dena said. "Insight doesn't store well, does it? It bubbles up, explodes, and then sort of fades to particles that glimmer, like stars in the sky. You can't remember precisely what you said, which is kind of frustrating, but you can feel the glimmering bits, there inside of you."

"Dena!" Tatum cried. "This is so incredible. *You're* incredible. You're turning into someone different, right before my eyes. A poet, a philosopher."

"Oh, stop," Dena protested, laughing.

"I'm serious!"

She grinned, feeling strangely proud of herself. "I guess climbing the walls gives you a great view of the bigger world, huh?"

"Everything you've said is so amazing. Listen. Let me write a blog piece on just that. What you said, and this whole new attitude of yours."

"Hmm." Dena paused to consider this. "No whistle-blower angle?"

"None."

"No dings against the WCBT or my artistic director?"

"You have my word. I'll just focus on the positive, a sidelined dancer whose determination and grace are an inspiration. Solace for anyone fighting to overcome obstacles in order to follow their dream."

"All right," Dena agreed. "Go for it."

The quiver of happy anticipation at seeing Misha for one of their twice-weekly dinners was replaced by shock when she swung open her apartment door that evening and saw him with his previously long hair now cropped short.

"Misha!" she gasped. "You look so... different."

He came in, rubbing his neck ruefully. "Bad?"

God, no. She couldn't believe how good it made him look. The visual emphasis fell more on his face now, the strong jawline and his deep brown eyes. More obscure things, too, like the back of his neck, now exposed, and the way she yearned to reach over and touch it, fingertips brushing against the curls forming at the base of the haircut.

"Not bad at all," she assured him. She closed the door, eyes taking in other changes, too. A new button-down shirt, white with navy stripes, which fitted the contours of his body more closely.

"Your shirt is new," she said.

"It is. So's yours." His gaze lingered on her bare arms.

She'd been putting extra attention into what she wore around him, since the Moss Beach weekend. She could almost hear David's voice, saying, *why the baggy clothes that hide your body?* each time she readied herself. Why not, after all, the sleeveless silk top and skinny jeans that Isabelle had bought her the last time she'd come up? While Rebecca had attended rehearsals, she and Isabelle had indulged in an unprecedented, mother-daughter shopping afternoon. Spending the whole afternoon with her mother, enjoyably, not arguing once, had been surreal. Their relationship was changing.

So was her relationship with Misha.

"You're getting more workouts in, aren't you?" he asked, studying her.

"I'm trying to. I take the advanced class at the ballet school, even though they're all terrified of me. There's a good Pilates class a few blocks from the theater. I try and make that a few afternoons. And then my little local gym, in addition to the fitness room at the studios."

"It shows."

You look hot.

That was what she longed to hear from him. No, actually, that would be horrifying to hear from him, because it wasn't part of their script. It was what David would have said. It amused her now, to consider David's list of "do not"s that he'd ticked off in Moss Beach. That she had a gorgeous body. That he'd wanted to tangle his hands in her hair. That she was hot. All said jokingly, in good fun. But the impact of the words still hovered between her and Misha, as if David had released some pheromone before departing, off to his next adventure.

"Are you ready to go?" Misha asked.

"Sure. You?" she asked, feeling self-conscious, as if this were a first date.

"I am. Let's go."

Every few weeks they picked a neighborhood to wander through, window shop, grab a bite to eat in. The Haight, Union Street, Upper Fillmore, the Mission District, North Beach. Tonight was Chinatown. Nearby street parking was easy after six o'clock, an added bonus. They strolled down Grant Avenue, past the shops lining both sides of the little street, punctuated by jade lampposts and pagoda facades. Balloon-y red lanterns hung from wires suspended across the street. By this hour most of the shops had closed, dispersing the crush of tourists. She and Misha peered into windows at the inventory within. Luggage, purses, ceramic figurines, plastic souvenirs, tee shirts, sweatshirts, scarves. Bins of dried mushrooms, herbs, teas. Shops selling food: cooked whole chickens and ducks, dangling from a rack, heads still intact, as the savory roasting smells and sound of Cantonese chatter wafted out.

Time spent with Misha seemed to carry a sense of urgency these days, a sweetly desperate feeling that the evening was passing too quickly. She found herself standing closer to him than she used to, allowing her shoulder and chest to brush against him. Her eyes lingered on his face when he spoke, taking note of the pleasing, well-formed shape of his lips. She made sure to keep her voice breezy, attitude as casual as his, so as not to betray her new feelings.

Misha didn't notice. Particularly tonight, where he seemed edgy, preoccupied.

"What's up with you?" she asked finally.

"I'm sorry. I'm being lousy company, aren't I?"

"Not in the least. But I can tell something's up."

He exhaled heavily. "It was a conversation I had with David. Last week he decided Northern California was too tame for him. Said he was going to travel for a spell. I was thinking, okay, L.A. or Seattle or something. Guess where he calls me from today?"

"Where?"

"Barbados. He just up and left for Barbados."

She had to laugh. "Talk about a free spirit."

"An irresponsible one. He pisses me off so much sometimes. I think he does it on purpose."

"He's a lively one, all right." In truth, David and his personality had won her over completely. Even his ploy to make her cry over music, jolt her out of her numb complacency, now seemed more inspired than cruel.

"He's so caught up in himself, what pleases and interests him alone," Misha said.

They'd stopped in front of one of the closed shops. In the window, half a dozen white, porcelain, fortune cat statues were waving their respective paws up and down, up and down.

"How did Barbados come up for him?" she asked.

"He'd met this group of people in Europe, all with deep pockets and few responsibilities, and charmed them all. One of them was his host in Rome. Now one of them has a vacation villa rental in Barbados, some posh place, and there goes David, off on another adventure with someone else taking the responsibility and footing the bill."

"Well. Lucky him. It all sounds like a fantasy."

"But that's just it. He pursues fantasies. That's the purpose of life to him. Have fun, do whatever, anything goes, as long as you avoid getting arrested."

"Not getting arrested is a good thing," she offered, even as she realized Misha was in no mood for joking around. That was David's department.

"And now," Misha continued, "he's bragging about his plan to eat out in little dive Barbadian restaurants, the dodgier and cheaper the better. It's like a contest, to see how much of himself he can risk. It's so stupid."

"Why? Because he's throwing himself into the flavors and spirit of a foreign culture?"

"He's risking his health. It's irresponsible."

"It's not irresponsible, it's refreshing. I wish more people would be like him."

Misha said nothing. He was silent so long, she glanced over at him. He was staring at the waving cat statues, his jaw tight. "I'm sorry I'm not like my brother, Dena," he said quietly.

"Oh, Misha," she stammered. "That's not what I meant to say."

Misha offered her a brittle smile. "It's okay. Having a brother like him, I'm used to the comparison."

How could she, of all people, have forgotten the bite of sibling competition?

"I'm sorry," she tried again, and he gave a wave of his hand.

"Nothing to apologize about. Sometimes I let my brother get the best of me."

This she could understand, as well. "Siblings," she said. "Such minefields."

He chuckled as they turned to resume their walk. "You said it."

"And when one sibling overshadows the other," she said, thinking of Rebecca, her beauty, its effect on Misha.

"Oh boy, and how."

She thought they were on the same page until he spoke again.

"It can't have been easy for Rebecca."

Rebecca?

"What are you talking about?" she protested. "Why Rebecca?"

"Sure. Living in your shadow. I mean, come on. You've had a pretty dramatic medical condition for a year now. Whether you want that spotlight or not in your family, I'm sure you have it. And in the ballet world, you're a rank higher. The older sister never promoted— that had to have hurt."

"But… she's beautiful. And smart. She's almost got her college degree. And besides…" She could feel The Wrong Retort forming in her mind, tumbling out of her mouth before she could figure out a way to keep it bottled in. "She's the one you have a crush on."

Oh, God. Oh, God.

But Misha didn't seem to catch the gaffe behind her accusation, which was probably a very good thing.

"A crush on Rebecca?"

He looked confused, as though she'd told him a joke but omitted the punch line.

"The first time I met you," she said, unsure whether it was worse to go on or change the subject. Likely the former, but here she was, like a bull in a china shop, charging forward. "You couldn't stop looking at her."

"Well, yes, she's beautiful. And that was eight months ago. Your point?"

Oh, the awkwardness. "Just… never mind." She jammed her fists into her jacket pockets.

A full minute passed as they strode down Grant, no longer noticing the colorful scenery, the other pedestrians, but when Misha spoke again, it was as if no time had elapsed.

"…And how do you think it made *me* feel, watching my brother ogle you all night?"

"Why should you care?"

"Why should I *care?*" His outrage seemed to double. "Because, because…" He cut himself off abruptly, eyes fierce, a flush staining his cheeks.

So awkward. For both of them.

Siblings.

Inescapable minefields. Whether they were present or not.

Chapter 24 – Rebecca

Three days before Program III opened, Rebecca sustained her third minor injury for the season. She tweaked something in her lower back, near her sacroiliac joint, while holding a pose in a rehearsal for the ultra contemporary *Symmetries Unknown to Them*. Bodies behaved differently in contemporary ballets; you had to isolate each part, the ribcage shifting this way while hips and thighs faced that way, balance often off axis, all while moving very, very fast. The choreography in *Symmetries* was full of sharp, angular abstraction, abrupt starts and stops, avoiding poetry in the movement much in the way the atonal Schoenberg score avoided any melodic intention. "Mr. Reijin likes to challenge both his dancers and his audiences," the choreographer's stager told the dancers, by way of explanation.

She hated the ballet. So did her body.

After a torturous two hours of *Symmetries*, it was a relief to end the day with a rational, likeable *Songs* rehearsal. She dosed up on ibuprofen and headed to the rehearsal studio early, clutching a foam roller that she'd use to help break up knots and fascia along her overworked quads, gluts and IT bands. She found a quiet corner spot where she could avoid human interaction, and positioned herself over the roller.

The other dancers wandered in, some of them stopping by the

bulletin board, an offshoot from the main call board. A few notes dangled, stabbed through with white pushpins. Jimmy inspected them. "Rebecca and Boyd, did you see there are notes for you here?" he called out.

Rebecca looked up and Jimmy gestured to the board.

She rose slowly, wincing in pain, and hobbled over to the board. The other dozen dancers in the room fell silent as she opened the folded note addressed to her. Inside was only a rubber-stamped message that said "used goods" in red ink. She turned it over, mystified. Nothing else.

"What does it say?" Jimmy asked.

"There's no message. Just this stamp."

"What does the stamp say?"

"Used goods."

"Well, what does that mean?" Jimmy asked.

"I don't have a clue."

"What does it say?" someone called out.

"Used goods." Jimmy pulled the message from Rebecca and held it up to the group.

"What could that be referring to, Rebecca?" Steph, who wasn't even in *Songs* and should have left for her own rehearsal, asked.

Someone emitted a snicker, and Rebecca's eyes darted over to the source. Charlotte, who was suddenly very busy lacing up her pointe shoes, tucking in the ribbon bits with great care.

Oh, shit.

Ernesto, one of the dancers who'd witnessed Rebecca's sleazy hallway episode, caught on at the same time. "Used goods, again! Oh, girlfriend, ouch!" he said, and began to laugh.

It didn't take the others long to figure out the reference either. Romantic relationships and ugly breakups in the company were visible to all. Laughter started up like popcorn in a microwave: a few chuckles, more, more, and soon almost everyone was sputtering with laughter. It felt like high school-level cattiness all over again.

Jimmy cast Rebecca a worried glance. "I'm sorry. I think maybe I shouldn't have done that, but I'm not sure what the joke is."

"It's okay," she said to him, and smiled, to cover up the fact that inside she wanted to curl up and die.

Boyd strode toward the bulletin board. "I got a message, too. Mine's an envelope." Everyone fell silent as he opened it and pulled out a letter.

"What does yours say?" Charlotte called out.

"'To Mr. Boyd Buchannan,'" he read, "'As per our negotiations, we're pleased to offer you a two-year contract in the capacity of soloist...'"

"Aiiiieeee!" Ernesto's scream tore through the air. "You're moving up! Soloist with a new company!"

The DBDs in the room—five in all, which was interesting because three of them weren't even in *Songs*—shrieked and cheered, and everyone else joined in.

Ben, running the rehearsal, entered the room and looked around, perplexed. "Glad you're so animated. Let's get right to work, then. Those of you who don't belong here, out. Starting from the top, let me see the second cast lead couple up front. Places, please."

Rehearsal sucked, plain and simple. Toward Boyd, Rebecca maintained a stony silence, but everyone else chuckled with him over the note prank. Ernesto seemed only too happy to enlighten every last person, via whispers and chortles, about what had happened the previous week. The others' amusement carried a jeering edge. Yes, they were still a company of dancers who got along, but the favoritism directed Rebecca's way of late had not endeared her to the others.

Ben noticed. At the end of rehearsal, he gestured for Rebecca to stay. Once everyone else had left, he turned to her. "Okay, so tell me what the private joke is. This 'may I use you?' line—are they making fun of what I said to you last week? And this new thing, the 'used goods.'"

"Boyd found out about Anders," she said in a low voice. "About Carmel."

"Oh, Becca." Ben's voice was soft with sympathy. "That's not fair."

"I deserve this," she continued, hating herself enough to share the truth with Ben so that he, too, had a reason to find her despicable. "I cheated on Boyd. That weekend."

She dared herself to look up, take the punishment. He was frowning, as she'd expected.

"It's no excuse."

"I know. I'm sorry."

"No, not you. Him. Bringing something personal into the studio, into the workplace. Bad call. And what the hell did he think he was doing, parading that acceptance letter around?"

"Please don't tell Anders about any of this. He'd blame me."

"I'm not going to say a word to anyone. Let Boyd shoot his own foot."

Which he did. Anders, upon hearing Boyd's news, particularly the way he'd informed the others so publicly first, promptly pulled him from rehearsals for future programs, including *Songs of Yesterday*. He remained only in a peripheral capacity in one of Anders' ballets, in Program III.

And Boyd's hatred of Anders quadrupled.

Two nights into the Program III run, tensions exploded. Rebecca, following a *Symmetries* performance, had returned to the dressing room, but raised voices outside in the hallway made her pause and peer out. Ernesto spied her. "Drama brewing backstage," he said. "Anders is in one of his moods. Boyd's taking the bait. C'mon."

Rebecca's breath caught. Abandoning her cleanup efforts, she hurried down the hall after Ernesto. Another dancer joined them. "What started it?" he asked Ernesto.

"Anders started sniping at Boyd in the wings, every time he exited stage right."

"Mid-performance?"

"Yup. Criticizing his footwork, his jumps. He called him an ox."

"Oh, man. How did Boyd react?"

"Looked like he wanted to kill the man. He had no choice but to stand there and take it, though, while waiting for his next cue."

The three of them hurried up one level to the backstage area, where a dozen dancers had congregated, out of the way of the performers and crew but close enough to listen in. Charlotte and Steph were already there.

In the dimness, one of Ernesto's friends beckoned him over.

"What did we miss?" Ernesto whispered.

"Boyd told Anders 'fuck you' a split-second before he leapt back onstage," he whispered back. "Anders just about had a coronary. Now we're all waiting for when Boyd has to come back."

They didn't have to wait long. Thirty seconds later, the four-member male ensemble came offstage, huffing, panting, wiping sweat off their faces. Anders stepped right up to Boyd, leaning into his face like a drill sergeant.

"Fuck you? You tell your artistic director 'fuck you'? How dare you speak to me that way!" His voice had risen to a shout; everyone backstage could hear, although no one in the audience could hear it over the music. "And out there, your sloppy execution. I will not have

298

you crucifying my choreography in this way. Those are *my* steps. You are damaging my property."

"Your property?" Boyd burst out. "I'm messing with *your* property. Oh, that's rich."

Anders scowled at Boyd. "What are you going on about?"

Time seemed to slow as Boyd's gaze swung out, past Charlotte, Steph, Ernesto, the other dancers, to focus on her, standing in the periphery, but clearly not peripheral enough. His eyes burned into her before he turned back to Anders. "You're a thief, that's what. You took what wasn't yours to take."

"*What?*"

Boyd spoke more slowly, his words loud and deliberate. "You took what did not belong to you. What belonged to *me.*"

Boyd looked over at Rebecca again. Anders followed the direction of Boyd's gaze. He stared at Rebecca, uncomprehending, but an instant later, his eyes narrowed with understanding.

Oh, no. Not this.

Anders turned back to Boyd. "Now you listen here—" he began, but Boyd cut him off.

"I don't have to listen to another word from you," Boyd said. "You know what? I'm out of here." He strode to the edge of the wings again, but instead of awaiting his cue, he took a half-dozen steps onstage, right in the middle of the lead couple's pas de deux, and assumed a preparatory pose, a full thirty-two counts early. He stood there, all confidence and smiles, gallant and regal, as if it were all part of the ballet.

She wouldn't have thought this kind of unhinged drama could take place during a professional performance. It was as unprecedented and agonizing to watch as a striptease by a hooker during a church service. Even Anders, for once, seemed to be at a complete loss for words.

Boyd turned his head, several counts before the corps men's actual entrance, with a grand, affected, *come join me, lads!* arm gesture to the three other dancers waiting. His eyes, settling on Anders' aghast face, mocked him.

Come get me, you bastard, the look said. *Come out here and show me who's boss, and ruin your ballet in the process.* He stood there in his green unitard costume, the lighting onstage having turned a dusky rose, making the green glow, as though it, and Boyd, were radioactive.

The dancers backstage pressed closer, watching in horrified fascination. The DBDs were gasping and laughing. "I love you, Boyd," Charlotte cried from her place in the wings, one section upstage from Anders. "You show him what you're made of!"

This shocked Rebecca further. Surely Charlotte knew Anders was nearby, and could hear her, even if the audience couldn't. Did she care that little?

Steph was more prudent. She stood further back, hand over mouth, shaking with laughter, with shock. More dancers crowded the wings to watch what was going on. Rick, the stage manager, shouted for them to back off, do not interrupt the show or the dancers or the crew.

The other corps men leapt on for their cued entrance, and Boyd continued on with them, as if nothing were awry. Anders moved away from the wings. Rebecca observed his expression fearfully. It was neutral, as if he'd gone beyond rage and now it was simply a matter of deciding on one of the many ways in which he might dismember Boyd. He walked over to Rick and the glowing control panel, exchanged a few words, and left the backstage area without a backward glance.

She remained backstage, even as the rest of the gawking crowd dispersed, now that the drama was over. Charlotte, too, stayed behind. When the ballet ended, the curtain came down, the dancers assembling themselves for curtain call. After two sets of bows and solo bows for the leads, the curtain dropped for the last time. The backstage work lights came on, the buzz of audience members' conversations grew louder, and now Boyd didn't look quite so confident.

Ben approached him. "Anders would like to speak with you in his annex office upstairs."

"I don't care what he says." Boyd raised his chin a notch. "I don't regret it."

"Save it for him, my friend," Ben said. "That's between you and your boss."

The brave look faded.

Charlotte glanced over at Rebecca. She was beyond upset, her eyes having taken on a wild look. "I'll get even with you for this, you bitch," she said in a low voice.

"Charlotte?" Ben called out.

She jumped, and swung around.

"Anders would like to speak to you, as well." He looked straight at Charlotte and avoided eye contact with Rebecca. Which scared her.

"Ben?" Rebecca asked in a voice gone wobbly.

"Get out of here. Finish up downstairs and leave." Ben motioned in the direction of the dressing rooms. "This isn't about you."

Of course it was about her.

Fifteen minutes later, makeup removed, she hunted down Ben and found him in the hallway. "I need to speak with Anders," she told him.

His short gold hair looked rumpled, like he'd run his hands through it in frustration. But his voice was as calm as ever. "He's in a state, Becca. I'd let him cool off. Tomorrow would be better."

"No. It'll be worse if I don't get in there right now."

Ben paused to consider this. "Fine. But I'll go in there with you."

"That's not necessary."

"Rebecca." He sounded harsher now. "My way or no way."

"Okay. I'm sorry, Ben. I'm sorry."

Another sigh, this one more resigned. "Let's get it over with," he said.

Together they took the elevator up, walked down the hallway that led to the annex office Anders used when at the theater. Rick, the stage manager, was leaving the room. He caught Ben's gaze and rolled his eyes, a *watch it, he's still toxic* alert.

Ben knocked, called out. Anders told him to come in. Rebecca crept in behind him, moving forward as Ben remained by the door.

Anders looked calm, leafing through papers that cluttered the desk, but she knew him. His body radiated rage.

"What the hell do you want?" he barked out finally, and she jumped out of nervousness.

"Anders," she tried. "I'm so sorry."

"You told him. You stupid, fucking little twat."

"Anders," Ben warned, standing by the door.

Anders glared at him. "Fuck you. Are you forgetting who's in charge here? Is this whole fucking company forgetting?"

Ben didn't reply. Rebecca stood frozen, afraid to move.

"Get the hell out of here," Anders shouted at Ben.

"No."

Anders looked incredulous. "No? *No?*"

"No."

"Who are you trying to protect?"

It sounded like an accusation. A threat.

"Both of you," Ben said.

A charged, silent exchange passed between them. A moment later Anders sighed and turned back to Rebecca, expression still murderous but more controlled.

"I'm sorry," she began again. "It slipped out during an argument about something else."

The muscles in his jaw ticked. "This is why an artistic director does not get involved with his dancers. This is precisely why. Do you think I need this shit? This pathetic waste of time and energy?"

She felt six inches tall. "I'm sorry, Anders. It won't happen again."

"Oh, you can be damned sure of that," he said in a cold voice.

Terrifying to ponder just what that meant. Severing all ties with her? Pulling her from *Songs* or *Arpeggio?* Firing her?

He shifted his focus to the papers on his desk. "Get out of here and leave me to my work," he said. "Both of you. Get the hell out."

Ben signaled her with his eyes.

Time to get out. Before worse happened.

Curtis taught company class the next morning. Rebecca found herself clinging to Dena's company and support. Dena, who'd been aghast to hear about the drama the night before, now seemed matter of fact about it. "This place is a drama factory," she said as she tucked her feet into her pointe shoes. "Next week, it'll be something else."

To Rebecca's relief, no one seemed to be singling her out today. They were all too preoccupied by what had happened. No Boyd today, of course. He'd been fired. Shockingly, Charlotte had been fired, as well.

"He can't do that!" Rebecca heard Steph say to the remaining DBDs in a low, outraged voice. "What did she do? Since when can you get fired for cheering? She's going to fight it, of course. Her dad's a lawyer. And we have union protection."

"That bastard, Gunst."

"This is war," Steph warned. "Are we agreed?"

"Yes!"

"We'll fight back," Steph said. "Somehow."

The conversation ceased when they realized Rebecca was listening in. Rebecca ignored their glares and turned to Dena.

"Having fun this morning, sis?"

Dena chuckled. "Actually, yeah. I'm well rested. How about you?"

"Pretty un-rested."

"Too bad!" Dena said cheerfully.

Anders called an all-company meeting after class. He let the group know, in no uncertain terms, that the previous night's drama had been an egregious display of misconduct, and if anyone ever tried that again, they'd meet the same fates of the others. He didn't look at Rebecca once. Then again, he hadn't fired her.

No one was meeting his eye in a defiant fashion. Not one DBD.

He called for Steph to follow him to his office. She looked terrified. Rebecca wondered if it meant Steph would be punished, too. But Steph arrived for the next rehearsal, ten minutes late, with a private smile on her face. And at five o'clock, when the next day's rehearsal lists were posted on the board, there was Steph's name, slated to rehearse a soloist role for Program IV. A role much like what Rebecca was doing in *Arpeggio*.

Anders Gunst was unknowable indeed.

Chapter 25 – Dena

Arpeggio rehearsal was set to begin, but the studio still seemed empty. Lexie looked around in bemusement. "Fine, this was only a second-cast rehearsal, but where are the others in your cast?" he asked the half-dozen dancers gathered, inclining his head toward the hallway to see if the *clop-clop* of pointe shoe-clad feet on the hallway's linoleum signaled an imminent arrival. No go. The steps receded, another dancer bound for another rehearsal.

Dena stood at the barre, where she'd développéd her leg to the side, taking her heel in hand in order to pull the leg closer against her upper torso. She exchanged shrugs with Rebecca, seated nearby, doing ankle stabilization exercises with a neon orange Theraband.

Sylvie had not yet arrived. Most of the understudies were missing, as was Lana's partner. "I think the clock on the wall is fast," Jimmy offered as Nicholas joined them, peeling off his bulky sweatpants in favor of the torn black cutoff tights beneath.

"Well, I'm ready to begin," Lexie said. "So's Johann." He gestured to the accompanist, already seated behind the piano, softly playing a Chopin mazurka to himself.

"We can still run it," Lana said, spreading her arms, smiling. "You've got *us*. The ones who matter. "

Rebecca rose to her feet. "Oh, *let's*. Lexie, let's run it with Dena

305

in Sylvie's place. She knows the part inside and out. That gives you five out of six of us."

Dena's heart gave a wild leap. She watched Lexie's face as he pondered this.

"You know what? I like the idea," he said, and looked over at her. "Dena, the early bird gets the worm, and you're overdue for a worm. Feel like giving it a shot?"

"Yes, I'd love it!"

"Then let's start. Maybe hearing the music will light a fire under the other dancers' butts."

Dena scurried into place, alongside Nicholas in the downstage right corner marked off on the floor. He reached over and gave her hand a squeeze. "Yay," he stage-whispered. "I get to dance again with my favorite partner."

They'd been having a little fun lately, playing around with partnering after rehearsal and during breaks. The first time had been when Sylvie's understudy had asked Dena to demonstrate a tricky eight-count passage for her. Dena had shown her, continuing along afterward out of habit. To her surprise, when it came time for a partner to pivot her around in a promenade, she felt Nicholas's hands on her waist. "Go for it," he told her from behind. The next sixteen counts flowed out automatically, from the overhead leap to the partnered pirouette that completed the passage. Nicholas's hands spun her, aided by the clean execution of her own pirouette turn. One rotation, two, three, four revolutions, effortless and precise.

"Wow, that was great!" Sylvie's understudy had cried, and the others watching had laughed and clapped.

So much fun, she and Nicholas had both agreed. Since then, they'd made it a point to practice a partnered lift or two every day. Fun, yes, but for her, a whole lot more.

"Let's take it from the opening," Lexie called out now.

For five minutes the group of them danced. Dena felt no performance anxiety; this was just for Lexie and the understudies, coming in one by one. Lana's partner ran into the room, dropped his dance bag at the door and leapt right into action, which made them all laugh. Sylvie hurried in and tried to do the same, but Lexie stopped her.

"Stay. We're letting Dena do it this time," he told her.

Sylvie scowled, gave her dance bag a theatrical shove with her foot, but remained there, arms crossed, watching.

Lexie allowed the group of them to dance the section to its end. They were all laughing by the end, Rebecca and Nicholas telling Dena she'd been right on the mark the whole time. Dena glanced guiltily at the still frowning Sylvie. Lexie noticed her too.

"Next time get here on time," he told Sylvie.

"I had a good reason," she shrilled. "Wardrobe needed me for a fitting and they were slow!"

"Well, you're here now, so get into place and let's move on. All right, everyone. Let's jump forward to the final ensemble section."

Just before they recommenced, with Dena now tucked in the back, Salim, Lucinda's assistant in public relations, appeared at the door. "Someone told me I might find Dena Lindgren here?" he called out, looking around.

All eyes swung to her. "Uh-oh," said Jimmy. "What'd you do?"

Everyone laughed. Everyone except her and Rebecca.

The question echoed in her head as she accompanied Salim to the administrative level, the brisk, intimidating, professionally dressed side of the WCBT. Lucinda, on the phone in her office, acknowledged Dena with a nod, gesturing to the chair in front of her desk. Dena took a seat and waited as Lucinda finished her call.

"So," she said, a second after hanging up. "What's going on,

Dena?" She gazed at Dena pointedly over the frames of her reading glasses.

"What do you mean?" Dena stammered, thinking of Nicholas, partnering up with him when she was neither an assigned dancer nor an understudy. She must have violated some rule in the company handbook.

"Did you start the rumor that you were Natalie Portman's double in *Black Swan?*"

"No!" Her tumbling thoughts rearranged themselves to accommodate this new, more understandable situation. "Why would I? I look nothing like Natalie Portman. Or Sarah Lane."

"No kidding. Only an idiot would be taken in by the rumor."

"I know."

"Well, there you have it. People are idiots." Lucinda glanced down at her notes. "So. It has come to my attention that, seemingly overnight, you're being mentioned all over the place. On the company website, clicks on your bio and your photo have gone through the roof, over a hundred a day, exceeding any of the other dancers. Even Javier and Katrina. What brought it on?"

Elation bubbled up, amid her unease. Tatum had told her to be patient, that noticeable results would follow, and they had. "I've just gotten more active in social media," Dena said. "I have a blog. A new Twitter and Instagram account."

"Yes, I know. And a Facebook fan page. And someone wrote an article about you that's being shared everywhere and striking a sentimental chord in people's hearts." She pointed to an adjacent stack of photocopies and letters. "Many of those people are inquiring about you now. Wanting to know why they haven't seen you perform this year. Wanting to know how soon they can."

Dena clenched and unclenched the fabric of the shorts she'd thrown on over her leotard and tights, back in the rehearsal studio.

"I'm sorry if that's become a nuisance."

"And now everyone knows you had a brain tumor."

Her hands stopped their clenching. Was she supposed to apologize over this as well? And if so, was the apology supposed to be for having had the acoustic neuroma, or letting on to such an unpretty anomaly?

"But that's the truth," she said in a small voice.

"Well, Katrina's got hemorrhoids that won't go away. That's the truth as well. Shall we blast that out to the press?"

"No."

Lucinda stabbed a finger at her. "And that fact does not leave this room. Word of it leaks out, you'll have me to answer to, young lady."

"Of course not. I mean, yes. Point taken." The hands resumed their clenching.

Lucinda turned away from Dena and studied her computer screen. She clicked, scanned the screen and sighed. Clicked, scanned and sighed. Dena realized she was looking over Dena's Google hits, now numbering over 45,000. A month earlier there had been 1900.

"I don't like it," Lucinda muttered to herself.

A wave of defensiveness rose in Dena. "Is there a problem?" she asked. "I'm being careful not to step on any toes here. I'm not speaking against the company or its administrators. But something difficult has happened to me, and if others are taking comfort from hearing about my struggle and I feel less alone, getting their support, what's the conflict?" She forced herself to meet Lucinda's eyes. Adrenaline had sent her heart banging wildly in her chest, like a loose shutter in a storm. She'd never talked back to an administrator in this way before.

Lucinda eyed her carefully before speaking.

"You have an online presence that's quite remarkable, given your short time in promoting it. Just be aware that I'm watching. And I'm watching how others react to you. That's my job. It's my job to protect you, and this company."

"Okay," she managed.

Lucinda handed her a printout on social media etiquette, followed by a list of "do not mention" items. She gave Dena another long, scrutinizing look, which intimidated her, which, most likely, had been its purpose. She couldn't wait to rant about all this to Tatum.

"Do we understand each other?" Lucinda asked finally.

On her lap, Dena's fingers curled into fists, but she smiled at Lucinda. "Yes."

"Fine. Good to hear."

She realized later, working off some of her frustration in the fitness room, that she couldn't say a word of this to Tatum. She'd pounce on it gleefully; she'd say to Dena, "Aha, do you see what I mean? They want you to hide what's wrong and they expect you to hide any evidence of what's less than perfect. They don't care about you, the person, they care about the illusion of perfection. And I think we need to shout that out to the world."

No. Best left unsaid, unshared. That was the company way.

Misha's call came the following Monday afternoon. "Dena," he said in a soft voice. "Oh, Deen. I'm so glad you picked up." It was such a departure from his usual breezy greeting, it shot an electric jolt through her. A sexy voice; a bedroom voice.

Only, not. Instead, a voice in shock, in the aftermath of cataclysmic news.

It was about David. David, on a motorcycle in Barbados, traveling down a highway. He'd been cut off by a pickup truck and flung into a ditch. Broken bones, internal bleeding. In surgery now, hovering between life and death.

She clutched at the phone, incapable of saying anything but a strained "no, no."

"I'm going out there," Misha said. "I'm flying out tonight, on the red-eye."

"Where are you right now?"

"Moss Beach."

"I'm coming out. I'll drive you to the airport tonight." She knew just how deeply shaken Misha was because he didn't protest.

"Thank you. That would be great, Deen."

Misha was on the phone when she arrived at his home an hour later. He opened the front door with his free hand, held out his arm. She fell against him and his arm went around her tightly, staying there. The contact warmed her, steadied her. "Thank you," he whispered to her during a pause in his phone conversation, and she sensed he felt the same.

He remained on the phone, with someone named Martine, who appeared to be David's girlfriend as well as the one paying for the Barbados vacation villa rental. Misha was translating medical terms for her. "...A ruptured viscus means they know some internal organ has been damaged and is bleeding," he told her. And, later, "...When you heard someone say he was 'bleeding out,' it meant he was bleeding internally. But it's okay, Martine. It sounds like they got him right into surgery, that's the crucial thing."

After the call, he phoned his mother and sister, giving them the information he knew. No, he told his mother, he wasn't sure if David had taken his advice to buy health insurance.

Misha studied Dena bleakly after he hung up. "The insurance thing. That was one of our bigger arguments. I told him he needed it, if only for situations exactly like this, and he laughed at me. Told me I took life too seriously and needed to lighten up."

His last words hit her like a slap. Hadn't she, herself, defended David's flighty hedonism, even hinted that she wished more people could be like that? Words that had wounded Misha.

"Maybe he took your advice anyway," she said faintly.

"Maybe."

Martine called Misha back once the surgery was over. The verdict: it was the spleen David had ruptured, which they'd removed. He'd sustained a fractured femur which the team had stabilized with pins; they'd work more on that once David's condition had stabilized. He was in the ICU, condition not yet stable.

The time arrived for them to leave for the airport. Dena insisted on driving so Misha could take and make calls. A good choice: bad news came while they were on the road. David's blood pressure had dropped and more internal bleeding was suspected. He'd gone back into surgery. Misha maintained a confident tone as he told Martine that this sometimes happened. A compromised blood vessel could have constricted, closed off during surgery, or a clip on a bleeding vessel could have fallen off, both resulting in the new bleeding. Being in surgery again meant they were on it and taking care of him, he assured her. But when he hung up, five minutes later, Dena could feel his sense of helplessness.

The tiniest grace: Martine had found papers in David's bags, back at the villa. David had gotten the insurance.

At the airport she insisted on parking and going in with Misha. Once he'd gotten his boarding pass, she excused herself to use the restroom; her left eye was taking on that hated grating, scratched feeling. She administered a heavy dose of the eyedrops, a viscous, gloomy liquid that blurred her vision for several seconds. She resented this dependence on the drops, as she did every difficult aspect of her new, compromised life.

But she had her life.

She clutched at the washbasin in front of her, regarding her blurred self in the mirror.

David might die. During her dark, doubting period in January, she'd believed that to not dance would be like a death. She'd been wrong. A death was a death. Not dancing still gave you your life. How luxurious, to weep over your life ending because your ability to be a professional ballet dancer might be ending. How humbling, to look at yourself and see the trite nature of your problem against the greater backdrop of life and death.

David couldn't die. He was too full of life. She blinked away the last of the eyedrop blur, drew a steadying breath and went back out to Misha.

She found him standing nearby, gazing at the pedestrian traffic around him. His fatigue and vulnerability were evident now, his hair mussed, his shoulders sagging. She touched his arm and he swung around to face her. The bewildered expression on his face cut right through to her heart. "He'll be fine," she said, arms going around him. "I just know it."

He buried his head in the crook of her neck, like a child. She stroked his shoulders, his neck, her fingers coming to rest at the nape of his neck, just below his hairline. His skin felt warm, silky, vital. They remained like that, meshed together, an intimacy both unfamiliar and instantly knowable, until finally Misha raised his head, met her eyes.

"I love my brother so much. Guys don't say things like that enough. Not until it's too late." He hesitated. "Oh God," he said in a choked voice, "if he—"

"Misha," she cut in. "This is David we're talking about. He's not going to give up without a fight. He's not going to let either of you off the hook so easily." She gave him a little shake for good measure, which made a wan smile break through his face.

His phone rang. Misha stepped back and fumbled to answer the call. Judging from his serious expression as he spoke, terse little "yeah"s and "okay"s, it was Martine. He hung up two minutes later, looking both strained and relieved. "He's out of surgery," he said. "The medical team found the source of bleeding and it's been stopped. Now we just wait, pray that he stabilizes."

"But that sounds good. Right?"

He nodded. "Good as we can hope for."

They held hands as they walked toward the security checkpoint. Clutched hands was a better description. Like two children walking through the dark forest, understanding they would be safe as long as they were together. As they approached the checkpoint, their steps slowed.

It was time to say goodbye. Another tight hug, one from which he seemed reluctant to release her, or was it that she couldn't let go? They pulled apart slightly. Her hand still rested on his hips, fingers looped into the belt-holes of his jeans. He reached over and cradled her face in his hands, like the time he'd studied the tarsorrhaphy and her blink reflex. Only this time, there was more than just scientific curiosity in his eyes. His thumbs softly caressed her cheeks. For a long moment neither of them spoke.

What could be said, after all? Break a leg? Bon voyage? Tell David I say hi?

A shadow flitted across his eyes, an instant of dread and uncertainty she could feel coming from him. Her heart swelled, contracted.

"I love you," she heard herself say, and before she could ponder the impact of the words—where had they *come* from?—his gaze had softened, eyes never leaving her face.

"I love you too."

They stared at each other, mute, until the noisy squawk of an airport announcement broke the trance. Over Misha's shoulder she spied a large group of people, a busload, from the looks of it, making a determined beeline for the security checkpoint. "Go," she said, gesturing to them. "Get in line before they do."

He picked up his carry-on bag, checked for his boarding pass and passport, and stepped into line just in time, seconds before the mass of people descended, filling the air with the buzz of conversation. She waited, glancing over the heads of the people who now obscured her view of Misha, until he reappeared a moment later, from the far right corner. He, too, was searching for her. She was able to catch his eye one last time, offer one last frantic wave. No chance for more words, but that was okay. The important ones had been said.

Chapter 26 - Rebecca

The new dressing room wasn't all that bad, Rebecca decided. It was oddly shaped, with one of the dressing tables angled off on its own, cutting off the natural flow of communication and camaraderie that normally passed between dressing roommates. Before Rebecca's move, the space had been vacant, used for storage. "Are you sure you want that space?" April had asked her when she'd made her request known. "You might feel isolated."

Protected was more like it. Away from the DBDs, and the dozen other dancers who'd blamed her, without having (or apparently needing) proof of any sort, for Boyd's and Charlotte's dismissals. She wouldn't have guessed the two of them had had so many friends in the company, but one thing was certain: she herself had few remaining friends. She shared the new dressing room with the youngest corps dancers, all of whom seemed a little afraid of her and jumped every time she asked for their help in hooking up her bodice from behind.

Dena had dropped by before the night's big performance to offer her support. They exchanged small talk as Rebecca finished applying her Pan-Cake foundation and started in on her eyes. A heating pad nestled against her still-tweaked lower back, and two ice packs tented over an ankle giving her trouble. Nothing a double dose of ibuprofen couldn't control, which would also help reduce the hip pain.

"Are you nervous?" Dena asked, as Rebecca searched her makeup case for new false eyelashes.

She considered this as she fished out the packet of eyelashes. "In a way. Knowing you and Mom will be out in the audience, it feels kind of weird. And okay, yes, I'm nervous about *Arpeggio* going right."

Anders had approved her casting in *Arpeggio*. She'd played the game with him right, after all. Two weeks earlier, she'd been so afraid she'd blown it, but here she was, prepping for her cast's opening night, just like she'd done those five years back. She and Dena, side by side at their dressing tables, scared yet so excited, thrilled to be dancing together as sisters.

She felt that sisterhood keenly once again. Ever since the night Dena had come into her room, three nights earlier, reaching over to touch her shoulder to wake her. Dena had been crying, saying something about how siblings had so much power over you, the capacity to ruin things, and yet, they were the most precious people in your life, and now Misha's brother might *die*, and oh, Becca, I love you and I'm so sorry I've taken you for granted. Dena was sobbing by the end, drawing in ragged breaths between sentences. Rebecca, now fully awake, had pulled herself up to sitting, turned on the bedside light, and made Dena tell her everything about what was going on with Misha's brother.

They stayed up together, waiting for news from Misha, although both of them fell asleep finally, to be woken up when Dena's phone rang out at six-thirty the next morning. David had made it through the night, Misha reported, and while still in critical condition in the ICU, he was stable. Since that call, Dena had stayed in constant contact with Misha via phone and email, as David's condition improved, slowly but surely. Rebecca could feel the intensity of Dena's connection to Misha, always there, the way her whole body seemed to curl around the phone when they talked, a sort of human bubble of protection and support.

Rebecca sized up Dena's reflection. She was wearing a sleek gold and black dress, all prepared to be an audience member that night. Her face was unsmiling. She did that a lot now, because if both sides of her face were expressionless they looked more symmetrical. It made Rebecca sad though, to see this unsmiling Dena, even as she understood it didn't always reflect her emotions.

"You'll do great tonight," Dena told her.

"I'm going to give it my best." She pressed the glued lashes into place.

"My sister, the soloist," Dena said.

Rebecca grimaced. "Oh, stop. It's just for this ballet. We both know that."

"No, we don't. Lana's promotion created an open spot for a soloist. Someone will get it."

She tried to ignore the frisson of hope that sprang up at Dena's words. "Deen. I'm too senior. My body's too used up. That's why this ballet means so much to me." She picked up an eyebrow pencil and studied it as she spoke.

"I don't know if I can explain, but there's this sense of pure sweetness in dancing this, against the bigger reality of how things really are. The bigger thing's going to win. The inevitability of it isn't something I can negotiate, or bully, or take Advil to alleviate. Dancing *Arpeggio* is like this precious gift that landed on my lap by mistake, and for a few fleeting onstage hours, I get to keep it. It's a dream come true. But the dream is temporary."

She looked up from the eyebrow pencil. She could see Dena trying to keep her expression neutral, but she couldn't stop her chest from heaving, nor the trail of tears leaking down the right side of her face.

"Oh, Dena, I'm so sorry. I didn't mean to rub it in—" she began, but Dena cut her off with a raised hand.

"It's okay. This is your time. It's totally your turn. And I couldn't be happier for you. Really."

Their eyes met in the mirror. "I wish, more than anything," Rebecca said softly, "that you could be performing it with me. If there was any way I could make it happen, any mountain I could move, I'd do it."

"I know you would. And I love you for that, sis." Dena lowered her head and swiped at the tears. When she looked back up, both sides were impassive once again. "But let's stick to reality. And I'll just say this. Enjoy the hell out of *Arpeggio*, Becca. Enjoy it for the both of us."

"I will," Rebecca promised.

During the cast's warm-up time onstage at intermission, Jimmy did his customary set of 100 push-ups, while Sylvie practiced pirouettes and Nicholas jogged the periphery of the stage. Lana and her partner ran through one of their passages, using fingers and hand gestures for the turns and lifts so as to spare their bodies the extra work. Rebecca stopped her own warm-up to observe the others. How beautiful and full of energy they all were. Brimming with optimism, and why shouldn't they be? They all had a staggering talent, the best of the best, and even at the elite level, these were the ones being noticed, getting promoted. None of them were immune to physical pain, of course. Nicholas had ongoing rotator cuff issues, and for Sylvie, it was her hip and periodic tendonitis. Lana had been wincing the past few days, rubbing her hamstring, keeping it warm now with a heat pack and double leg warmers over the tender spot.

A surprising surge of affection for all of them came over Rebecca. What incredible, resilient creatures dancers were. What tortured, driven, stubborn, exhausted marvels.

Arpeggio was a neoclassical ballet, which meant it was plotless, somewhat abstract, although the choreography adhered to classical conventions. Sets were minimalist. *Arpeggio* utilized a neutral backdrop that would change colors via lighting gels, from mango to turquoise and later, sunset pink. Three oversized panels hung from the rigging, like oversized portraits, textured abstracts in charcoal and gold. The colors resurfaced in the women's costumes, a glittery gold, ivory and crimson bodice with transparent straps and a multilayered chiffon skirt featuring the same colors as the backdrop hues.

Curtain. Orchestra. Lights. Dancers go.

Sylvie and Nicholas opened the ballet with a quick-moving pas de deux, repeating a sequence that the other couples would join in on. All Rebecca could see was how Sylvie compared to Dena in the role. Dena with her signature turbocharged movements, her playfulness, her astonishing range of moods and colors. She visualized Dena, not Sylvie, there with Nicholas, whose finesse and control in jumps and turns produced sighs of satisfaction from the audience.

Jimmy, standing by her side in the upstage left wing, turned to her. "Just about ready to kick some *Arpeggio* ass?"

Focus, she told herself. Not focus on how she wished things were, but how they actually were. This fleeting moment, this treasure of a role.

Enjoy it for the both of us, sis.

She smiled at Jimmy, loving his youthful energy, his talent, his sweet, likeable face, his incurable optimism. Leaning over, she planted a kiss on his cheek. "Ready."

They leapt into the light and activity onstage for the ensemble vignette. Four minutes later they returned backstage, panting, while Lana and her partner danced the second vignette. She and Jimmy took the center in the third. It wasn't her best night of dancing ever; her back pain was still dogging her and she had to fight for sufficient energy on the brisk, Balanchine-esque passages with their lightning quick footwork and rapid shifts from one movement to the next. But, as in Arabian Dance, Jimmy's support and enthusiasm gave her the push needed for them to finish strong. In a later vignette, Lana charmed audience and her three male suitors with her insouciance and spirited dancing. An all-male vignette followed, an all-female one after that. In the penultimate movement, Sylvie and Nicholas returned for a slower, more tender pas de deux, reaching, supporting and intertwining. The added poignancy came, no surprise, from the now-familiar aching thought.

Dena should have been the one dancing.

By the ballet's end, after a final ensemble vignette, both Rebecca's body and mind were spent. The curtain call, with its separate bows for each couple, was always a thrill, but tonight it seemed bittersweet, which she couldn't understand. This wasn't farewell, she reminded herself. It was only the first performance of a six-show run, three of which belonged to her.

Meeting her mother and Dena after the show, she saw that Dena, too, looked drained. "Thanks for toughing it out," she murmured to Dena, giving her hand a squeeze. "I know it couldn't have been easy."

"No, it was worth it. You looked great. You all did."

Isabelle, unlike her daughters, was full of energy. Her eyes sparkled; she'd spent the past week nursing Dan through a bout of ill health, and was happy to be back in the city for the night. She seemed disappointed to hear that neither of them wanted to extend the night's excitement by going out for a cocktail, a late meal. "Oh, you two are no fun," she protested, mock-pouting.

It was tiring having such a young-acting, vivacious mother. The comment "she could be your sister!" used to fill Rebecca with pride. Tonight, the thought only irritated her.

"How about thinking of Dena's needs for a change, Mom?" she

said. "Late nights and crowds and noise are difficult for her."

Even as the rebuke came out, it appalled her. What had possessed her to sound so harsh and critical? She made an effort to soften her words. "I care about her, that's all. About how she's feeling."

But the second comment had no impact. Isabelle's face had gone slack with hurt.

"Think about my daughters' needs for a change?" Isabelle repeated. "Is that how you see me and my life, Rebecca, that it's been all about me?"

Before she could find the right reply, she heard Anders' voice.

"Why the long face on such a beautiful woman?"

The three of them turned to see him approaching, smiling at Isabelle.

Isabelle tried to smile back. "My eldest is chastising me for my insensitivity. These two want to rest and I want to play. Shameless behavior for a mother, I now see."

"Hardly shameless," he said with a frown he managed to direct to Rebecca, even as his eyes never left Isabelle's. "Exemplary. I wish all women over forty would take a look at you, how beautiful and full of energy you continue to be, year after year."

Isabelle's shoulders relaxed. "That's very sweet of you to say," she told Anders, who smiled back at her.

It was a special kind of horrible to watch the two of them interact, regarding each other so intensely, like no one else in the room mattered. If she'd found her mother's effervescent spirits difficult to be around a minute earlier, that was nothing compared to this.

Dear God, was she jealous of her mother? Vying with her for the warmth of Anders' gaze?

"And I propose an easy solution," Anders was saying to Isabelle. "They rest, you play. Why don't you join me and my group? I've got a table over at L'Orange."

This was getting worse and worse.

The sparkle had returned to Isabelle's eyes. "Thank you," she said. "I would enjoy that."

"Good. So will I."

He glanced over at Rebecca, his brow knitted with reproof. "You. Go home. Rest up. Good job tonight, by the way."

Without waiting for a reply from Rebecca, Anders turned back to Isabelle to discuss where to find him in twenty minutes' time.

"Becca?" Dena reached over and touched her arm. "Let's go have dinner by ourselves back at the apartment. I'll make it while you give yourself a hot soak. You don't need that." She gestured toward Isabelle and Anders, still talking. "Any of that."

Because now that Dena knew the story behind her and Anders, she could see everything.

"Mom's always been that way," Dena said in a low voice. "You've just never noticed before."

Beautiful, ageless, energetic, indomitable Isabelle Lindgren. When their parents had divorced, years back, Rebecca had been so sure their father had been the villain, Isabelle the hapless victim. But the woman now laughing and chatting with Anders was no victim. Dena had known that about their mother all along.

Going to bed at a reasonable hour spared her the experience of chatting with her mother when she returned to the apartment well past midnight, humming a little tune to herself. The following morning, Rebecca avoided her by leaving early for the studio. Isabelle returned to Los Gatos but called and left Rebecca a message, enthusing about what a wonderful time she'd had, and for her to call back so they could talk about it more.

Like hell, Rebecca thought. She didn't need her mother making her feel any older or more run down.

After a Saturday matinee performance, only one more *Arpeggio* remained for their cast. Late morning on Tuesday, Lana pulled Rebecca aside. She looked anxious.

"You didn't hear this from me, okay?" she murmured. "But Sylvie's acting sick. Like she might not be able to perform tonight. Only, she wants to, so she's trying to hide it." She glanced around nervously. "I gotta run. I just thought you should know."

Rebecca studied Lana's retreating form in confusion, but a moment later the implications exploded in her mind.

She watched Sylvie through the day after that, who, sure enough, seemed off. Most dancers strove to hide their infirmity; it was far more important to perform than to be in perfect health. The day's last rehearsal had the corps and soloists working together, so Rebecca was able to watch her more closely. Sylvie had grown more sluggish, marking steps instead of dancing full out whenever possible. Through the rehearsal, her pallor worsened. She had to excuse herself twice to use the bathroom. During one of the breaks, Rebecca overheard Javier tell one of the other principals that Anders had an off-site function that night and that Ben would be in charge during the performance.

She couldn't believe her luck. It was as if all the Fates had converged to decree that this thing should happen.

Sylvie returned from the bathroom and the rehearsal continued, but once the rehearsal ended, she was off again. A moment later, Rebecca followed her out into the hallway. Nicholas stood waiting outside the ladies' room for Sylvie. He looked concerned.

She liked Nicholas. He was a good guy, one of the higher-ranked dancers who still "saw" the corps dancers, who would tell the women they looked nice on the days they did indeed look nice, who wished people happy birthday and commiserated with someone having a tough day. She'd seen how he'd gone out of his way to be kind to Dena.

Insecurity washed over her. The idea was too far-fetched. Even if Nicholas agreed to the plan, the whole thing would most likely either fizzle out or get her into trouble.

It didn't matter. She had to try.

She drew a deep breath and strode over to Nicholas. "Can I have a word with you?"

Nicholas frowned, but at her softer "please, just for a second?" he nodded and followed her twenty feet down the hallway.

"What is it?" he asked, glancing back at the restroom door.

"Sylvie's sick."

His smile seemed both friendly and wary. "She's just a little under the weather. We think maybe it's something she ate last night. But she'll be fine for tonight's performance. Don't worry about her."

She wouldn't waste one ounce of breath worrying about Sylvie.

"Well, in truth, it's someone else I'm thinking about," she said.

"Yes?" he prompted.

"It's about Dena." Her voice cracked. "It's about giving her a chance that she won't get again for a long time."

He caught on quickly. At first, he only studied the floor and frowned. She saw herself for what she was: an aging corps dancer trying to persuade a respected, responsible soloist to go against authority and listen instead to her plan. He'd never go for it.

He looked up and their eyes met. "Tell me what you have in mind. Quick. Before Sylvie comes back out."

Chapter 27 – Dena

The phone call from Rebecca came while Dena was preparing chicken stir-fry for dinner. She'd just ended a long call with Misha, where he'd reported that David, now out of the ICU, was progressing well. Like all the calls from Misha, it had been absorbing, nourishing and charged with this new feeling growing between them. The "I love you" had not yet been discussed, but it was there, hovering in the air between them, connecting them. It lent a new softness to Misha's voice, a lower purr to her own whenever they discussed non-David matters.

She was dicing celery and red bell peppers in a happy, dazed reverie when Rebecca's call pulled her back to reality. "Get in here," Rebecca told her in a low, urgent voice. "Bring a good pair of pointe shoes."

"You mean for you?"

"No. For you."

"Becca. Why?"

"Don't ask questions. Just get here, fast. Gotta go."

Rebecca disconnected and Dena stared at the phone in her hand, baffled. She nonetheless did as she was told, and thirty minutes later, she arrived at the theater. The performance had already begun. She flashed her ID badge to the security guard at the backstage entrance and hurried to the dressing room area. Rebecca had changed into her costume for *Arpeggio*, the night's second ballet, and was pushing the final hairpins into her bun when she saw Dena. Her eyes filled with relief.

"Dena! Hi!" Rebecca said in a falsely surprised voice. She leaned in and murmured in a low voice. "You came by just to wish me merde, okay? And watch the performance from the wings."

"What's this about?"

Rebecca ignored the question. "Go say hi to your dressing-room mates," she said in the same bright, loud voice. "They'll be glad to see you."

"Who?!"

"You know. Lana. And Sylvie. Go see how Sylvie is doing."

Dena didn't move. "Why?"

"Here, I'll go with you. I need to talk to them anyway."

Dena grabbed Rebecca's arm as they walked down the hallway. "What the hell's going on?" she hissed.

"Sylvie's not feeling well, that's what," she hissed back.

"But what does that have to do with me?"

"Just trust me here."

No more words were exchanged as they passed other dancers in the hallway. In the soloists' dressing room, Sylvie sat at her dressing table, in costume, putting finishing touches on her makeup. Lana sat there, too, fully prepped, looking worried.

"Oh, you're feeling better," Rebecca said to Sylvie in what could only be called disappointment.

"Yes," Sylvie said. "I'm feeling better." Lana said nothing, but gave Rebecca a quick "no way" shake of the head.

A closer look at Sylvie told Dena that she was not well. She had an unhealthy pallor, even under the makeup, and a dullness to her bloodshot eyes.

Rebecca turned to Lana. "Go," she said in a harsh voice. "You played no part in this, do you hear me? Leave. And stay away from me backstage."

The cruel words shocked Dena, but before she could protest, Lana, even more surprisingly, merely nodded. She flashed Rebecca a look of gratitude and slipped out. It made no sense.

A moment later Nicholas, in costume, appeared at the door. He sized up Sylvie, turned to Rebecca and nodded in resignation. He turned back to Sylvie.

"Sylve?" He reached over to massage her shoulder. "Consider what we all talked about. For your sake as well as hers."

Dena watched, baffled, at the interplay between the three of them, until it became clear: Nicholas and Rebecca wanted Sylvie to give her night's performance to Dena. The news exploded in her mind. Except that dancers didn't cast the ballets. They didn't assign substitutes. What the hell was Rebecca thinking? Anders would never go for it.

But Anders wasn't there that night.

A shiver of fear came over her at the brazen nature of Rebecca's plan. "I don't think this is a good idea," she said, and Sylvie swung toward her, pointed at her, and nodded.

"Trust me here, Deen," Rebecca said.

Nicholas turned to Dena. "Are you up to this? If Rebecca can get Ben to approve it?"

Terror battled with excitement. She would never get such a chance again this season.

"I... I think I am. Yes. I am."

The first ballet had just ended. The drenched, panting dancers made their way toward the dressing rooms while the *Arpeggio* dancers pushed through to get onstage and warm up. They had twenty minutes of intermission time.

Dena's heart hammered in her chest as she tried to assume a neutral expression, tell her fellow dancers hi, yes, watching the production yet again tonight. Can't get enough of *Arpeggio*. She was still clad in street clothes, hair down, all but invisible among the more exotic, glittery creatures around her.

Sylvie came onstage, in costume, her gait unsteady. She refused to look at either Rebecca or Dena as she made her way over to where a portable barre had been set out for warming up. Midway there, however, she swayed and groaned. Making an about-face, she clutched at her abdomen and hurried offstage to the bathroom.

"That's it. Go get April or Ben," Rebecca said to Dena. "Now."

Dena bumped her way through the milling dancers, the backstage crew, searching for Ben. She found him in a corner talking to members of the lighting crew, chuckling over someone's comment. Dena grabbed at his arm.

"Sylvie's sick," she said, and before she could explain, Ben was moving, striding right over to where the others had congregated.

He sized up Sylvie, back from the bathroom. "Oh, boy. You're sick, all right."

"I'll be fine."

"Wrong. You're not going onstage like that."

Before she could reply, he turned to consult with April, who'd joined the onstage huddle. April was shaking her head. "Grete is the understudy, but she's already left for the night," she said to Ben.

"Mimi takes this part in cast one. Where is she?"

"Off tonight."

"All right, that's a no go as well." Ben's voice remained calm but in his eyes Dena saw worry.

Rebecca stepped forward. "Dena knows it. All of it. She's been attending rehearsals and running through some of the passages."

Faces swung toward Dena. "You remember everything?" April said. "You can dance it?"

"Of course she can," Rebecca said before Dena could reply. "She and I did this, five years ago. Sylvie has what was Dena's part."

"Rebecca," Ben said. "Let Dena speak for herself."

Dena drew a shaky breath. "Yes. I can dance it."

Ben, however, didn't look convinced. "I just don't know. Too risky, I think."

"Ben," Rebecca said, "it makes perfect sense. She and Nicholas work great together. They ran through the whole first section in rehearsal last week, and it was perfect. Ask Lexie. *Call* Lexie. He'd agree in a heartbeat that she could do it."

Ben offered no reply as he mulled over the situation.

"Dancers in ballet two, ten minutes," Rick the stage manager's amplified voice boomed overhead. "All others off the stage, please."

"Ben." Rebecca's voice shook. "You have to let her do this. Please. I'm begging." She stepped closer to him and now her hands were resting on his upper arms. "Please," she repeated in a softer voice. To Dena's astonishment, she reached up to touch his face, like they were lovers.

Were they?

An electric moment passed between Rebecca and Ben, which made Dena decide yes, they were lovers, because how else had Rebecca come to exert such a hold on him? Ben's eyes had taken on a helpless look, locked with Rebecca's as if she'd pulled him in, along with his soul, with a tractor beam of strong will.

But only for an instant. "Stop that, Rebecca," Ben said roughly. He grabbed Rebecca's hands and pushed them away as he stepped back from her. He turned to Sylvie, studied her again, shook his head.

"You're not dancing like this. You shouldn't be here. Why didn't you notify us earlier?"

"I was sure I'd be fine by now," she gasped. "And besides. Rebecca made me wait." She managed a righteous glare in Rebecca's direction.

Ben shot Rebecca an incredulous look. "You knew she was feeling poorly, putting her performance at risk, and you told her to keep quiet about it?"

"It's not like it sounds," Rebecca protested.

Fury came over Ben's face. "So you made your own decision? You should have come to us with your concerns, Rebecca. There still would have been time to contact her understudy. She should have had the opportunity, not Dena."

Sylvie's tight-lipped smile of vindication shifted abruptly and she once again raced to the bathroom. Just as quickly, the discussion ended. There was a show to run. Fast. In two minutes.

"Dancers in place for the next ballet." Rick's voice sounded angry now. "Others, *clear the stage*. Ben. What's going on? I need answers."

"Let her do it, Ben," Rebecca said. "Please."

Ben looked over at Lana, who'd crept up to the group, and at Nicholas. "What do you two think?"

"She's up to it, Ben," Lana said. "This is Dena we're talking about, after all."

Ben remained unconvinced. "Nicholas, you'd need to anticipate every spot that she might need help in."

Nicholas nodded. "We can do it. I'm sure of it."

A rush of gratitude toward Lana and Nicholas passed over Dena, so intense it made her breath catch.

Ben strode over to Rick and his assistant, hovering over the control panel, and murmured with them. The dancers waited in silence, Rebecca and Lana exchanging worried glances. There was the crackle of walkie-talkies, Ben calling others, listening to their response.

Everything happened at once. "It's a go," Ben called out to April, who repeated it to Dena, and like that, helpers from all departments swooped in. The wardrobe and makeup people from downstairs appeared seconds later, charging the wings in search of Dena.

Tights. Pointe shoes. Hair. Makeup. Costume transferred in a backstage changing room from Sylvie to Dena. It was possible, then, to go from street attire to performer in sixty seconds. It helped when a team of six people, including a driven older sister, worked together.

"Call Tatum," Dena told Rebecca. "She's on my cell phone redial. Tell her what's going on."

"Done." Rebecca sped off.

As Lana laced up Dena's pointe shoes for her, the makeup artist set to work on Dena, sponging on Pan-Cake foundation. An assistant stood at the ready with pencils and concealers and blushes and false eyelashes. Five minutes later the makeup artist told Dena to smile, the tiniest bit, on the right side, as she worked busily on Dena's left side. "There," she said, stepping back when she was done. "Smile small, just like that, when you're onstage."

Rebecca, returning, stopped in her tracks. "Holy shit," she said in a stunned voice. "You're smiling."

The mirror held to Dena's face revealed perfect shadowing and contouring and there it was, a little smile on her paralyzed left side, even laughter wrinkles around her eyes to show merriment.

"Oh," Dena whispered, and tears welled up on her good side.

"No tear, no tears!" the makeup artist exclaimed. "Don't mess up the makeup!"

April had been at work behind Dena, fastening the tiny hooks down the back of her costume, tsk-ing in disapproval when the bodice didn't fit. "Christ, Dena, you've gained weight. You've got boobs."

"Sorry," Dena gasped, which made Betty, the generously built wardrobe mistress, laugh. From her kit, she whipped out an extra piece of the glittery gold, ivory and crimson bodice fabric, along with needle and thread. Dena was fitted and hand-sewn into the costume as the orchestra began to tune up. She was walked to the wing, downstage right, the hairdresser giving her hastily assembled bun a heavy dose of hairspray. Betty still worked on sewing as an assistant tucked in a satin pointe shoe ribbon tip that poked out on one ankle. Dena stopped by Nicholas's side. As the last thread was tied and clipped, she heard a voice from the theater's public address system, announcing the substitution. Dena Lindgren, performing in place of Sylvie Thibodeaux. It was a thrill above all thrills, as was the smattering of applause that following the announcement.

She and Nicholas would be the first dancers out. There'd been no time to think, to analyze what was about to happen. Just enough time for her to do a rapid warm up as the orchestra tuned up, and make sure her eye had enough moisture. She handed her eyedrops to Rick's assistant to pass to her every time she came offstage.

The familiar, effervescent Mendelssohn music began. A sudden bout of stage fright cut off her air supply, but the moment she ran out onto the brightly lit stage, Nicholas by her side, instinct took over. The brisk pas de basque steps, chaîné turns and partnered overhead lifts flowed out effortlessly. Two minutes later, Rebecca and Jimmy joined them. Lana and her partner. Two minutes beyond that, she and Nicholas exited stage right.

April and Ben anxiously sized her up.

"I'm fine," she assured them. "I'm great."

Nine vignettes, alternating duets, trios, full ensemble, quartets. On, off. Breathe. Accept eyedrops. Don't think, just dance. One thought did slip in, however. In the seventh vignette, she joined Rebecca and Lana onstage, the three of them giddy as young girls, cavorting and dancing for themselves alone, clasping and releasing hands.

Had it ever felt so joyous, so perfect before? For a split-second, time evaporated and it felt like five years earlier, thrilled to be in *Arpeggio*, so full of delight in the movement, in what the three of them were sharing. No tumor. No promotion. Just sisters beaming at each other, their joy so propulsive, it made their dancing explode with energy.

Rebecca raced toward her now from upstage left. Lana shot out from upstage right, and the three of them met in the center of the stage, joining hands for a lightning fast "ring around the rosy." She met Rebecca's excited eyes.

This precious gift, this fleeting moment. All thanks to her sister.

The rest of the ballet grew more and more challenging. No surprise; the energy required for performing was considerable, and she hadn't performed in ten months. Adrenaline took over, in the way you heard of dancers spraining their ankle in the first leap onstage and they danced on it the entire ballet, never allowing the infirmity to dictate the quality of the night's performance. She clung harder to Nicholas, who caught on and modified his own movements to better support her. Their final pas de deux became not just a slow, graceful pairing of body and movement, it became a testament to how beautiful support amid tension could be. Once they'd finished and left the stage, the applause from the audience grew thunderous, never ending. She saw Rick, at the control panel, exchange bemused looks with Ben as the applause went on and on.

"The applause has got to stop before we can cue the music for the next section," Rick said.

"They liked it." Ben chuckled. "How you doing, Dena?"

Really bad, in truth. Ready to pass out, or throw up, or sink to the cool floor and stay there. "Fine," she heard herself tell Ben calmly.

"You're a warrior, all right."

"Finally," Rick grumbled, as the applause gradually petered out.

"Orchestra, last movement. Go."

How she powered through the ensemble finale in strong form would remain a mystery. She made it through curtain calls, too, a deep curtsy of gratitude to the audience—oh, they had no idea. Afterward, Nicholas's arm encircled her waist, supporting her, as she limped backstage. She hadn't had time to tape any of her toes and she could feel blisters, formed and torn while she'd been dancing. The now-raw skin rubbed against her tights and burned like fire. Dizziness overcame her, with a fringe of dark around the edges. People were crowding around even as Rick was saying, "give her breathing space" and someone handed her bottled water which she took with shaking hands, gulped, and promptly retched up into a nearby trash can.

Rebecca held her in a long embrace until Dena felt ready to walk to the dressing room, but it was Rebecca's dressing room because Dena didn't have her own spot, her own theater trunk with its creams and lotions and degreasers and towels, and she realized how punchy she was getting, and even that was all right because her big sister was in charge again and she'd make sure everything was okay.

What she couldn't figure out, was that Rebecca seemed so upset. She was all but crying by the end of their cleanup, apologizing, saying it had been too much of a risk, that Conrad would kill her, what had she done, are you all right, Deen?

Dena told her to shut up, that it had been the chance of a lifetime, and they'd pulled it off, even though now she felt like shit, except no, she felt like a million dollars.

No, this: she felt like a professional ballet dancer, exhausted by a hard night of performing.

There was no sweeter feeling in the world.

Chapter 28 – Rebecca

Nothing was too big a price to pay for what she'd done for Dena, Rebecca told herself. Whatever Anders doled out, she could handle. What she hadn't seen coming was Ben's wrath.

"Don't you ever, *ever*, test or challenge my authority again, Rebecca. Do you understand?" Ben stood by Anders' side behind the desk, tall and terrible.

"Yes, sir." She'd never called Ben "sir," except as a joke, but now the title seemed mandatory.

"We are the sole authorities on who gets cast, who gets substituted in, what should happen in the event of an emergency. You are a corps dancer. You have no authority there. You are to shut up at a time like that and do what we say. And that goes for presuming to tell another dancer how to manage their infirmity. You had *no* business interfering with Sylvie's poor health."

"Yes, sir. I mean, no, sir."

He continued on. Anders leaned back in his chair, pen in one hand, clicking it from time to time, swiveling to regard Ben one moment and Rebecca the next. He let Ben finish his rant before he took over.

He studied Rebecca and gestured with his head to Ben. "What he said," was his only comment. Had the situation not have been so terrifying, so painful, it might have been cause for laughter.

Anders shifted his attention to Dena and his expression grew kinder. He wanted to know how Dena was doing, how she'd felt physically, how the orchestral levels had sounded, whether she'd ever felt hindered. She told him she'd gotten used to her compromised hearing, and her instincts about the musicality had gone a long way in correcting the errors she'd made last spring. She heard the music in a different way now, but it was no less effective. The fact that she'd known the choreography from years back had helped.

Rebecca offered up a silent prayer of thanksgiving that the risk had paid off, physically, for her sister. More than once the previous night, Rebecca had worried that it was all too much, that she'd put her little sister at terrible risk. She hadn't known fear like that before. Just before Dena leapt onstage with Nicholas, Rebecca had seen the flash of terror cross Dena's face, which had made Rebecca feel sick with remorse. But then Dena bounded onstage and instantly she became that other Dena. The one with superstar abilities. The one who could beat any odds and excel. Toward the end, watching the way Dena struggled—she knew her sister and saw it even as Dena, like a cat, managed to show no pain or weakness—she berated herself again. Conrad would have had every right to shout at her this time.

Was Rebecca a hero or a tyrant? She pondered that question now. No answers came.

"And your eye?" Anders was asking Dena.

"I used drops when I was offstage. That protected the cornea. I was scared some speck of dust would fly into my bad eye that I couldn't blink away, but that never happened."

"Your energy level?" he asked.

"A little scary," Dena admitted. "It took a lot of energy. I did it, I could do it, but it seemed… challenging." She gave a miserable shrug. "I think I've still got a long way to go."

Anders nodded. "I don't want you performing right now. I'm standing firm on that. I'm proud of you for how you fared; I've been told you pulled it off very well. But I don't want it happening again."

"It won't." Dena lowered her gaze to the floor.

"Darling girl," he said in a gentler tone, one so kind and loving, it cut right through Rebecca. "I'm not trying to punish you. I care deeply about what's right for you physically. What's best for you in the long run."

Dena offered him a brave half-smile. "Thank you."

His gaze grew cooler as he glanced over at Rebecca. "Enough said. You two are free to leave."

Ben, his anger having subsided to chilliness, didn't say a word. He didn't look Rebecca's way.

That troubled her most of all.

With the end of Program IV, the rehearsal schedule eased over the following days. Conrad called on Thursday morning and left a message. "Well, sounds like you were tricky again, Rebecca. But this time for your sister. That's my good girl. I like seeing you two supporting each other." He chuckled. "I imagine you got an earful from the boss. You didn't let that stop you, though, did you? You can be pushy that way." Before she could bristle over that, his voice softened and he ended the message with, "Love you, sweetie. You take care." She saved the message in her phone archives, so she could play it again and again, and bask in the unfamiliar pleasure of hearing praise from a loving father.

She didn't have a rehearsal in the final slot on Thursday afternoon and managed a return to the apartment before five o'clock. The living room was quiet. "Dena?" she called out. No reply. When the apartment phone rang, Rebecca picked it up absently, thinking it might be Dena.

"Hello, Rebecca Anne," her mother said in a dry tone, and Rebecca cursed herself for not checking caller ID. "Why haven't you called me back? And what's this Dena's telling me, that you got her on stage the other night? Can you please clarify?"

She explained the situation in as few words as possible. She didn't want to engage in cheerful banter with her mother. When Isabelle commented on this, Rebecca flared up.

"It's *you,* Mom. Your behavior that night, leaving your daughters to go to a lounge with Anders. With our *boss.*"

She braced herself for the verbal lashing sure to come, but Isabelle surprised her.

"I understand where you're coming from, Becca. I do. You see a mom-type who shouldn't be allowed to play. Someone who should continue to put her needs and interests behind those of her children's. Her adult children, I might add. Your father used to see something equally prosaic and bland. Mother of his children. Free labor. Dan? Of late, he sees a caretaker. Anders? He sees *me.* The woman behind the duties. The other night, I needed that."

It was eerie, this conversation. Its intimacy made Rebecca uncomfortable.

"He always has," Isabelle continued. "All those years back, living out here, with the two of you finishing up your training, he saw my loneliness and paid me some attention. I'll always be grateful to him for that. Is it such a crime to spend an evening visiting with him again?"

"You and Anders together at L'Orange. Mom, what are people supposed to think?"

"Oh, nonsense. It was in perfect innocence this time."

"This time. Because, not like the other times."

In the electric moments of silence that followed, during which time she seemed incapable of regaining her breath, she better

339

understood what Boyd had gone through. The innocent question you pose that explodes in your face, revealing that which your mind simply can't process. No. It wasn't possible. It couldn't be true.

It was.

Two occasions, Isabelle confessed. The first, back when Rebecca had joined the company, from apprentice to full corps member. Not so much a love affair as finding some physical comfort during a very lonely time in her life. Rebecca had moved out, Dena was hostile, Conrad ever-absent. Anders alone had seen this, the dear man, and was such a sweetheart, taking her out to dinner one night, all attention and consideration. He'd told her he found her beauty irresistible. What woman didn't melt at such words? This, coupled with two bottles of wine, and, all right, she'd been no saint that night. The second time had been just after Dena joined the company and Rebecca turned twenty-one, and Isabelle knew it was time to go back to Chicago and her unloving husband. A final, fond evening together, a memory she would always treasure.

A flashback came to Rebecca, almost too painful to contemplate, of her twenty-one-year-old self, posing nude for Anders, trying to seduce him to her bed that first night in Carmel. His amused, benevolent rejection. Because he'd already found someone to meet those needs. Her mother.

Isabelle mistook Rebecca's stunned silence for disapproval. "I'm not proud of what I did, Becca. I violated my wedding vows over a fling and never came clean over it. Your father, in truth, had more integrity. He loved Janey. He couldn't live with the infidelity so he left me to marry her. I can respect him for that now."

The rest of the conversation was just noise. Rebecca finally escaped from it on the pretext of having plans. She hung up the phone and moved like a zombie into the bathroom. Hands shaking, she splashed her face with water, meeting her eyes in the mirror.

Those deep-set brown eyes, her *mother's* eyes. The daughter who was a carbon copy of her mother; this was what Anders had seen. She drew in noisy gulps of air, half-sobs, and asked herself just how one proceeded from here.

Even though there was no performance that night, she left the apartment at the usual time, leaving a message for Dena that she'd taken the car. Once out, she drove aimlessly, her goal mostly to get away from what was inside her. A left on Van Ness Avenue, a right on California Street, a left on Stockton, heading toward Fisherman's Wharf. En route, a car vacated a parking space on her right, just off Washington Square. She took it. Even though she hadn't planned to stop in North Beach, when you found parking in North Beach, you grabbed it, with euphoric gratitude.

Coit Tower was walking distance, and she needed to walk, ascending the treacherously steep sidewalks up Telegraph Hill, welcoming the way the effort burned her quads and stole her breath. Five minutes later, the panoramic view of the San Francisco Bay was her reward.

Straight ahead, from her perch on the steps of Coit Tower, stood the Golden Gate Bridge and the Marin headlands. To the east, the Bay Bridge with rush hour traffic, people returning home to their calmer families and their calmer lives. The sun had commenced its descent, casting gold light over the surrounding East Bay hills and houses. To the west, lay a neat grid of city streets, the Presidio and the Pacific Ocean beyond it. Everything concise and orderly. Nothing fucked up, the way she felt inside.

Descending Telegraph Hill, she walked the streets of North Beach, its bars and Italian restaurants still relatively quiet, the tawdry, bustling neon of Broadway's strip joints not yet drawing in its nightly crowd of revelers. Further down Columbus Avenue, she stopped at a small Italian restaurant, where she picked at a plate of pasta before returning to her walk. A left on Chestnut, through a residential area, a street with a steep ascent that rendered her breathless long before the hill crested several blocks later, at Hyde.

Russian Hill. Where Anders lived.

She went to a nearby wine bar and ordered a glass of red, sipping it slowly until they closed for the evening, shooing her out.

Which meant there was only one place left to go.

His home was a cream two-story Edwardian with gold fixtures in a posh, well-tended neighborhood. She knew the address and when she saw the row house it looked just as she'd expected. No doubt in her mind that he was home and still awake.

In a trance of sorts, she approached the door, until prudence made her stop to consider things.

This was beyond taboo, an uninvited visit, violating a rule set in stone. What gave her the right? Was it because the night that he called her a fucking little twat, he, too, had broken a rule, come down to the dancers' level, revealed a different kind of intimacy? Or was it because things had grown so unhinged, so lawless of late, that this was simply one more sacred rule she was about to prove could be broken?

There wasn't a chance she would reconsider, however. This was like challenging someone to a duel. You just couldn't go on, knowing what you knew.

Maybe this was how Boyd had felt, when he'd stepped out onto that stage.

She walked the last few steps to Anders' door and sounded the bell. Moments later, he opened the door. He stood there, frozen in his surprise. She offered no explanation.

"Come in," he said finally.

He led her to the living room. She sat. The room was elegant, with plush, tasteful furniture, Persian rugs on the floor, original artwork on the walls, Delft plates arrayed on their own built-in shelves. He sat across from her. "Is it Dena?" was the first thing he asked.

"No."

"Your mother?"

She began to laugh, a sound cut off by something more akin to a sob. "Yes. You might say this is about my mother."

"Rebecca. What is it?"

"You slept with her."

He angled his head in confusion. "I'm sorry?"

She repeated it and still he seemed to not make the connection.

"Your mother has not fallen ill? Been in some accident?"

"No."

"You came here to tell me this, accuse me in this way?"

She lifted her chin. "Yes."

He rose, strode to the door and flung it open. "Leave," he said. "Now."

Something in her snapped.

"No."

"Oh, yes, Miss Lindgren."

Adrenaline began to surge through her. "I don't think so, Mr. Gunst."

She wasn't strong enough to attack him with her fists. The greatest assault on him appeared to be her intrusion into his personal life. And right then, she wanted to go for maximum assault.

"Get out of my house!" His voice rose to a roar.

She matched its volume. "Just try and make me!"

He swung his door shut and the thunder of it seemed to shake the whole room. He marched toward her, the fury in his face unleashing a terror inside her that reverberated through her. She leapt up on legs gone weak, darted around him with the agility of a cat, and dashed up the nearby staircase, to the even-more-forbidden second level. Behind her came the pound of his footsteps and it was like the chase games she used to play with Dena when they were little. Dena, even then, was so fierce, so determined as she ran after Rebecca, that Rebecca would scream in that kid's mix of terror and delight, darting into a room, hands shaking as she tried to barricade herself from Dena's battering entry.

She burst into one of the rooms and looked around.

His bedroom.

As she leaned against the now-closed door, she drank in every detail, the reds and golds, soft lighting coming from a lamp in the corner, a pair of armchairs, the bed. This most private place of all, this place where he slept, where he fucked the beautiful women he desired, women he'd chosen from the throngs who desired him, most of whom didn't have enough of what he was seeking to be invited here.

Her *mother* had probably been in this room. The thought made her dizzy. She swayed, lost her momentum for a split second, and that was all it took for Anders to catch up with her.

The door burst open, making her stumble. He came in, terrifying in his wrath, eyes wild with rage. Grabbing her arm, he gave it a yank.

"Get out of here! You little bitch. Get the hell out of my room."

A tug of war ensued, Rebecca digging her heels into the carpet, grabbing at anything she could, the corner of the chest of drawers, the bedpost. He was strong. Her arm felt like it was going to be pulled out of its socket, but still she held on.

But Anders was clever. He made an abrupt shift, stepping toward her, not away from her, which made her lose her balance. He gave her arm one last great tug, back in the direction of the hallway.

She tried to catch herself, anchor herself to a part of the room again, but she failed. In a last-ditch attempt to go anywhere beside through the door, she lunged to the left. The sudden twist of weight confused Anders, made him stumble as well. He released her arm at the moment she made yet another lunge and the force of his release sent her flying sideways, unmoored and unprotected.

Her arms pinwheeled as she fell. The corner of his chest of drawers came at her too fast for her to react, and with a *bam* and an explosion of pain, her face made contact with it before she continued her downward fall to the floor.

She didn't have it in her to get up. She huddled there, weeping, cradling her cheekbone, which now seemed on fire with pain. He offered her a hand, a tap against her shoulder. She ignored it.

"Come on," he said. "Get up." Two hands appeared. She slapped them away.

"Rebecca. Snap out of it."

Without rising from her huddle, she gave him a vicious kick that hit its mark with a tactile thud. "Don't you tell me when I can or can't snap out of my pain."

He sighed and hunkered down beside her. "Look at me," he commanded, and even now, he was an authority she couldn't ignore. She looked up and he took her face in his hands, angling it in a professional manner that allowed him to see the throbbing cheekbone.

"Oh, Christ," he muttered. "*For fanden da også.*"

He rose. "You need ice. I'll be right back. At least get up from the damned floor. Go sit in the chair. Or on the bed. I don't care. You'll just do what you want anyway."

She was too dispirited to reply.

She chose one of the chairs. He returned with a tray that held a bottle of scotch, two glasses, a towel and a gel ice pack, which he angled, with the towel, over the point of swelling. Her cheekbone throbbed and burned as if she'd broken something. She sat there, holding the pack in place, so spent and passive now that he could have shoved her out the door, rolled her down the stairs, nudged her outside, and she would have offered no resistance.

He poured two glasses of scotch, an antique single malt type that went down as smoothly as cognac. He sat in the chair beside her and in silence they sipped. When Rebecca finally found the energy to speak, she focused her gaze on the glass, the amber liquid that glinted through the crystal facets.

"My mother commented on your compassion and warmth, the way you alone had seen her loneliness. I think hearing that shocked me the most of all. That you were capable of such sensitivity toward a woman. Here I've been thinking you were one of those superhuman artistic geniuses, trapped in your own mind, incapable of intimacy because of who you were. And I loved you, in spite of it. Or maybe because of it. And as it turns out, you *were* capable of reciprocating. Of giving. Just not to me."

She could feel tears working their way out, marring the sense of control she so wanted to maintain in front of him.

"Rebecca," Anders said. "I want you to know. I do love you, in my own way. You are very special to me. You always will be."

He rose from his chair and left the room, returning a moment later with an 8x10 framed work of art, a gorgeously rendered charcoal sketch. It featured the bare backside of a female, perched on a bed, the silken sheets rumpled, the morning light from a nearby window making the contours of her body glow. Her head was angled, chin visible, as if she were listening to something very important, being whispered in the room next door. With a jolt, Rebecca realized it was her. From last spring's Carmel trip. Her throat cramped up.

He propped it against the dresser and returned to his seat.

Together, they studied it. The only sound was the soft clink of ice in their glasses as they sipped the scotch.

The throat cramp eased. "It's beautiful," she said finally.

"It is. One of my best. The only one I've felt compelled to frame."

He reached for the bottle of scotch and trickled a little more into each of their glasses. In silence, they sipped and studied the charcoal a moment longer.

"What happened to my beautiful, compliant girl?" he asked finally. "Where did she go?" He sounded genuinely baffled.

She turned and met his eyes over her drink. "I guess she grew up, Anders," she said. *Into a woman,* she wanted to add, à la Alice Willoughby, but decided against it. She was no Alice.

"I think you're right," he said.

How ironic. In losing everything, she'd just been granted her greatest wish.

Two adults, weary from storm, talking, connecting. Equal minds. Like Alice and him.

Which he only did when the other relationship was over.

Chapter 29 – Dena

"Did you see the big numbers on my Facebook post about you?" Tatum asked Dena during their phone catch-up Thursday night. It was late, but Tatum was a night owl, and they were both energized by the excitement generated over Tuesday night's *Arpeggio* performance and the social media response.

"I did!" Dena exclaimed. "You know, when your article about me a few weeks ago got shared almost 200 times, I was impressed. These 400 shares and 3000 likes just blow that number out of the water. And the views on my blog since the article came out—amazing. Yesterday I got over 1000 views."

"Everyone who knows your story—and that's a lot of people by now—went crazy over the news that you'd gone back onstage for one night," Tatum said. "You've got people caring about what happens to you. See? *See?*" Her voice rose in triumph. "I told you something was going to happen."

"All those visits to my blog sort of intimidate me, though. What I write is so humble and pedestrian. It's like a letter you'd send to a relative."

"That's why people find you so relatable, Dena. Don't change a thing. Just keep being yourself, dropping a few lines on Twitter, Facebook and your blog."

They agreed to talk in another five days' time. After they'd disconnected, Dena looked at her watch. It was past midnight, and Rebecca was still out, which concerned her. Rebecca's scrawled-out "taking the car" message had been terse, like she'd had an argument with someone. She hoped Rebecca wasn't still catching grief over the *Arpeggio* replacement. Dena tried calling her, but the call rolled over to voice mail. She texted a "where r u?" that drew no response.

Even though it was late, she felt wide awake. She thought of Misha, because, these days, she never stopped thinking about Misha. But it was 3:00am there in Barbados.

Happy Friday morning, she texted him, knowing he'd see the text when he woke up. To her surprise, her phone rang less than a minute later. A buttery rush of pleasure filled her when she saw it was Misha calling.

"What are you doing, making phone calls when you should be sleeping?" she mock- scolded him.

"I'm wired so that I wake up when important things happen."

"I'm so sorry. I should have waited to text you."

"No, no, it's okay. I love it."

"You were sleeping. I can tell by your voice."

When he spoke again, his voice had grown even lower and sleepier. "I was. I was in the middle of a great dream. An impossibly wonderful one."

"Oh?" she said, trying to sound casual. "Do tell."

"A beautiful woman was pressed up close to me, telling me she loved me."

Here it was, then. Her heart began to jackhammer. "That's some dream," she offered. This made him laugh, which gave her time to compose her thoughts.

"Deen," he said softly.

She licked her lips, opened and closed a mouth gone dry.

"I want you to know that I haven't stopped thinking about that, about you, since I left you that night. Even throughout David's drama, the hospital situation, being here in Barbados. It's been there. And I hope to God you're not going to tell me not to get the wrong idea. David said, well, he told me he thought maybe you… That you felt… Oh, crap. I guess I should stop right here and just come out and ask. Am I way off the mark here, making an idiot of myself, in thinking you might have been thinking about me, too? In the same way?"

A roaring had filled her ears, but amid it, she found her voice. "No. You're not off the mark. I haven't stopped thinking about you either."

He exhaled. He didn't say a word. She was afraid to analyze the silence.

"Wow," he said. "You should hear how my heart is pounding right now."

"Mine too," she said through a choked laugh.

They stuttered through their next words in an attempt to transition from the sublime to the pedestrian. The weather in Barbados, what he'd had for dinner. The success of her and Tatum's social media campaign. David's cheerful misbehavior in the hospital.

"All right, so here's the biggest news," Misha said. "It looks like David will be discharged tomorrow or the next day, and he has officially ordered me to go home. Only one slacker allowed per family and he told me he'd called it, and for me to get back to work."

"Misha! When are you flying back?"

"Right now, it looks like it'll be Saturday."

"Oh, that's such good news. Will you let me come pick you up?"

"That would be great, Deen. Are you sure you don't mind?"

Euphoria welled up in her. "Positive."

"Is there any chance I can persuade you to hang around in Moss

Beach afterward? Maybe, like, for the rest of the weekend?"

She squeezed her eyes shut, fearful of letting anything burst this bubble of too-good-to-be-true. "Yes. Definitely the weekend. I would love that."

"Good. Fantastic. I can't wait, Deen."

It was no surprise that sleep, following their conversation, eluded her. She was still wide awake when Rebecca finally arrived. She looked tired, dazed, as if she'd been crying.

"Becca, where were you?" Dena asked. "I was starting to worry."

Rebecca's hair was down and when she lowered her gaze, it hid half her face. "Doesn't much matter," she said, studying the carpet. "I'm back."

"But… what were you doing?"

"I was walking. Doing a lot of walking. North Beach. Russian Hill."

"This late?!"

Rebecca looked at her watch as if noticing the hour for the first time. "Oh. Well, I stopped by to talk with someone. Discuss something."

She eyed Rebecca suspiciously. "Who?"

"Doesn't matter." Rebecca glanced at her from beneath the curtain of hair.

Anger replaced Dena's concern. "God, Rebecca, would you give me some straight answers?"

Rebecca stood there, swaying. "Look, Deen. I had a bad night, okay?" To Dena's astonishment, she began to cry. "I just want to go escape into sleep. Can we talk tomorrow?"

"Sure. Okay. I'm sorry I yelled."

Rebecca managed a smile through her tears. "It's okay. It's your right as a sister."

"Damned straight. And don't you forget."

Rebecca's attempt at a second smile fell short. "Anyway, good night," she said.

"Good night."

Rebecca retreated to her bedroom and Dena wandered over to her computer. Even more sleepless than before, she went online and scrolled through her Facebook and Twitter feeds, her acoustic neuroma forum.

She thought of Misha's call and smiled, letting the thrill of his words wash over her all over again. Then she thought of Rebecca's distress, the mystery of where she'd been, and the good feelings disappeared.

North Beach, fine, that was a good walking neighborhood, a good place to get dinner. But Russian Hill? It was residential. Quiet and more private.

It was where Anders lived.

She didn't need to know anything more. She understood, immediately, that Rebecca had gone over there and that they'd had words. He'd rejected or berated her, and sent her out.

She returned to her Twitter home page. She took a deep breath, wrote and posted, along with Tatum's suggested hashtags, what was on her mind.

"Why was it so necessary to take my sister down after she moved mountains to give me my chance?"

And a second one, five minutes later: *"While my sister's methods and actions may be considered unorthodox, is that any reason to crush her?"*

Over a scrambled egg breakfast the next morning, the two sisters didn't talk. Rebecca looked frail and washed out, utterly defeated. It was frightening to observe. She touched a discolored spot on her cheekbone and winced.

Dena stared, stunned. She hadn't noticed it the night before. "What the hell happened?" she demanded.

"I fell."

"You were at Anders' last night, weren't you?"

Rebecca looked awake for the first time. Guarded. "Why do you say that?"

"Because I'm smart and you're my sister and I know you."

"Fine. Whatever."

"No, not 'whatever.' Goddamn it, did he *hit* you?"

"No, I told you. I fell."

"Bullshit!"

"Drop it, Deen. It's way too complicated."

Before Dena could say anything more, Rebecca rose abruptly from the table, scrambled eggs untouched, and headed to her room. Dena followed her, watched as Rebecca flung herself back on her bed and covered herself with the blankets. "Go away," Rebecca said, her voice now thick with tears.

"What are you doing? It's just about time to leave for company class."

"I'm not going. I'm not well."

"Becca, come on. Where's your spirit?"

"Just leave me alone with this!"

It was a piteous howl, like a mortally wounded animal might make, and the pain and grief behind it frightened Dena most of all. She wouldn't have believed someone could take down her sister like this. "Okay, okay." She tried to sound soothing, accommodating. "I'll just leave, give you some quiet, then."

"Thank you."

She had time to get dressed, arrange the contents of her dance bag, grab a Luna Bar and banana, with a minute to spare. All the time she needed.

At the computer, she sent an email to Tatum.

Help me get the word out. I think he hit my sister.

Next, Twitter.

She wrote it before she could change her mind.

And we won't talk about my sister's bruise. Mustn't mention that. Not when image is everything.

She added all of Tatum's recommended hashtags, included Tatum's Twitter handle, and pressed "Tweet."

There. Posted.

Salim, Lucinda's assistant, came to fetch her in the middle of company class. This time, she didn't have to pause and ask herself why. Together they walked in silence down the hall, took the now-familiar route from elevator to administration level to Lucinda's area. Lucinda, formidable today in a tailored black suit, was standing outside her office next to Megann, the director of human resources. She looked murderous. "Get your ass in there," she said, gesturing violently to the conference room adjacent to her office.

Megann, a tall, light-skinned African-American also dressed in a suit, shook her head. "Lucinda," she warned in a low voice.

"Fine. Get your ass in there, *please.*" The word dripped with sarcasm.

Megann offered Dena a wan smile. "Dena. As you can tell, we need to talk."

Little prickles of unease rose on the back of her neck. She followed Megann into the room, grateful for her calmer presence.

Lucinda shut the door behind her and began her attack.

"These tweets, boy oh boy, do you have explaining to do. Do you have any idea what kind of damage your words created?"

She slapped the papers in her hand against the desk. They appeared to be copies of Dena's tweets and other online activity.

"And this was an hour ago. It's going to be worse now," Lucinda said as she opened her laptop and began clacking away.

"Lucinda," Megann said, "I'm more concerned here that Dena has a grievance."

Lucinda ignored Megann's words. "No less than two dozen bloggers are talking about you this morning. Each post has likes and shares in the hundreds. You've been tagged on every social media avenue possible. Your little tweet has been retweeted two thousand times. And the comments throughout, people's analyses, are just sickening. Have you read them?" she demanded.

"No," Dena said, trying to keep her voice from shaking. "I haven't gone online since I left my apartment."

Lucinda tapped at her keyboard again and a moment later gestured for Dena to approach. Over Lucinda's shoulder, she read a few.

The comments were awful. They accused Anders of hitting his dancers frequently, of being a tyrannical autocrat. They accused him of sleeping with favored dancers, firing those who didn't bow to his will or his dictates. They compared him to Joseph Stalin and made Boyd and Charlotte out to be martyrs sacrificed to the cause.

"This is horrible," she cried. "People are just saying these things without any authority or information. They don't have a clue what's really going on."

Lucinda rolled her eyes. "Welcome to the Internet, Dena."

Megann spoke, more gently. "Dena, do you have a grievance against the company?"

"No!"

"Then what the hell are these?" Lucinda banged her pen on the photocopies. "They sound distinctly like a threat."

"Lucinda," Megann warned, louder this time. She turned back to Dena. "Is it true that Rebecca has a bruise?"

Dena hesitated. "Yes."

Megann looked solemn. "You don't have to be afraid to speak up here. If you feel compelled to report an accident that's being covered up, if you have knowledge of any employee harassment, I'm the one to tell. A bruise is a big deal. We aren't going to take that lightly, nor will your dancers' union. I'm surprised we haven't heard from the AGMA representative already."

"Give him a few more hours," Lucinda said darkly.

Salim appeared at the door, holding it open for another meeting participant.

Anders.

Oh, God. She hadn't seen this coming.

He took a seat as Lucinda continued her attack on Dena.

"The *Chronicle*'s been calling. The *New York Times*. A dozen online journals and reporters from all over the map. I'm offering no comment, of course. There is no news here. This is gossip and speculation and this is precisely, *precisely* what I warned you against."

"And *you.*" She swung around to Anders. "What do you know about this? A bruise, Anders? *A bruise?* Do you know how people are eating this up?"

"Lucinda," Megann cut in. "Deep breath. This is not an interrogation." She turned to Dena, with a soothing, accommodating Human Resources smile. "What do you think happened to Rebecca that she has a bruise?"

Dena bit her lower lip.

"It's not what you think, Deen," Rebecca had said to her about the bruise.

But how could it have been anything else?

"Rebecca told me she fell," Dena said to Megann. "My feeling is that she's gotten careless of late. Not looking where she's going, not considering the consequences of her actions. But that still shouldn't matter." She looked over at Anders, addressing her next words to him alone. This man, her hero, who'd done so much for her. "She got hurt, and that bothers me. Upsets me. And I blame you, Anders, for not protecting her from it. I blame you for it all."

He didn't try and offer a defense. He held her gaze, and on his face she saw the same grief and sorrow she'd seen in Rebecca's.

He had not hit Rebecca. No one could look you in the eye in such a way and be guilty.

"Dena," he said, "please tell Rebecca how sorry I am. For the way I failed to protect her. For any pain I've caused her."

There was no guile in his words, no agenda. This was the real man before her, vulnerable and humbled.

Where did that put her and her grievances now?

Megann asked him a question and the two of them began talking in low voices that excluded Lucinda and her. Lucinda glowered at her, lips compressed.

"Well, young lady. It appears you've made a fine mess of things. Don't think there aren't going to be consequences."

"You can't fire me for speaking honestly," Dena quavered.

Or could they?

Imagine surviving this terrible year, only to throw her career away, right here, right now. Over this.

Then she thought of Rebecca's terrible grief. All that Rebecca had risked to help her.

It was worth it. However this ended, she'd stand by her choice.

Megann finished her conversation with Anders and asked Dena a few more questions, jotting down the replies. Finally Megann dismissed her with a reassuring, *we aren't going to fire you* smile that clashed with Lucinda's *boy are you in trouble* glower.

"I want you to get your ass back onto Twitter," Lucinda said to

Dena, "and clarify your position on the situation, stressing your administration's support and cooperation on the matter."

"I will," Dena said, edging out of the room.

"And you tell that Tatum Monroe to back off, as well. Don't try and tell me she's not part of this. I know a social media expert at play when I see one."

Clever Lucinda. She was good.

"I will," Dena repeated.

Once outside the room, she heard Lucinda recommence her attack on Anders.

"Oh, no, not you. Sit back down. You are not out of hot water here, Mr. Gunst. You still owe us answers. About your treatment of Rebecca Lindgren. About the necessity of Charlotte Darracott's firing. Her grievance is being taken quite seriously by her AGMA representation. Goddamn it, we've run a clean ship up to now, beyond reproach, and I will not have you bringing us down in the public's eye. Not now, in this culture, this economy, when so much is at stake for all of us."

One almost had to pity Anders right then. Answering to Lucinda was no easy task. Even for an artistic director, it would appear.

She sent Tatum a *big news, let's talk* text, which Tatum replied to with a *great, but in meeting, 90 mn okay?* request.

No problem, she texted back to Tatum.

Any regrets? Tatum texted a moment later.

She considered her own reply before responding.

Nope.

She left the WCBT building, drawing in big gulps of the cool, bracing spring air outside. The tweet, she decided, could wait, until she was sitting, relaxing.

A coffee at Celia's would be perfect. She thought of Rebecca, likely still at the apartment. She needed to know about the public relations storm brewing. Dena had never thought to warn her about what she'd done.

Whoops.

Dena called her. "Uh, I might have gotten you into a little trouble," she told Rebecca. "Or out of trouble. I'm not sure which."

"Can you please elaborate?"

Dena summarized the morning's events. Silence followed. Then Rebecca began to laugh, an odd reaction for something so serious, from someone in such a state of trauma. Dena began to laugh, too, in relief as much as anything.

"Want to meet me at Celia's in twenty minutes?" Dena asked.

"Count me in," Rebecca said. "I'll be the one wearing dark sunglasses."

Which set them off laughing again.

Her warrior big sister would be just fine.

Chapter 30 – Rebecca

Being a company pariah had its advantages. In company class, Rebecca had plenty of space around her at the barre, which Dena always loyally tried to fill. During center work it didn't matter if she went with the first group or the second because either way, no one besides Dena, Lana, and the ever-friendly Jimmy acknowledged her. People didn't care—nor did she—whether she overheard comments like, "what a troublemaker she turned into, dragging Anders' good name through the mud" or "it's because she's jealous of her sister's bigger talent and had to act out" and "such a media whore. I hear she hacked Dena's Twitter account to post those messages."

Anders ignored the gossip and ignored her; she hadn't expected otherwise. She'd known, that night at his house three weeks earlier, that she'd been saying goodbye to him in more ways than one. Safe to say her own infatuation with him was over. For good. What she felt now was sorrow, even distaste. Not for anything he'd done so much as what she'd done to herself. Now, she impassively watched him watch Steph, who'd succeeded at her eleventh-hour soloist role in Program IV, picking up steps and nuances fast and proving confident and graceful when performing them. When *The Sleeping Beauty* was cast, Steph and not Rebecca received a demi-soloist part. On the rehearsal sheet for the season's final program, there in a prominent place was Steph's name, not Rebecca's. This, then, was how it would be. She longed to turn to the only other person beside Dena who might understand her pain, but Ben's coolness toward her had continued.

There'd been only one personal interaction with Ben, just after the incident, when he'd pulled her aside and asked, in a strained voice, if she'd really gotten the bruise from falling. When she'd confirmed this, and that no, Anders had not hit her, the concern left his eyes. He nodded, his expression returning to neutral.

To lose Ben in this way was an ache that wouldn't go away.

Another day of uninspiring rehearsals, her aching, aging body protesting it all. Another. An early evening rainstorm midweek drenched her as she made her way wearily back to Dena's apartment. Dena greeted her at the door with a mysterious look on her face. "Come to the mirror," she said, and hurried into the living room. Bemused, Rebecca shucked her soggy jacket, dropped her dance bag next to her water-clogged shoes, and followed her.

Misha was there, as well. Misha had been around a lot, ever since his return from Barbados. Most days, in fact. And nights. He and Dena were inseparable, utterly besotted.

"What is it?" Rebecca asked.

"Look." Dena gestured to the mirror, angling her face so Rebecca saw only the paralyzed side.

Nothing.

Wait.

The tiniest bit of a smile, a hint of a lifting around her mouth and lower cheek. And her eyebrow. It moved, *it moved.*

All weariness was forgotten. "Oh my God. Your muscles are returning," Rebecca said in a hushed voice.

Dena met her eyes in the mirror. "I know. I mean, only the tiniest bit, right? But my face has been tingling—I woke up from a dream, slapping it, thinking it was a bee or something. It's felt sort of warm and tingly for the past week, especially around the mouth and the eye."

"I told her last week that something was happening," Misha said as he encircled his arms around Dena's waist and rested his chin on her shoulder. "She didn't believe me. But now she does. Now she's all smiles." He reached up and with one finger, stretched her flaccid cheek into a broad smile. "Will you look at that?" he said, smiling at her now-beaming reflection in the mirror, which made both of them laugh.

Oh, the sweet sound of her little sister's laughter. It was a new Dena once again, morphing before Rebecca's eyes. For the first time in the past three awful weeks, she felt good about something.

"Congratulations," she choked out, turning to hug Dena, who hadn't quite detached herself from Misha, so the three of them shared a goofy cluster hug, Dena in the middle, all of them laughing. Because what a wondrous thing it was, this nerve that had been severed in two, then grafted and presumed unsuccessful all these months, only to surprise them all in the end.

Ben was in a terrible mood the next day. It was contract renewal season, which made everyone edgy, but Ben had always seemed immune in the past. While teaching company class, he snapped at the dancers in a way only Anders usually did. When Anders appeared at the door with Curtis, gesturing for Ben to let Curtis take over so Ben could leave with him, everyone heaved a sigh of relief. Curtis covered Rebecca's first rehearsal, as well, but Ben appeared at the door midway, irritably eyeing the dancers. "Rebecca," he called out, voice terse, during a pause. "Meet me in Anders' office at the beginning of lunch hour."

Dear God. It was something bad.

She pushed her way somehow through the rest of the rehearsal. An hour later she knocked at Anders' door, feeling queasy and weak in the knees. Ben called for her to come in. He was alone in the office, standing behind Anders' desk. He motioned for her to take a seat, across from him. A desk separated them, which scared her more. The old Ben would have taken the seat beside her.

"Is it the contracts?" she said through numb lips.

Ben sank to the chair behind the desk. "In a way."

"Not... Dena's contract?"

Please, God, no.

Surprise crossed Ben's face. He shook his head. "Dena's fine, for some time to come. He's renewing her contract for the soloist's full three years."

A colossal weight fell from her shoulders.

"Is it my contract?" she asked next.

"No. Your contract is to be renewed, as well. For two years."

"Ben. What is it, then?"

He sighed, rubbed his forehead before looking up at her again. "Before you sign the new contract, you should be aware of this. Anders reinstated Charlotte. She has a contract for two years as well."

Her stomach took a sickening plunge. "It gets worse," Ben told her.

She looked at him helplessly. "What?"

"He's promoting Steph to soloist."

She heard the words but it took a moment for them to impact her, like when you watch your priceless Ming vase get tipped from its stand and fall, as if in slow motion, before it finally reaches the ground and shatters into a thousand pieces.

End of vase.

End of hope.

"Oh, God," she whispered, clutching her middle as if the words had been a fist that had made perfect contact with her most vulnerable abdominal spots.

"Why?" She looked over at Ben. "Why is this happening?"

"The pressure to reinstate Charlotte came from administration. It was either do it, or suffer the consequences. As for Steph, she's up to the task." He expelled his breath in a sharp exhale. "Well, enough."

His tone had changed. She glanced up. "Ben?" she asked.

He gazed at her impassively, as if trying to decide whether to remain the cool, formal Ben or resume some of his warmth. He let the question hang in the air as he rose, went to the door, locked it and returned, this time to the seat next to her. "I am sharing private information with you," he said tersely. "I trust that you'll keep it between us."

"Of course."

"Anders resisted the mandate to reinstate Charlotte. She's a troublemaker and she'll feel like she's won. But he had to do it, so he did. Promoting Steph to soloist was, in his mind, the perfect solution. She'll never again side with Charlotte against him. I disagree with his decision. I think it's too soon. She should continue to be tested as a soloist and at the end of season he could more objectively judge. And what's more, it hurts you."

"Well. Thank you for thinking of me," she said in a curt voice.

"You're welcome."

Those two words were all her former confidante and friend and support buddy were going to offer.

Somehow, she managed to rise gracefully and face him. "Gosh, thank you for letting me know this! Yes. I might have to seriously consider what I want to do with that contract. Because, to be honest, I'm not sure if I can continue on with the company under these circumstances."

She made it to the door successfully. She had a hand on the doorknob when she hesitated, realizing there was no way she could walk out of the room, walk through the halls, amid the other cheerful oblivious dancers on lunch break, and pretend that her world hadn't come to an end.

Because this really was the end. This moment here.

"Rebecca," he said from behind her. "I'm sorry."

"You're sorry. Thank you. How proficient and... administrative of you. Tell me. Did Anders give you this task to perform, telling me this news?"

"No, Rebecca. He did not."

She swung around to face him. "You know, I'm remembering a time—it was when you rescued me in San Mateo after Carmel—when you said you'd be there for me, always. Well, guess what, Ben. You're not here."

"I am."

"Bullshit. And I have to tell you, it's killing me. Because I need that friend now. He's gone and I miss him so bad."

She couldn't go on. Instead something let loose in her and she began to cry, the tears rolling down one after the other, her shoulders shaking with sobs.

Worse was the fact that he didn't hurry over and give her a hug. The old Ben would have done that, cheered her up within minutes. Instead he took his time, procuring a box of Kleenex, and offering her one a minute later.

"Thank you," she sniffed, and grabbed one, and another, and another.

They stood there in a misery-drenched silence.

"Becca," he began, then stopped. When he spoke again, he sounded irritable. "It's lunch hour. Let's go. I don't want to have this conversation here. Are you free?"

"Yes," she managed.

They walked out of the office without another word. She ducked behind him, kept her gaze down. The last thing she wanted was for any of the dancers to see her tearstained face. They'd think she'd been fired. And they'd be glad.

He took her to a little Thai restaurant tucked off a side street a few blocks away. It was small enough to be intimate, large enough that no one could overhear their conversation. The owner seated them at a quiet corner table. She looked around for a menu. "They don't let you choose," Ben told her. "They just bring out food."

"That's fine. I'm not in this for the food."

She felt calmer now, more composed. "Ben. Whatever you have to say, I just want to say this first. I know you hate me for what I did that night Dena went onstage."

"I don't hate you, Rebecca."

"Stop. Let me say my bit."

"All right."

"It was for Dena. All of it. I saw a chance to help her and I grabbed it. I used the fact that you and I have grown closer. I'm so sorry. I don't know what that says about me, that I would do something like that to you."

"It says you're a hell of a sister."

"I don't know about that."

The waiter approached with salad plates and set them down.

"Will you forgive me?" she asked Ben. For the first time since leaving Anders' office, she met his eyes. To her relief, he smiled.

"Yes, Rebecca. I forgive you."

She poked at her salad for a few moments before speaking again. "I won't be signing that contract," she said, surprising herself.

He studied her. "You sound serious."

"Dead serious." She sighed and laid down her fork. "You were right in your thinking. I couldn't thrive under those circumstances. To hell with thriving—I couldn't survive, period. I'd just wilt, and die inside."

A helpless look crossed Ben's face. "I wish there was something I could do to help you."

"There's not."

"No, you're right. Not anymore."

The waiter brought two bowls of fragrant coconut-chicken soup to the table. She stared gloomily at the mushroom bobbing at the surface.

"If it's any comfort," Ben said, "I might be leaving too."

She looked up, astonished. "Ben! Why?"

His jaw tightened. "This. You."

"What do you mean?" she stammered.

"The ways he was handling this new promotion. And the cavalier way he's been treating you. He wasn't going to tell you in advance. He was going to let you find out through the grapevine. When I protested, he reminded me of the way I let you manipulate me."

"Ben—" she began.

"No, this time I have to talk. He started in on me. Cited my weakness around the issue of you. Jeered at me. Told me I needed to learn to toughen up. We had words—it got ugly, actually. Somehow, incomprehensibly, he hadn't realized I'd had strong feelings for you. The man *leered* when he figured it out. I wanted to hit him. He told me you dancers were easy come, easy go. I disagreed. I told him that if it came down to a choice, I'd choose the girl over the job. He told me I couldn't be serious. Not when the girl was just a corps dancer, to boot."

Saying this, he looked so angry, she was afraid to move.

"So I wrote out my resignation right there and handed it to him."

No one had ever fought for her before. No one had ever defended their feelings for her so fiercely before.

He had feelings for her.

Strong feelings.

She reached out and took his hand. Clutched it. He looked over at it, this little hand of hers against his much bigger one. His hand rotated, palm up, and closed again, this time around her hand. The firm warmth of it, the strength behind it, made something in her sag in relief, letting go of a tension she hadn't even realized she'd been holding.

Neither of them spoke. Neither of them paid attention to the food that kept accruing on the table, the waiters slipping away silently once they'd set the platters down. It seemed as though the world had shrunk to this: the two of them, holding hands.

This paradigm shift; this whole new world unfolding.

She was leaving the company.

She had a chance to keep Ben.

"Anders isn't going to let you leave," she said finally.

"You're right," Ben admitted. "He took my written resignation, tore it into bits, and told me to cut the theatrics and get back to work."

In spite of herself, she laughed. He did too. As if on cue, they released hands and started in on their food.

Sitting there eating, she missed his touch already, and nudged her chair closer so their thighs touched. She could almost feel the strength flowing from him to her, and immediately felt better.

"I'm going to leave the company." She tested the words out loud.

"Give it some thought. A day or two."

"No, I know. I feel it in my bones." Her aching, compromised, nine-years-in-the-corps bones. "And, come on. I see the writing on the wall. I saw what Anders did to Pam. He stopped using her except for the big corps de ballet ensemble parts. Why wait to have that happen to me?"

"Would you go to another company, like Pam?"

"No." She shook her head. "My body's spent. I've almost got my college degree. Time for a change."

She'd always thought such a pronouncement would be accompanied by weeping, a sick feeling in her gut that would go on and on. Okay, that might come later. Likely it would. Right now, though, what she felt was free.

"Do you have any other thoughts?"

"Something where I can use my brain more. I've really enjoyed some of my college classes. Especially the business one. It's like this whole new world is opening up, somewhere inside my brain. Discovering how this company operates just fascinated me. It made me want to learn as much as I could. I'm just not sure what comes after the courses are all finished."

He speared some chicken. "You know who could help you there?"

She knew instantly. "Alice," she said, and he smiled at her.

"You read my mind."

"Do you think she would?"

"Definitely. Back in the day, she had a tough time of deciding to leave. She struggled through a lonely year of transition. She'd be glad to help another dancer through it all. I'll give her a ring right now. What would you think about the three of us meeting up for a drink after work tonight?"

Relief bubbled up from within her. "Oh, Ben, that would be great."

He reached into his pocket and pulled out his phone. Here he hesitated, met her eyes.

"Rebecca. This is a big decision. Once you take it beyond this table, there's no turning back. Is this the path you want to take?"

His thigh pressed into hers, and retreated. Because, really, he was asking about both things.

"Yes," she told him. "Absolutely yes."

Alice answered her phone, and Ben exchanged a few pleasantries with her. "Listen," he said finally, "Rebecca and I are wondering if you're free to talk after work tonight." His eyes remained on Rebecca as he spoke. "Rebecca's considering leaving the company—"

She nudged him. "Rebecca has decided," she cut in, and Ben grinned.

"Rebecca has decided to leave the company and feels that you would be an excellent source of information on how to move forward in the professional world. And I concur. So we're hoping you might be free for drinks."

As she watched him, she felt the world open up within her. Tightness inside eased with each breath, and it dawned on her just how free she was, to make any number of choices.

Free. A woman empowered.

She reached over and laid her hand on Ben's thigh. Because she could. And it felt great. Even better when his hand covered hers a moment later.

He was grinning at something Alice was saying. "No," he protested, and began to laugh. "Stop saying that. Be good."

Was Ben *blushing*?

"We are fine with meeting at your house." Ben glanced at Rebecca in query and she nodded. "We will bring over wine for the adults, and some sugar-laden beverage for your dear little rug rat, so we can watch him race around the room."

It was all going to happen.

Wait till Dena heard the news.

Acknowledgements

This novel took a long time to write. Correction: it took a short time to write. It just took a long time to revise and re-revise until I got it right. At all stages of its evolution, I owe thanks to those who helped. To my agent, Anne Hawkins, thank you for believing in the premise and seeing it through its development into the final revisions shopped in 2012 and 2013 respectively. Heaps of thanks to Sandra Kring, who took a look at the 2013 "final" version two years later, offered suggestions and gently told me that although it was a great story, it could be made even better, particularly if I took my time, deadlines be damned. Great advice. To my son Jonathan, thank you for letting me go all manic and frantic during your summer vacation in order to finish this twelve-month revision. To my husband Peter, you are a saint and I am so grateful you don't mind a sloppy house and uncooked dinners. I love you both so much.

Thank you, early readers Tara Staley, Kelly Mustian, Kathleen Hermes and MarySue Hermes. Many thanks to Chris Graham, Karen Dionne and the attendees of the 2013 Salt Cay Writers Retreat, for allowing me to read an excerpt from this novel one night, and for clapping, not booing.

Books that educated me and enriched my writing include *Apollo's Angels: a history of Ballet,* by Jennifer Homans; *Private View: Inside*

Baryshnikov's American Ballet Theatre, by John Fraser; Zippora Karz's *The Sugarless Plum;* Steven Manes's *Where Snowflakes Dance and Swear: Inside the Land of Ballet;* Misty Copeland's *Life in* Motion; Christine Temin's *Behind the Scenes at Boston Ballet;* Janice Ross's *San Francisco Ballet at Seventy-Five,* and the ballet fiction of Adrienne Sharp. Online research became a joy and a delicious distraction through watching YouTube clips and mini-documentaries provided by dance companies around the world, including Anaheim Ballet, The Australian Ballet, Pacific Northwest Ballet, San Francisco Ballet and The Royal Ballet. American Ballet Theatre's comprehensive online glossary of ballet terms was a tremendous help as I set about creating my own, somewhat irreverent glossary of terms.

In the spring of 2006 my sister was diagnosed with an acoustic neuroma, and shortly thereafter underwent a craniotomy and translab procedure to have it removed. Dena's plight and slow post-op recovery were very much like hers. The Mayo clinic website and articles from Johns Hopkins School of Medicine were an excellent source of information. The most authentic story detail, however, came from my sister's experience and others who shared their stories at the discussion forums of the Acoustic Neuroma Association. To all the ANA posters, I offer my gratitude and thanks. It humbles me to no end to ponder the random stroke of fate that allowed me to walk away from my fictionalized account unscathed, while the rest of you continue to struggle with this massive paradigm shift in your lives. Thank you, Annette Hadley, for your medical/surgical acumen and step-by-step description of treating a traumatic internal injury and what a ruptured spleen entailed.

Outside the Limelight features a secondary character who is a blogger. What seemed exotic and unfamiliar to me in 2011 when I first penned this story has now become my own livelihood. I am tremendously grateful for the network of supportive dance bloggers and writers that includes Nichelle Suzanne, Kristen Gillette, Rachael McKinley, Grier Cooper, C. Leigh Purtill, Johanna Aurava, Lorry Trujillo Perez, Geri Jeter, Nancy Lorenz, Teri McCollum and Jen Romano. Other performing arts writers who've been a great help to me include Lauren E. Rico (classical music!) and Laurie Niles, founder of Violinist.com. Hugs to my fellow former dancers of the Kaw Valley Dance Theater, as well, particularly artistic director Kristin Benjamin and fellow company members Ken Stewart and Jerri Niebaum Clark. To Donna Zimmerman, thank you for your encouragement and lifelong support of both my dancing and my writing.

Heartfelt thanks to Lauren Baratz-Logsted and Polgarus Studio, respectively, for excellent copyediting and formatting. For gorgeous cover art, a second time in a row, I am indebted to James T. Egan of Bookfly Design.

Lastly, to my five sisters: Kathleen, MarySue, Annette, Laura, and, most importantly, we would all agree, our wounded warrior sister, Maureen. How I wish I could have written you a happier ending. Know that all of us, your sisters, love you so much.

Characters in Outside the Limelight

There are lots of characters in this story. That's what happens when you chronicle a year in a fifty-five member professional dance company. So many people coming together to make it all happen, from backstage crew, lighting and scenic design, stage management, wardrobe and myriad upstairs administrators. All the dancers with their dynamic, diverse personalities. The medical people Dena meets and interacts with. New friends outside the ballet world, for Dena and Rebecca both. If you've read OFF BALANCE, you'll know several of these characters already. If you didn't, maybe this page will help.

The Lindgren Family
Rebecca
Dena
Conrad
Isabelle
Janey - Conrad's second wife
Dan - Isabelle's partner

The DBDs
Pam
Boyd
Joe
Steph
Charlotte
[2 others unnamed]

Other corps de ballet dancers mentioned

Lauren

Ernesto

Courtney - former company member, character in *Off Balance*

Gabrielle - Javier's ex-girlfriend, former company member, character in *Off Balance*

Soloists mentioned

Nicholas – Dena's favorite partner and first romantic love from three years earlier

Sylvie – new to the company in fall of 2009

Lana – joined the company five years earlier as a soloist.

Jimmy – recently promoted to soloist

Principals mentioned

Katrina

Mimi

Javier

Administrators

Anders Gunst – artistic director

Ben – assistant artistic director, ballet master and former company principal

April – former principal and ballet master

Curtis – senior ballet master

Rick – stage manager

Betty – wardrobe mistress

Jenny – in-house massage therapist

Lorraine – in-house physical therapist

Lucinda – director of public relations

Megann – director of human resources

Salim – Lucinda's assistant in public relations

Gil - director of development, Alice's former boss and Lana's fiancé

Medical

Dena's neurotologist (also called a neuro-otologist)

Dr. Vanderhaven – oculoplastic surgeon

Academics

Misha – biology professor who becomes Dena's close friend

Nell – Rebecca's philosophy/aesthetics professor

Others

Alice – former company dancer and administrator, still friends with Ben and Katrina

Andy Redgrave – billionaire arts philanthropist and WCBT donor

Celia – owner of Dena's favorite coffee house

Tatum – Celia's friend, freelance writer, social media consultant and blogger

David – Misha's brother

Alison – waitress at the Moss Beach Roadhouse and a friend of David and Misha's.

Glossary of Ballet Terms

Taken from "Ballet Terms Made Simple"
© 2016 The Classical Girl

Okay, we all know you came here to find out ASAP what a certain word or phrase means, before jumping back into your reading. You don't need the long, involved answer, right? You don't even care about the pronunciation. I mean, you're not reading the story out loud (are you?) and likely you don't plan to engage in a conversation that will include, say, "dégagé" or "glissade" in the near future. So, here you go. Definitions made plain, fast, simple.

A

Adagio – slow, sustained movement. A section in a ballet, or in the center during class. Pretty to watch. Can also be called an adage.

Attitude (devant or derrière) – one leg goes up at an angle, preferably with the knee way high and the foot just a little lower and nothing dangling downward like a bird's broken wing.

Arabesque – the non-standing leg lifts in back and holds, nice and straight, somewhere between a ninety and 120 degree angle.

À la seconde – refers to a body and leg position, which here would be to the side.

Assemblé – a jump movement where one foot/leg sort of swings out to the side and then both feet/legs "assemble" midair just before you land in fifth position. Commonly linked to a glissade.

B

Barre – that wooden railing affixed to the wall that you see in every ballet studio. Also the term for the first part of ballet class, which takes place—you guessed it—at the barre.

Battement – "beat." Petit battements are these little foot beats at the ankle you do midway through barre, and grand battements are these big, leg-swinging kicks you do to the front, side and back, at the end of barre.

Ballet master – the guy (or female, who is sometimes called a ballet mistress) who does things like supervise rehearsals, teach class, serve as the dude in charge when the artistic director is not around.

Ballon – wow, I could write an essay on this one. Translated as "bounce," this coveted trait, most commonly noted in male dancers (mostly because they tend to be the big jumpers), refers to a sense of lightness and ease when doing jumps. A dancer with great ballon will seem to sort of linger in the air, defying gravity for an instant. To use it in a sentence, and thus impress others with your newfound ballet acumen, you might say, "wow, did that guy have great ballon, or what?"

Bourré – a busy little foot skitter en pointe that makes it look like the dancer (always female—males *totally* don't bourré) is skimming across the stage. Used to great effect in the "Wili" scene in *Giselle*. Also part of a pas de bourré.

C

Cambré – an arch back with one arm overhead. Usually done while at the barre, during a port de bras. A very iconic movement in *La Bayadère*'s "Kingdom of the Shades."

Chaîné turns – a moving "chain" of quick revolutions, usually en pointe.

Choreographer – the person (usually a male; why is that?) who created the ballet, although if he's busy and/or quite established (or dead), he'll send out his representatives, called stagers, to teach the ballet to the dancers.

Corps de ballet – the entry level rank into a ballet company, above apprentice, below soloist and principal. Not the most coveted place to spend your whole dance performance career.

Chassé – a movement step, from fifth position, where one foot sort of "chases" the other while doing this little baby leap/hop. Ideally the feet sort of slap together midair. Commonly paired up for a chassé sauté.

D

Dégagé – a movement at the barre where your foot goes out, like in a tendu, but "disengages" from the ground, a few inches, before returning to a closed first or fifth position.

Demi-plié – demi means half and plié means "bent." At the barre, the plié exercise you begin class with usually includes a few demi-pliés tossed in. All jumps begin with a demi-plié preparation.

Devant – "front." It's a floor position, a body position, that gets tacked on to other terms, such as in "attitude devant" where your attitude leg is in its pretty shape in front of you, not back.

Derrière – "back." Otherwise, pretty much the same definition as the one above.

Développé à la seconde – tell me you don't need me to translate the French here. A leg lift, where the toe traces a path from ankle, to knee, before developing out to the side and up. Some dancers can développé their leg way high, like close to 180 degrees. Pretty crazy to watch.

Downstage – back in the day, stages were raised in back, or "raked," which meant downstage, closest to the audience, was literally down from the back part of the stage.

E

Échappé – this jumpy thing where your feet are in first/fifth position and they "escape," while you're in the air, out to second position. And then in the next jump, the feet go back to first/fifth.

En l'air – "in the air," and it's usually paired with something like rond de jambe, which means your leg's in the air as it does the rond de jambe.

En pointe – on full point, when you're wearing pointe shoes.

Entrechat – a jump from fifth position, where the feet switch positions, and there's a sort of midair meeting of the feet before they land in their new spot. An entrechat quatre (French for "four") means you double up the midair action, so the feet go back and then front before landing. An entrechat six (pronounced CEES) means there's yet one more meet-up happening, before the feet land. Guys with great jumps can do entrechats huit ("eight") and story has it Rudolf Nureyev could do entrechats dix ("ten"). Whoa!

F

First [position] – when your heels are together, toes turned out, usually 150 to 180 degrees, depending on how turned out your hips are. (See Turnout)

Fifth [position] – a foot position where the hips are doing the turned-out thing (see Turnout) so that the right heel fits snugly up against the left big toe and the left heel is behind the right toes.

First cast – the casting everyone craves. You are the top dog. You will likely perform on opening night, which is when most of the critics come to review, so you are lucky and fabulous, but likely you already know it, and so does your artistic director.

G

Giselle – the classic 1841 story ballet about Giselle, this village girl betrayed by love, who dies and becomes a Wili, one of a band of vengeful maiden spirits, but nonetheless tries to protect her beloved from being killed by them. The story motif of "bereaved, betrayed, innocent maiden sent to the spirit world" would make its way in several more story ballets (see *La Bayadère*).

Glissade – translated as "glide," it's this movement that starts in demi-plié, fifth position, and, well, *glides*, with a teeny, weeny leap-but-not, into another fifth position. A common prep step for glissade assemblé.

Grand allegro – the big run combination across the diagonal at the end of a ballet class. Big fun. Classical Girl's favorite part of class.

Grand battement – a big giant beat (see Battement). Basically, big kicks at the end of barre, that you do to the front, side and back.

Grand jeté – a big-assed leap. Comes at the end of a few prep steps, most commonly a tombé, pas de bourré, glissade, and voilà. I don't know a single dancer who doesn't *love* doing this combination. It's what dance is all about. All dancers, regardless of age and/or physical condition, secretly long to do this every time we walk down a long, wide, empty hallway. Kudos to those who actually do.

Grand jeté lift – when the guy lifts his partner, either waist-high or overhead, and she does the leap in the air. Overhead is the most common. Cool to watch. This is why male dancers must be very, very strong. It's a HUGE myth that male dancers are wimpy. Couldn't be further from the truth. Basically, they bench press girls. And they do it without those grunts or face contortions you see on some guys at the gym. But I digress. Sorry.

H

High fifth – this relates to the arm position, not the foot position. High fifth means arms are curved and overhead, like you're holding a big beach ball over your head.

J

Jeté – "thrown." Most common use is "grand jeté," that leap where you just throw yourself into the movement.

L

La Bayadère –another 19th century story ballet about Nikiya, an innocent, young temple dancer, betrayed in love, who dies, and becomes a Shade, and her love, Solor, smokes himself into an opium stupor so he can follow her into the Kingdom of the Shades. Sounds a little like *Giselle*, huh? (See Giselle.)

Low fifth – an arm position, like high fifth. Low fifth, however, looks more like a guy wanting to cup his nuts in his two hands but his hands are politely hovering six to eight inches from his torso, arms curved all nice and pretty.

Lines – this refers to the pleasing coordination of the arms and legs in relation to the torso and head. Think of an artist sketching the initial lines of a perfect person's body. You might hear someone say, "she has gorgeous lines" about a dancer (usually the lean, leggy ones).

M

marley [floor] – once a name brand, now a generic term for a type of sturdy black vinyl flooring that covers dance performance stages and quite a few studios, too. Good, slip-free surface to dance on. You can roll it up and transport it.

Merde - French for "shit" and what dance people tell each other before performing, because of course you'd never say "break a leg" to a dancer, and theater/dance people love their little superstition good-luck customs.

Mixed bill – this kind of program means the night's performance will include two to four short ballets versus one long story ballet. Most times there are three.

P

Pas – "step."

Pas de bourré – this step thingy, three small steps, that serves as a transition to bigger thingies. Like a tombé, pas de bourré, glissade, grand jeté.

Pas de deux – "step of two." Basically, a more elegant way to say "a duet." Most ballets have a few pas de deux thrown into them, almost always male/female, but in today's contemporary ballets, hey, anything goes.

Pas de basque – you don't expect me to keep repeating "step," do you? And this one, it's "step of the Basque" and I dunno, it's a folksy, jaunty, steppy thing. It's fun to do, if that helps.

Passé – position on one leg where the knee is out to the side and the toe is touching the other knee, sort of "passing" through, like from a front attitude to back.

Penché – translated as "leaning" or "inclining," it's affiliated with an arabesque. Basically the back arabesque leg goes way high while the chest dips way low, and the gaze remains forward. Lovely to watch. Very *Giselle* Act II.

Petit allegro – fun, busy stuff with the feet, and also a designated portion of the ballet class. (Generally, a combination of several steps within eight or sixteen counts). Hard to do the busy stuff if you're a relative beginner, but SO much fun to watch a professional do it. YouTube it.

Plié – "bent." Every barre starts with pliés. Every new student starts with pliés. Every professional does about a million of them. It's like death and taxes: no way to avoid 'em.

Piqué – "pricked," a deliberate step into something, like an arabesque.

Piqué turn – kind of like chaîné turns, but the non-supporting leg is in a passé or back retiré position.

Piqué arabesque – instead of bouncing up into an arabesque en pointe, you deliberately step into it.

Pirouette – turns in place with the non-supporting leg up in passé or retiré. Good dancers can do triples effortlessly. Really good dancers can do a half-dozen revolutions (guys, for whatever reason, seem to be able to do more). Partnered pirouettes are when the guy spins the girl's waist, which doesn't mean she's not doing any of the work. She is. It's just that a good partner can make a good spinner go four or five revolutions.

Port de bras – movement of the arms.

Promenade – a movement during an adagio where a dancer moves in a circular direction on one leg while the other is doing something fabulous, like a back arabesque or a back attitude. A partnered promenade is where the male moves his partner around while she's en pointe in aforementioned arabesque or attitude, either holding her waist or her hand.

R

Répétiteur – okay, so different people apply different meanings to the term. Some say it's interchangeable with the term "stager," others say it's someone who rehearses the dancers after they've learned the ballet's steps. Then some say it's the person who merely schedules all the rehearsals. Meanwhile, a ballet master often acts as a répétiteur. Whatever. You get the idea; take your pick.

Retiré – this position the non-standing leg takes, like a passé where the toe is at the knee, but instead of "passing" through, well, it "retires" there, in front. Or in back.

Rond de jambe (plural: ronds de jambe) – during barre, the foot traces a slow half-circle on the floor.

Rond de jambe en l'air – the thing described above, in the air. (See "en l'air.")

S

Sauté – "jump." I like the image of cooking, when you sauté onions on a too high heat and they jump. Yeah, that's a good image. (BTW, even though I said I wasn't going to mess with pronunciation, you really do need to know that this one is pronounced like "sew" as in sewing, versus "saw" like sautéed onions. I can hear your mistake from all the way over here, and it hurts my ears. Just saying.)

Second cast – the lesser cast, that won't get opening night, but will still get a good number of performances, so, hey, it's still a great thing. Beats being the understudy cast.

Shade – spirit maiden dancer from *La Bayadère*, Act II, Kingdom of the Shades.

Sisonne – another jump thingy where the dancer springs off both feet and midair the legs "scissor" open. One foot lands a split second before the other, into a closed fifth position. They can be done from front to back, back to front, or side to side. Can be done as a partnered lift for more dramatic effect.

Stager – a choreographer's representative, who will teach the dancers the ballet before leaving rehearsals to the ballet masters (or the mystery-laden répétiteur). Generally, they themselves will have performed the ballet many times, with aforementioned choreographer. No Balanchine ballet can be professionally performed without it first being taught by a stager from the Balanchine Trust, all of whom have a close connection to either him or his choreography.

Story ballet – also called an evening-length ballet. Tends to be one of the classics, like *Giselle, Swan Lake, Don Quixote, The Nutcracker,*

etc. Will be the sole ballet performed that evening. Big
moneymakers for companies.

T

Tendu – its official name is "battement tendu" but no one bothers
with the first word. In a tendu, you slide your foot out, point the
toe, and slide it back in. It's one of the most elementary steps at the
barre, right after pliés. It's the thing every little girl learns on her
first day of ballet class and will thereafter demonstrate to you daily.
Hourly.

Turnout – this is mostly referring to how your hip joints were
built. Although anyone can turn their feet out when they're in first
position, having great turnout means your hips will allow a 180
degree pose without twisting the hell out of your knee joints. Either
you're born with it or you're not.

U

Upstage – see "downstage" for explanation; I don't feel like writing
it out twice.

W

Wili – maiden spirits [from the ballet *Giselle*] who died before their
wedding day and now wander the forest by night, exacting revenge
on unsuspecting men by dancing them to death.

About the Author

Terez Mertes Rose is a writer and former ballet dancer whose work has appeared in the *Crab Orchard Review, Women Who Eat* (Seal Press), *A Woman's Europe* (Travelers' Tales), the *Philadelphia Inquirer* and the *San Jose Mercury News*. She is also the author of *Off Balance*, Book 1 of the Ballet Theatre Chronicles (Classical Girl Press, 2015). She reviews dance performances for Bachtrack.com and blogs about ballet and classical music at The Classical Girl (www.theclassicalgirl.com). She makes her home in the Santa Cruz Mountains with her husband and son.

CPSIA information can be obtained
at www.ICGtesting.com
Printed in the USA
LVOW11s1821090217
523759LV00004B/780/P

9 780986 093432